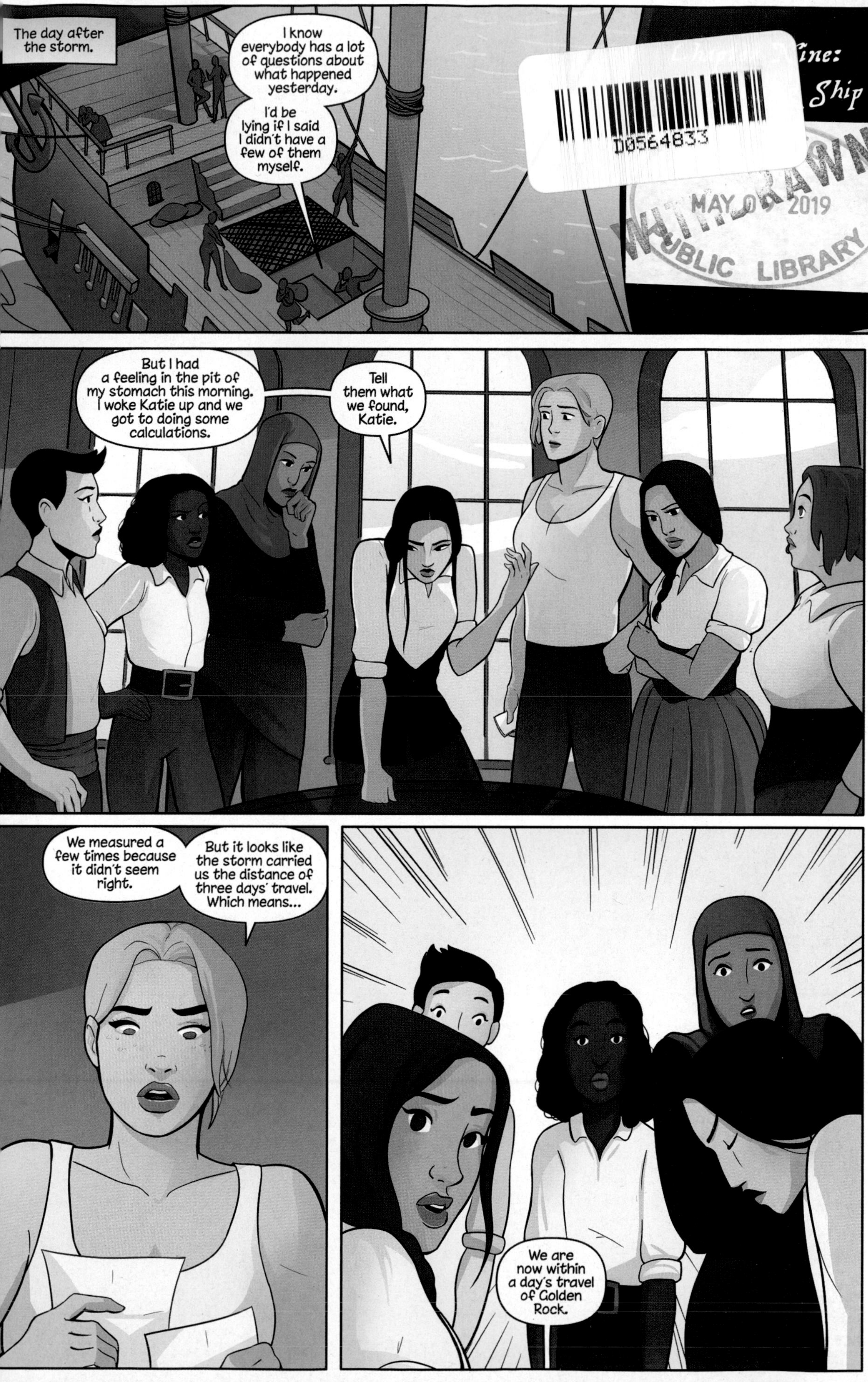
The day after the storm.
I know everybody has a lot of questions about what happened yesterday.
I'd be lying if I said I didn't have a few of them myself.
But I had a feeling in the pit of my stomach this morning. I woke Katie up and we got to doing some calculations.
Tell them what we found, Katie.
We measured a few times because it didn't seem right.
But it looks like the storm carried us the distance of three days' travel. Which means...
We are now within a day's travel of Golden Rock.

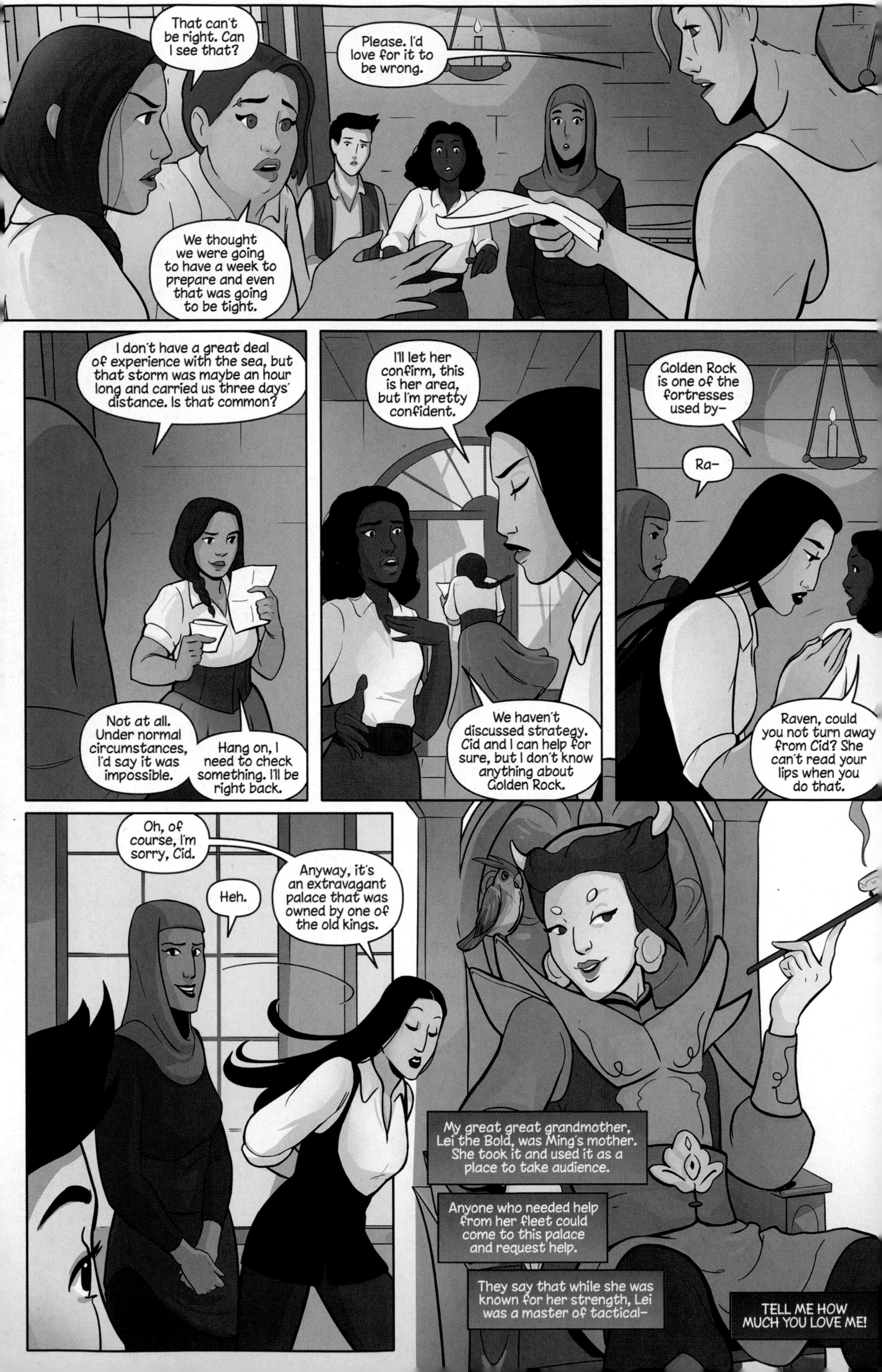
That can't be right. Can I see that?
Please. I'd love for it to be wrong.
We thought we were going to have a week to prepare and even that was going to be tight.
I don't have a great deal of experience with the sea, but that storm was maybe an hour long and carried us three days' distance. Is that common?
Not at all. Under normal circumstances, I'd say it was impossible.
Hang on, I need to check something. I'll be right back.
I'll let her confirm, this is her area, but I'm pretty confident.
We haven't discussed strategy. Cid and I can help for sure, but I don't know anything about Golden Rock.
Golden Rock is one of the fortresses used by–
Ra–
Raven, could you not turn away from Cid? She can't read your lips when you do that.
Oh, of course, I'm sorry, Cid.
Heh.
Anyway, it's an extravagant palace that was owned by one of the old kings.
My great great grandmother, Lei the Bold, was Ming's mother. She took it and used it as a place to take audience.
Anyone who needed help from her fleet could come to this palace and request help.
They say that while she was known for her strength, Lei was a master of tactical–
TELL ME HOW MUCH YOU LOVE ME!

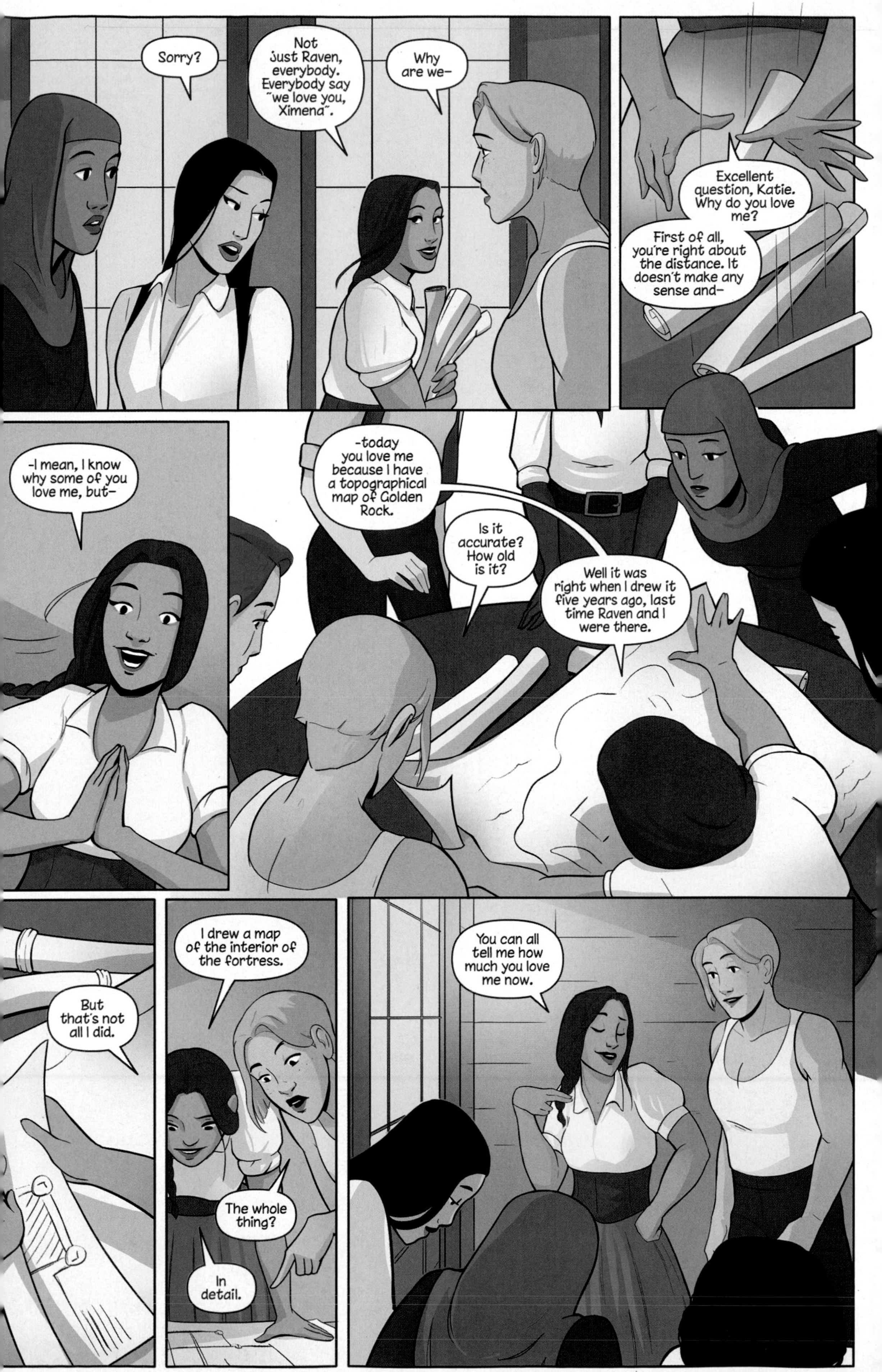
Sorry?
Not just Raven, everybody. Everybody say "we love you, Ximena".
Why are we-
Excellent question, Katie. Why do you love me?
First of all, you're right about the distance. It doesn't make any sense and-
-I mean, I know why some of you love me, but-
-today you love me because I have a topographical map of Golden Rock.
Is it accurate? How old is it?
Well it was right when I drew it five years ago, last time Raven and I were there.
But that's not all I did.
I drew a map of the interior of the fortress.
The whole thing?
In detail.
You can all tell me how much you love me now.

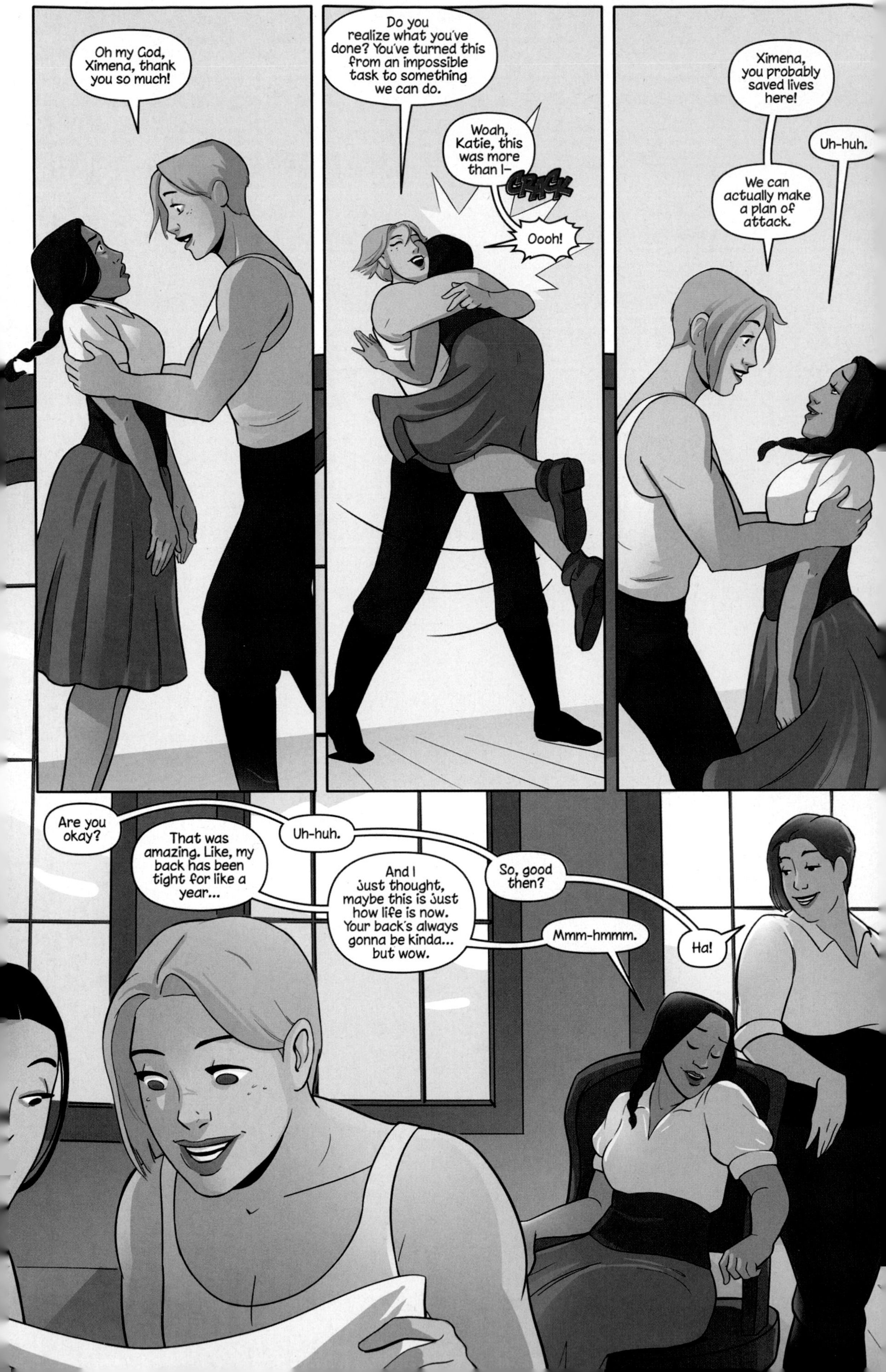

Oh my God, Ximena, thank you so much!
Do you realize what you've done? You've turned this from an impossible task to something we can do.
Woah, Katie, this was more than I–
CRACK
Oooh!
Ximena, you probably saved lives here!
We can actually make a plan of attack.
Uh-huh.
Are you okay?
Uh-huh.
That was amazing. Like, my back has been tight for like a year...
So, good then?
And I just thought, maybe this is just how life is now. Your back's always gonna be kinda... but wow.
Mmm-hmmm.
Ha!

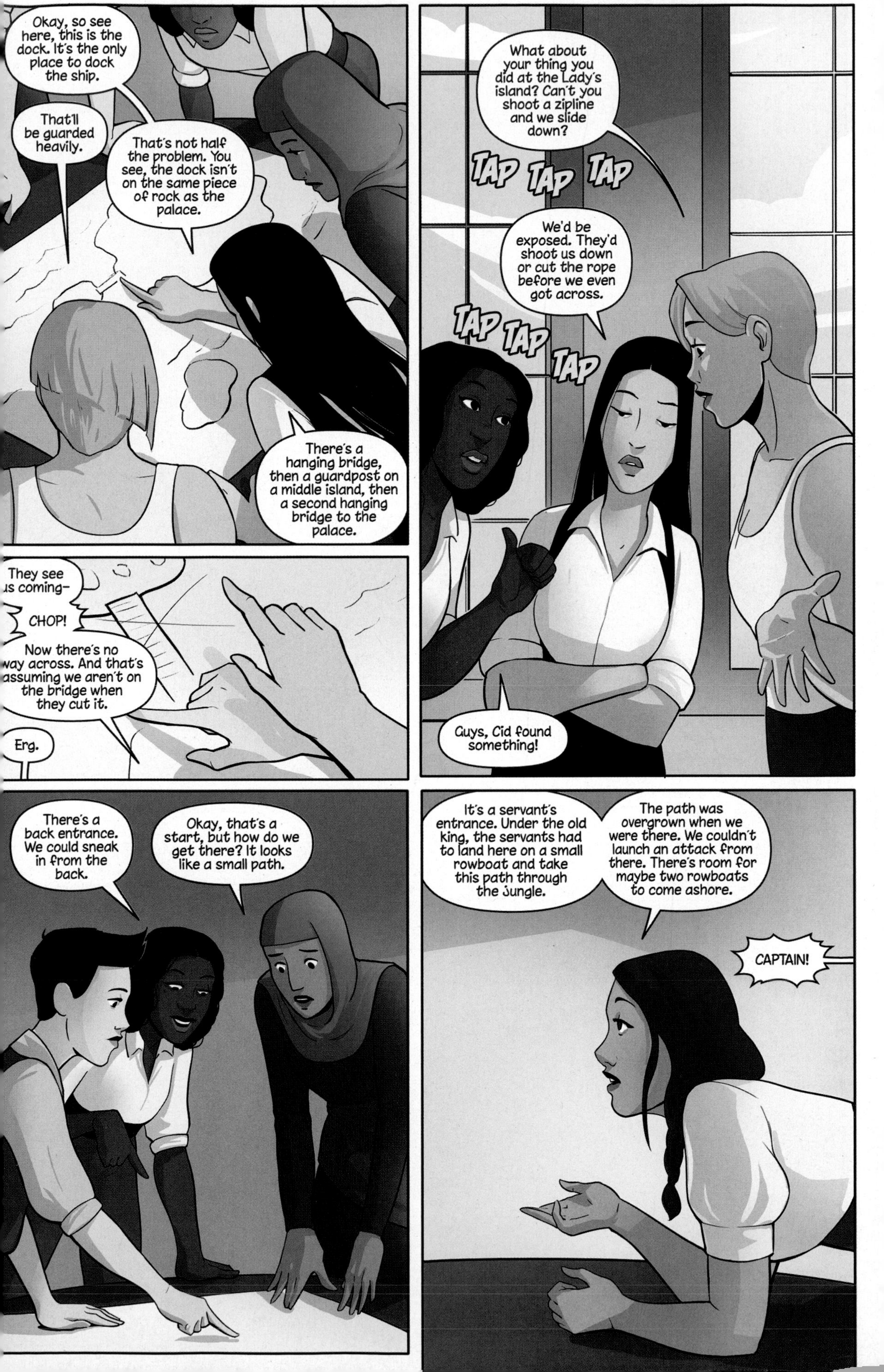

Okay, so see here, this is the dock. It's the only place to dock the ship.
That'll be guarded heavily.
That's not half the problem. You see, the dock isn't on the same piece of rock as the palace.
There's a hanging bridge, then a guardpost on a middle island, then a second hanging bridge to the palace.
They see us coming–
CHOP!
Now there's no way across. And that's assuming we aren't on the bridge when they cut it.
Erg.
What about your thing you did at the Lady's island? Can't you shoot a zipline and we slide down?
TAP TAP TAP
We'd be exposed. They'd shoot us down or cut the rope before we even got across.
TAP TAP TAP
Guys, Cid found something!
There's a back entrance. We could sneak in from the back.
Okay, that's a start, but how do we get there? It looks like a small path.
It's a servant's entrance. Under the old king, the servants had to land here on a small rowboat and take this path through the jungle.
The path was overgrown when we were there. We couldn't launch an attack from there. There's room for maybe two rowboats to come ashore.
CAPTAIN!

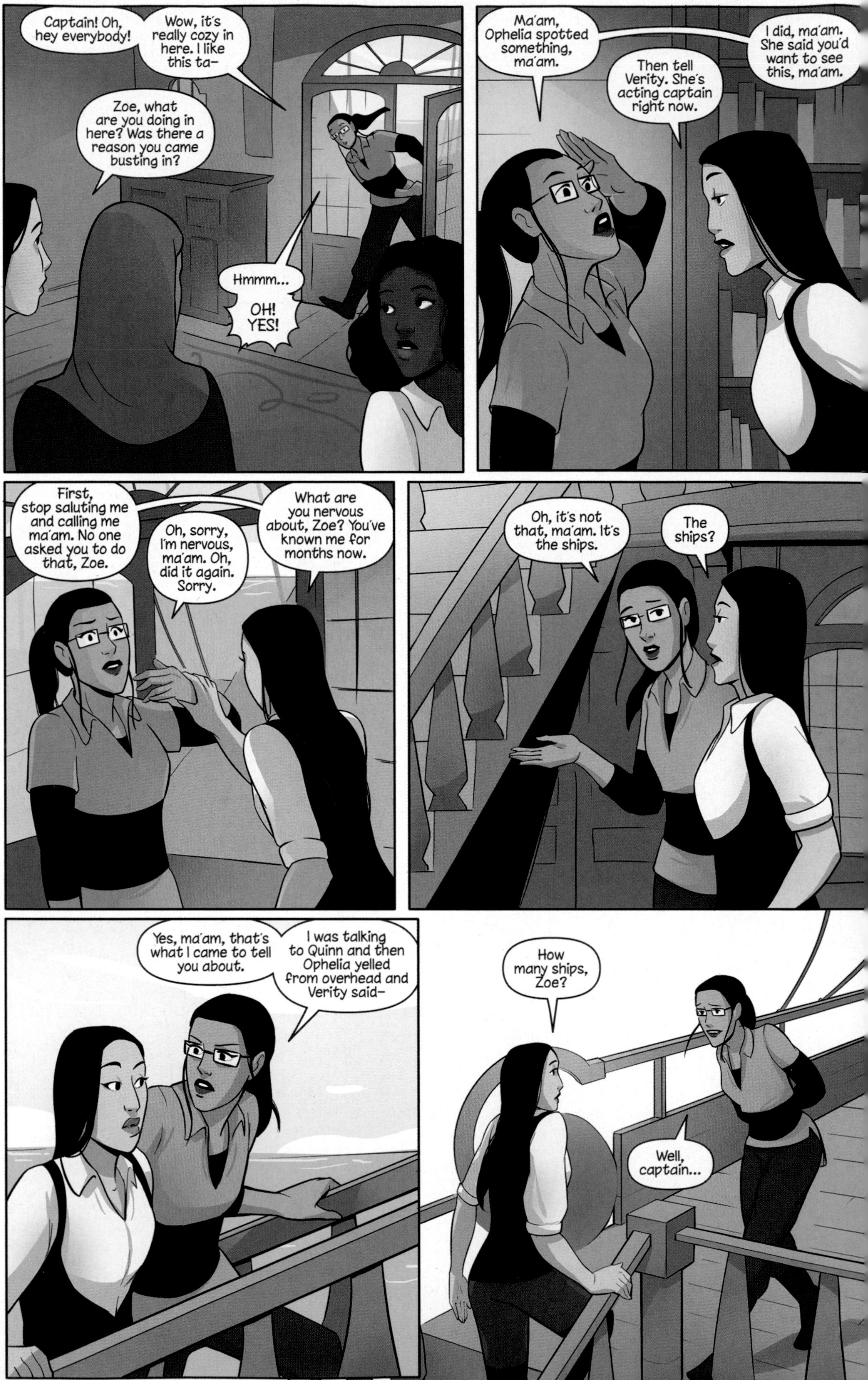
Captain! Oh, hey everybody!
Wow, it's really cozy in here. I like this ta-
Zoe, what are you doing in here? Was there a reason you came busting in?
Hmmm...
OH! YES!
Ma'am, Ophelia spotted something, ma'am.
Then tell Verity. She's acting captain right now.
I did, ma'am. She said you'd want to see this, ma'am.
First, stop saluting me and calling me ma'am. No one asked you to do that, Zoe.
Oh, sorry, I'm nervous, ma'am. Oh, did it again. Sorry.
What are you nervous about, Zoe? You've known me for months now.
Oh, it's not that, ma'am. It's the ships.
The ships?
Yes, ma'am, that's what I came to tell you about.
I was talking to Quinn and then Ophelia yelled from overhead and Verity said-
How many ships, Zoe?
Well, captain...

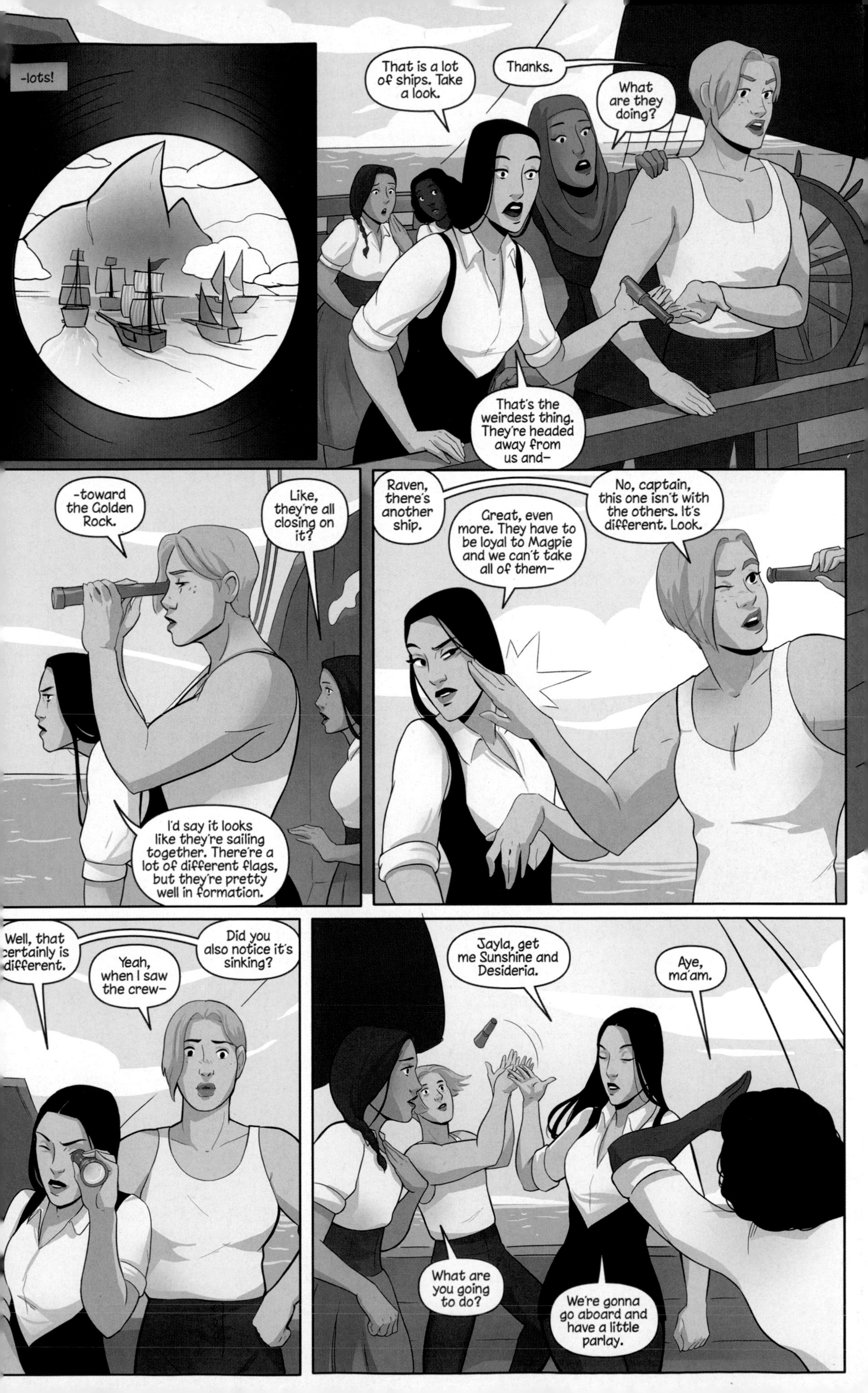
-lots!
That is a lot of ships. Take a look.
Thanks.
What are they doing?
That's the weirdest thing. They're headed away from us and-
-toward the Golden Rock.
Like, they're all closing on it?
I'd say it looks like they're sailing together. There're a lot of different flags, but they're pretty well in formation.
Raven, there's another ship.
Great, even more. They have to be loyal to Magpie and we can't take all of them-
No, captain, this one isn't with the others. It's different. Look.
Well, that certainly is different.
Yeah, when I saw the crew-
Did you also notice it's sinking?
Jayla, get me Sunshine and Desideria.
Aye, ma'am.
What are you going to do?
We're gonna go aboard and have a little parlay.

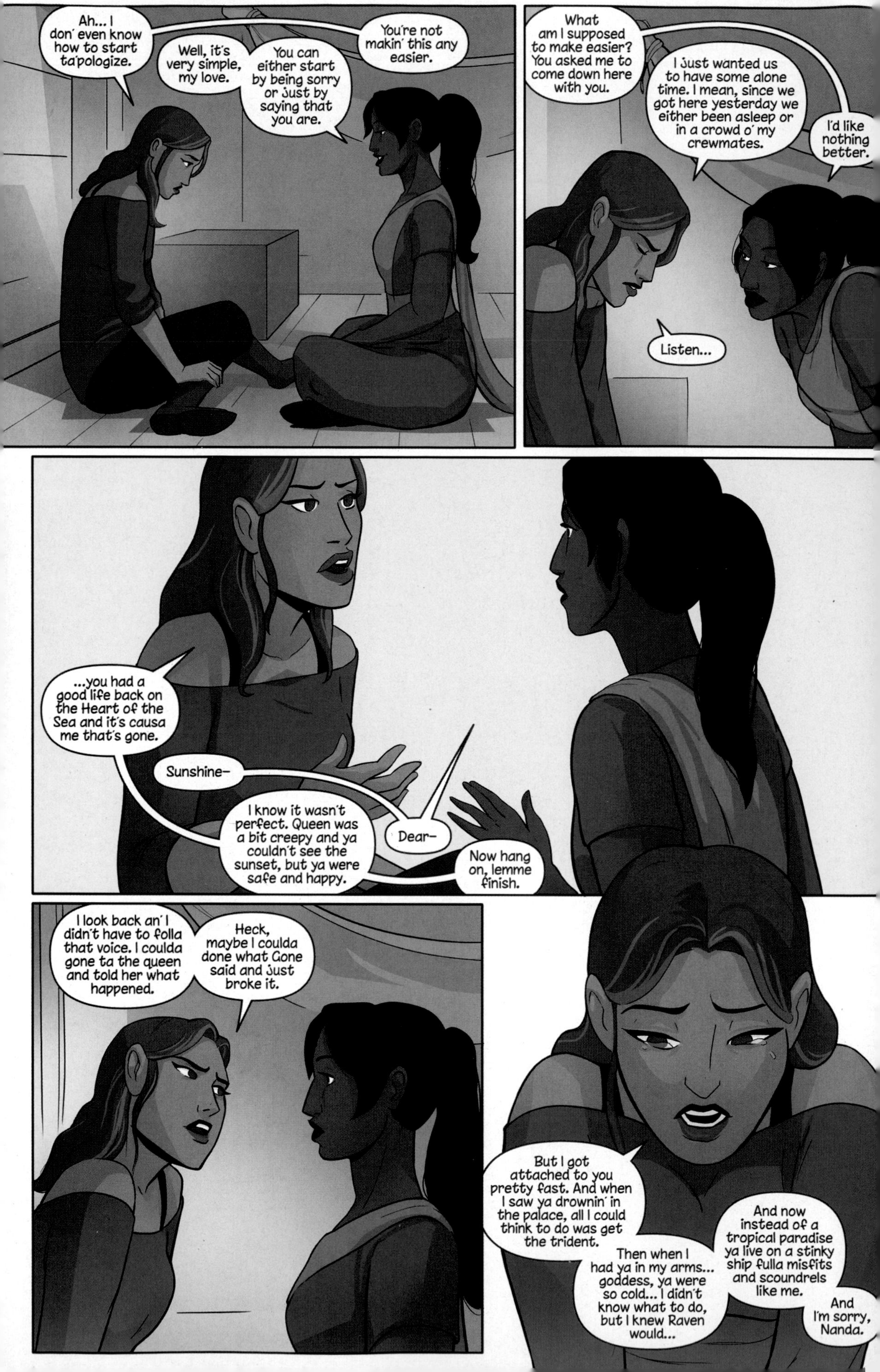
Ah... I don´ even know how to start ta´pologize.
Well, it´s very simple, my love.
You can either start by being sorry or just by saying that you are.
You´re not makin´ this any easier.
What am I supposed to make easier? You asked me to come down here with you.
I just wanted us to have some alone time. I mean, since we got here yesterday we either been asleep or in a crowd o´ my crewmates.
I´d like nothing better.
Listen...
...you had a good life back on the Heart of the Sea and it´s causa me that´s gone.
Sunshine-
I know it wasn´t perfect. Queen was a bit creepy and ya couldn´t see the sunset, but ya were safe and happy.
Dear-
Now hang on, lemme finish.
I look back an´ I didn´t have to folla that voice. I coulda gone ta the queen and told her what happened.
Heck, maybe I coulda done what Gone said and just broke it.
But I got attached to you pretty fast. And when I saw ya drownin´ in the palace, all I could think to do was get the trident.
Then when I had ya in my arms... goddess, ya were so cold... I didn´t know what to do, but I knew Raven would...
And now instead of a tropical paradise ya live on a stinky ship fulla misfits and scoundrels like me.
And I´m sorry, Nanda.

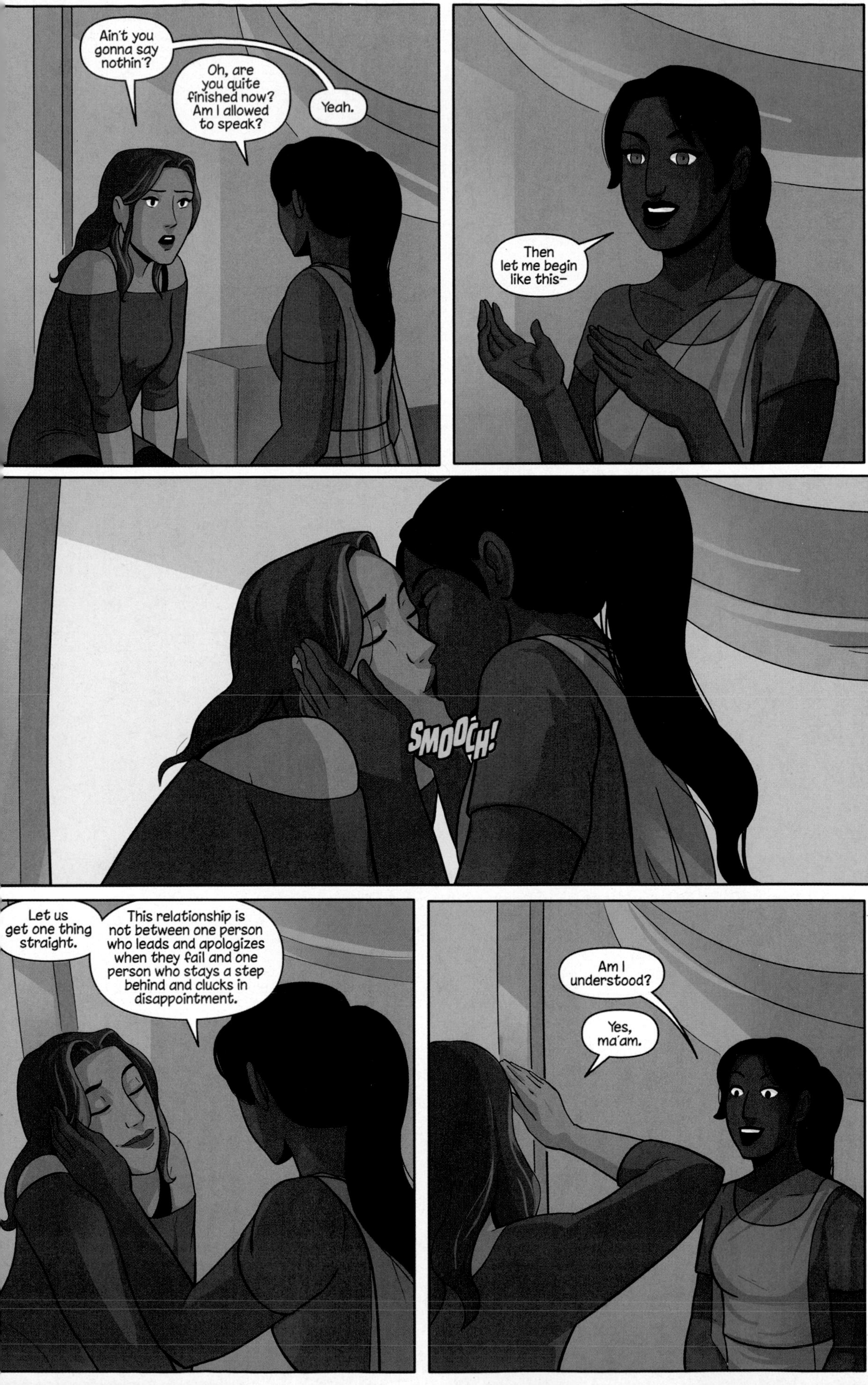

Ain't you gonna say nothin'?
Oh, are you quite finished now? Am I allowed to speak?
Yeah.
Then let me begin like this–
SMOOCH!
Let us get one thing straight.
This relationship is not between one person who leads and apologizes when they fail and one person who stays a step behind and clucks in disappointment.
Am I understood?
Yes, ma'am.

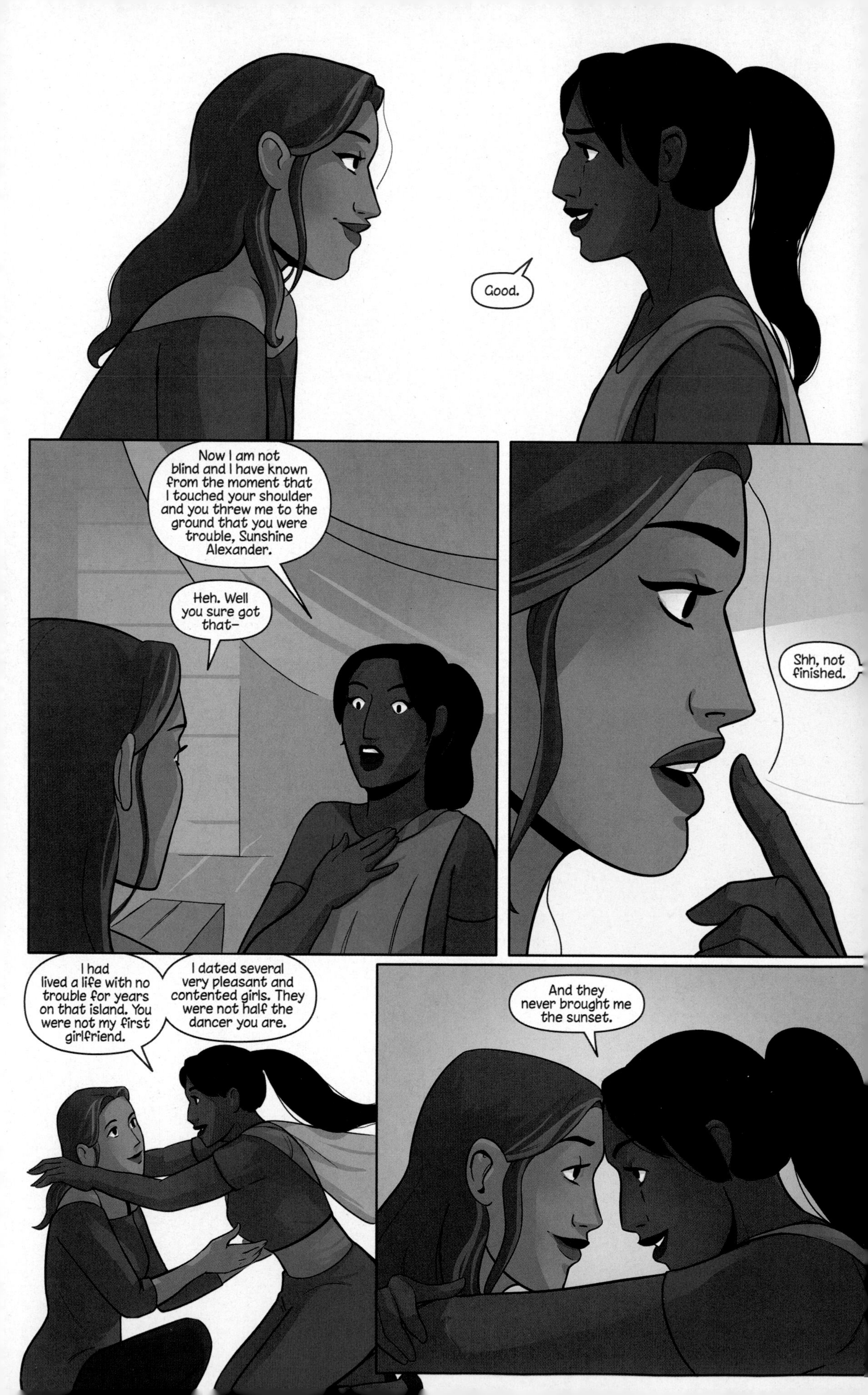
Good.
Now I am not blind and I have known from the moment that I touched your shoulder and you threw me to the ground that you were trouble, Sunshine Alexander.
Heh. Well you sure got that–
Shh, not finished.
I had lived a life with no trouble for years on that island. You were not my first girlfriend.
I dated several very pleasant and contented girls. They were not half the dancer you are.
And they never brought me the sunset.

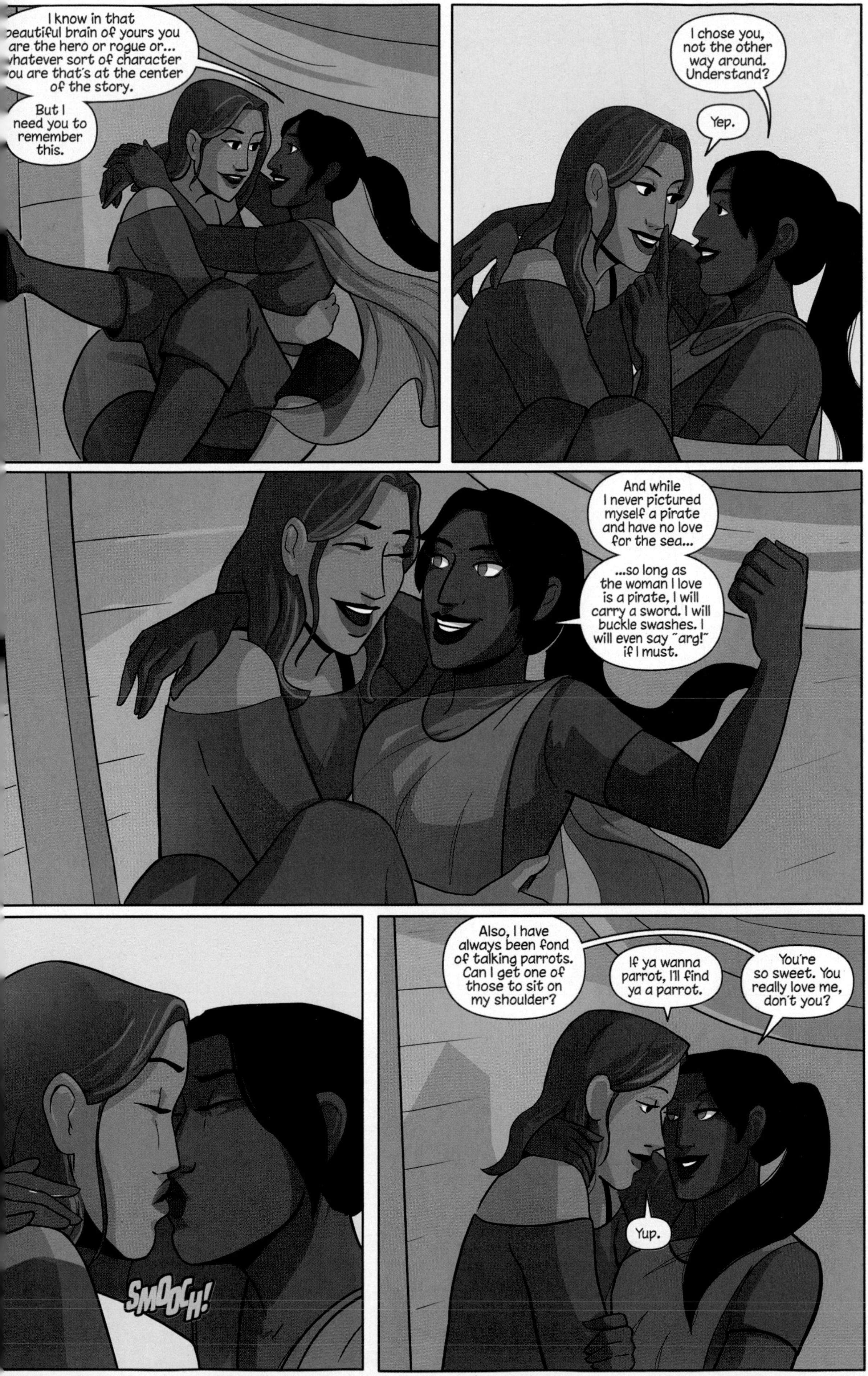
I know in that beautiful brain of yours you are the hero or rogue or... whatever sort of character you are that's at the center of the story.
But I need you to remember this.
I chose you, not the other way around. Understand?
Yep.
And while I never pictured myself a pirate and have no love for the sea...
...so long as the woman I love is a pirate, I will carry a sword. I will buckle swashes. I will even say "arg!" if I must.
SMOOCH!
Also, I have always been fond of talking parrots. Can I get one of those to sit on my shoulder?
If ya wanna parrot, I'll find ya a parrot.
You're so sweet. You really love me, don't you?
Yup.

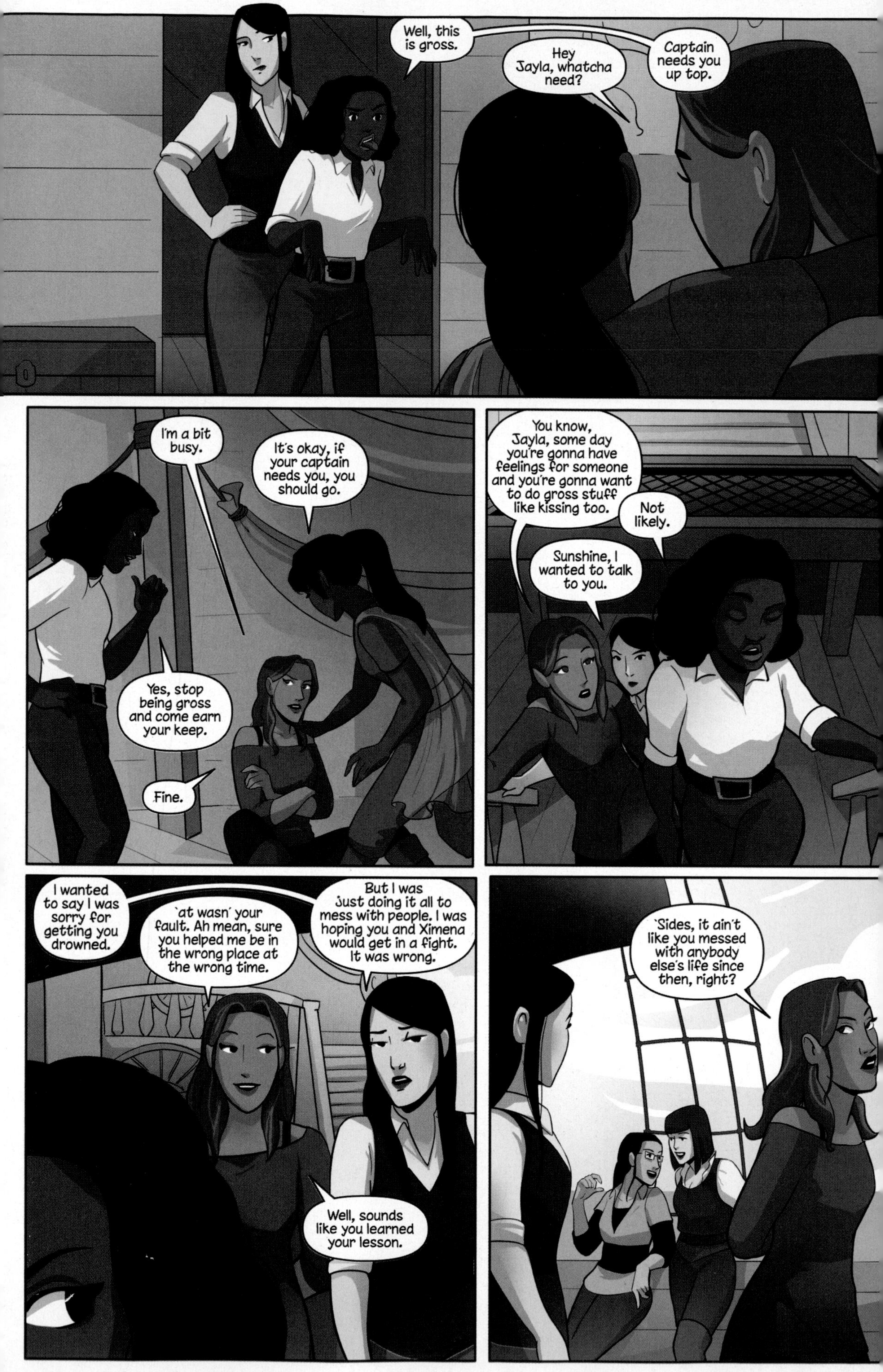
Well, this is gross.
Hey Jayla, whatcha need?
Captain needs you up top.
I'm a bit busy.
It's okay, if your captain needs you, you should go.
Yes, stop being gross and come earn your keep.
Fine.
You know, Jayla, some day you're gonna have feelings for someone and you're gonna want to do gross stuff like kissing too.
Not likely.
Sunshine, I wanted to talk to you.
I wanted to say I was sorry for getting you drowned.
`at wasn' your fault. Ah mean, sure you helped me be in the wrong place at the wrong time.
But I was just doing it all to mess with people. I was hoping you and Ximena would get in a fight. It was wrong.
Well, sounds like you learned your lesson.
`Sides, it ain't like you messed with anybody else's life since then, right?

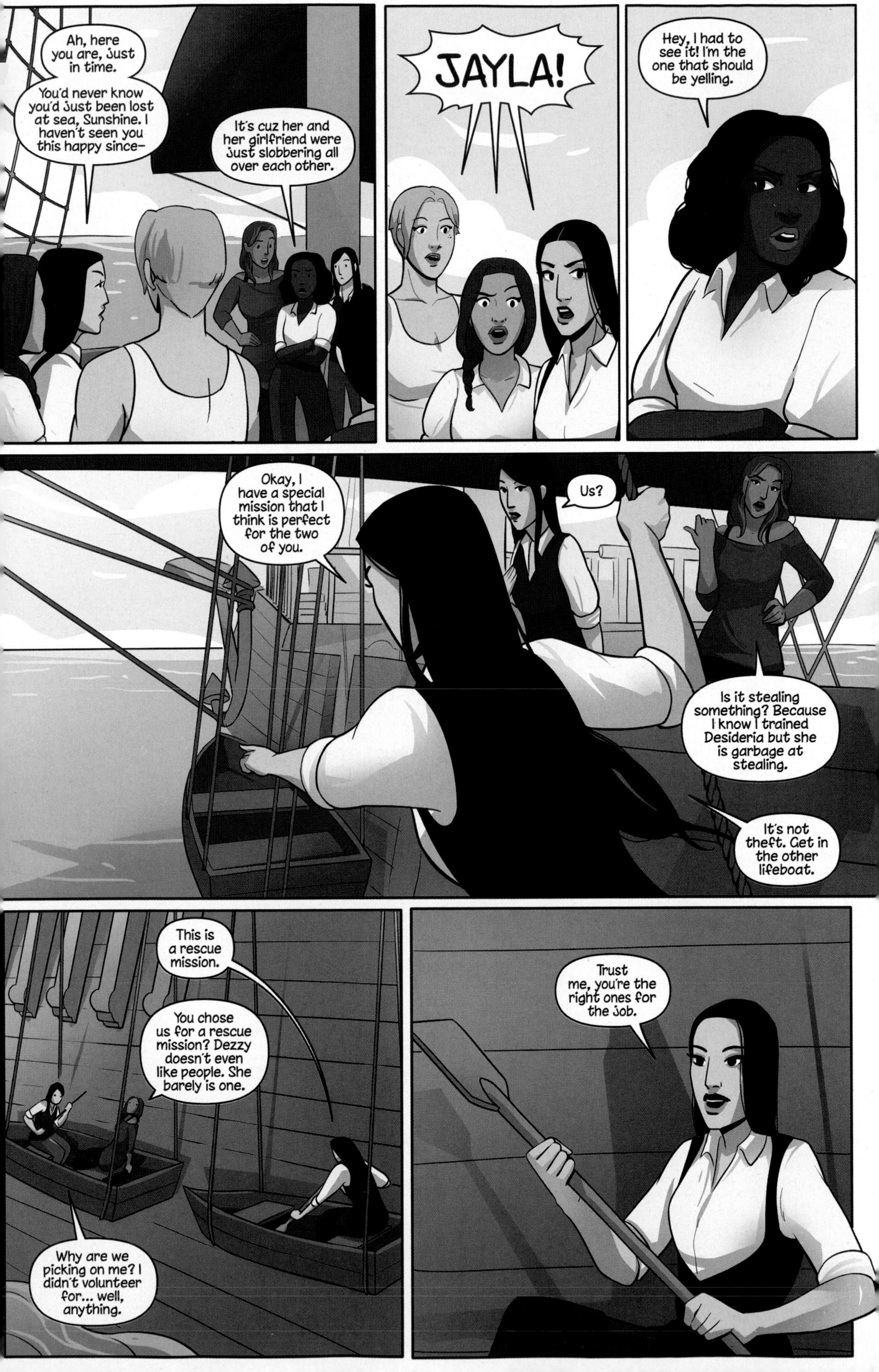
Ah, here you are, just in time.
You'd never know you'd just been lost at sea, Sunshine. I haven't seen you this happy since–
It's cuz her and her girlfriend were just slobbering all over each other.
JAYLA!
Hey, I had to see it! I'm the one that should be yelling.
Okay, I have a special mission that I think is perfect for the two of you.
Us?
Is it stealing something? Because I know I trained Desideria but she is garbage at stealing.
It's not theft. Get in the other lifeboat.
This is a rescue mission.
You chose us for a rescue mission? Dezzy doesn't even like people. She barely is one.
Why are we picking on me? I didn't volunteer for... well, anything.
Trust me, you're the right ones for the job.

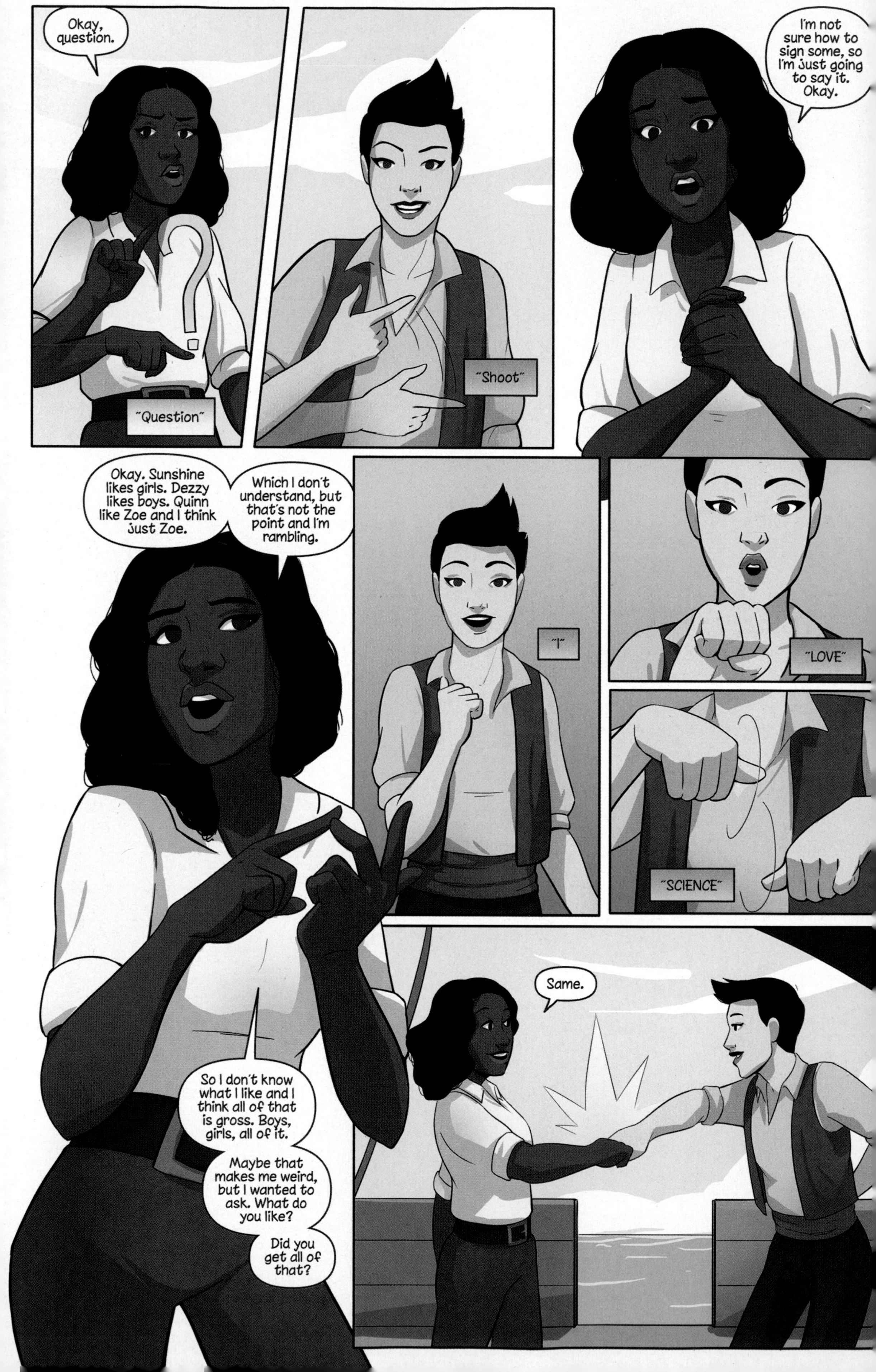
Okay, question.
"Question"
"Shoot"
I'm not sure how to sign some, so I'm just going to say it. Okay.
Okay. Sunshine likes girls. Dezzy likes boys. Quinn like Zoe and I think just Zoe.
Which I don't understand, but that's not the point and I'm rambling.
So I don't know what I like and I think all of that is gross. Boys, girls, all of it.
Maybe that makes me weird, but I wanted to ask. What do you like?
Did you get all of that?
"I"
"LOVE"
"SCIENCE"
Same.

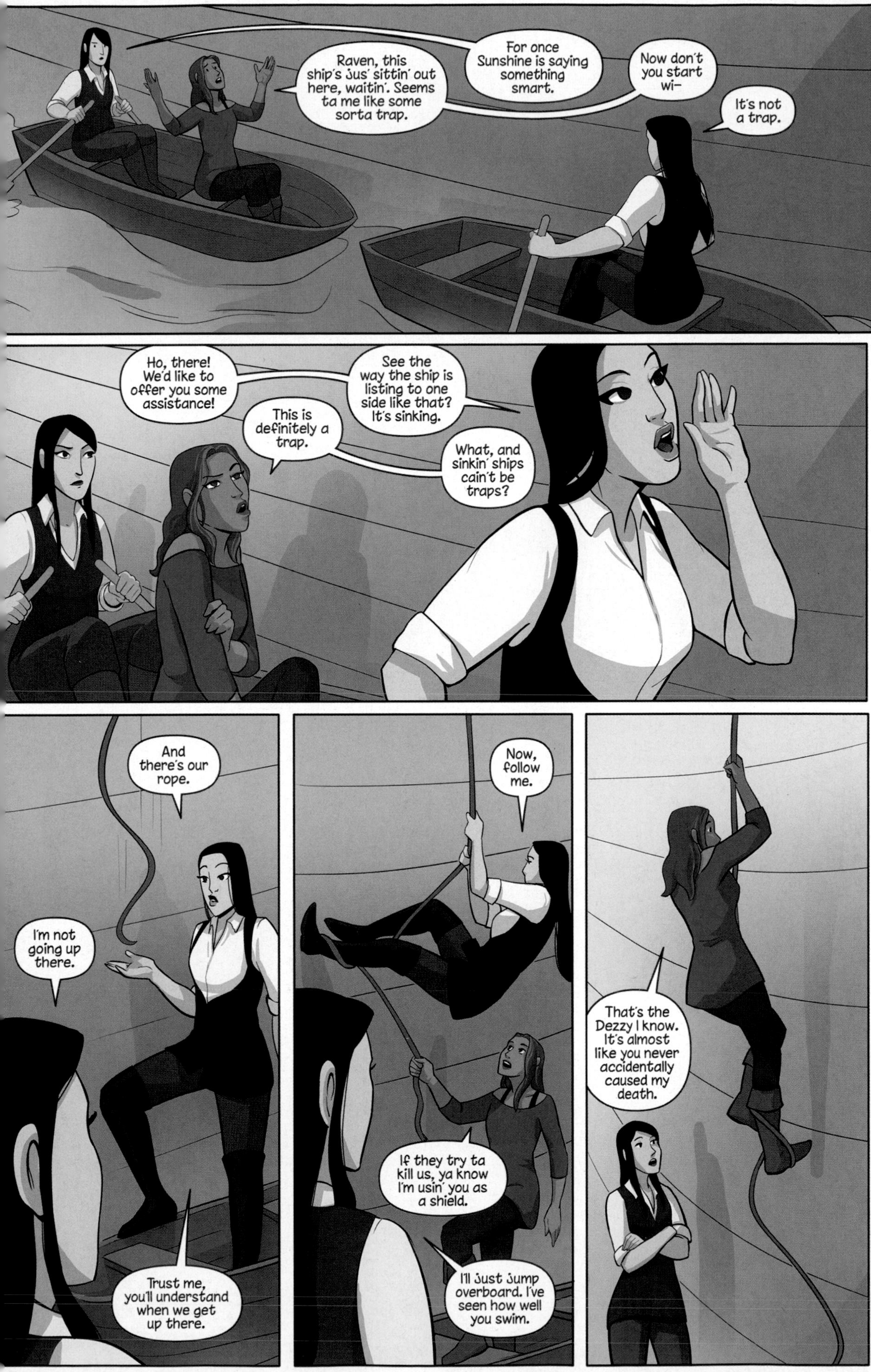
Raven, this ship's jus' sittin' out here, waitin'. Seems ta me like some sorta trap.
For once Sunshine is saying something smart.
Now don't you start wi–
It's not a trap.
Ho, there! We'd like to offer you some assistance!
See the way the ship is listing to one side like that? It's sinking.
This is definitely a trap.
What, and sinkin' ships cain't be traps?
And there's our rope.
I'm not going up there.
Trust me, you'll understand when we get up there.
Now, follow me.
If they try ta kill us, ya know I'm usin' you as a shield.
I'll just jump overboard. I've seen how well you swim.
That's the Dezzy I know. It's almost like you never accidentally caused my death.

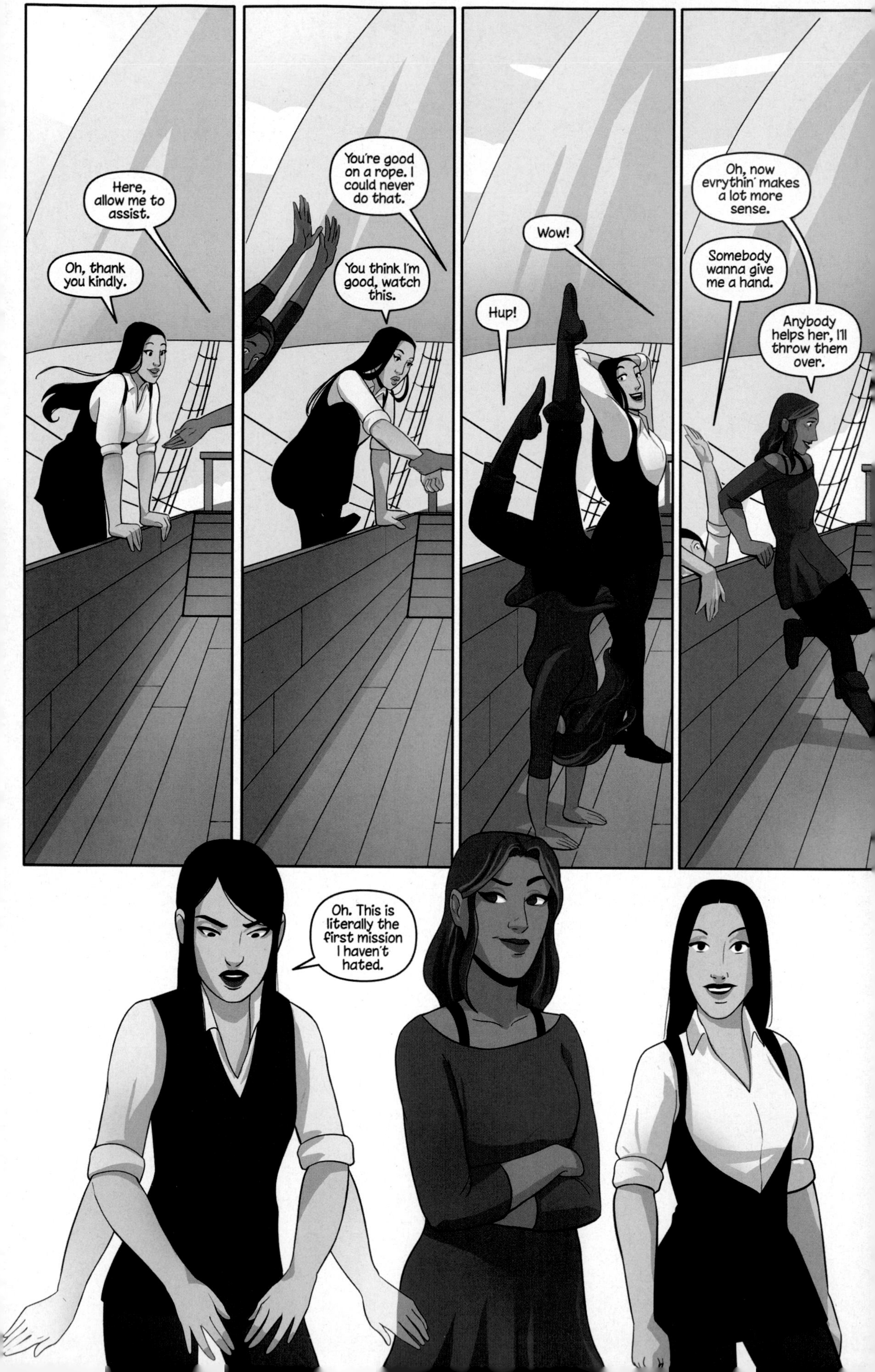
Here, allow me to assist.
Oh, thank you kindly.
You're good on a rope. I could never do that.
You think I'm good, watch this.
Wow!
Hup!
Oh, now evrythin' makes a lot more sense.
Somebody wanna give me a hand.
Anybody helps her, I'll throw them over.
Oh. This is literally the first mission I haven't hated.

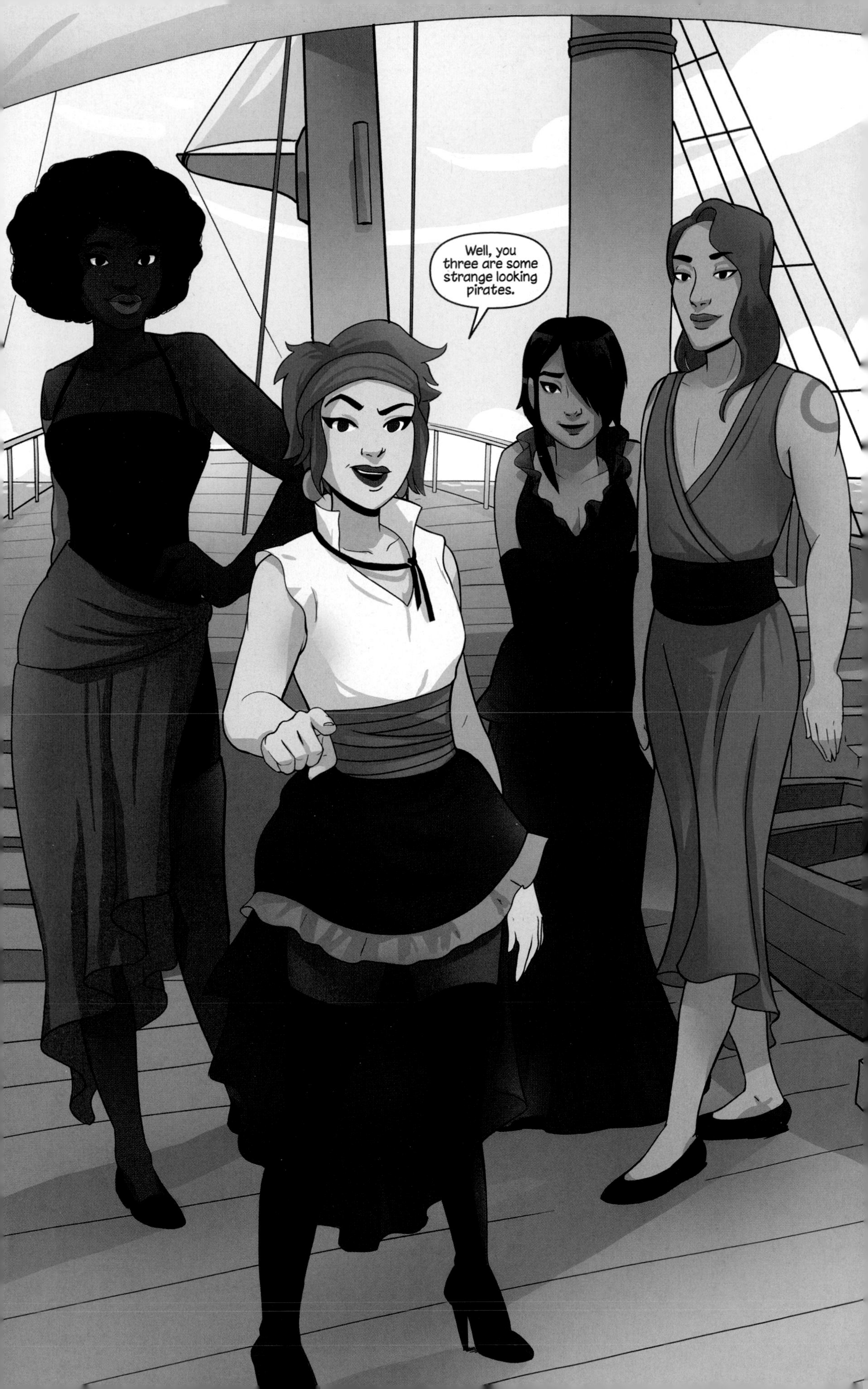
Well, you three are some strange looking pirates.

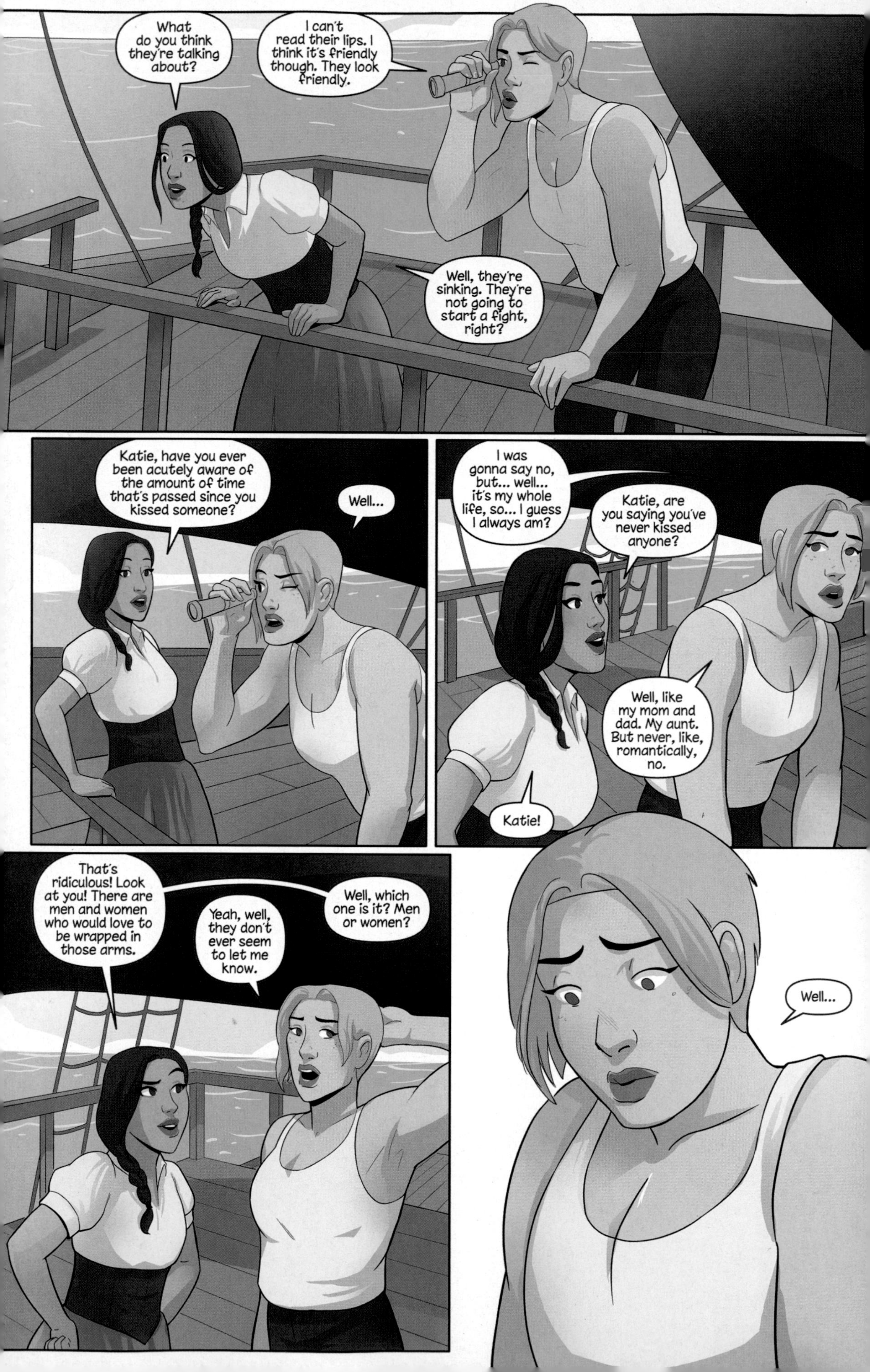
What do you think they're talking about?
I can't read their lips. I think it's friendly though. They look friendly.
Well, they're sinking. They're not going to start a fight, right?
Katie, have you ever been acutely aware of the amount of time that's passed since you kissed someone?
Well...
I was gonna say no, but... well... it's my whole life, so... I guess I always am?
Katie, are you saying you've never kissed anyone?
Well, like my mom and dad. My aunt. But never, like, romantically, no.
Katie!
That's ridiculous! Look at you! There are men and women who would love to be wrapped in those arms.
Well, which one is it? Men or women?
Yeah, well, they don't ever seem to let me know.
Well...

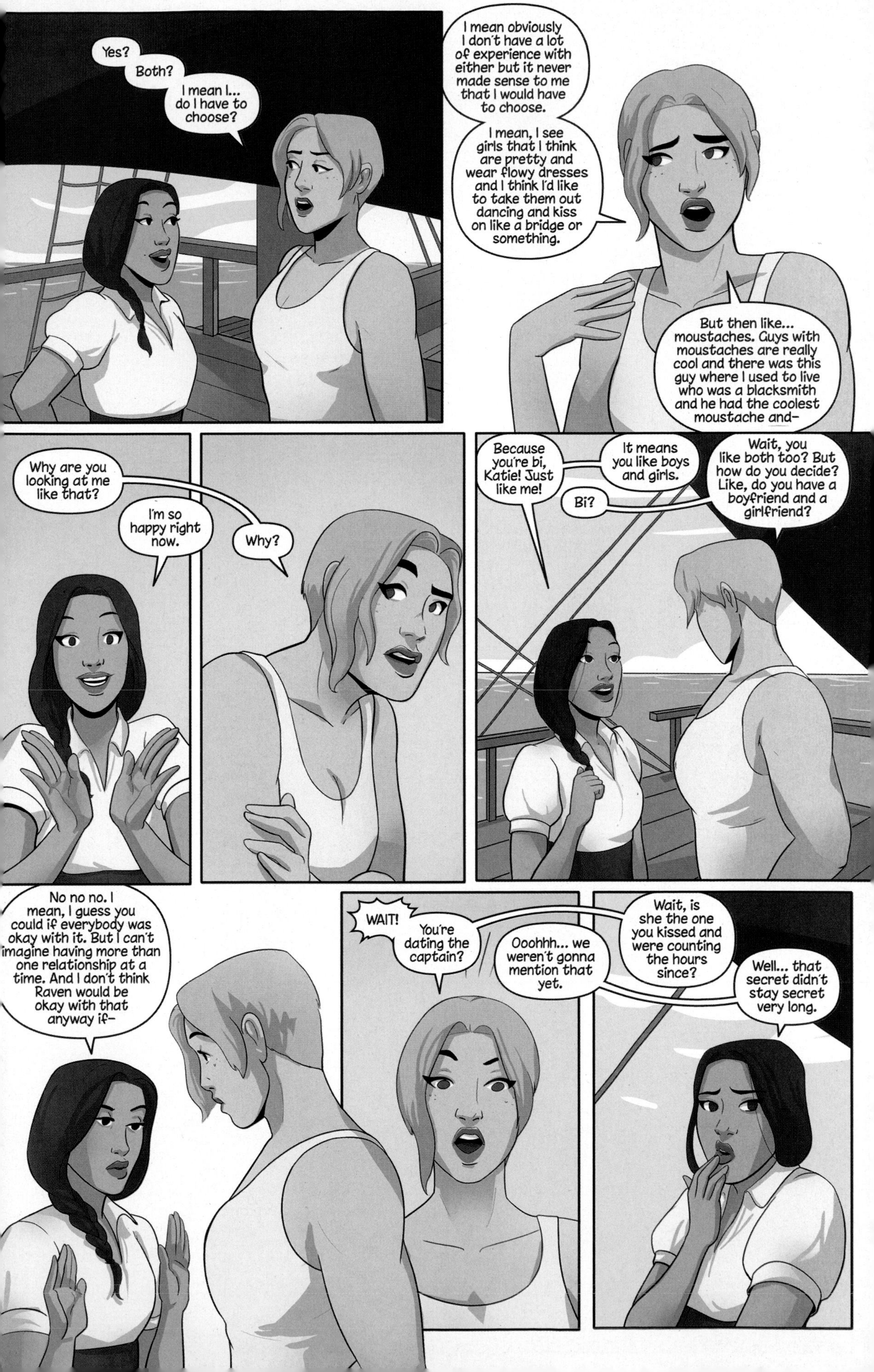
Yes?
Both?
I mean I... do I have to choose?
I mean obviously I don't have a lot of experience with either but it never made sense to me that I would have to choose.
I mean, I see girls that I think are pretty and wear flowy dresses and I think I'd like to take them out dancing and kiss on like a bridge or something.
But then like... moustaches. Guys with moustaches are really cool and there was this guy where I used to live who was a blacksmith and he had the coolest moustache and–
Why are you looking at me like that?
I'm so happy right now.
Why?
Because you're bi, Katie! Just like me!
Bi?
It means you like boys and girls.
Wait, you like both too? But how do you decide? Like, do you have a boyfriend and a girlfriend?
No no no. I mean, I guess you could if everybody was okay with it. But I can't imagine having more than one relationship at a time. And I don't think Raven would be okay with that anyway if–
WAIT!
You're dating the captain?
Ooohhh... we weren't gonna mention that yet.
Wait, is she the one you kissed and were counting the hours since?
Well... that secret didn't stay secret very long.

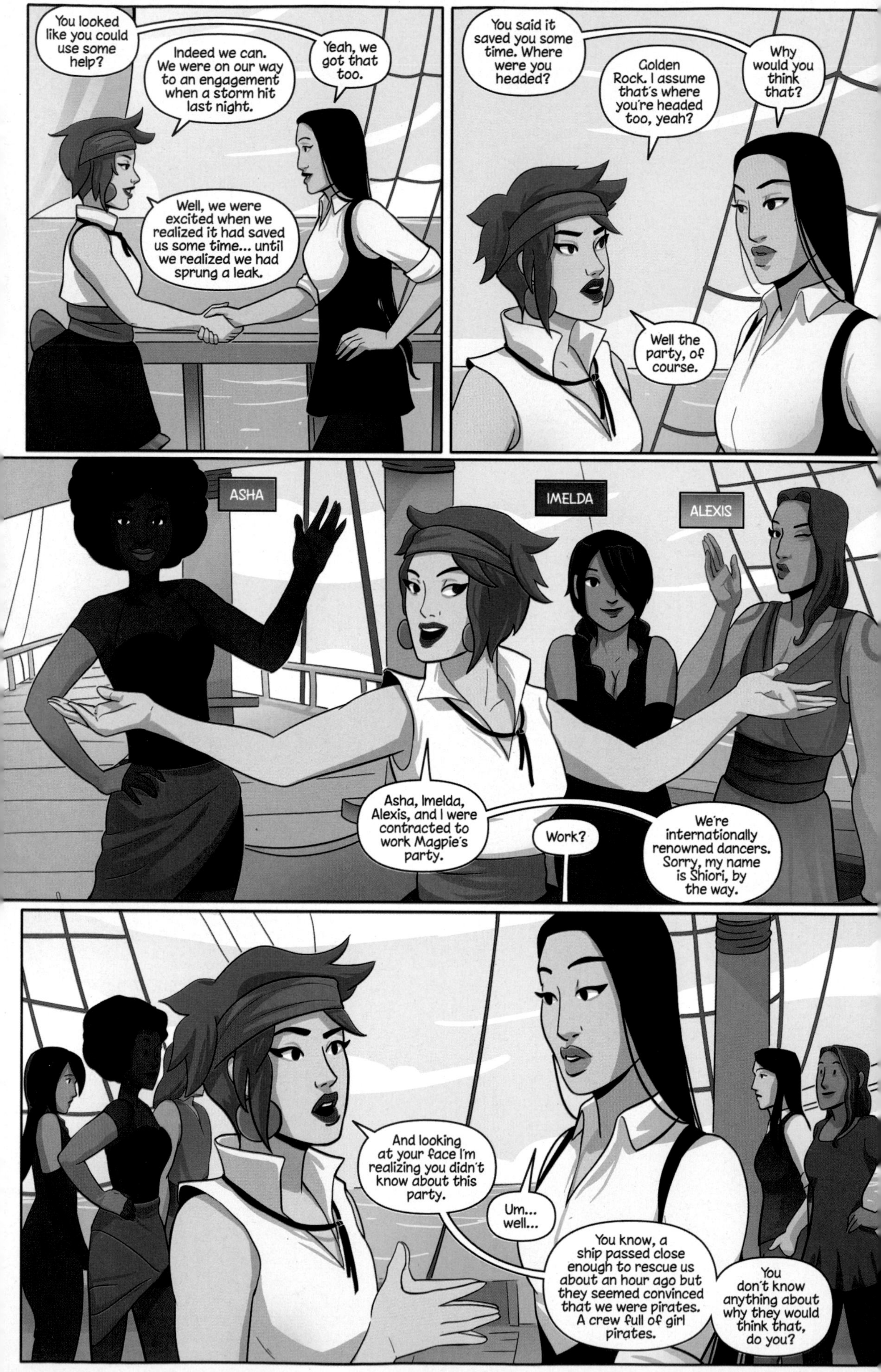
You looked like you could use some help?
Indeed we can. We were on our way to an engagement when a storm hit last night.
Yeah, we got that too.
Well, we were excited when we realized it had saved us some time... until we realized we had sprung a leak.
You said it saved you some time. Where were you headed?
Golden Rock. I assume that's where you're headed too, yeah?
Why would you think that?
Well the party, of course.
ASHA
IMELDA
ALEXIS
Asha, Imelda, Alexis, and I were contracted to work Magpie's party.
Work?
We're internationally renowned dancers. Sorry, my name is Shiori, by the way.
And looking at your face I'm realizing you didn't know about this party.
Um... well...
You know, a ship passed close enough to rescue us about an hour ago but they seemed convinced that we were pirates. A crew full of girl pirates.
You don't know anything about why they would think that, do you?

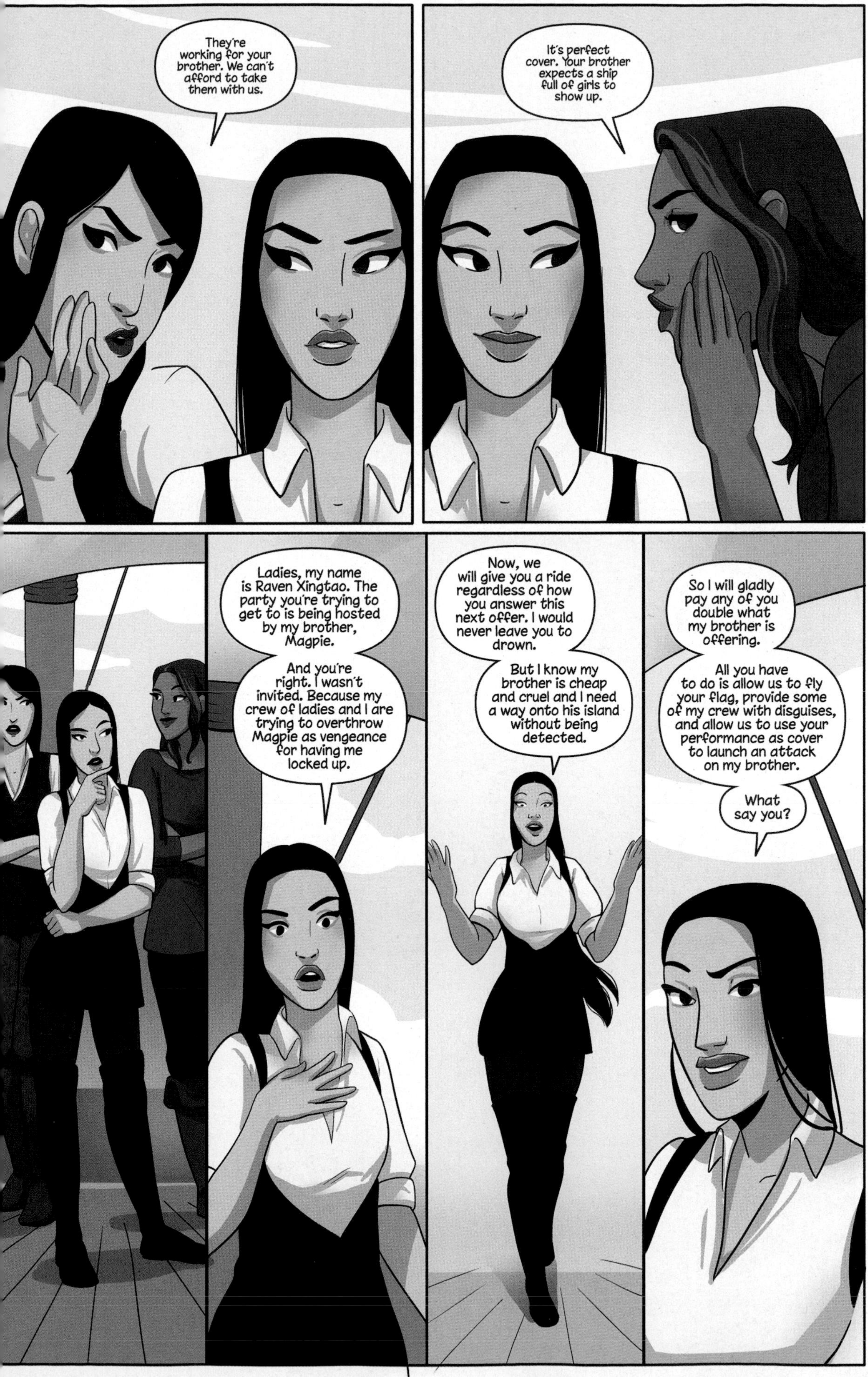
They're working for your brother. We can't afford to take them with us.
It's perfect cover. Your brother expects a ship full of girls to show up.
Ladies, my name is Raven Xingtao. The party you're trying to get to is being hosted by my brother, Magpie.
And you're right. I wasn't invited. Because my crew of ladies and I are trying to overthrow Magpie as vengeance for having me locked up.
Now, we will give you a ride regardless of how you answer this next offer. I would never leave you to drown.
But I know my brother is cheap and cruel and I need a way onto his island without being detected.
So I will gladly pay any of you double what my brother is offering.
All you have to do is allow us to fly your flag, provide some of my crew with disguises, and allow us to use your performance as cover to launch an attack on my brother.
What say you?

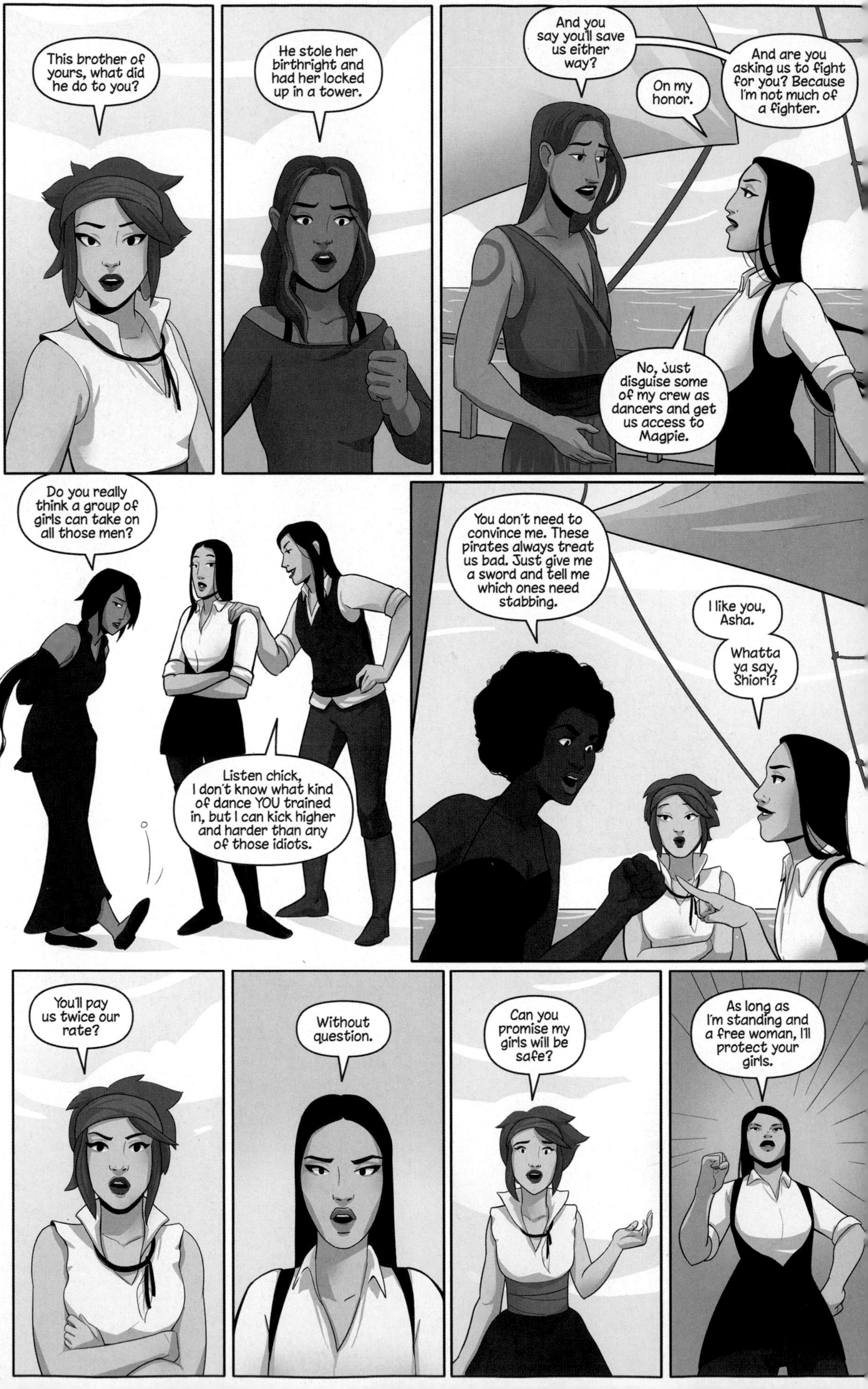
This brother of yours, what did he do to you?
He stole her birthright and had her locked up in a tower.
And you say you'll save us either way?
On my honor.
And are you asking us to fight for you? Because I'm not much of a fighter.
No, just disguise some of my crew as dancers and get us access to Magpie.
Do you really think a group of girls can take on all those men?
Listen chick, I don't know what kind of dance YOU trained in, but I can kick higher and harder than any of those idiots.
You don't need to convince me. These pirates always treat us bad. Just give me a sword and tell me which ones need stabbing.
I like you, Asha.
Whatta ya say, Shiori?
You'll pay us twice our rate?
Without question.
Can you promise my girls will be safe?
As long as I'm standing and a free woman, I'll protect your girls.

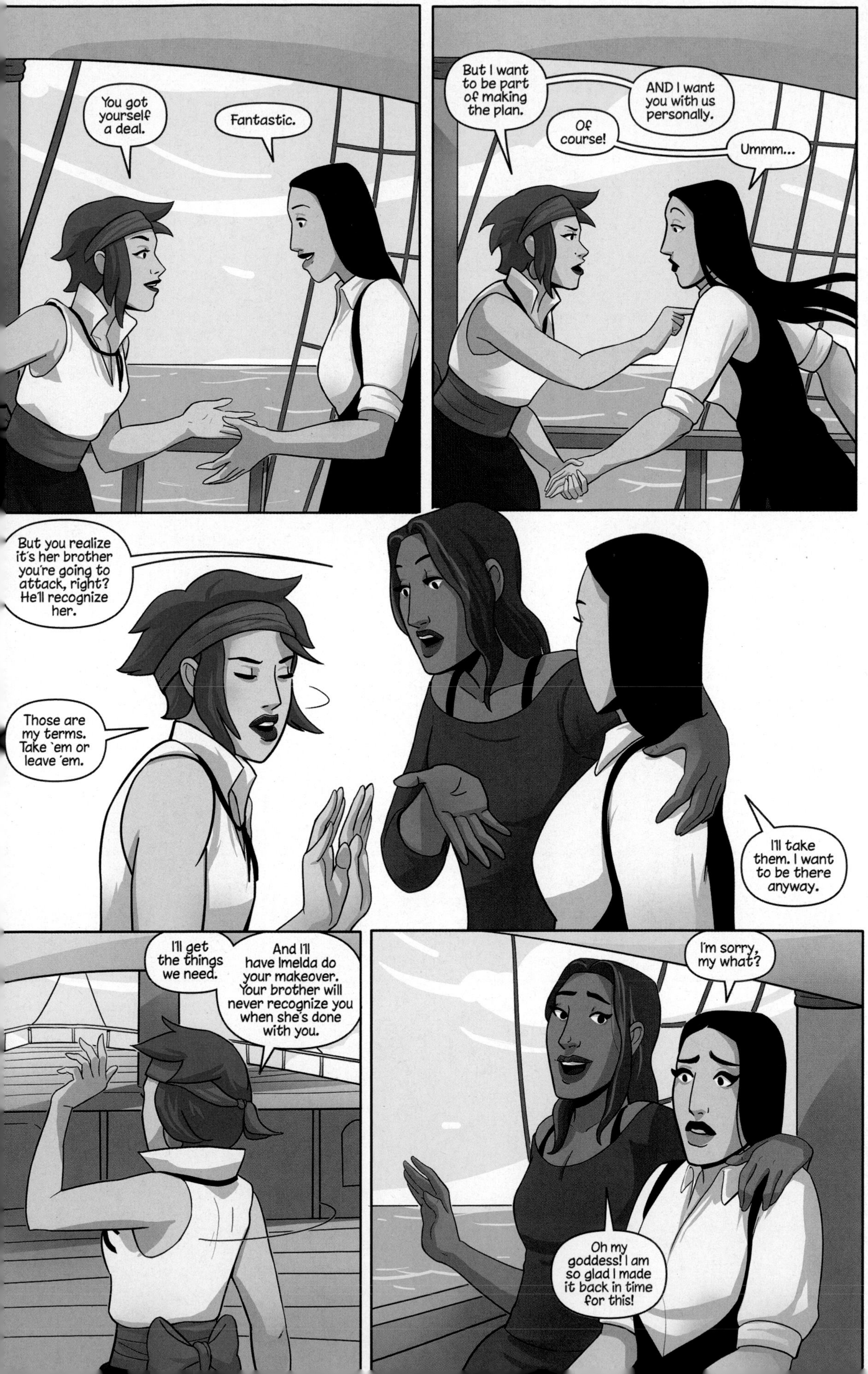
You got yourself a deal.
Fantastic.
But I want to be part of making the plan.
AND I want you with us personally.
Of course!
Ummm...
But you realize it's her brother you're going to attack, right? He'll recognize her.
Those are my terms. Take 'em or leave 'em.
I'll take them. I want to be there anyway.
I'll get the things we need.
And I'll have Imelda do your makeover. Your brother will never recognize you when she's done with you.
I'm sorry, my what?
Oh my goddess! I am so glad I made it back in time for this!

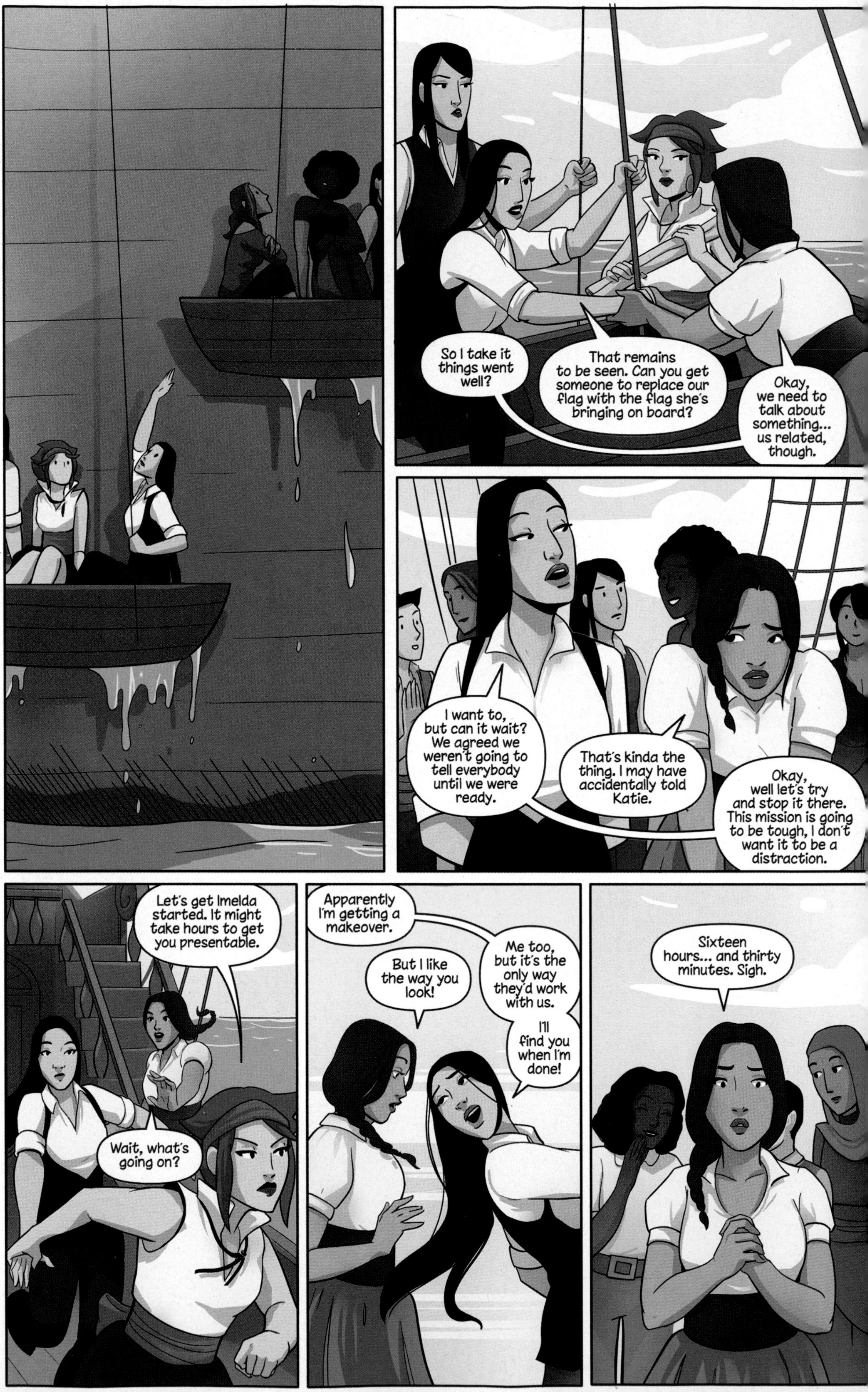
So I take it things went well?
That remains to be seen. Can you get someone to replace our flag with the flag she's bringing on board?
Okay, we need to talk about something... us related, though.
I want to, but can it wait? We agreed we weren't going to tell everybody until we were ready.
That's kinda the thing. I may have accidentally told Katie.
Okay, well let's try and stop it there. This mission is going to be tough, I don't want it to be a distraction.
Let's get Imelda started. It might take hours to get you presentable.
Wait, what's going on?
Apparently I'm getting a makeover.
But I like the way you look!
Me too, but it's the only way they'd work with us.
I'll find you when I'm done!
Sixteen hours... and thirty minutes. Sigh.

Princess
RAVEN
THE PIRATE PRINCESS

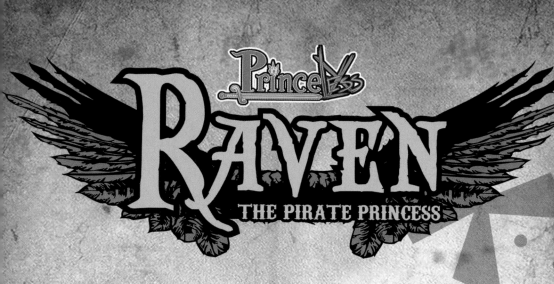

Year Two: Love and Revenge

Chapter Ten: Distraction, Infiltration, Extraction

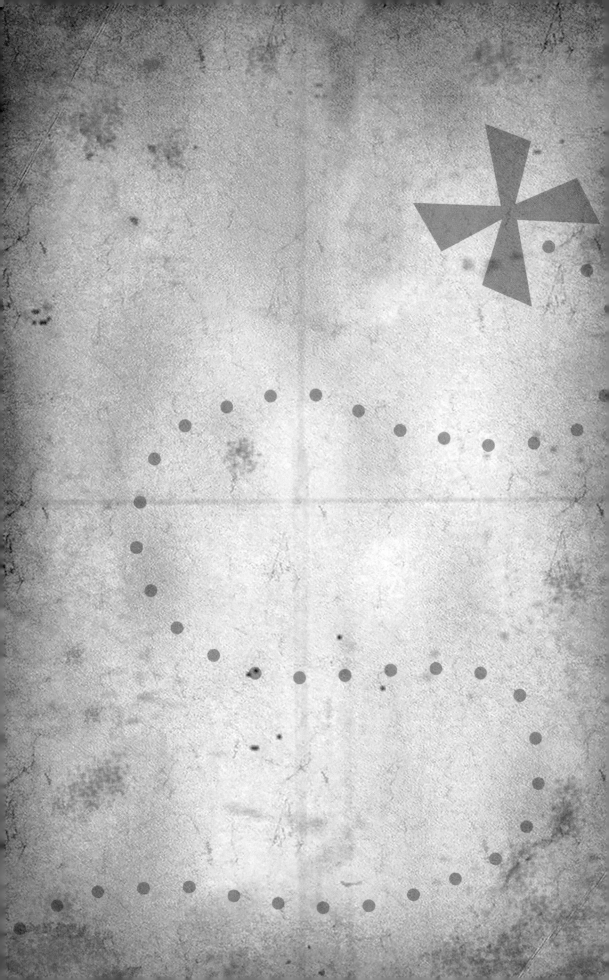

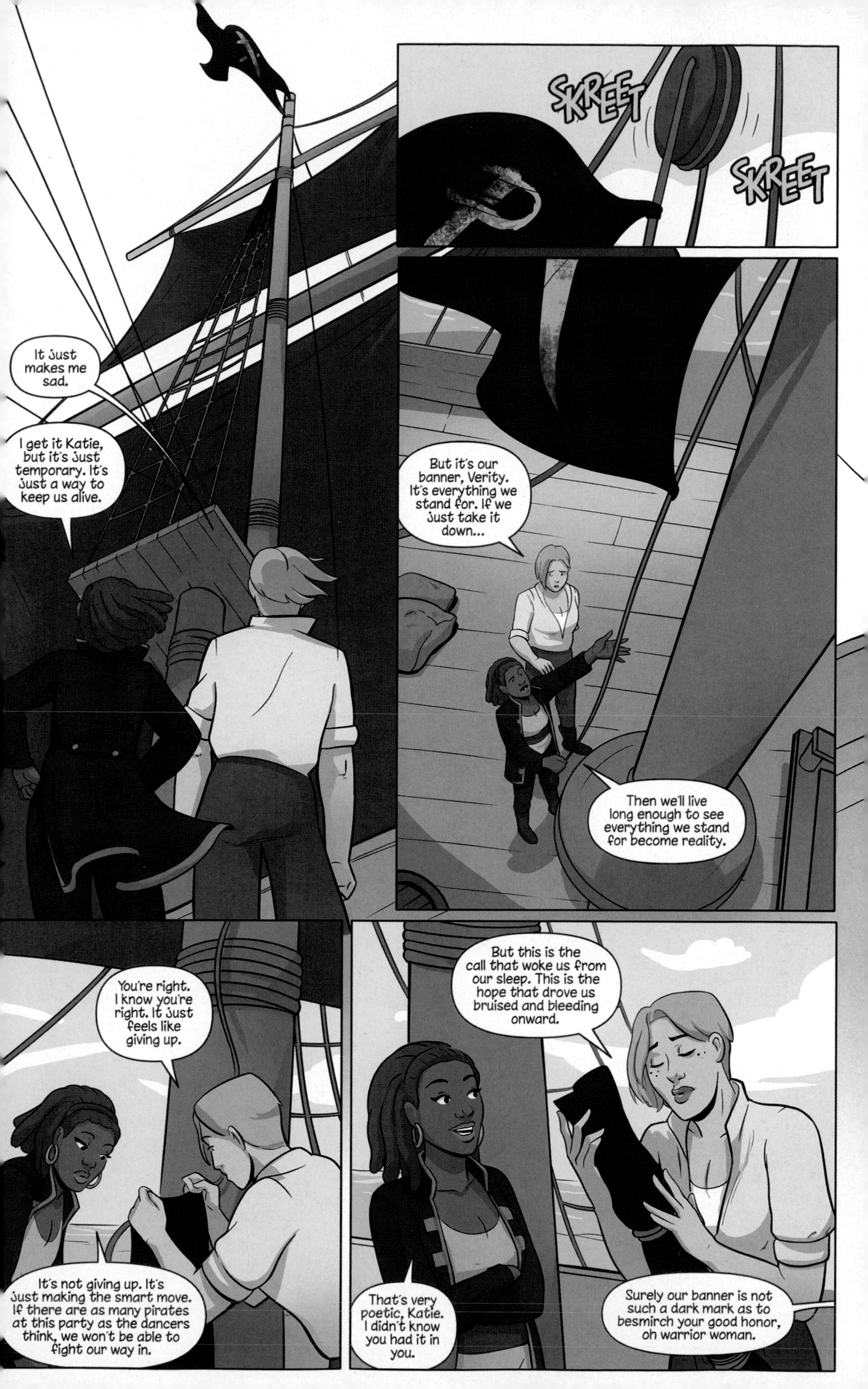
SKREET
SKREET
It just makes me sad.
I get it Katie, but it's just temporary. It's just a way to keep us alive.
But it's our banner, Verity. It's everything we stand for. If we just take it down...
Then we'll live long enough to see everything we stand for become reality.
You're right. I know you're right. It just feels like giving up.
It's not giving up. It's just making the smart move. If there are as many pirates at this party as the dancers think, we won't be able to fight our way in.
But this is the call that woke us from our sleep. This is the hope that drove us bruised and bleeding onward.
That's very poetic, Katie. I didn't know you had it in you.
Surely our banner is not such a dark mark as to besmirch your good honor, oh warrior woman.

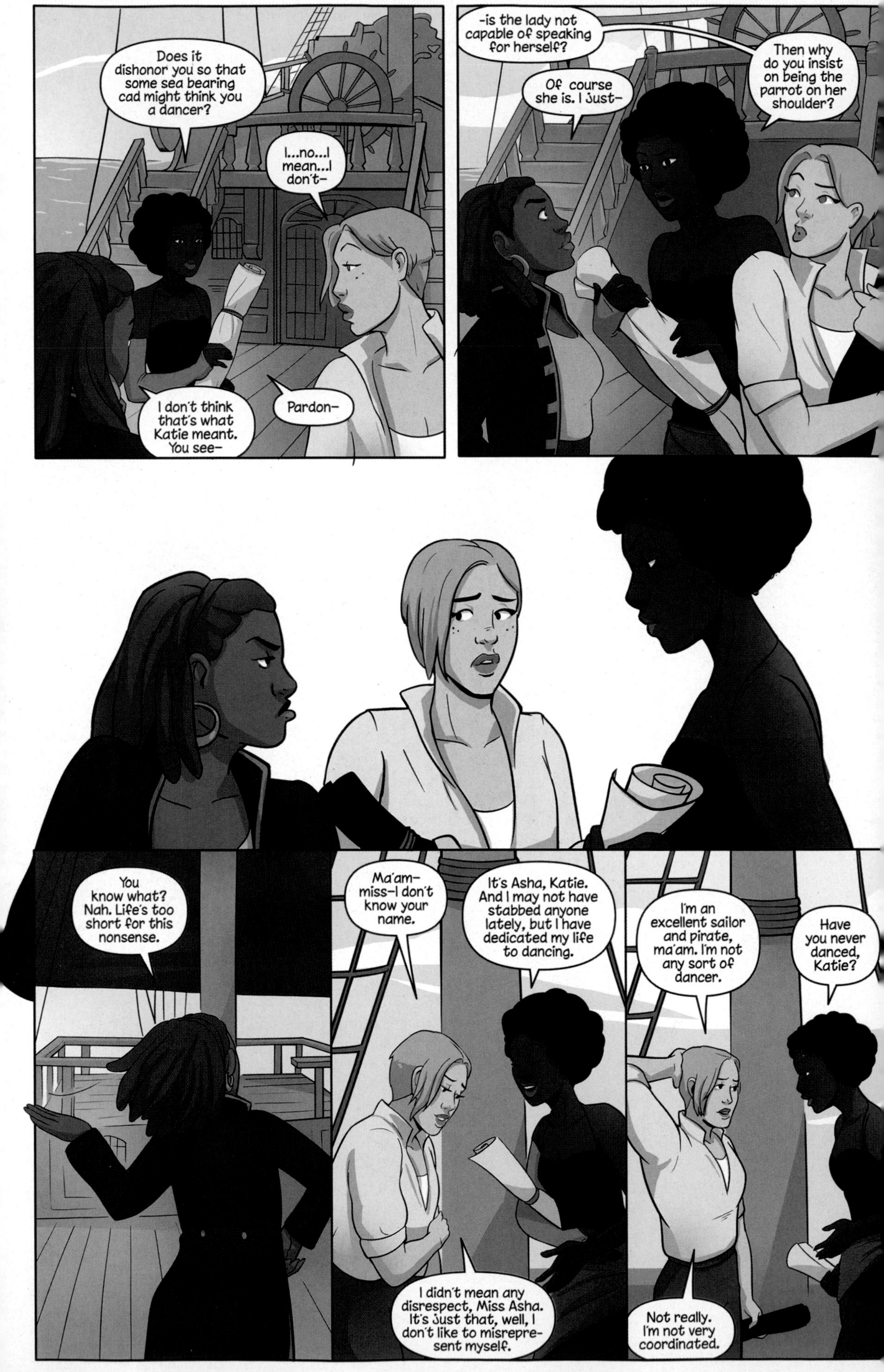
Does it dishonor you so that some sea bearing cad might think you a dancer?
I...no...I mean...I don't-
I don't think that's what Katie meant. You see-
Pardon-
-is the lady not capable of speaking for herself?
Of course she is. I Just-
Then why do you insist on being the parrot on her shoulder?
You know what? Nah. Life's too short for this nonsense.
Ma'am-miss-I don't know your name.
It's Asha, Katie. And I may not have stabbed anyone lately, but I have dedicated my life to dancing.
I didn't mean any disrespect, Miss Asha. It's just that, well, I don't like to misrepresent myself.
I'm an excellent sailor and pirate, ma'am. I'm not any sort of dancer.
Have you never danced, Katie?
Not really. I'm not very coordinated.

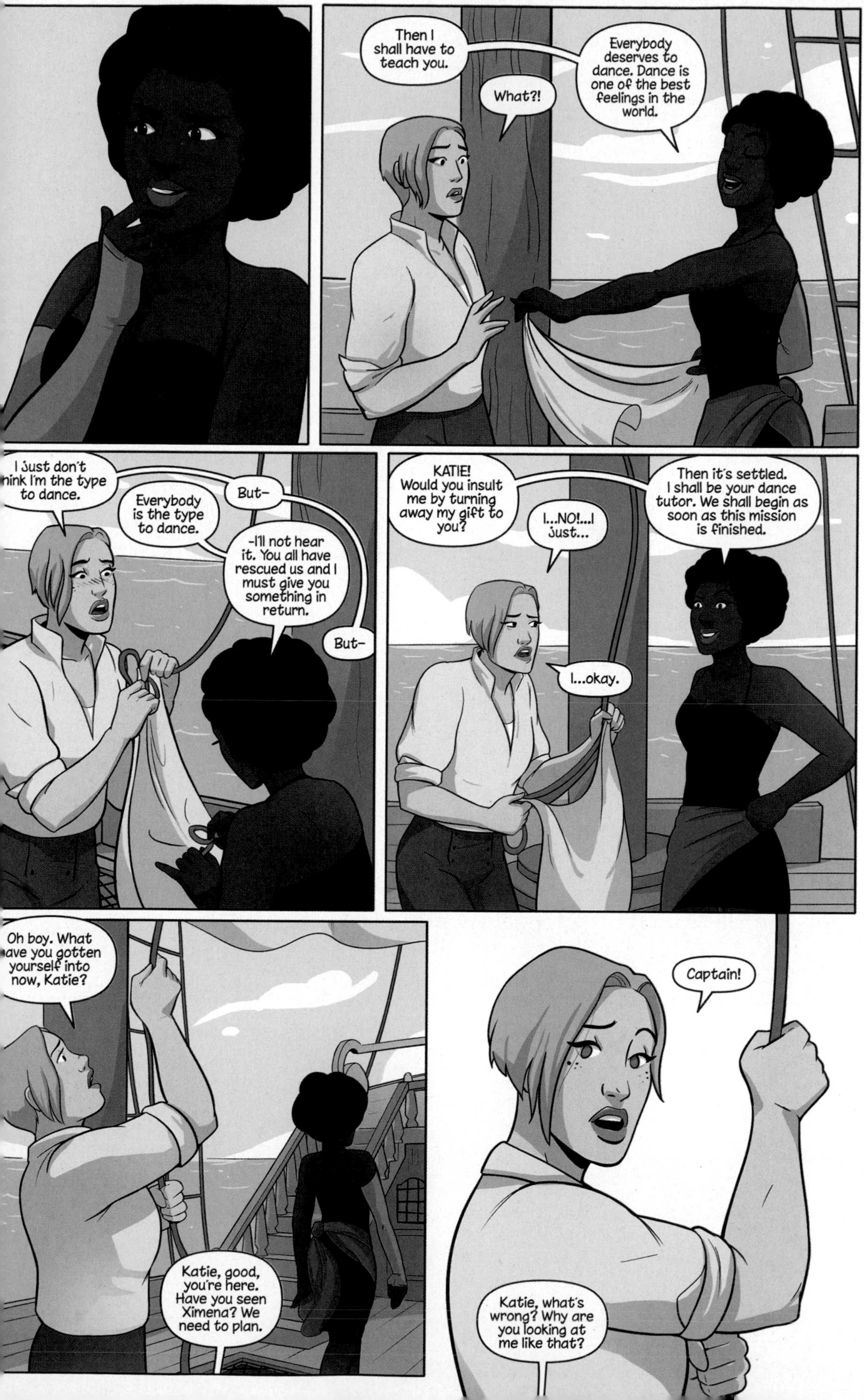

Then I shall have to teach you.
What?!
Everybody deserves to dance. Dance is one of the best feelings in the world.
I just don't think I'm the type to dance.
Everybody is the type to dance.
But–
-I'll not hear it. You all have rescued us and I must give you something in return.
But–
KATIE! Would you insult me by turning away my gift to you?
I...NO!...I just...
Then it's settled. I shall be your dance tutor. We shall begin as soon as this mission is finished.
I...okay.
Oh boy. What have you gotten yourself into now, Katie?
Katie, good, you're here. Have you seen Ximena? We need to plan.
Captain!
Katie, what's wrong? Why are you looking at me like that?

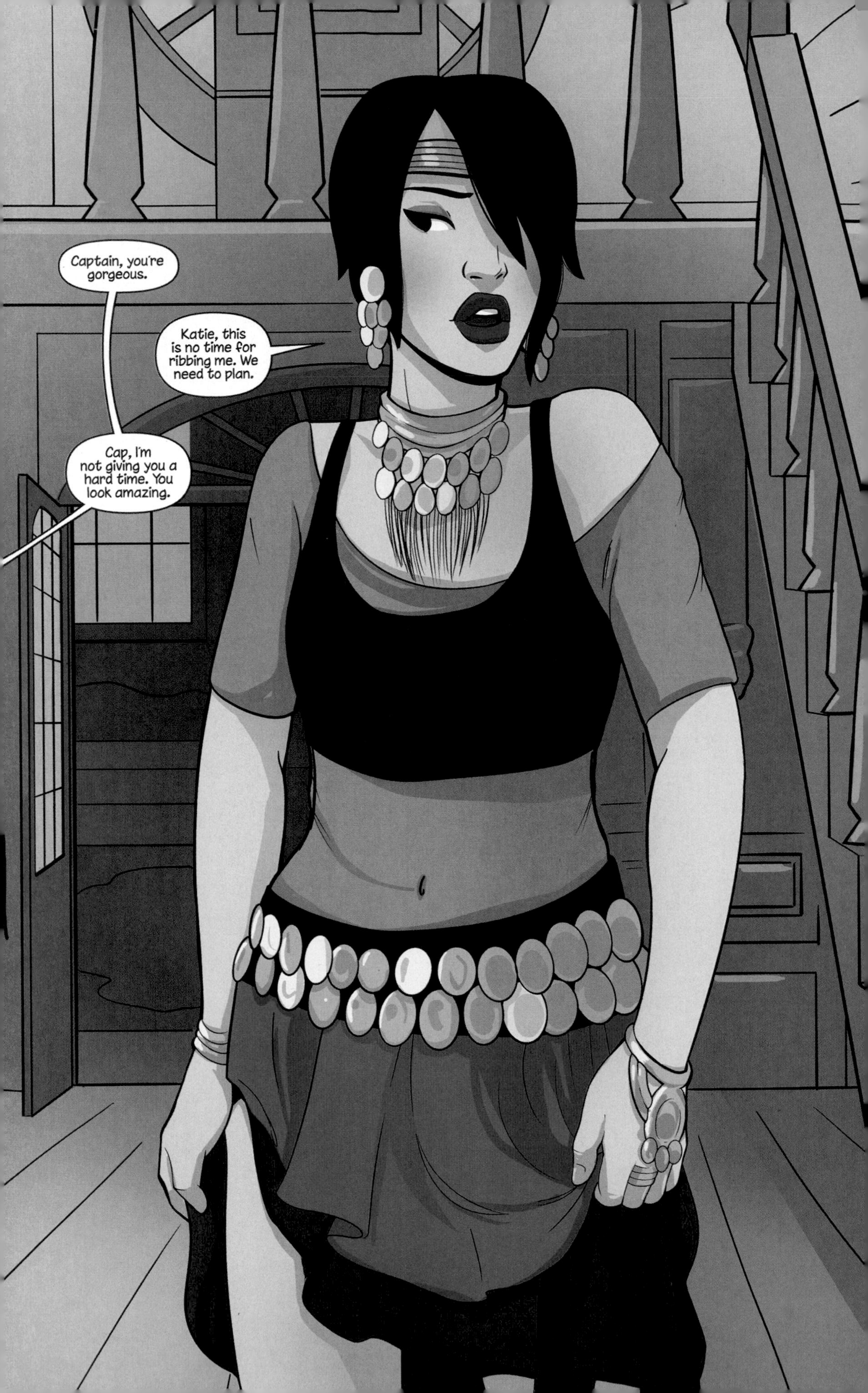
Captain, you're gorgeous.
Katie, this is no time for ribbing me. We need to plan.
Cap, I'm not giving you a hard time. You look amazing.

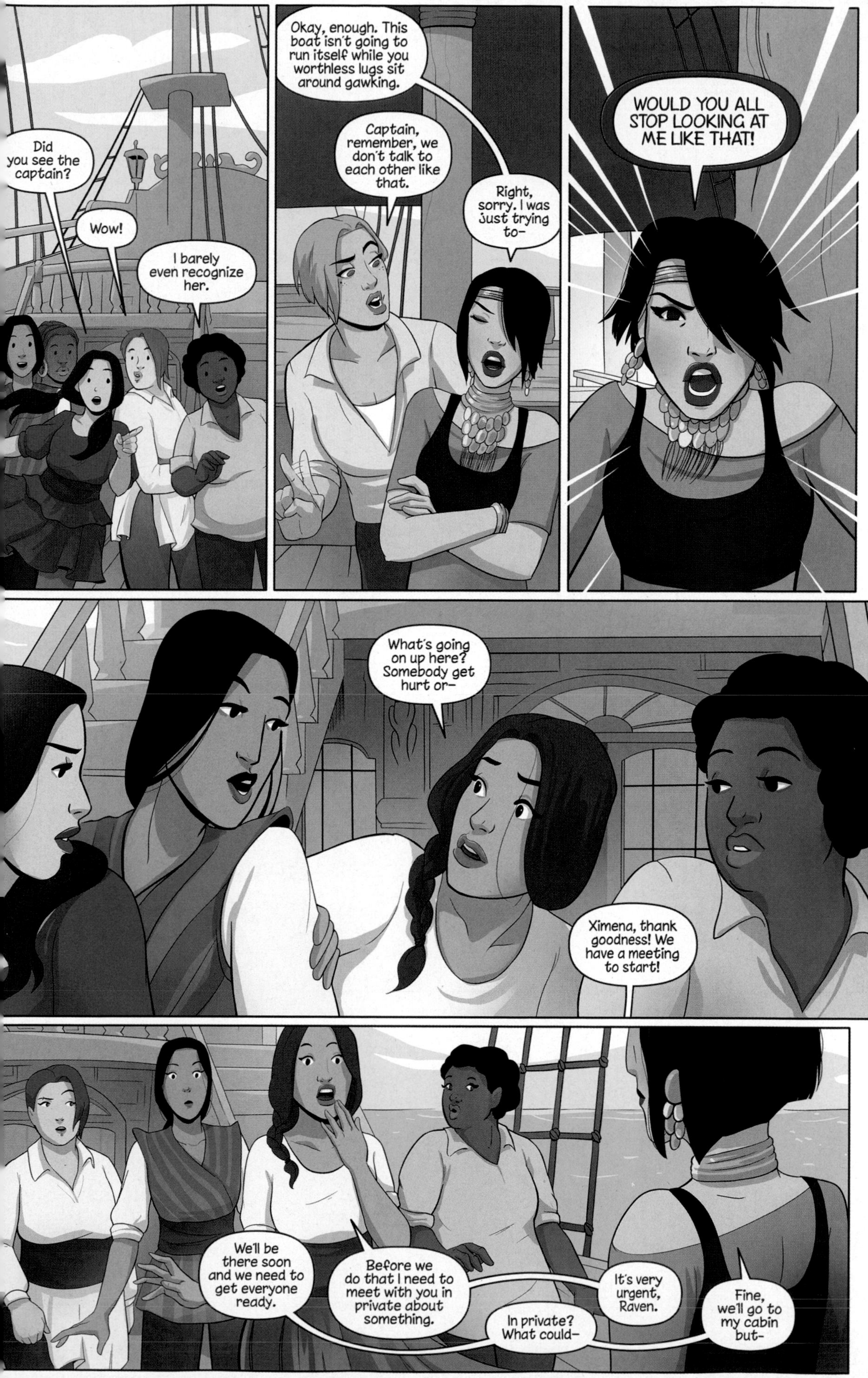
Did you see the captain?
Wow!
I barely even recognize her.
Okay, enough. This boat isn't going to run itself while you worthless lugs sit around gawking.
Captain, remember, we don't talk to each other like that.
Right, sorry. I was just trying to-
WOULD YOU ALL STOP LOOKING AT ME LIKE THAT!
What's going on up here? Somebody get hurt or-
Ximena, thank goodness! We have a meeting to start!
We'll be there soon and we need to get everyone ready.
Before we do that I need to meet with you in private about something.
In private? What could-
It's very urgent, Raven.
Fine, we'll go to my cabin but-

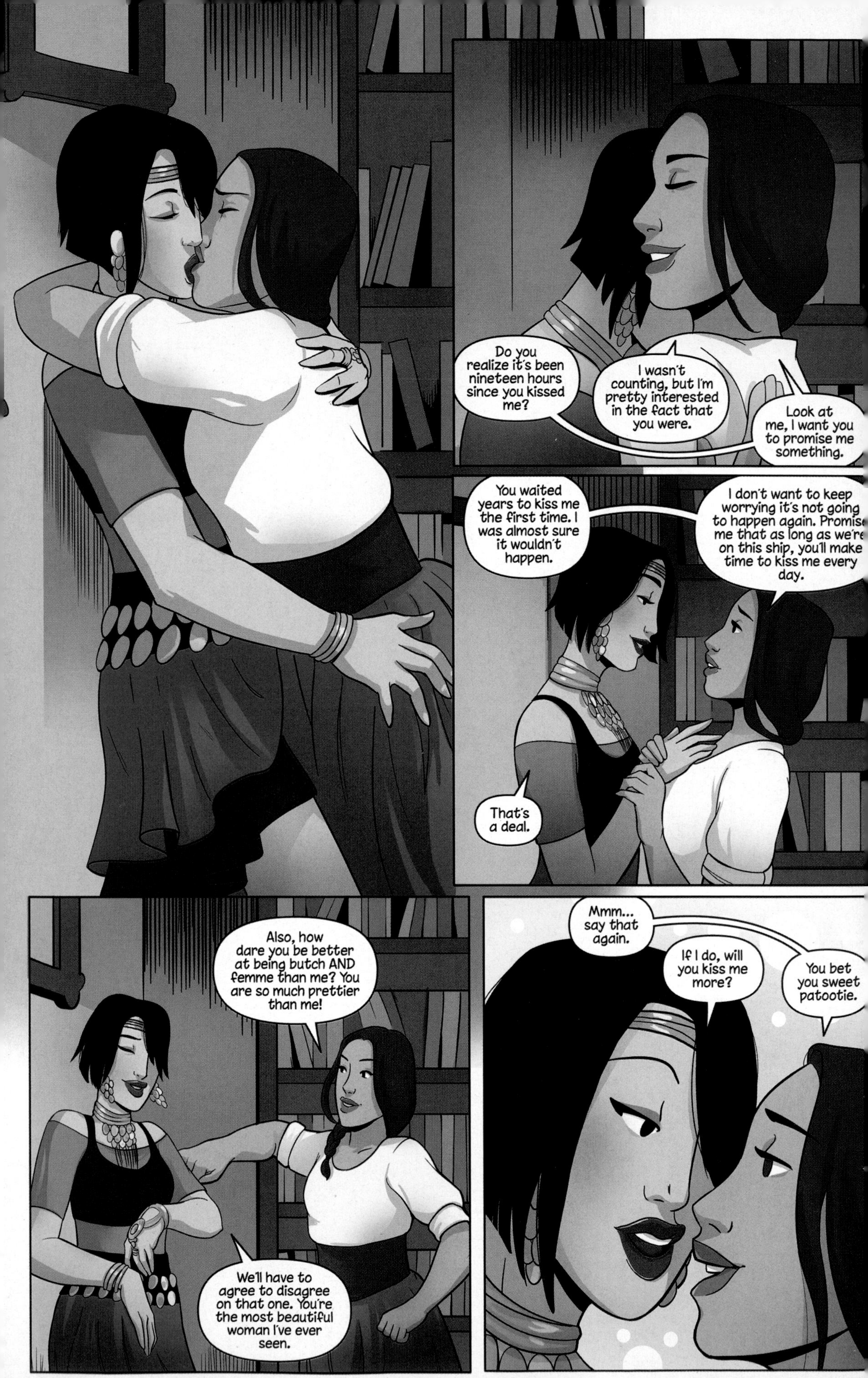
Do you realize it's been nineteen hours since you kissed me?
I wasn't counting, but I'm pretty interested in the fact that you were.
Look at me, I want you to promise me something.
You waited years to kiss me the first time. I was almost sure it wouldn't happen.
I don't want to keep worrying it's not going to happen again. Promise me that as long as we're on this ship, you'll make time to kiss me every day.
That's a deal.
Also, how dare you be better at being butch AND femme than me? You are so much prettier than me!
We'll have to agree to disagree on that one. You're the most beautiful woman I've ever seen.
Mmm... say that again.
If I do, will you kiss me more?
You bet you sweet patootie.

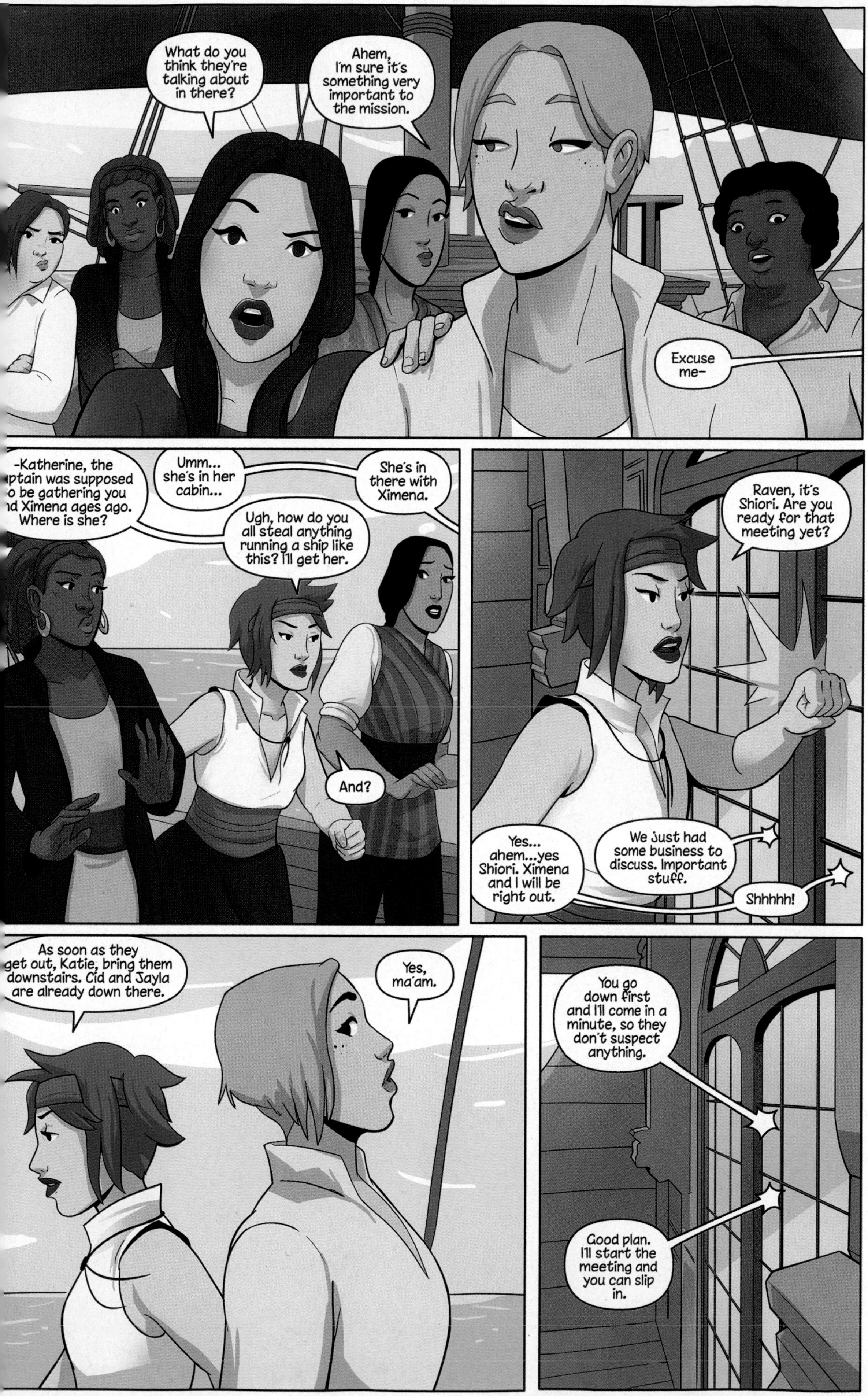
What do you think they're talking about in there?
Ahem, I'm sure it's something very important to the mission.
Excuse me-
-Katherine, the ptain was supposed o be gathering you nd Ximena ages ago. Where is she?
Umm... she's in her cabin...
She's in there with Ximena.
Ugh, how do you all steal anything running a ship like this? I'll get her.
And?
Raven, it's Shiori. Are you ready for that meeting yet?
Yes... ahem...yes Shiori. Ximena and I will be right out.
We just had some business to discuss. Important stuff.
Shhhhh!
As soon as they get out, Katie, bring them downstairs. Cid and Jayla are already down there.
Yes, ma'am.
You go down first and I'll come in a minute, so they don't suspect anything.
Good plan. I'll start the meeting and you can slip in.

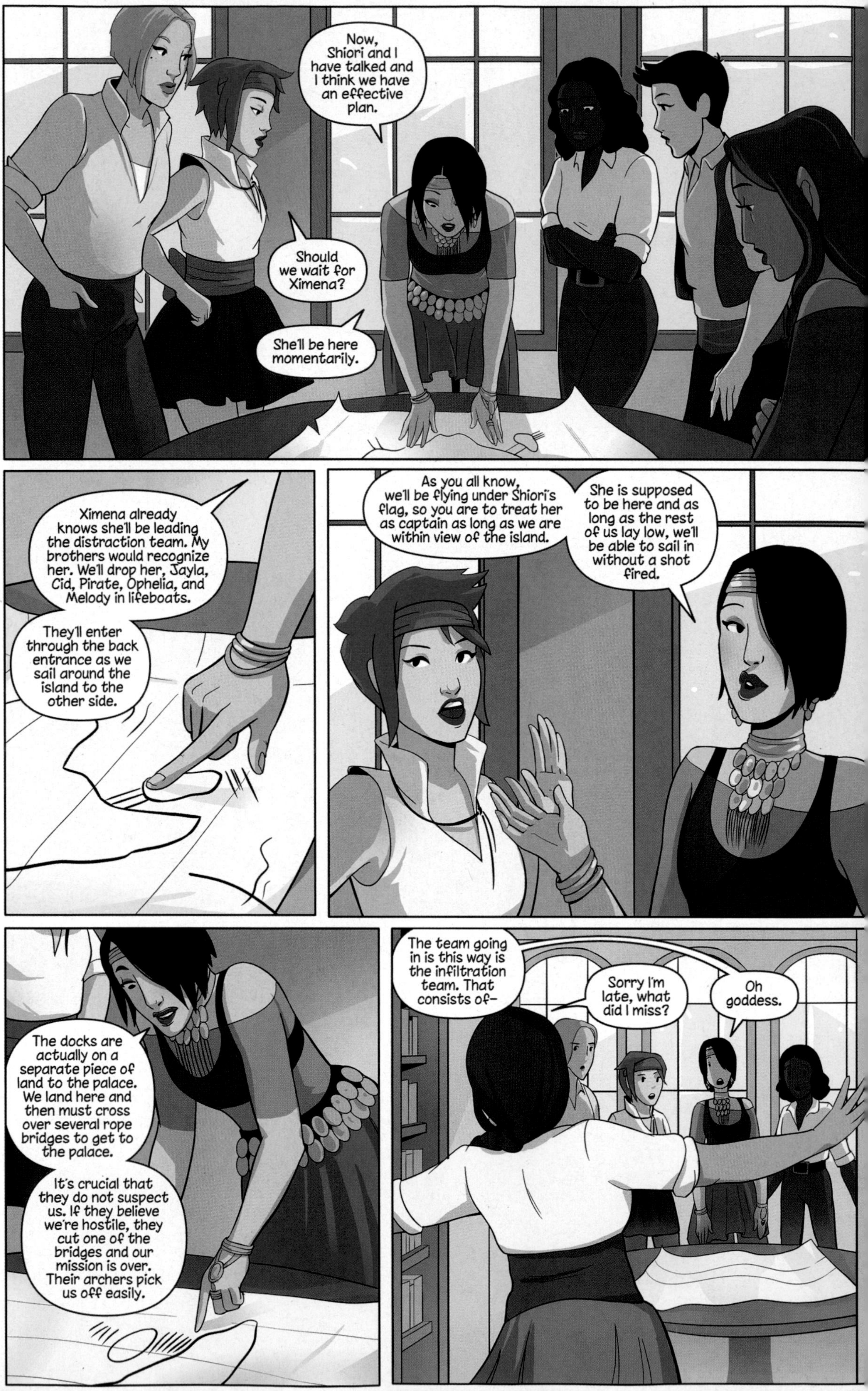

Now, Shiori and I have talked and I think we have an effective plan.
Should we wait for Ximena?
She'll be here momentarily.
Ximena already knows she'll be leading the distraction team. My brothers would recognize her. We'll drop her, Jayla, Cid, Pirate, Ophelia, and Melody in lifeboats.
They'll enter through the back entrance as we sail around the island to the other side.
As you all know, we'll be flying under Shiori's flag, so you are to treat her as captain as long as we are within view of the island.
She is supposed to be here and as long as the rest of us lay low, we'll be able to sail in without a shot fired.
The docks are actually on a separate piece of land to the palace. We land here and then must cross over several rope bridges to get to the palace.
It's crucial that they do not suspect us. If they believe we're hostile, they cut one of the bridges and our mission is over. Their archers pick us off easily.
The team going in is this way is the infiltration team. That consists of–
Sorry I'm late, what did I miss?
Oh goddess.

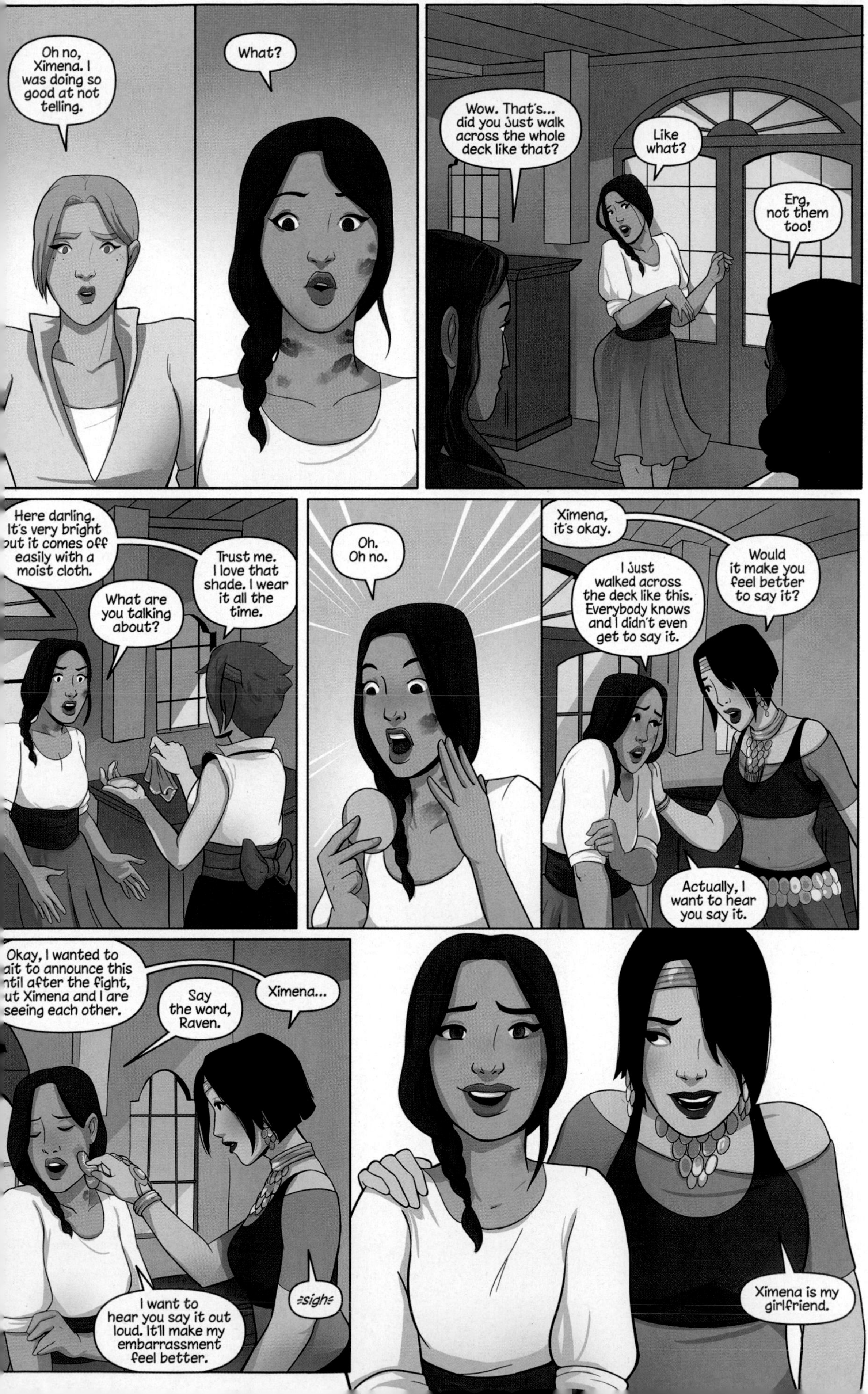
Oh no, Ximena. I was doing so good at not telling.
What?
Wow. That's... did you just walk across the whole deck like that?
Like what?
Erg, not them too!
Here darling. It's very bright but it comes off easily with a moist cloth.
What are you talking about?
Trust me. I love that shade. I wear it all the time.
Oh. Oh no.
Ximena, it's okay.
I just walked across the deck like this. Everybody knows and I didn't even get to say it.
Would it make you feel better to say it?
Actually, I want to hear you say it.
Okay, I wanted to wait to announce this until after the fight, but Ximena and I are seeing each other.
Say the word, Raven.
Ximena...
I want to hear you say it out loud. It'll make my embarrassment feel better.
sigh
Ximena is my girlfriend.

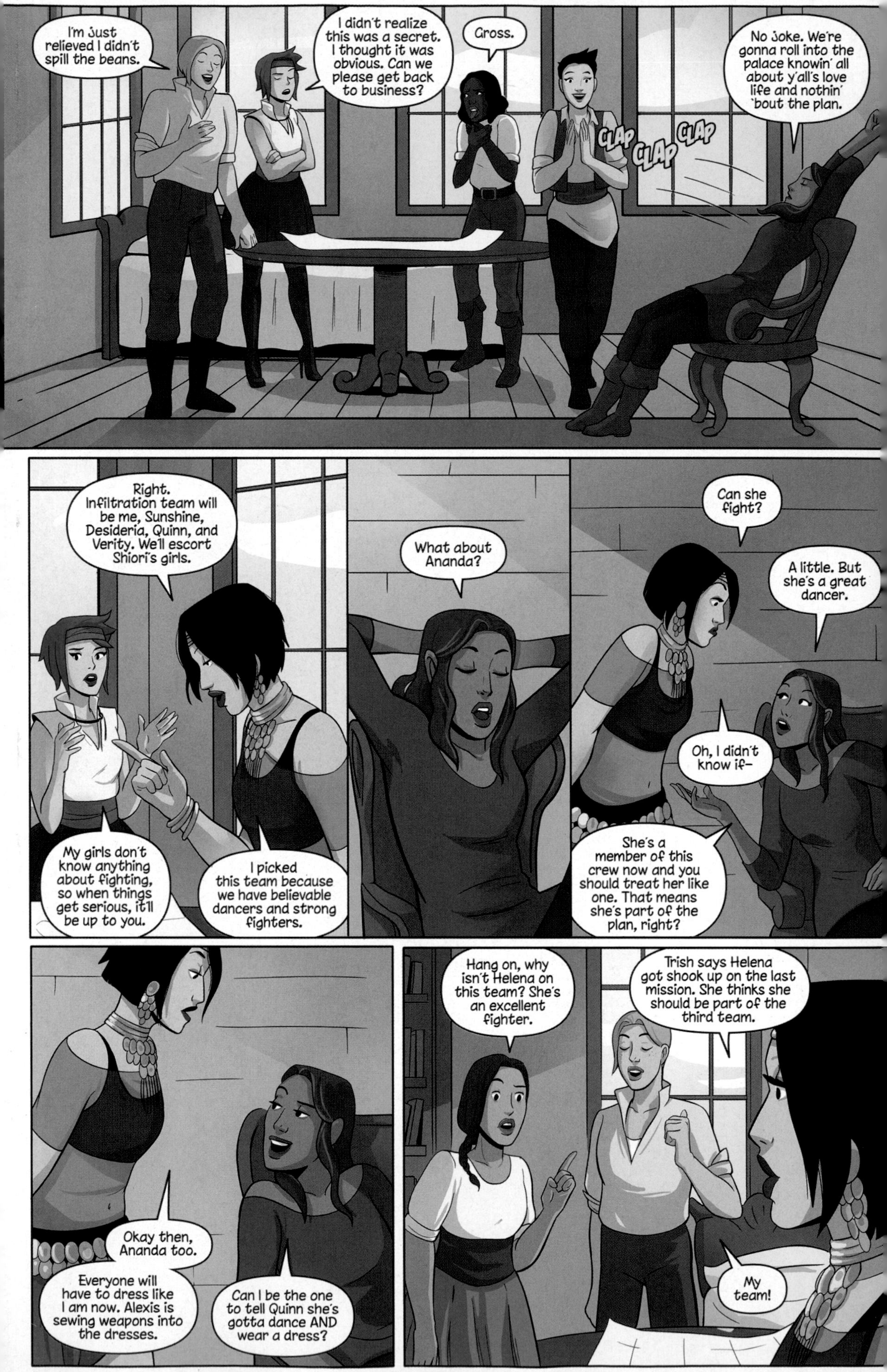
I'm just relieved I didn't spill the beans.
I didn't realize this was a secret. I thought it was obvious. Can we please get back to business?
Gross.
CLAP CLAP CLAP
No joke. We're gonna roll into the palace knowin' all about y'all's love life and nothin' 'bout the plan.
Right. Infiltration team will be me, Sunshine, Desideria, Quinn, and Verity. We'll escort Shiori's girls.
My girls don't know anything about fighting, so when things get serious, it'll be up to you.
I picked this team because we have believable dancers and strong fighters.
What about Ananda?
Can she fight?
A little. But she's a great dancer.
Oh, I didn't know if–
She's a member of this crew now and you should treat her like one. That means she's part of the plan, right?
Okay then, Ananda too.
Everyone will have to dress like I am now. Alexis is sewing weapons into the dresses.
Can I be the one to tell Quinn she's gotta dance AND wear a dress?
Hang on, why isn't Helena on this team? She's an excellent fighter.
Trish says Helena got shook up on the last mission. She thinks she should be part of the third team.
My team!

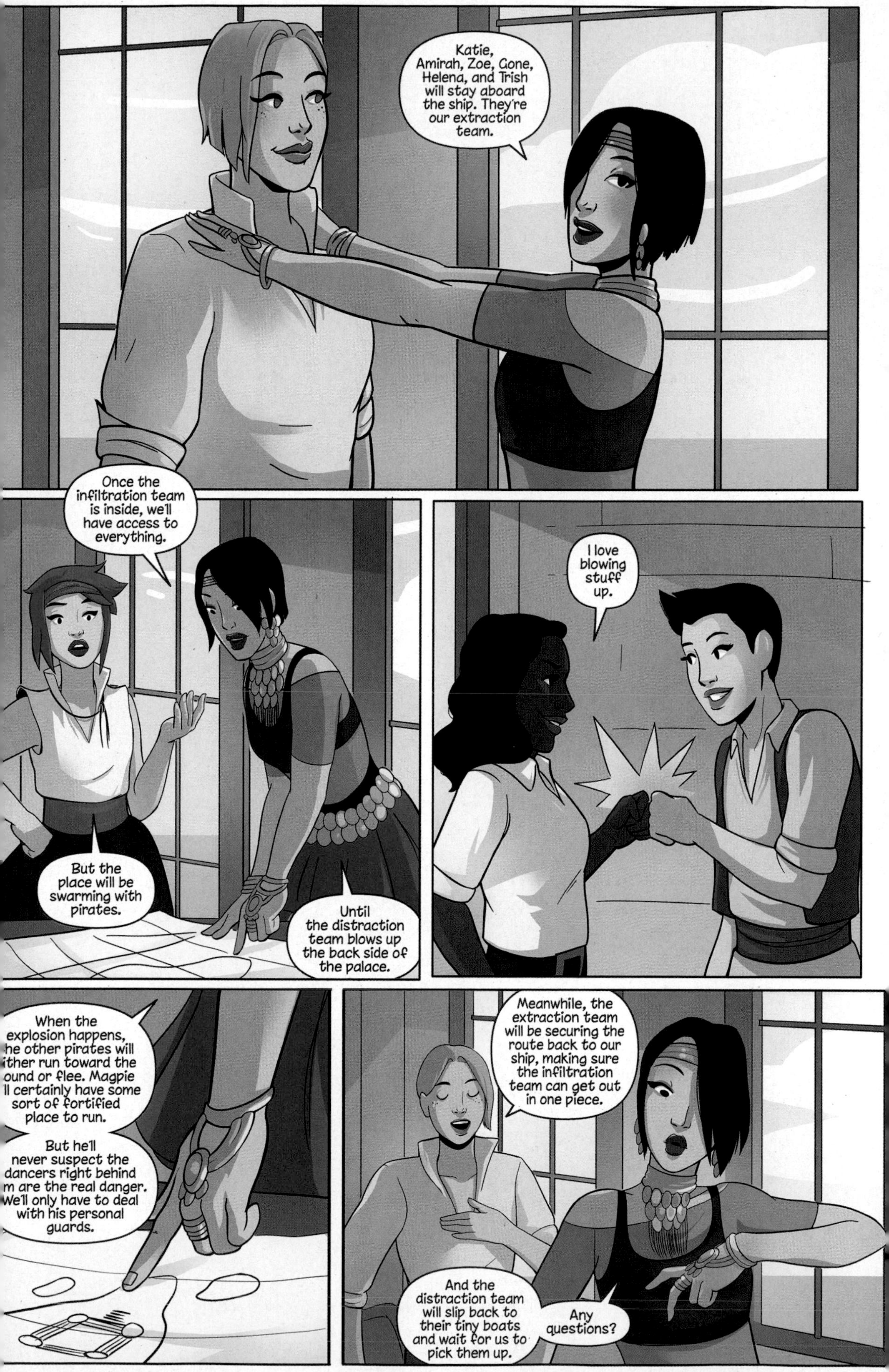

Katie, Amirah, Zoe, Gone, Helena, and Trish will stay aboard the ship. They're our extraction team.
Once the infiltration team is inside, we'll have access to everything.
But the place will be swarming with pirates.
Until the distraction team blows up the back side of the palace.
I love blowing stuff up.
When the explosion happens, he other pirates will ither run toward the ound or flee. Magpie ll certainly have some sort of fortified place to run.
But he'll never suspect the dancers right behind m are the real danger. We'll only have to deal with his personal guards.
Meanwhile, the extraction team will be securing the route back to our ship, making sure the infiltration team can get out in one piece.
And the distraction team will slip back to their tiny boats and wait for us to pick them up.
Any questions?

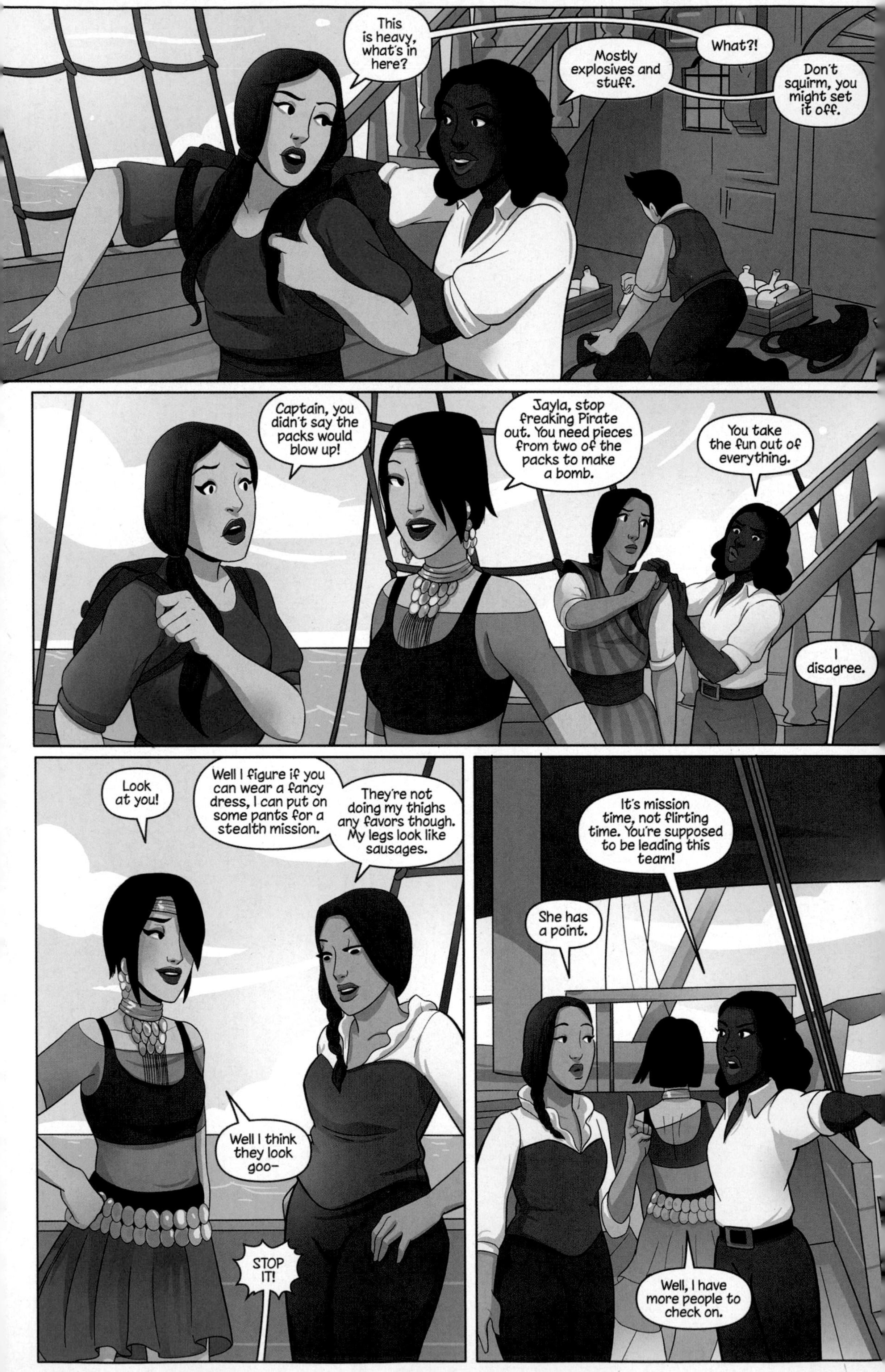
This is heavy, what's in here?
Mostly explosives and stuff.
What?!
Don't squirm, you might set it off.
Captain, you didn't say the packs would blow up!
Jayla, stop freaking Pirate out. You need pieces from two of the packs to make a bomb.
You take the fun out of everything.
I disagree.
Look at you!
Well I figure if you can wear a fancy dress, I can put on some pants for a stealth mission.
They're not doing my thighs any favors though. My legs look like sausages.
Well I think they look goo–
STOP IT!
It's mission time, not flirting time. You're supposed to be leading this team!
She has a point.
Well, I have more people to check on.

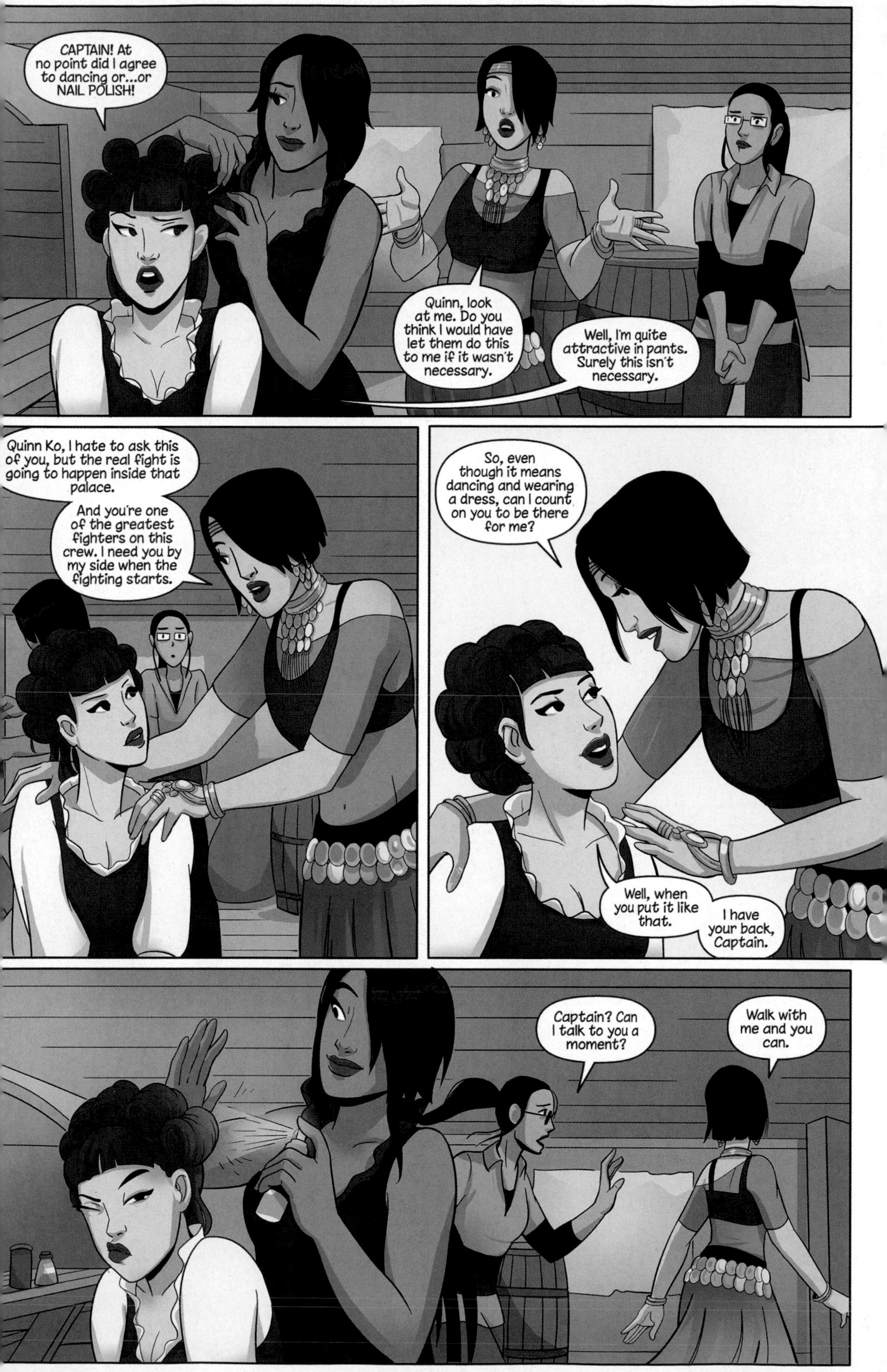
CAPTAIN! At no point did I agree to dancing or...or NAIL POLISH!
Quinn, look at me. Do you think I would have let them do this to me if it wasn't necessary.
Well, I'm quite attractive in pants. Surely this isn't necessary.
Quinn Ko, I hate to ask this of you, but the real fight is going to happen inside that palace.
And you're one of the greatest fighters on this crew. I need you by my side when the fighting starts.
So, even though it means dancing and wearing a dress, can I count on you to be there for me?
Well, when you put it like that.
I have your back, Captain.
Captain? Can I talk to you a moment?
Walk with me and you can.

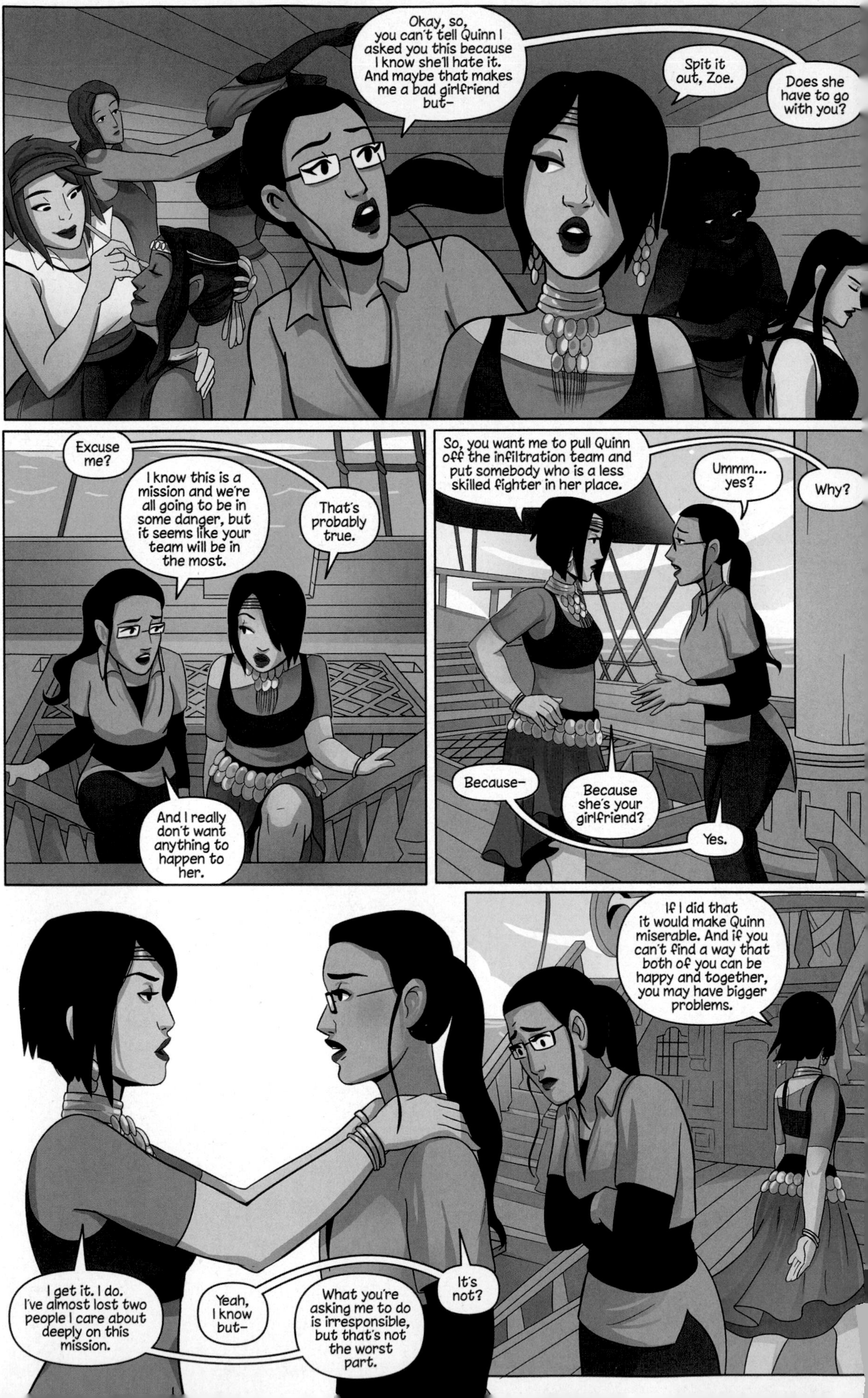
Okay, so, you can't tell Quinn I asked you this because I know she'll hate it. And maybe that makes me a bad girlfriend but–
Spit it out, Zoe.
Does she have to go with you?
Excuse me?
I know this is a mission and we're all going to be in some danger, but it seems like your team will be in the most.
That's probably true.
And I really don't want anything to happen to her.
So, you want me to pull Quinn off the infiltration team and put somebody who is a less skilled fighter in her place.
Ummm... yes?
Why?
Because–
Because she's your girlfriend?
Yes.
I get it. I do. I've almost lost two people I care about deeply on this mission.
Yeah, I know but–
What you're asking me to do is irresponsible, but that's not the worst part.
It's not?
If I did that it would make Quinn miserable. And if you can't find a way that both of you can be happy and together, you may have bigger problems.

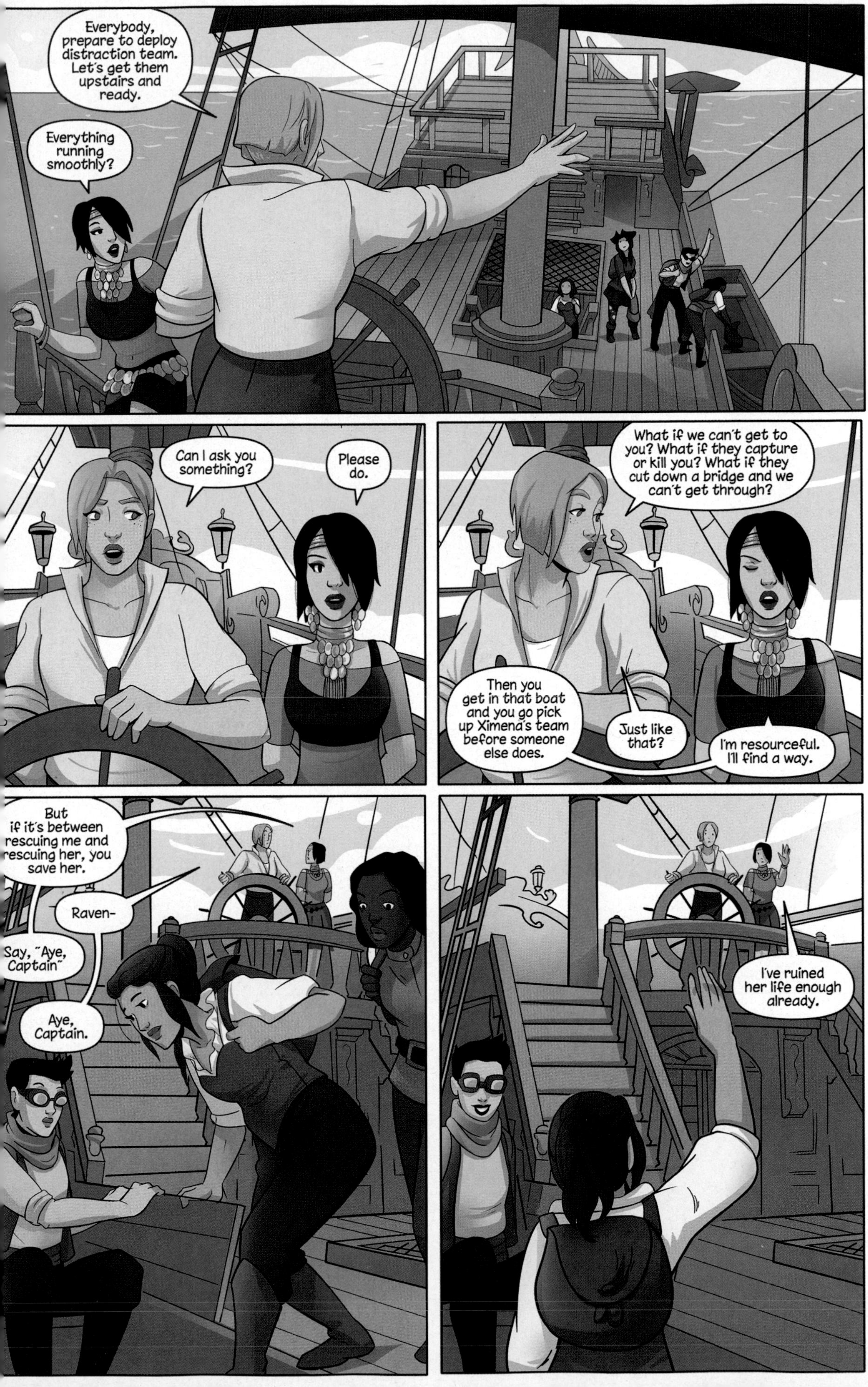
Everybody, prepare to deploy distraction team. Let's get them upstairs and ready.
Everything running smoothly?
Can I ask you something?
Please do.
What if we can't get to you? What if they capture or kill you? What if they cut down a bridge and we can't get through?
Then you get in that boat and you go pick up Ximena's team before someone else does.
Just like that?
I'm resourceful. I'll find a way.
But if it's between rescuing me and rescuing her, you save her.
Raven-
Say, "Aye, Captain"
Aye, Captain.
I've ruined her life enough already.

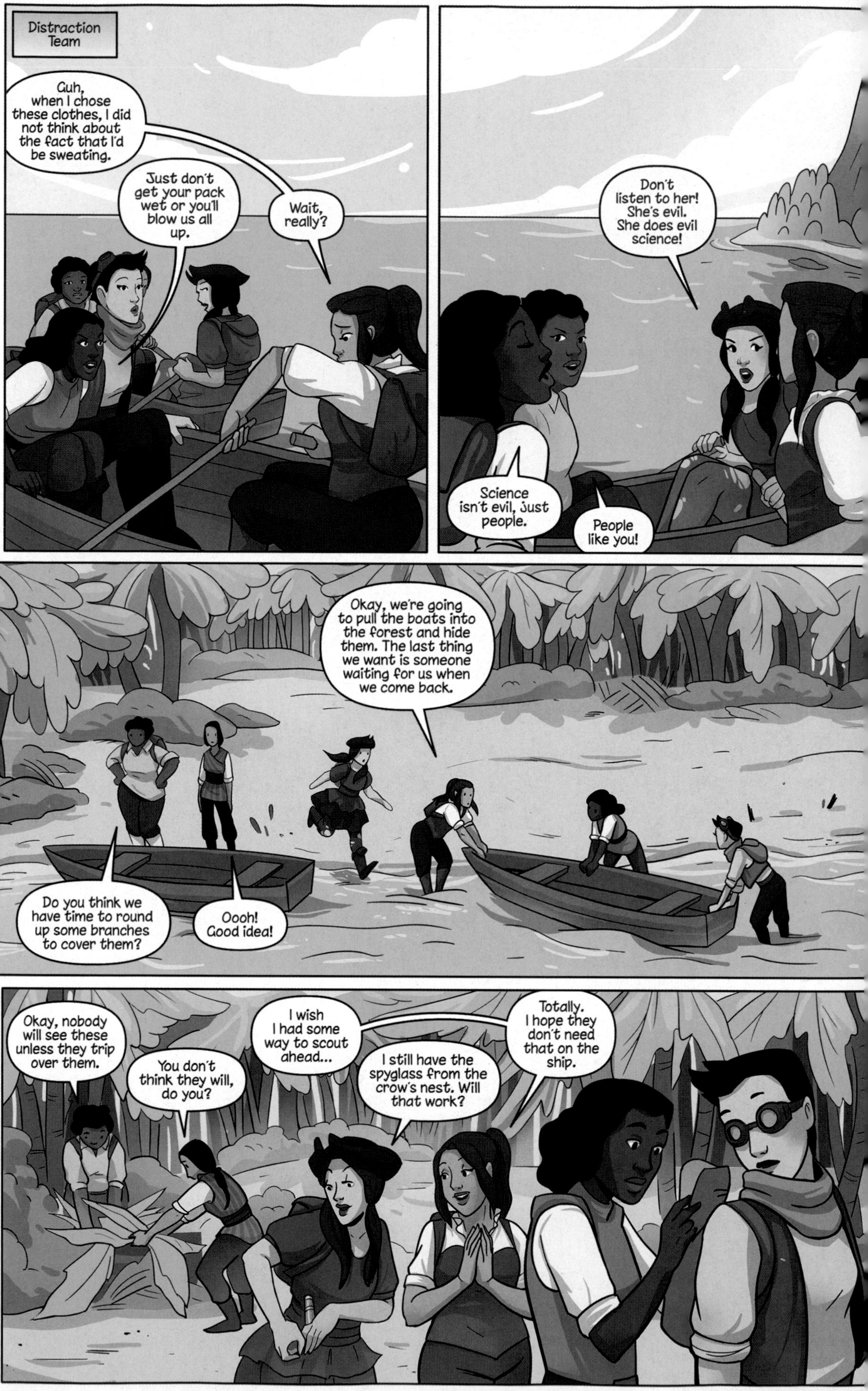
Distraction Team
Guh, when I chose these clothes, I did not think about the fact that I'd be sweating.
Just don't get your pack wet or you'll blow us all up.
Wait, really?
Don't listen to her! She's evil. She does evil science!
Science isn't evil, just people.
People like you!
Okay, we're going to pull the boats into the forest and hide them. The last thing we want is someone waiting for us when we come back.
Do you think we have time to round up some branches to cover them?
Oooh! Good idea!
Okay, nobody will see these unless they trip over them.
You don't think they will, do you?
I wish I had some way to scout ahead...
I still have the spyglass from the crow's nest. Will that work?
Totally. I hope they don't need that on the ship.

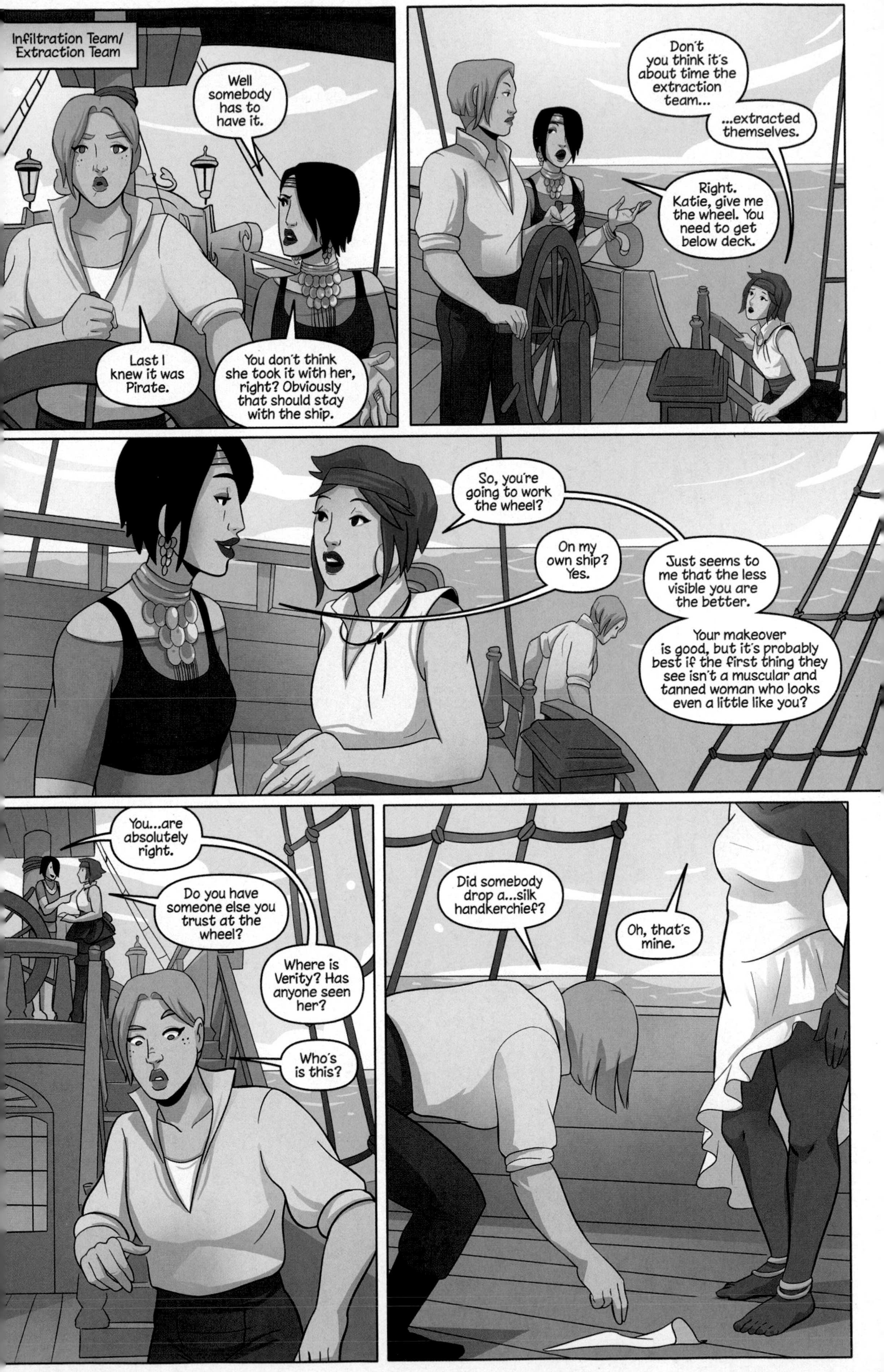
Infiltration Team/ Extraction Team
Well somebody has to have it.
Last I knew it was Pirate.
You don't think she took it with her, right? Obviously that should stay with the ship.
Don't you think it's about time the extraction team...
...extracted themselves.
Right. Katie, give me the wheel. You need to get below deck.
So, you're going to work the wheel?
On my own ship? Yes.
Just seems to me that the less visible you are the better.
Your makeover is good, but it's probably best if the first thing they see isn't a muscular and tanned woman who looks even a little like you?
You...are absolutely right.
Do you have someone else you trust at the wheel?
Where is Verity? Has anyone seen her?
Who's is this?
Did somebody drop a...silk handkerchief?
Oh, that's mine.

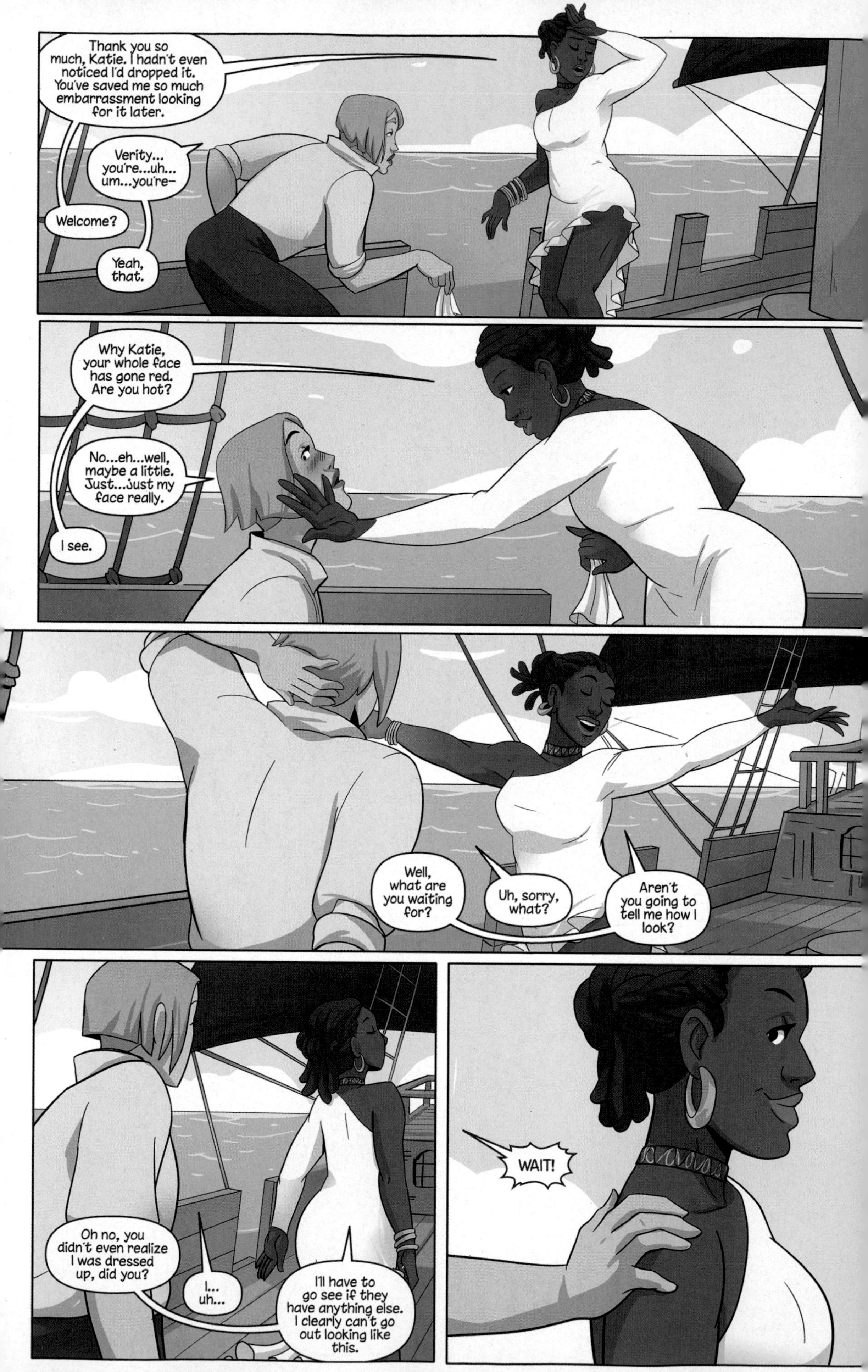
Thank you so much, Katie. I hadn't even noticed I'd dropped it. You've saved me so much embarrassment looking for it later.
Verity... you're...uh... um...you're—
Welcome?
Yeah, that.
Why Katie, your whole face has gone red. Are you hot?
No...eh...well, maybe a little. Just...just my face really.
I see.
Well, what are you waiting for?
Uh, sorry, what?
Aren't you going to tell me how I look?
Oh no, you didn't even realize I was dressed up, did you?
I... uh...
I'll have to go see if they have anything else. I clearly can't go out looking like this.
WAIT!

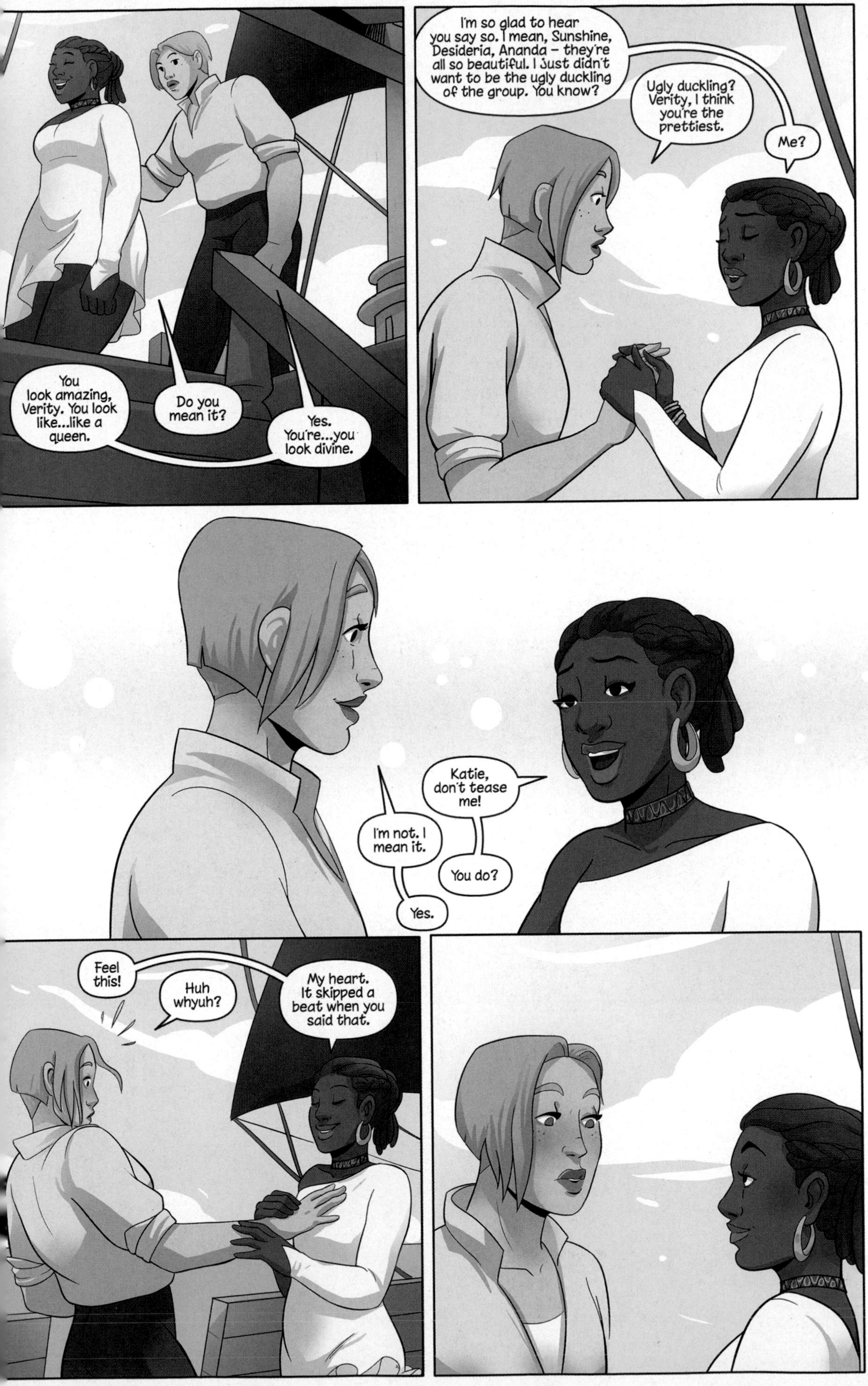
You look amazing, Verity. You look like...like a queen.
Do you mean it?
Yes. You're...you look divine.
I'm so glad to hear you say so. I mean, Sunshine, Desideria, Ananda – they're all so beautiful. I just didn't want to be the ugly duckling of the group. You know?
Ugly duckling? Verity, I think you're the prettiest.
Me?
Katie, don't tease me!
I'm not. I mean it.
You do?
Yes.
Feel this!
Huh whyuh?
My heart. It skipped a beat when you said that.

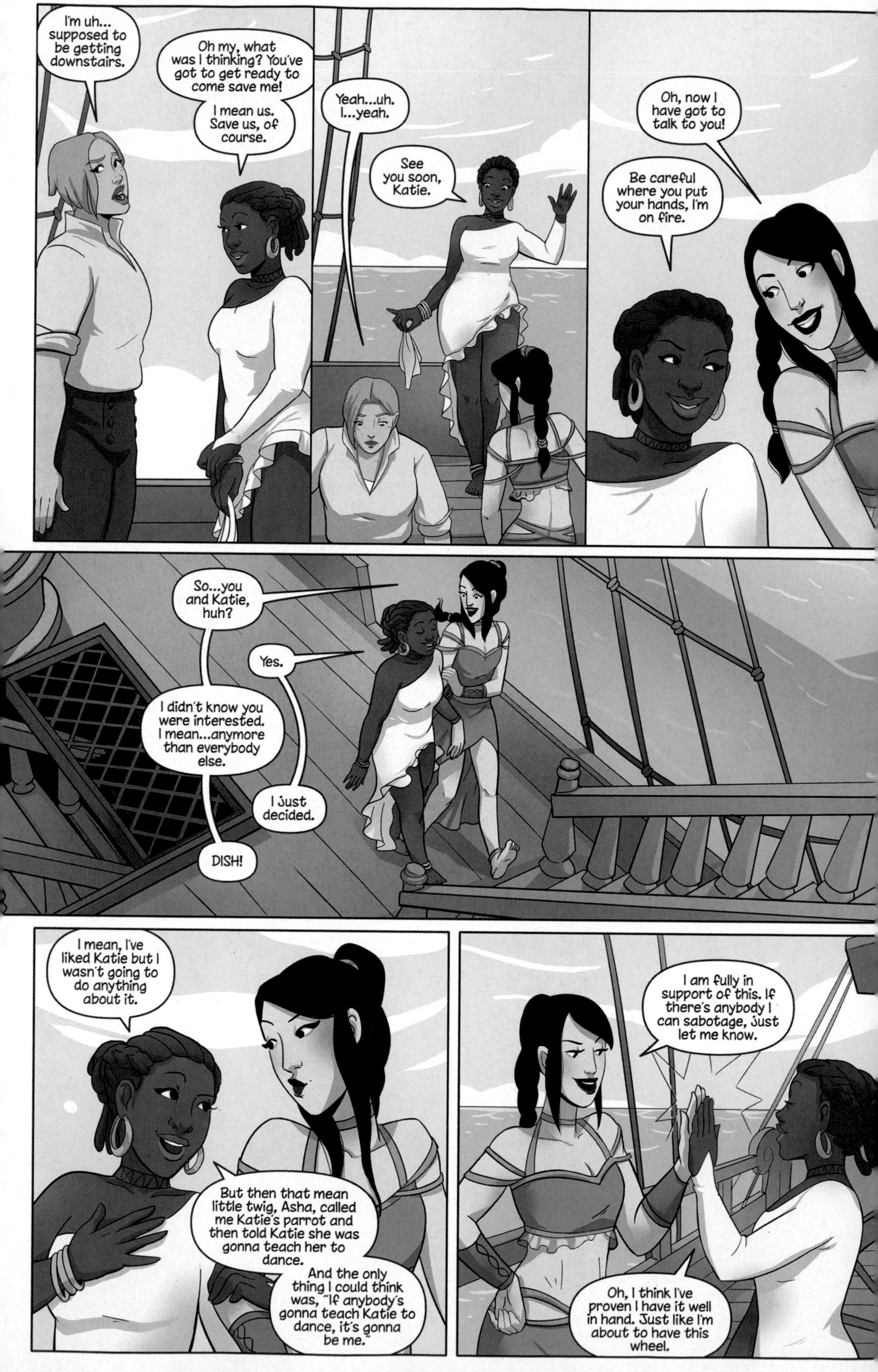

I'm uh... supposed to be getting downstairs.
Oh my, what was I thinking? You've got to get ready to come save me!
I mean us. Save us, of course.
Yeah...uh. I...yeah.
See you soon, Katie.
Oh, now I have got to talk to you!
Be careful where you put your hands, I'm on fire.
So...you and Katie, huh?
Yes.
I didn't know you were interested. I mean...anymore than everybody else.
I just decided.
DISH!
I mean, I've liked Katie but I wasn't going to do anything about it.
But then that mean little twig, Asha, called me Katie's parrot and then told Katie she was gonna teach her to dance.
And the only thing I could think was, "If anybody's gonna teach Katie to dance, it's gonna be me."
I am fully in support of this. If there's anybody I can sabotage, just let me know.
Oh, I think I've proven I have it well in hand. Just like I'm about to have this wheel.

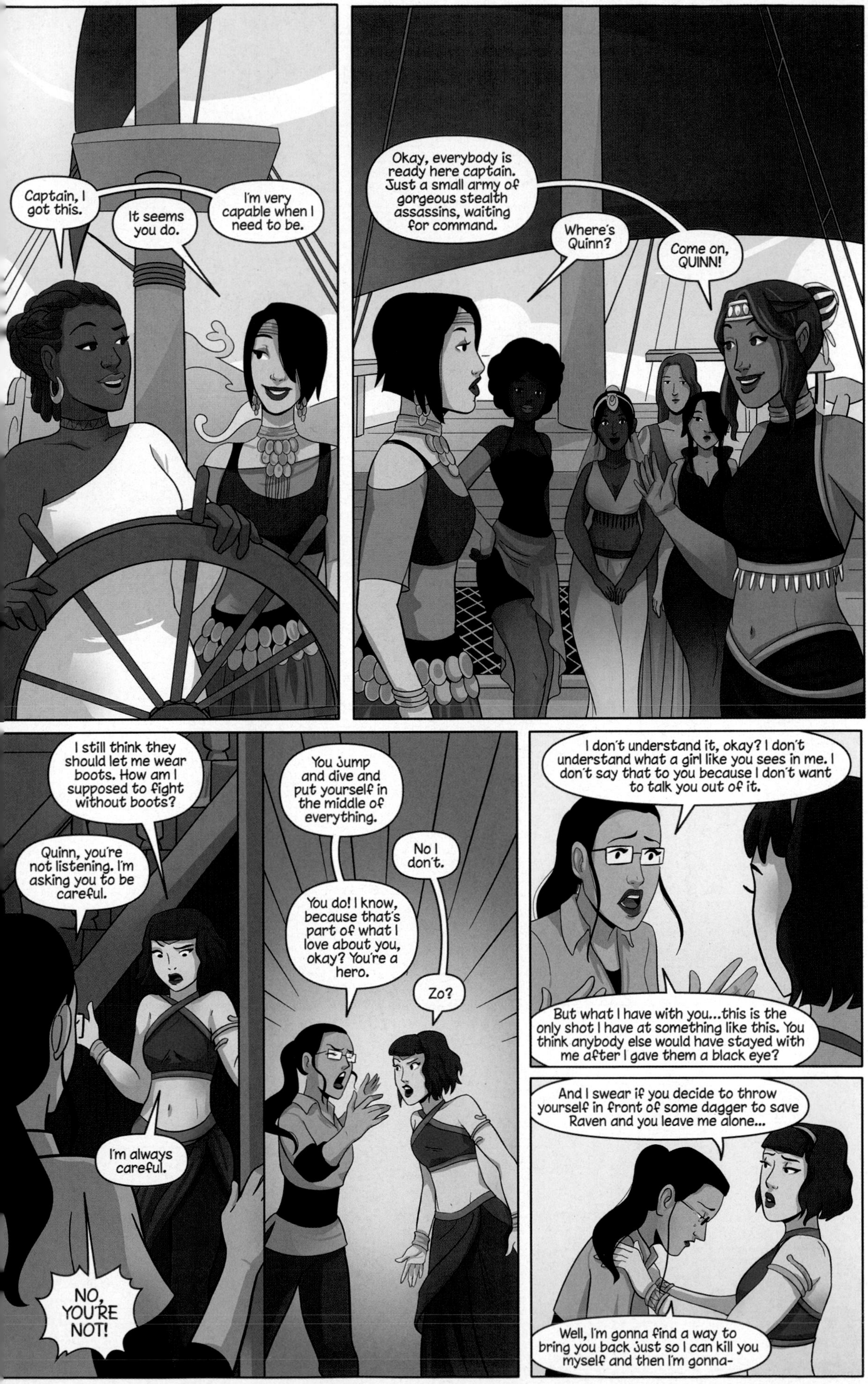
Captain, I got this.
It seems you do.
I'm very capable when I need to be.
Okay, everybody is ready here captain. Just a small army of gorgeous stealth assassins, waiting for command.
Where's Quinn?
Come on, QUINN!
I still think they should let me wear boots. How am I supposed to fight without boots?
Quinn, you're not listening. I'm asking you to be careful.
I'm always careful.
NO, YOU'RE NOT!
You jump and dive and put yourself in the middle of everything.
No I don't.
You do! I know, because that's part of what I love about you, okay? You're a hero.
Zo?
I don't understand it, okay? I don't understand what a girl like you sees in me. I don't say that to you because I don't want to talk you out of it.
But what I have with you...this is the only shot I have at something like this. You think anybody else would have stayed with me after I gave them a black eye?
And I swear if you decide to throw yourself in front of some dagger to save Raven and you leave me alone...
Well, I'm gonna find a way to bring you back just so I can kill you myself and then I'm gonna-

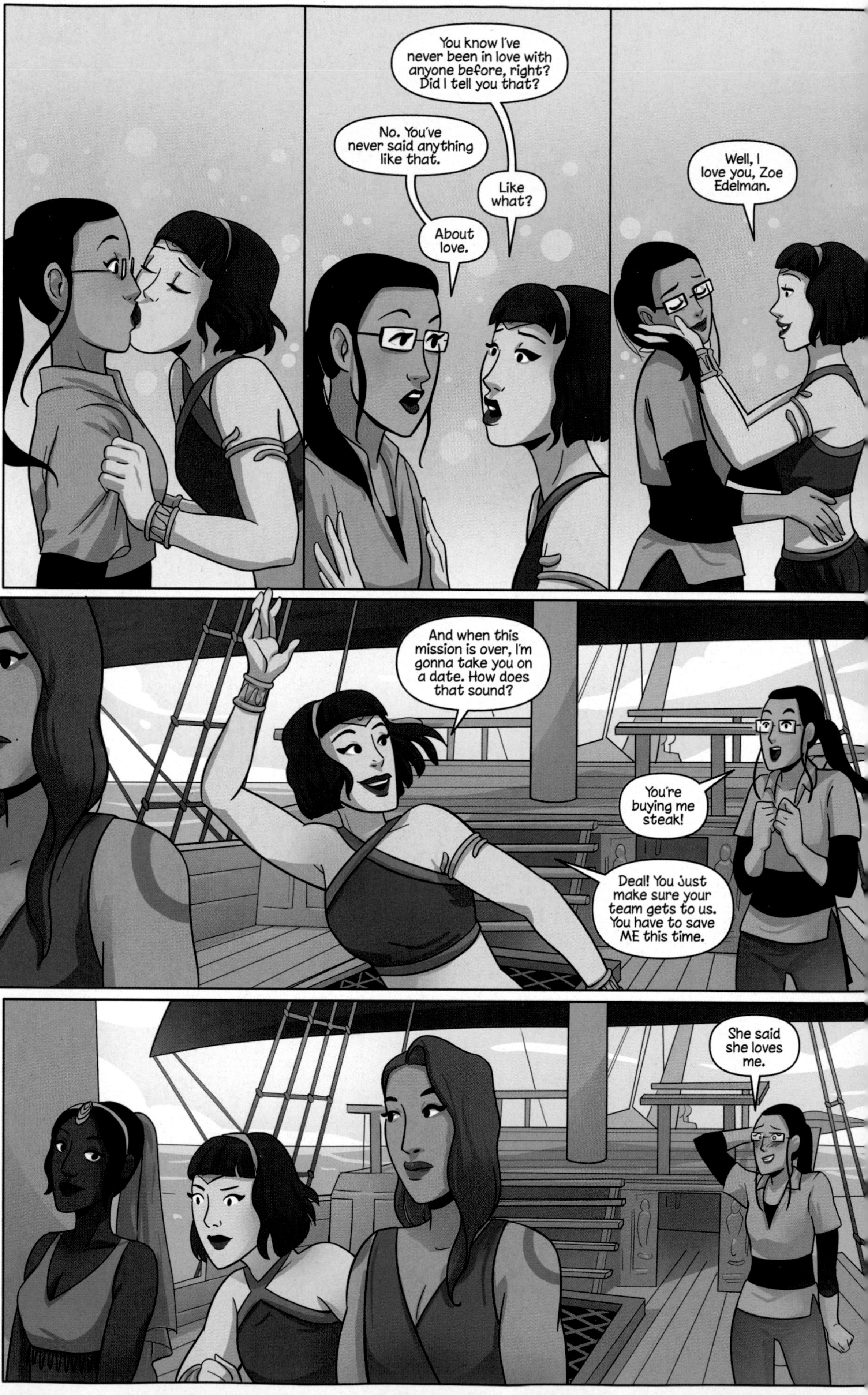
You know I've never been in love with anyone before, right? Did I tell you that?
No. You've never said anything like that.
Like what?
About love.
Well, I love you, Zoe Edelman.
And when this mission is over, I'm gonna take you on a date. How does that sound?
You're buying me steak!
Deal! You just make sure your team gets to us. You have to save ME this time.
She said she loves me.

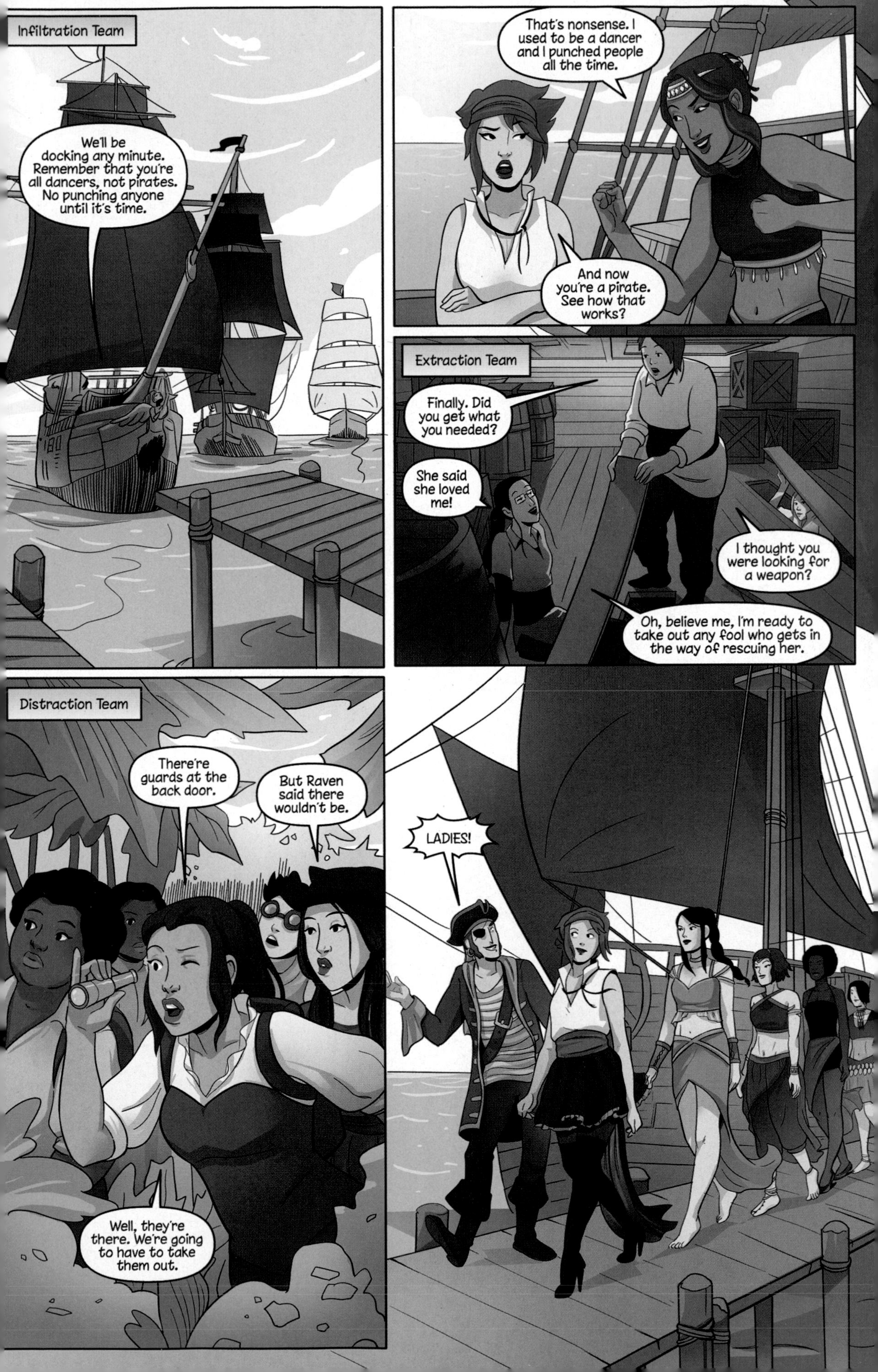
Infiltration Team
We'll be docking any minute. Remember that you're all dancers, not pirates. No punching anyone until it's time.
That's nonsense. I used to be a dancer and I punched people all the time.
And now you're a pirate. See how that works?
Extraction Team
Finally. Did you get what you needed?
She said she loved me!
I thought you were looking for a weapon?
Oh, believe me, I'm ready to take out any fool who gets in the way of rescuing her.
Distraction Team
There're guards at the back door.
But Raven said there wouldn't be.
Well, they're there. We're going to have to take them out.
LADIES!

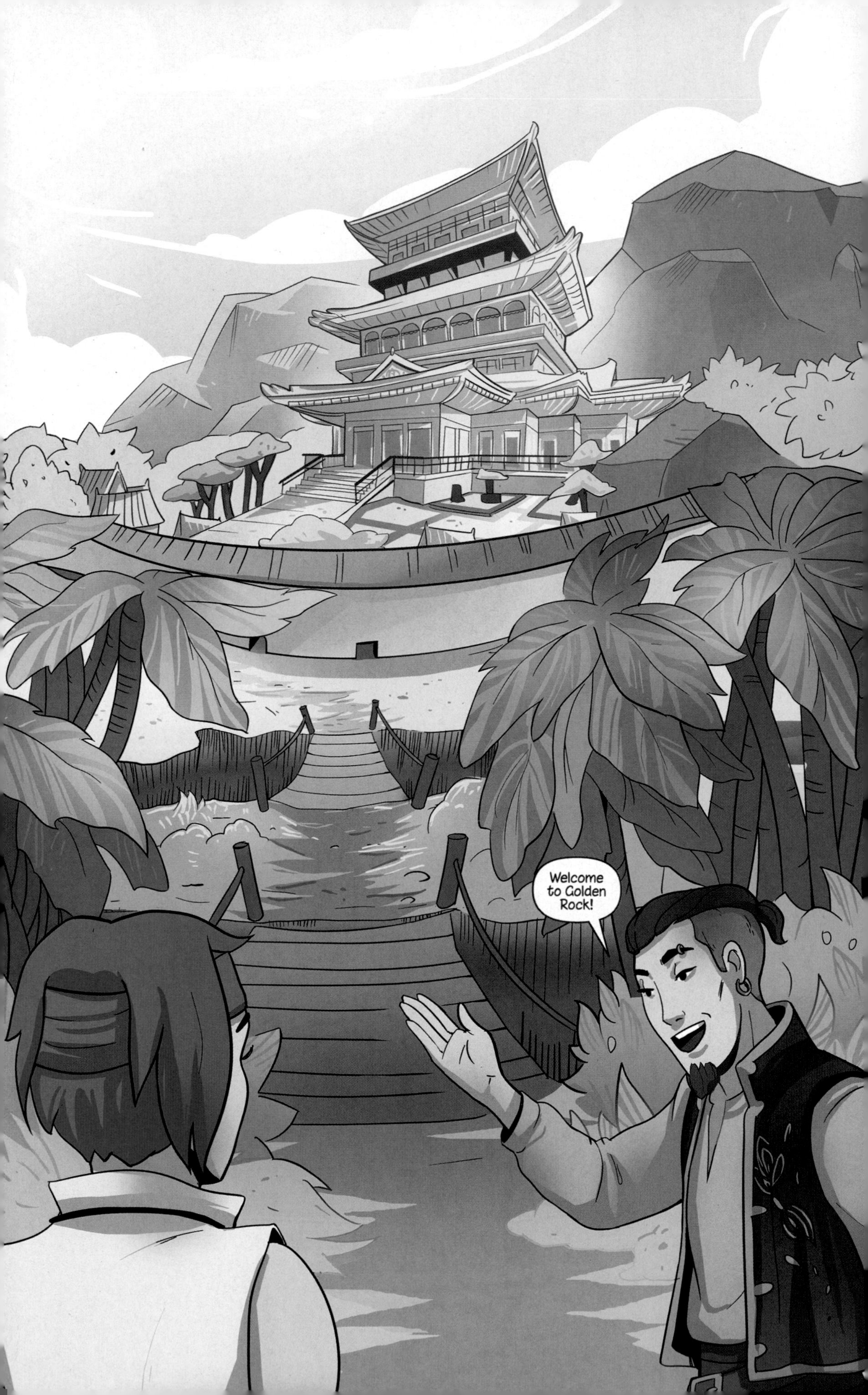
Welcome to Golden Rock!

Princess

Raven

THE PIRATE PRINCESS

Year Two: Love and Revenge

Chapter Eleven: Things, including plans and castles, fall apart

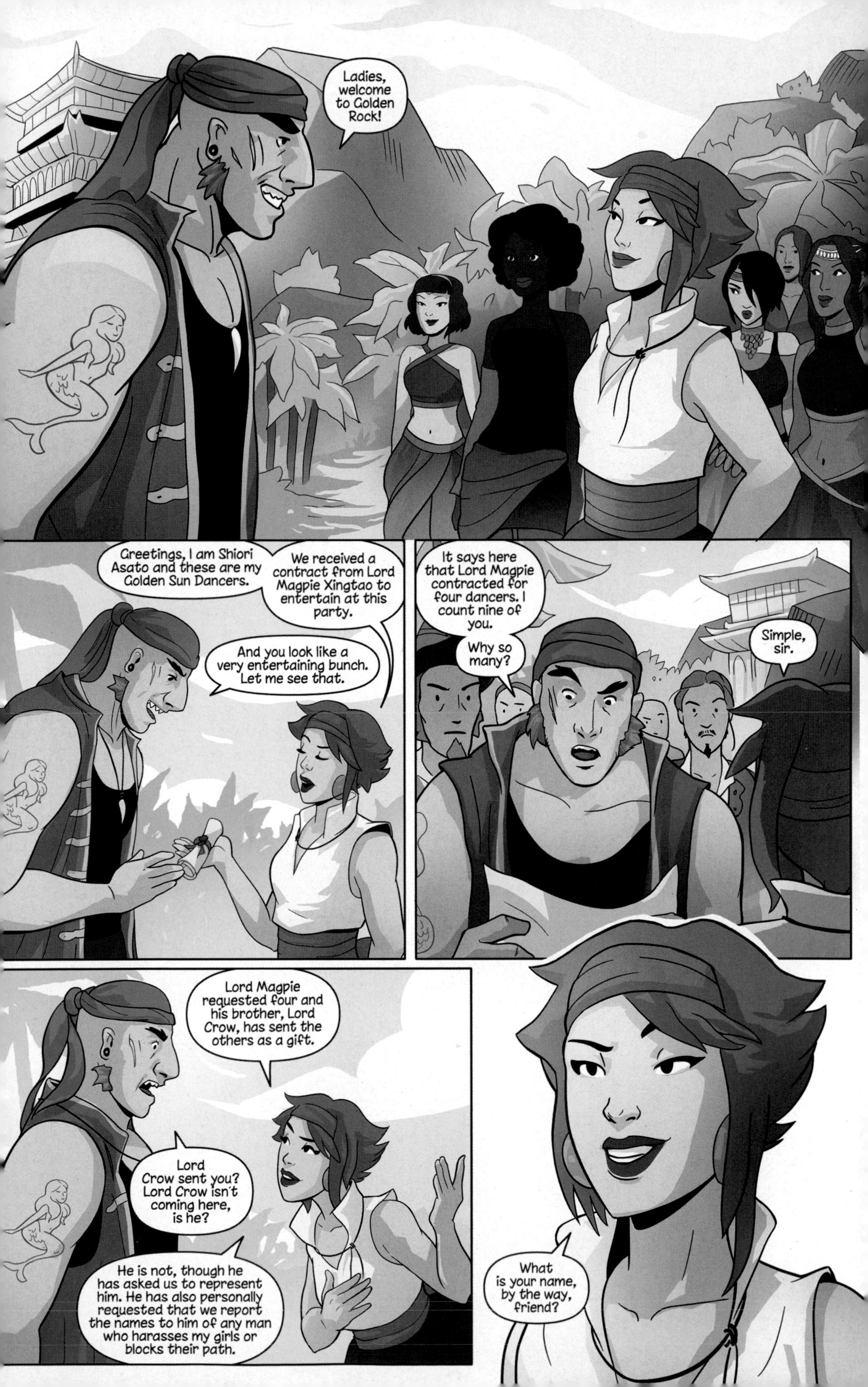
Ladies, welcome to Golden Rock!
Greetings, I am Shiori Asato and these are my Golden Sun Dancers.
We received a contract from Lord Magpie Xingtao to entertain at this party.
And you look like a very entertaining bunch. Let me see that.
It says here that Lord Magpie contracted for four dancers. I count nine of you.
Why so many?
Simple, sir.
Lord Magpie requested four and his brother, Lord Crow, has sent the others as a gift.
Lord Crow sent you? Lord Crow isn't coming here, is he?
He is not, though he has asked us to represent him. He has also personally requested that we report the names to him of any man who harasses my girls or blocks their path.
What is your name, by the way, friend?

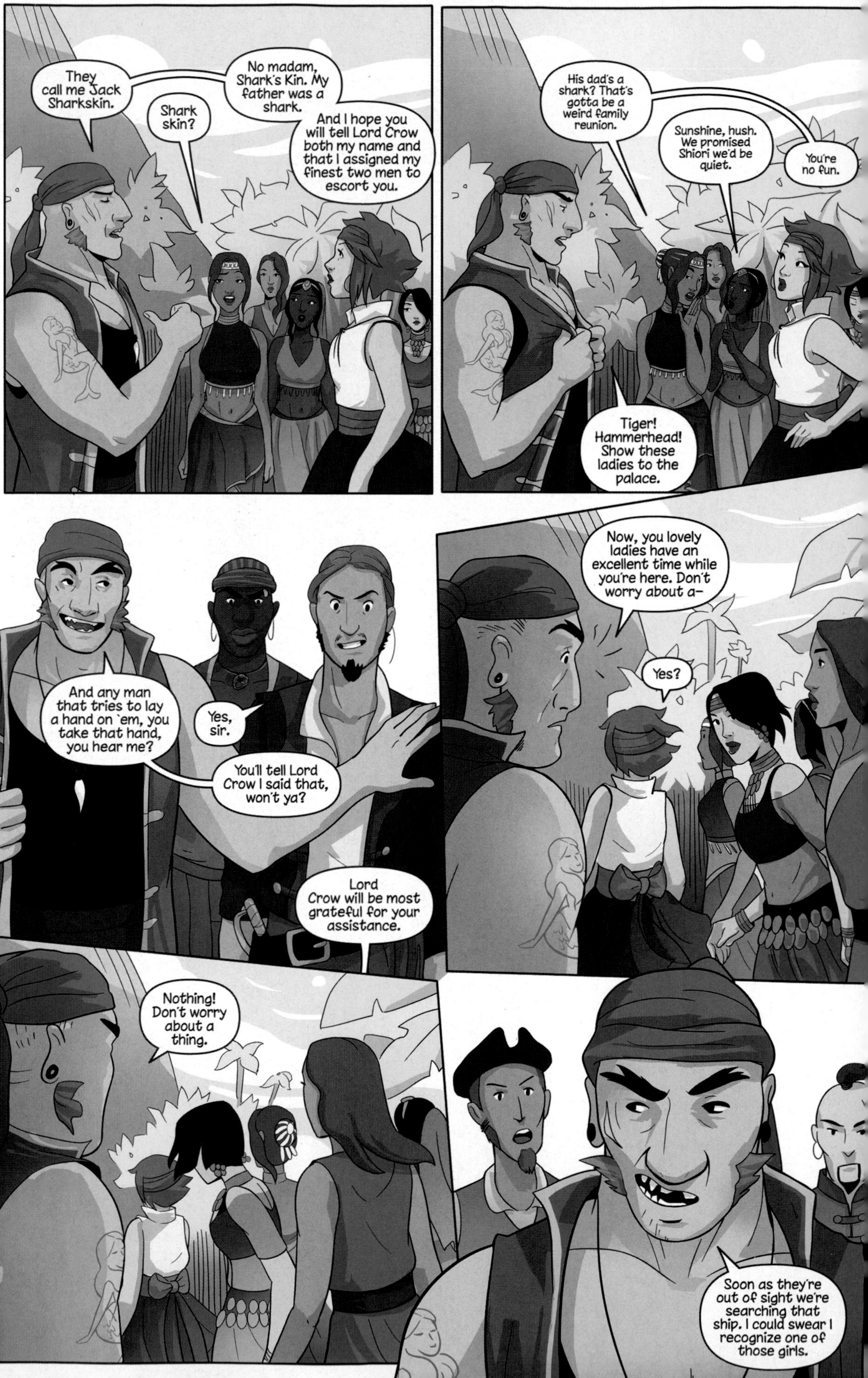
They call me Jack Sharkskin.
Shark skin?
No madam, Shark's Kin. My father was a shark.
And I hope you will tell Lord Crow both my name and that I assigned my finest two men to escort you.
His dad's a shark? That's gotta be a weird family reunion.
Sunshine, hush. We promised Shiori we'd be quiet.
You're no fun.
Tiger! Hammerhead! Show these ladies to the palace.
And any man that tries to lay a hand on 'em, you take that hand, you hear me?
Yes, sir.
You'll tell Lord Crow I said that, won't ya?
Lord Crow will be most grateful for your assistance.
Now, you lovely ladies have an excellent time while you're here. Don't worry about a–
Yes?
Nothing! Don't worry about a thing.
Soon as they're out of sight we're searching that ship. I could swear I recognize one of those girls.

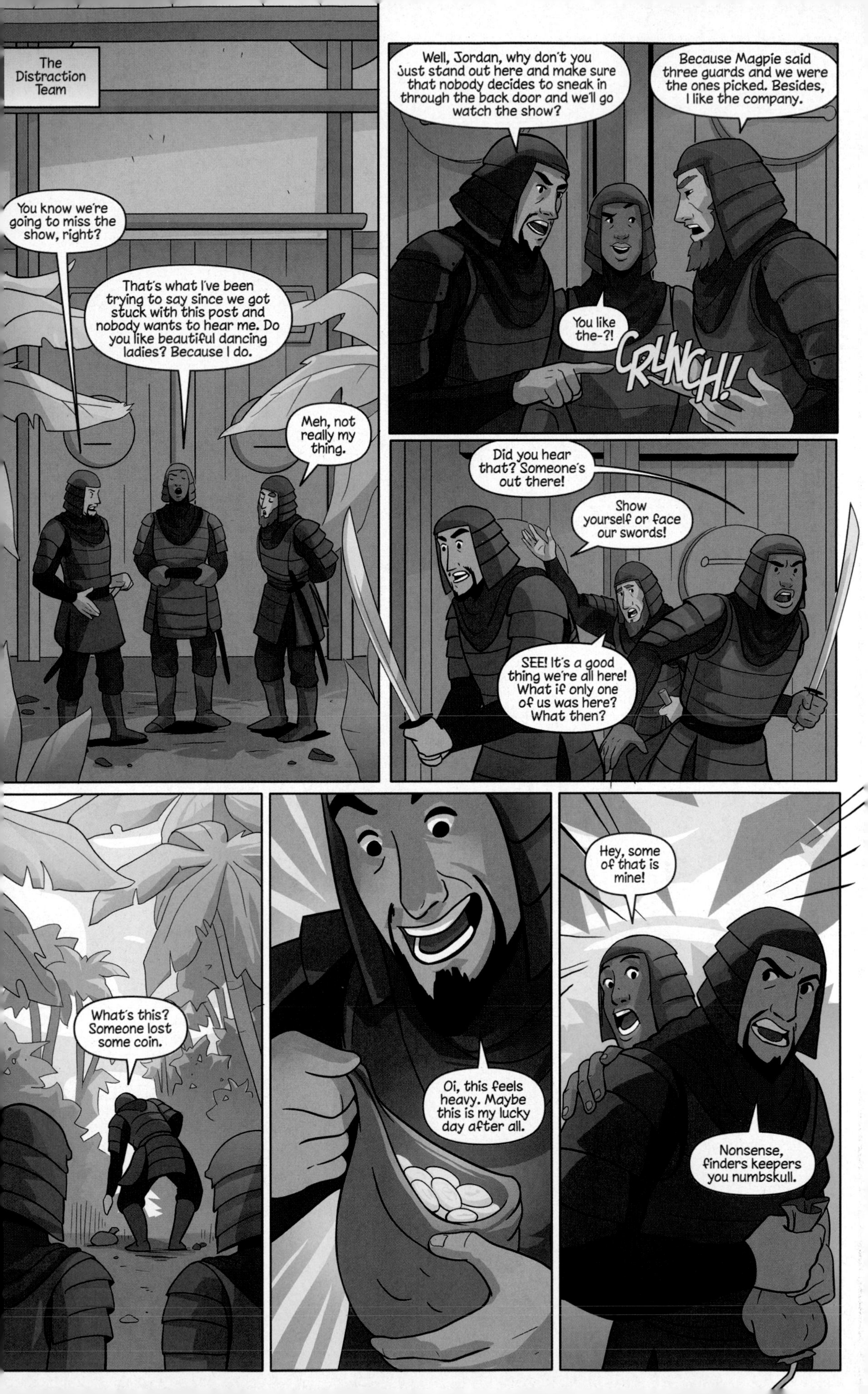
The Distraction Team
You know we're going to miss the show, right?
That's what I've been trying to say since we got stuck with this post and nobody wants to hear me. Do you like beautiful dancing ladies? Because I do.
Meh, not really my thing.
Well, Jordan, why don't you just stand out here and make sure that nobody decides to sneak in through the back door and we'll go watch the show?
Because Magpie said three guards and we were the ones picked. Besides, I like the company.
You like the-?!
CRUNCH!
Did you hear that? Someone's out there!
Show yourself or face our swords!
SEE! It's a good thing we're all here! What if only one of us was here? What then?
What's this? Someone lost some coin.
Oi, this feels heavy. Maybe this is my lucky day after all.
Hey, some of that is mine!
Nonsense, finders keepers you numbskull.

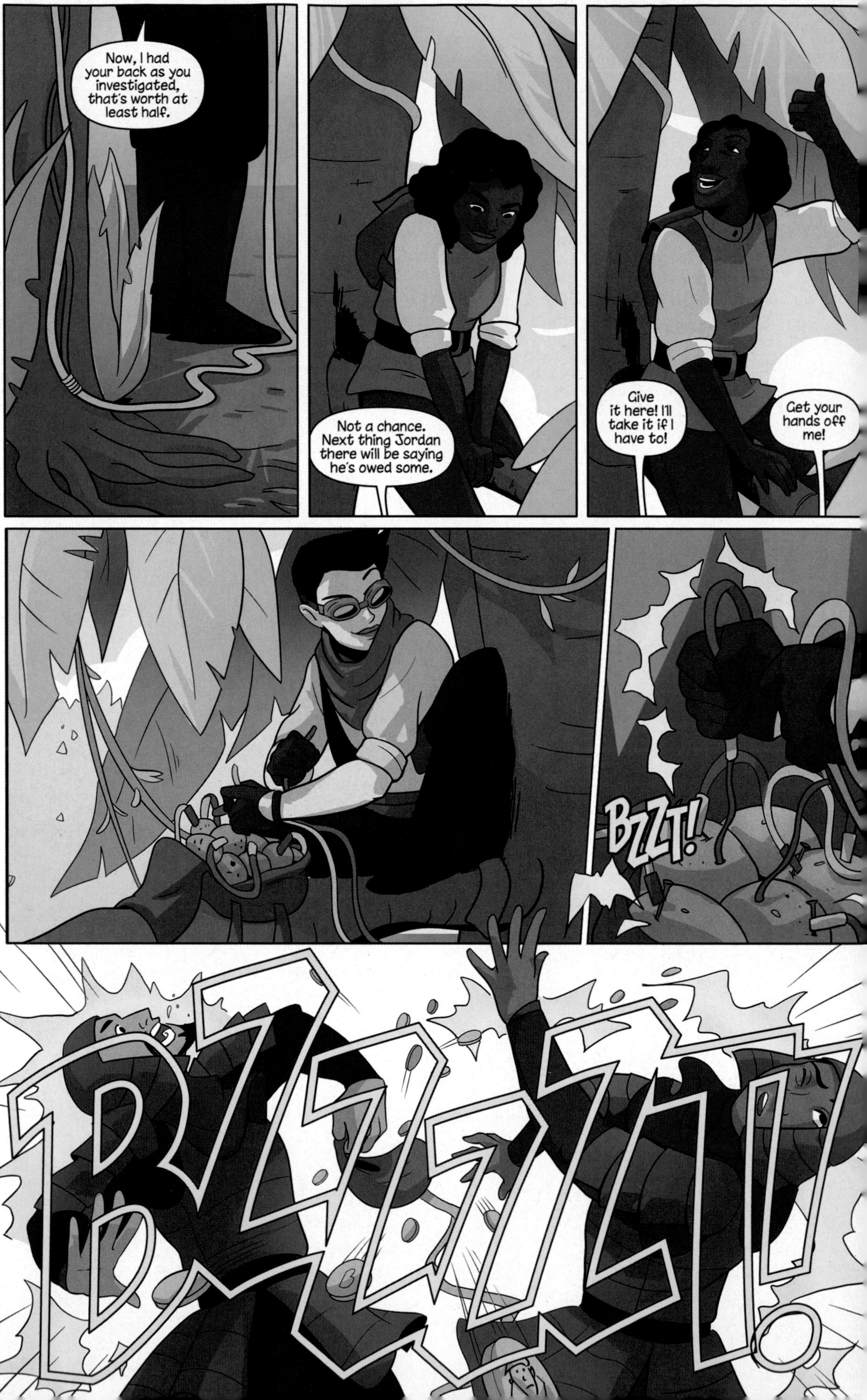
Now, I had your back as you investigated, that's worth at least half.
Not a chance. Next thing Jordan there will be saying he's owed some.
Give it here! I'll take it if I have to!
Get your hands off me!
BZZT!
BZZZZT!

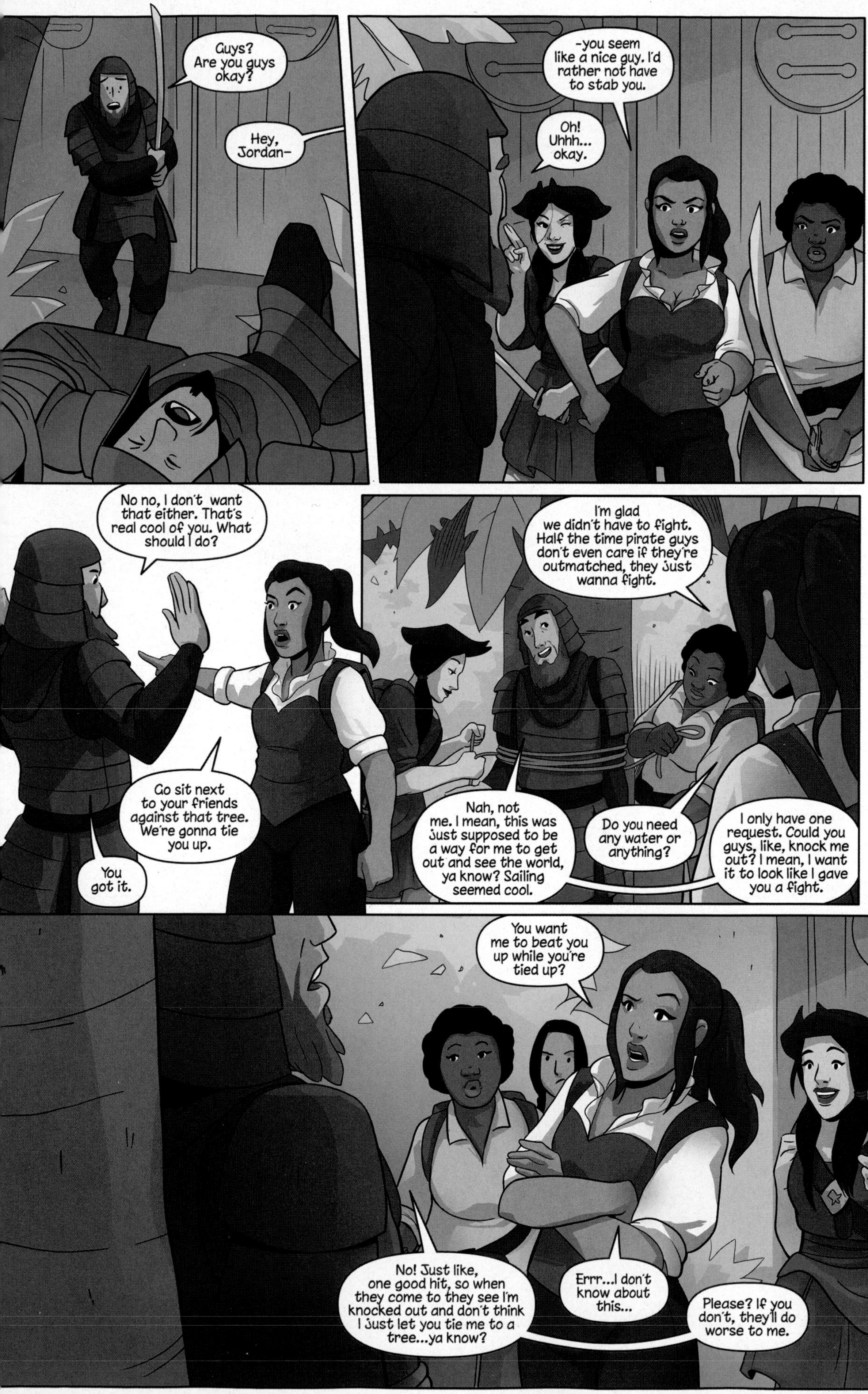
Guys? Are you guys okay?
Hey, Jordan-
-you seem like a nice guy. I'd rather not have to stab you.
Oh! Uhhh... okay.
No no, I don't want that either. That's real cool of you. What should I do?
Go sit next to your friends against that tree. We're gonna tie you up.
You got it.
I'm glad we didn't have to fight. Half the time pirate guys don't even care if they're outmatched, they just wanna fight.
Nah, not me. I mean, this was just supposed to be a way for me to get out and see the world, ya know? Sailing seemed cool.
Do you need any water or anything?
I only have one request. Could you guys, like, knock me out? I mean, I want it to look like I gave you a fight.
You want me to beat you up while you're tied up?
No! Just like, one good hit, so when they come to they see I'm knocked out and don't think I just let you tie me to a tree...ya know?
Errr...I don't know about this...
Please? If you don't, they'll do worse to me.

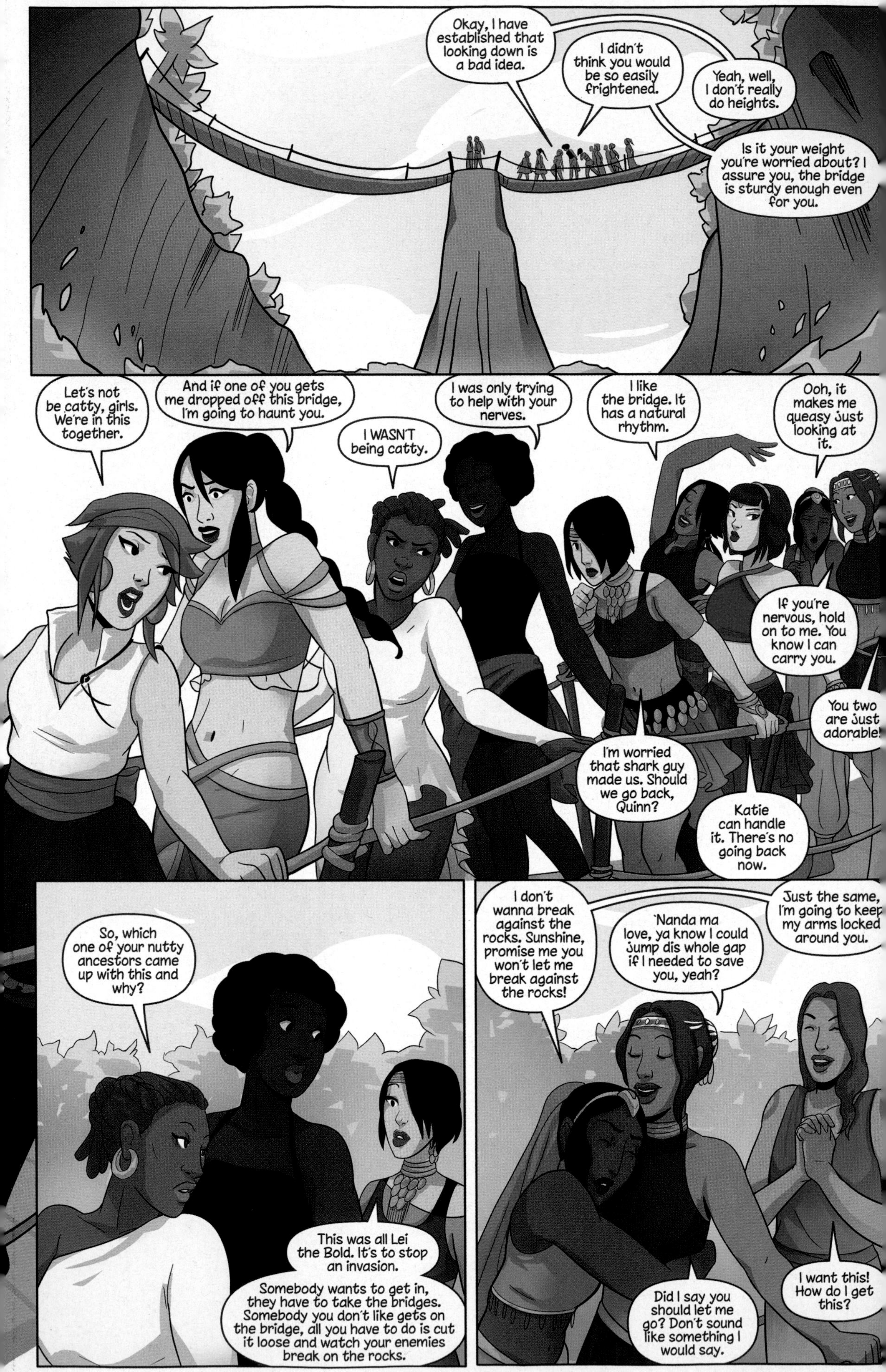
Okay, I have established that looking down is a bad idea.
I didn't think you would be so easily frightened.
Yeah, well, I don't really do heights.
Is it your weight you're worried about? I assure you, the bridge is sturdy enough even for you.
Let's not be catty, girls. We're in this together.
And if one of you gets me dropped off this bridge, I'm going to haunt you.
I WASN'T being catty.
I was only trying to help with your nerves.
I like the bridge. It has a natural rhythm.
Ooh, it makes me queasy just looking at it.
If you're nervous, hold on to me. You know I can carry you.
You two are just adorable!
I'm worried that shark guy made us. Should we go back, Quinn?
Katie can handle it. There's no going back now.
So, which one of your nutty ancestors came up with this and why?
This was all Lei the Bold. It's to stop an invasion.
Somebody wants to get in, they have to take the bridges. Somebody you don't like gets on the bridge, all you have to do is cut it loose and watch your enemies break on the rocks.
I don't wanna break against the rocks. Sunshine, promise me you won't let me break against the rocks!
'Nanda ma love, ya know I could jump dis whole gap if I needed to save you, yeah?
Just the same, I'm going to keep my arms locked around you.
Did I say you should let me go? Don't sound like something I would say.
I want this! How do I get this?

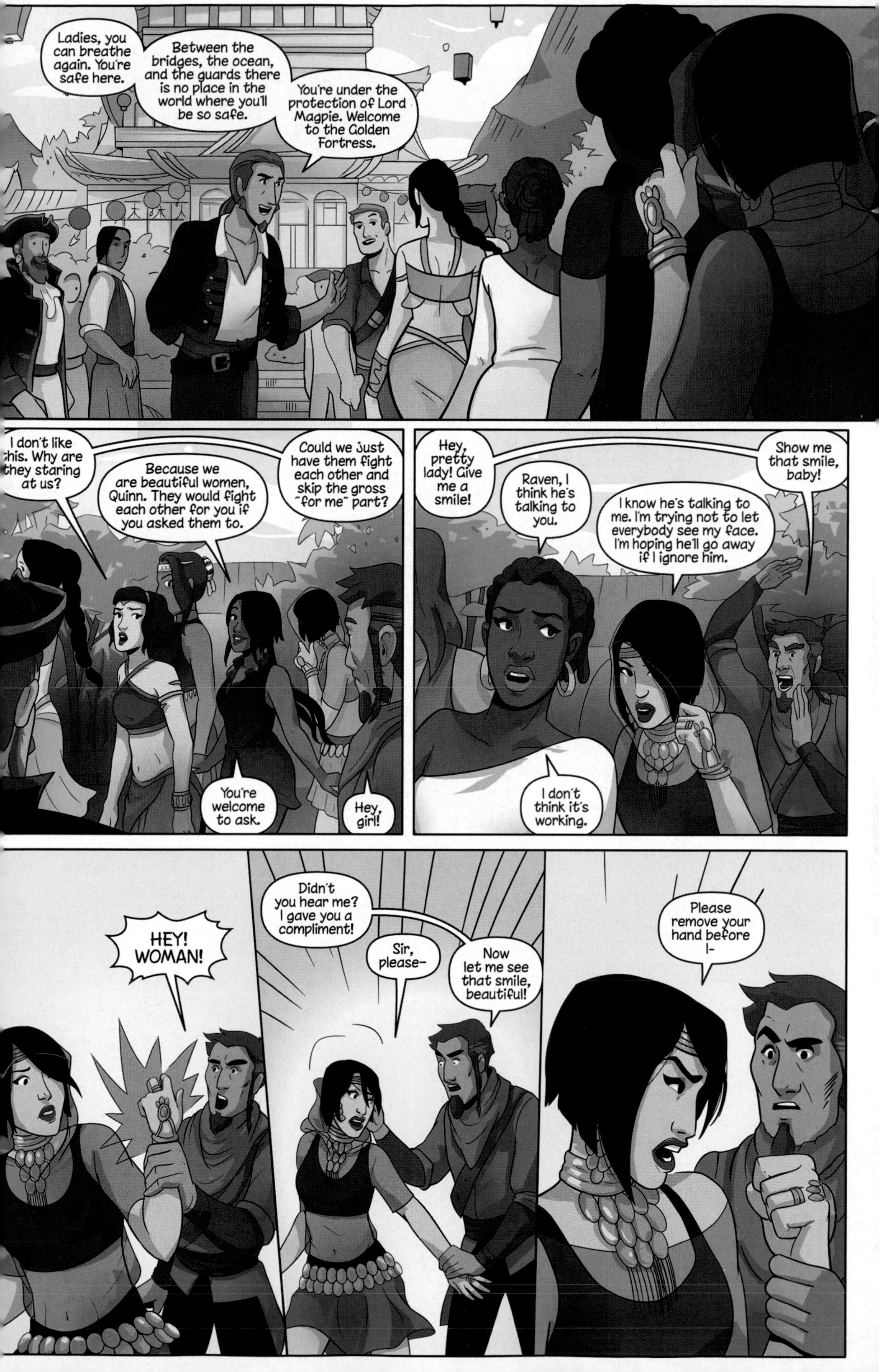
Ladies, you can breathe again. You're safe here.
Between the bridges, the ocean, and the guards there is no place in the world where you'll be so safe.
You're under the protection of Lord Magpie. Welcome to the Golden Fortress.
I don't like this. Why are they staring at us?
Because we are beautiful women, Quinn. They would fight each other for you if you asked them to.
Could we just have them fight each other and skip the gross "for me" part?
You're welcome to ask.
Hey, girl!
Hey, pretty lady! Give me a smile!
Raven, I think he's talking to you.
Show me that smile, baby!
I know he's talking to me. I'm trying not to let everybody see my face. I'm hoping he'll go away if I ignore him.
I don't think it's working.
HEY! WOMAN!
Didn't you hear me? I gave you a compliment!
Sir, please-
Now let me see that smile, beautiful!
Please remove your hand before I-

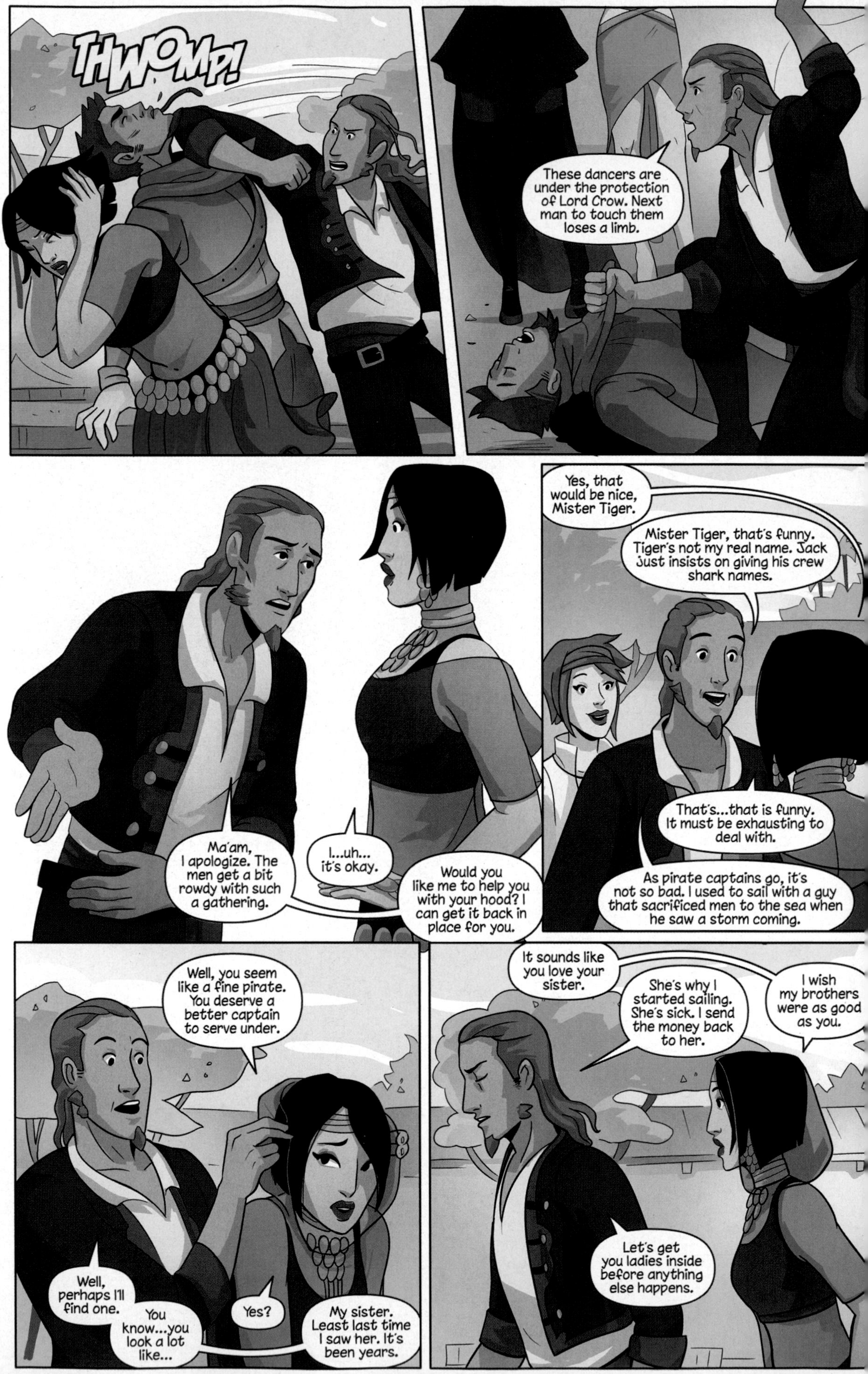
THWOMP!
These dancers are under the protection of Lord Crow. Next man to touch them loses a limb.
Ma'am, I apologize. The men get a bit rowdy with such a gathering.
I...uh... it's okay.
Would you like me to help you with your hood? I can get it back in place for you.
Yes, that would be nice, Mister Tiger.
Mister Tiger, that's funny. Tiger's not my real name. Jack just insists on giving his crew shark names.
That's...that is funny. It must be exhausting to deal with.
As pirate captains go, it's not so bad. I used to sail with a guy that sacrificed men to the sea when he saw a storm coming.
Well, you seem like a fine pirate. You deserve a better captain to serve under.
Well, perhaps I'll find one.
You know...you look a lot like...
Yes?
My sister. Least last time I saw her. It's been years.
It sounds like you love your sister.
She's why I started sailing. She's sick. I send the money back to her.
I wish my brothers were as good as you.
Let's get you ladies inside before anything else happens.

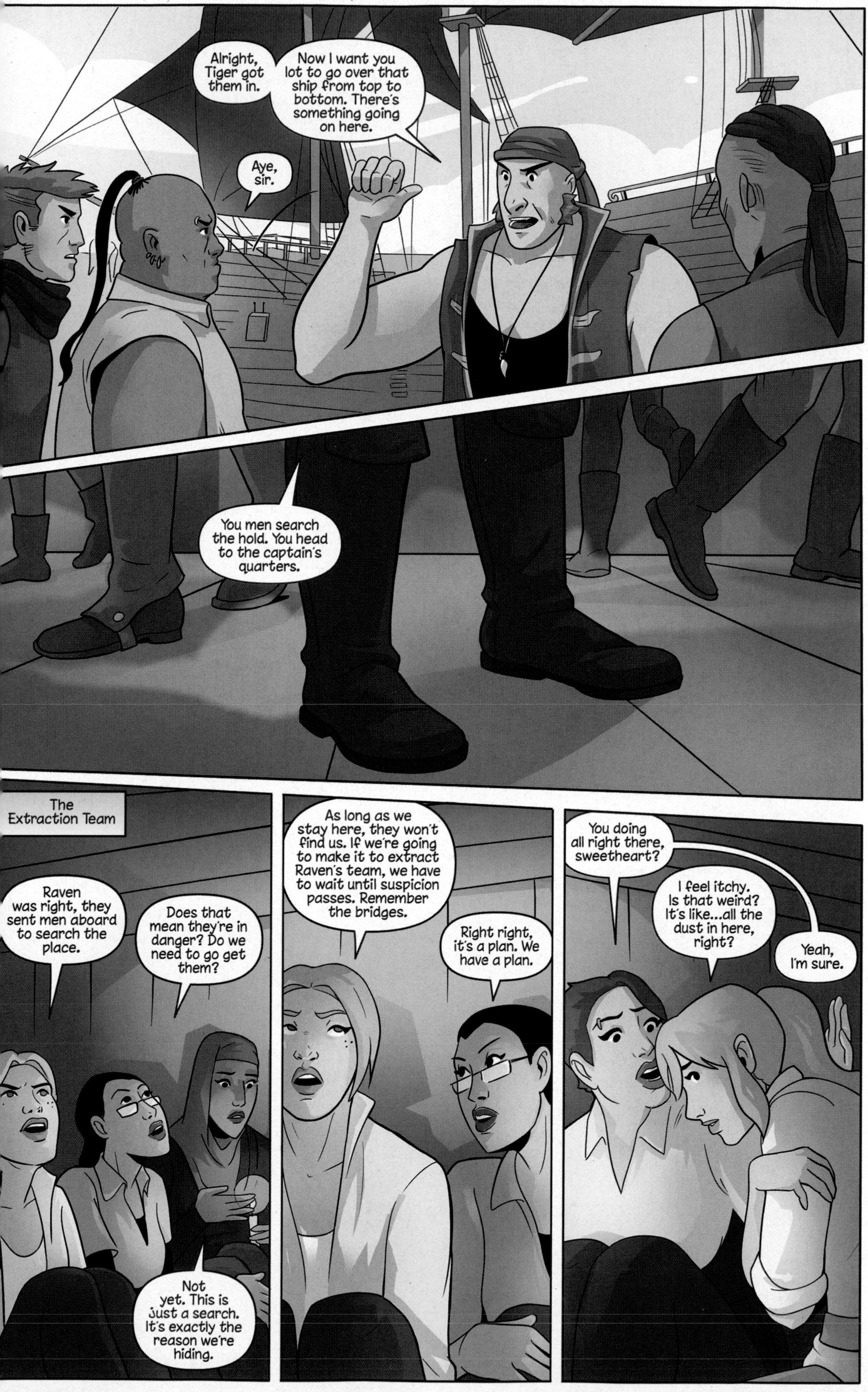
Alright, Tiger got them in.
Now I want you lot to go over that ship from top to bottom. There's something going on here.
Aye, sir.
You men search the hold. You head to the captain's quarters.
The Extraction Team
Raven was right, they sent men aboard to search the place.
Does that mean they're in danger? Do we need to go get them?
Not yet. This is just a search. It's exactly the reason we're hiding.
As long as we stay here, they won't find us. If we're going to make it to extract Raven's team, we have to wait until suspicion passes. Remember the bridges.
Right right, it's a plan. We have a plan.
You doing all right there, sweetheart?
I feel itchy. Is that weird? It's like...all the dust in here, right?
Yeah, I'm sure.

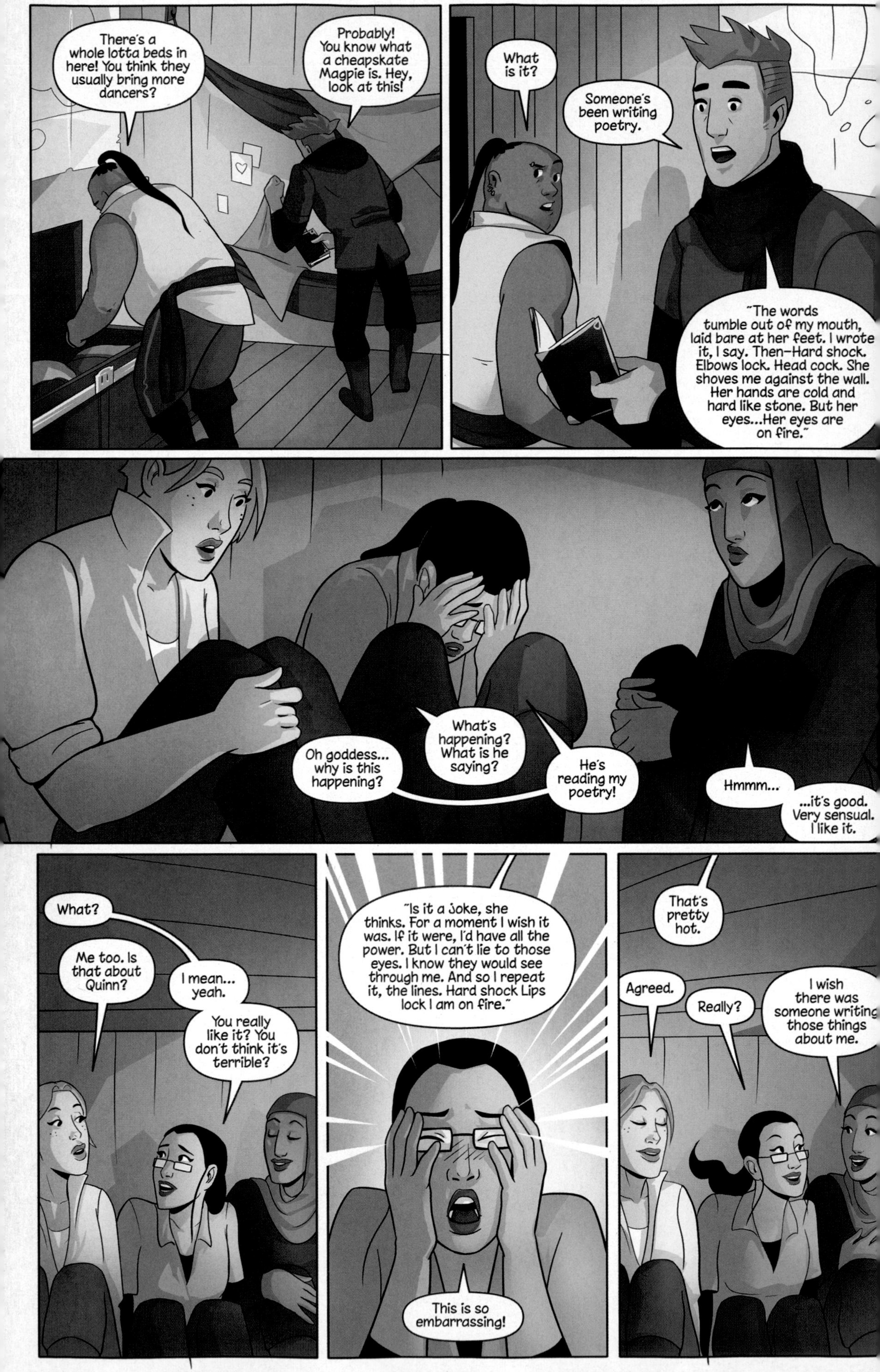
There's a whole lotta beds in here! You think they usually bring more dancers?
Probably! You know what a cheapskate Magpie is. Hey, look at this!
What is it?
Someone's been writing poetry.
"The words tumble out of my mouth, laid bare at her feet. I wrote it, I say. Then—Hard shock. Elbows lock. Head cock. She shoves me against the wall. Her hands are cold and hard like stone. But her eyes...Her eyes are on fire."
Oh goddess... why is this happening?
What's happening? What is he saying?
He's reading my poetry!
Hmmm...
...it's good. Very sensual. I like it.
What?
Me too. Is that about Quinn?
I mean... yeah.
You really like it? You don't think it's terrible?
"Is it a joke, she thinks. For a moment I wish it was. If it were, I'd have all the power. But I can't lie to those eyes. I know they would see through me. And so I repeat it, the lines. Hard shock Lips lock I am on fire."
This is so embarrassing!
That's pretty hot.
Agreed.
Really?
I wish there was someone writing those things about me.

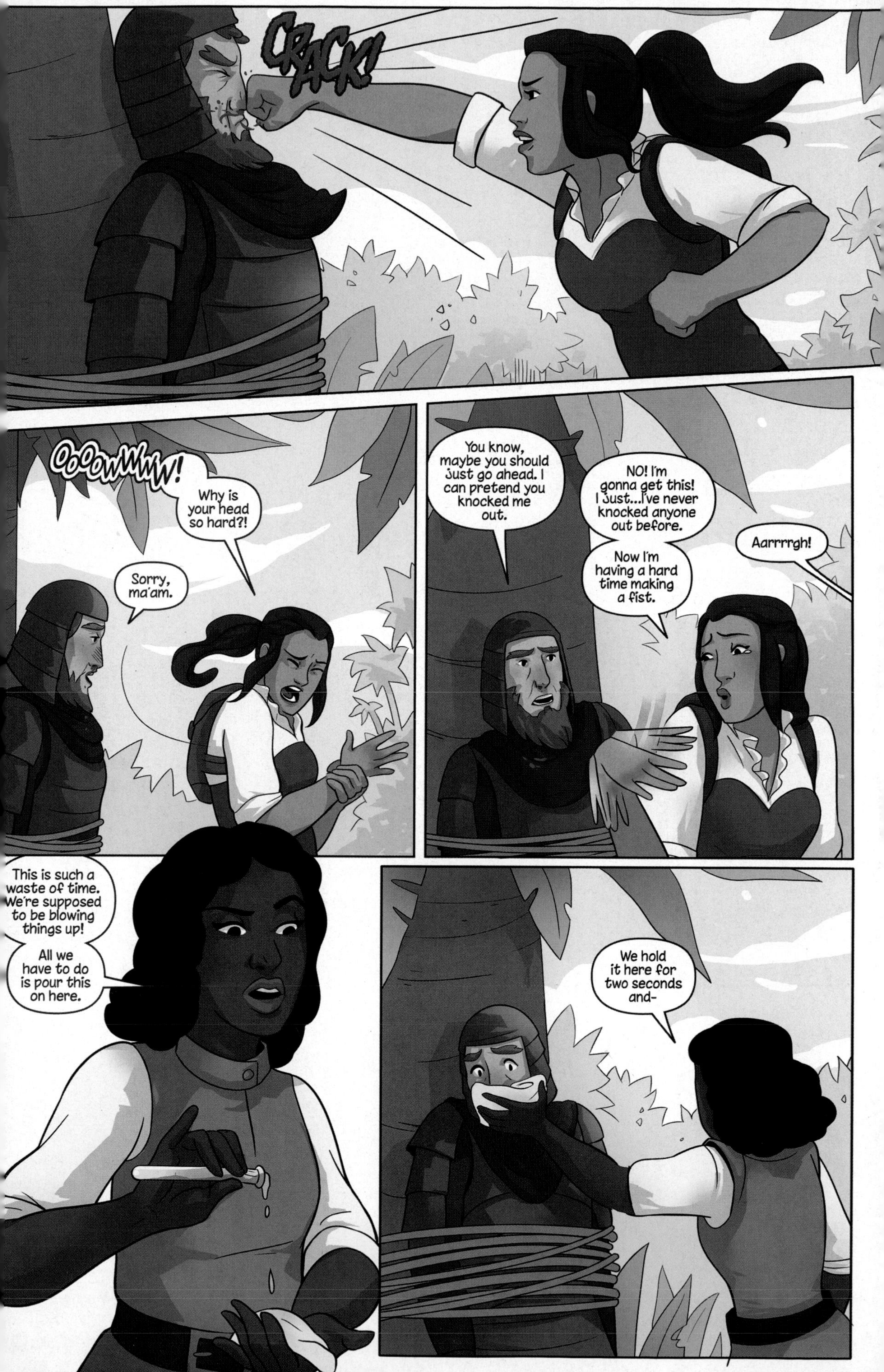
CRACK!
OoOoWWW!
Why is your head so hard?!
Sorry, ma'am.
You know, maybe you should just go ahead. I can pretend you knocked me out.
NO! I'm gonna get this! I just...I've never knocked anyone out before.
Now I'm having a hard time making a fist.
Aarrrrgh!
This is such a waste of time. We're supposed to be blowing things up!
All we have to do is pour this on here.
We hold it here for two seconds and-

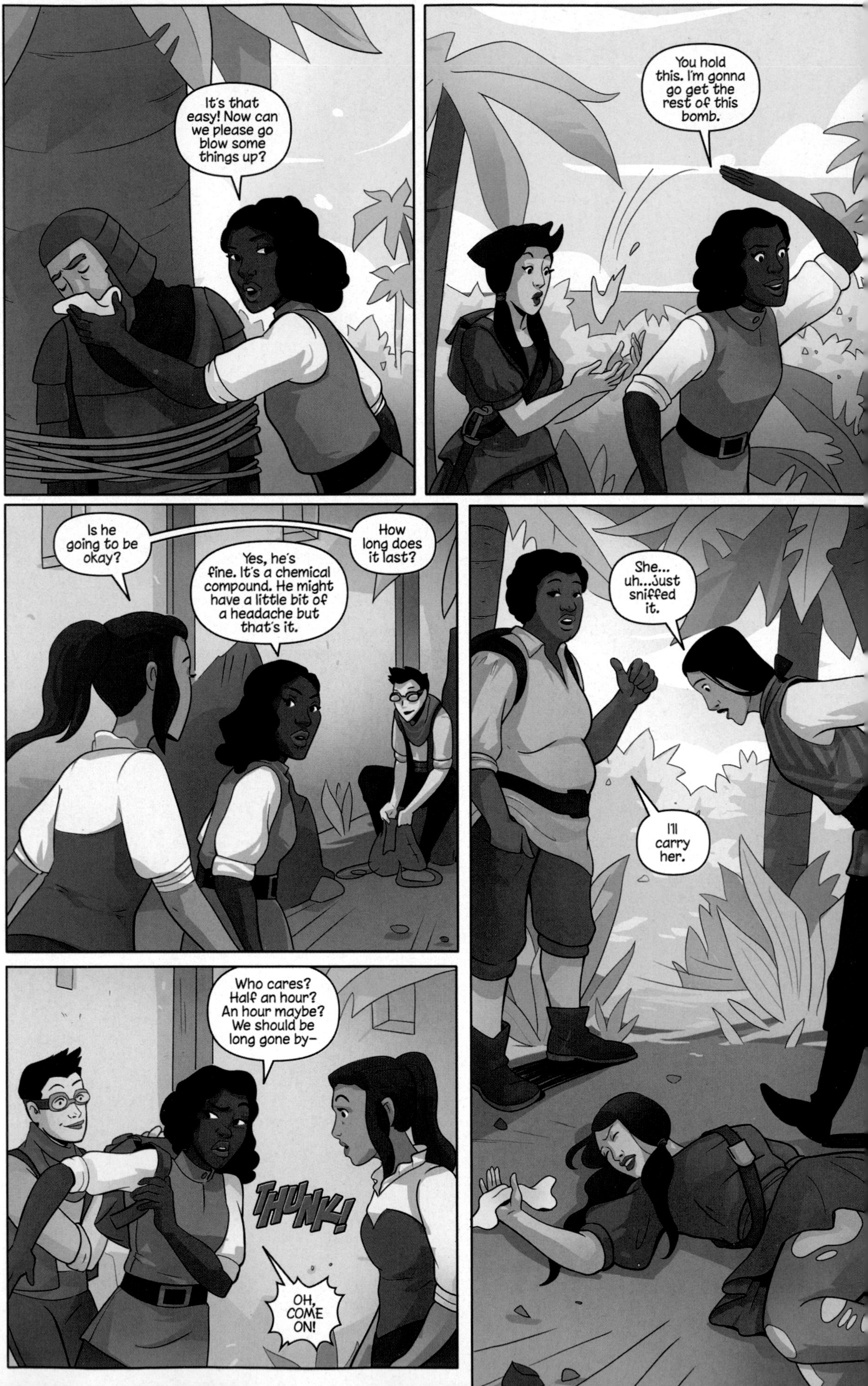
It's that easy! Now can we please go blow some things up?
You hold this. I'm gonna go get the rest of this bomb.
Is he going to be okay?
How long does it last?
Yes, he's fine. It's a chemical compound. He might have a little bit of a headache but that's it.
Who cares? Half an hour? An hour maybe? We should be long gone by–
THUNK!
OH, COME ON!
She... uh...just sniffed it.
I'll carry her.

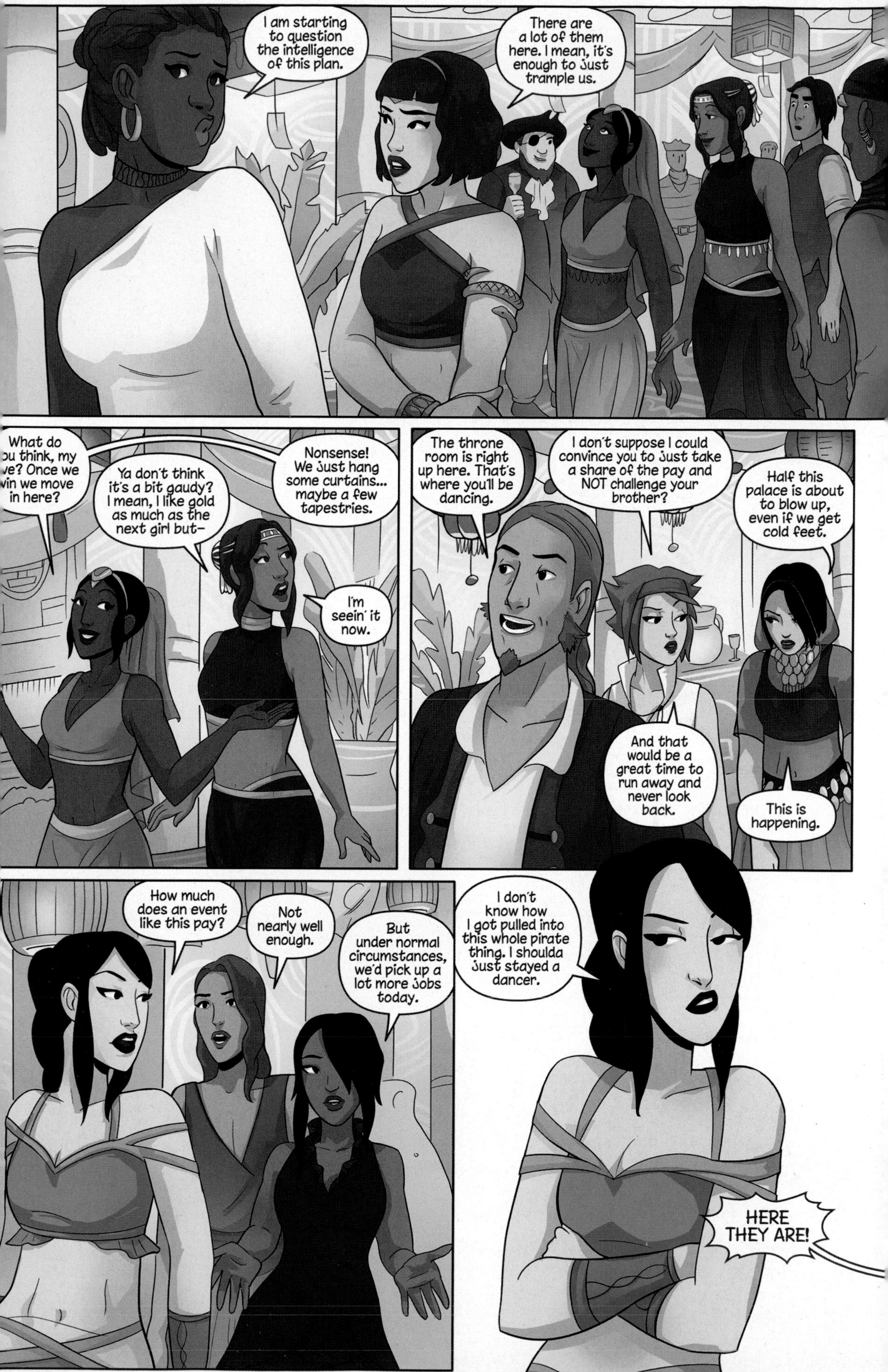
I am starting to question the intelligence of this plan.
There are a lot of them here. I mean, it's enough to just trample us.
What do ou think, my ve? Once we win we move in here?
Ya don't think it's a bit gaudy? I mean, I like gold as much as the next girl but–
Nonsense! We just hang some curtains... maybe a few tapestries.
I'm seein' it now.
The throne room is right up here. That's where you'll be dancing.
I don't suppose I could convince you to just take a share of the pay and NOT challenge your brother?
Half this palace is about to blow up, even if we get cold feet.
And that would be a great time to run away and never look back.
This is happening.
How much does an event like this pay?
Not nearly well enough.
But under normal circumstances, we'd pick up a lot more jobs today.
I don't know how I got pulled into this whole pirate thing. I shoulda just stayed a dancer.
HERE THEY ARE!

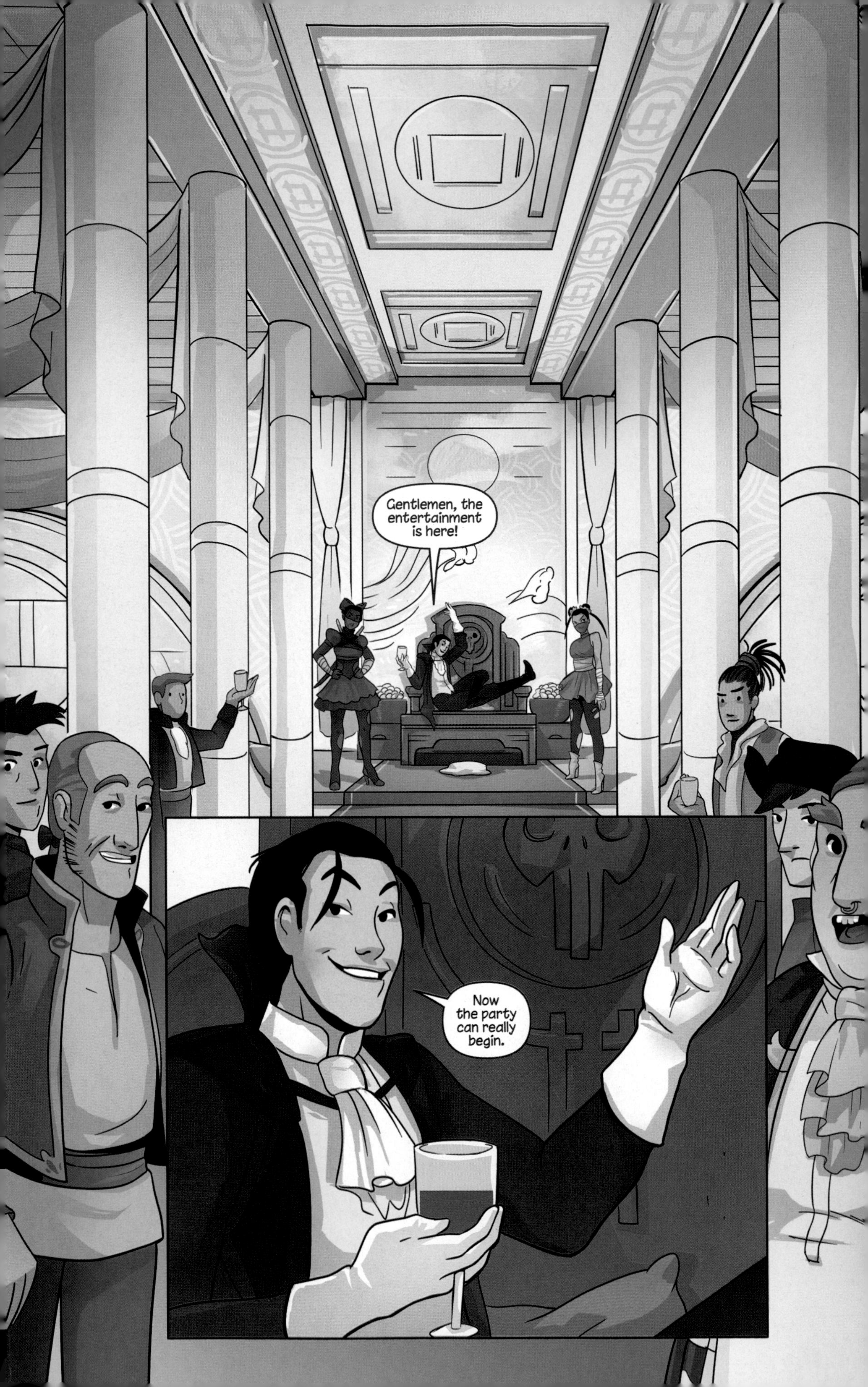
Gentlemen, the entertainment is here!
Now the party can really begin.

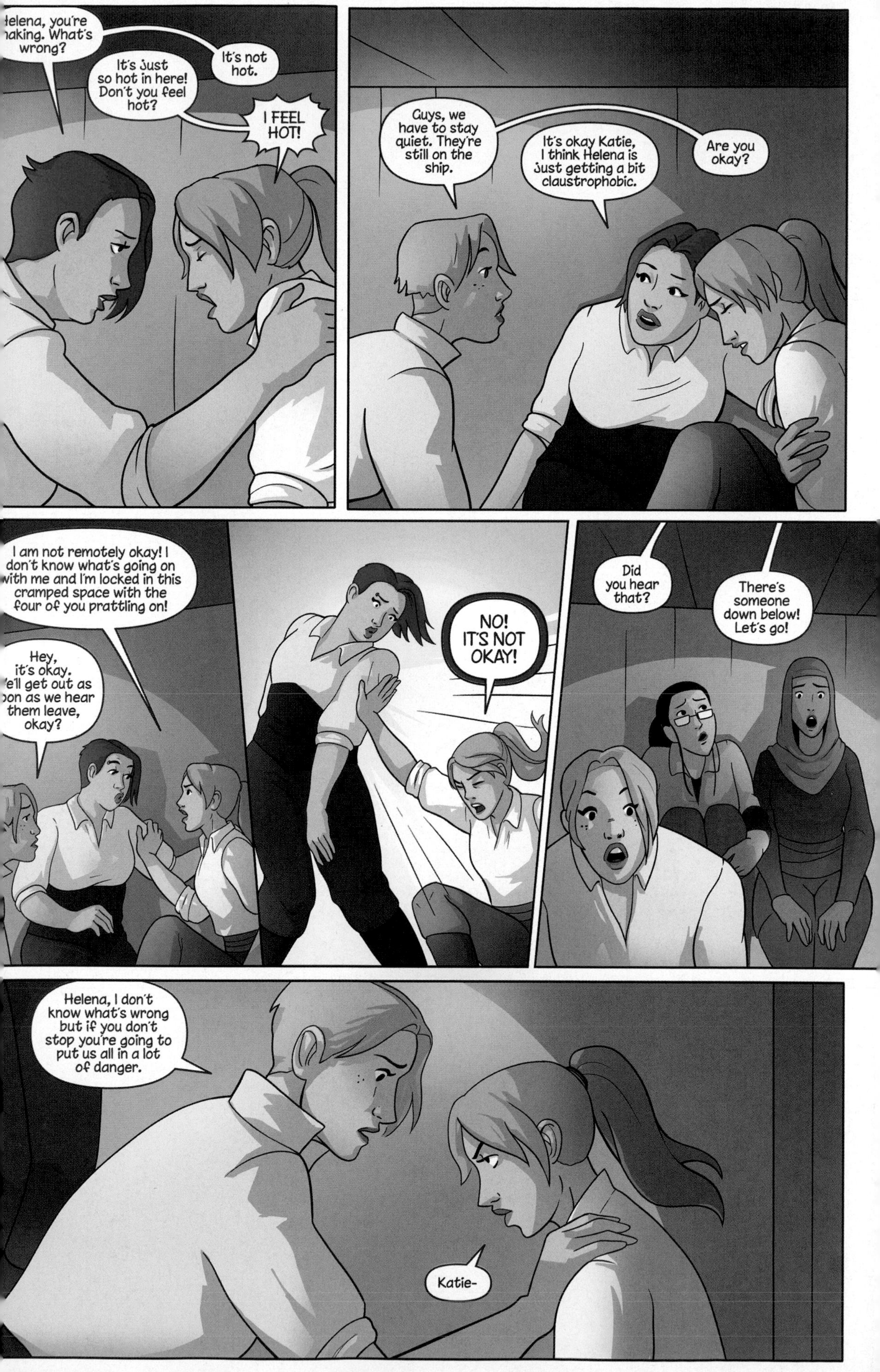

Helena, you're
shaking. What's wrong?
It's just so hot in here! Don't you feel hot?
It's not hot.
I FEEL HOT!
Guys, we have to stay quiet. They're still on the ship.
It's okay Katie, I think Helena is just getting a bit claustrophobic.
Are you okay?
I am not remotely okay! I don't know what's going on with me and I'm locked in this cramped space with the four of you prattling on!
Hey, it's okay. We'll get out as soon as we hear them leave, okay?
NO! IT'S NOT OKAY!
Did you hear that?
There's someone down below! Let's go!
Helena, I don't know what's wrong but if you don't stop you're going to put us all in a lot of danger.
Katie-

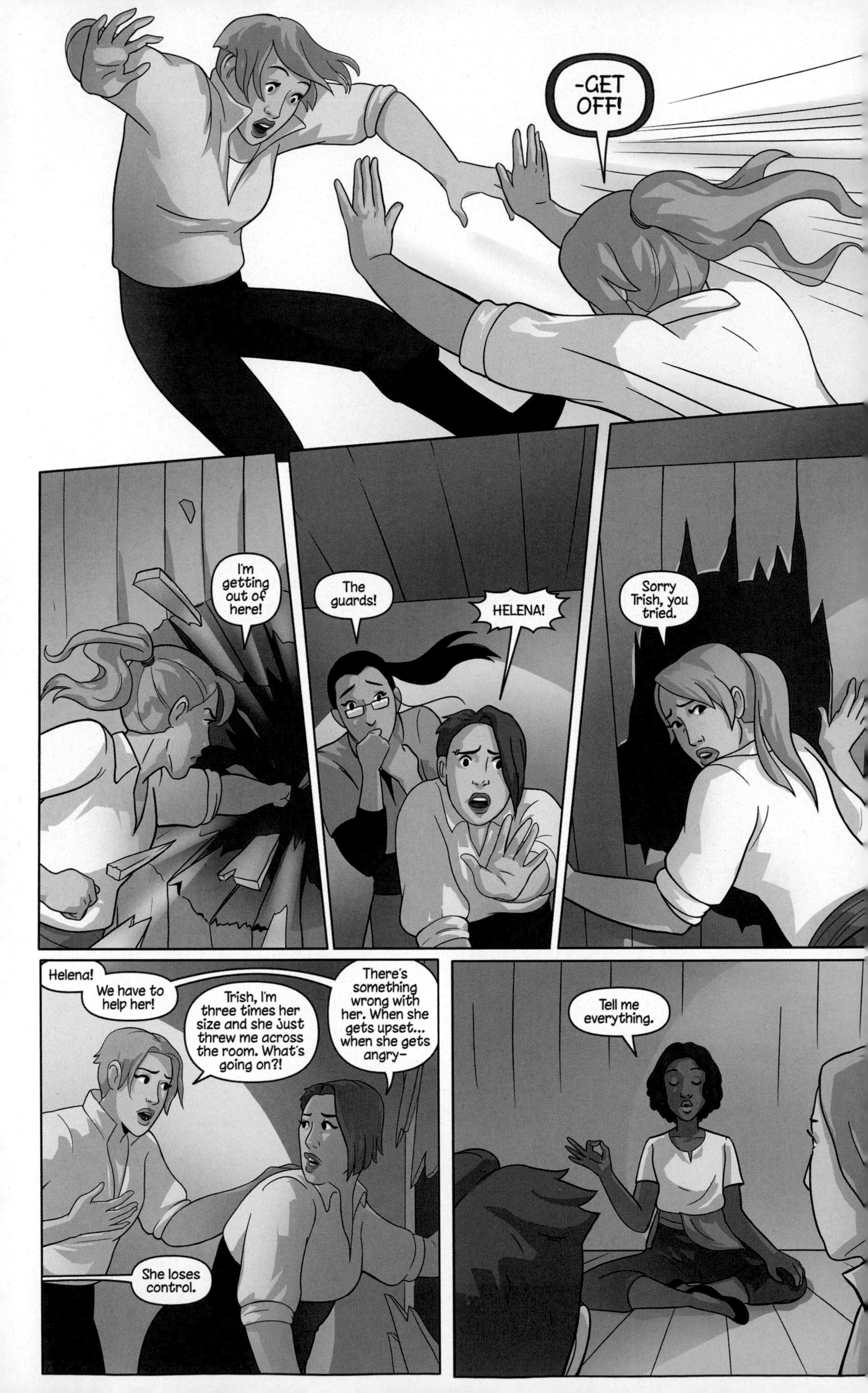
-GET OFF!
I'm getting out of here!
The guards!
HELENA!
Sorry Trish, you tried.
Helena!
We have to help her!
Trish, I'm three times her size and she just threw me across the room. What's going on?!
There's something wrong with her. When she gets upset... when she gets angry-
She loses control.
Tell me everything.

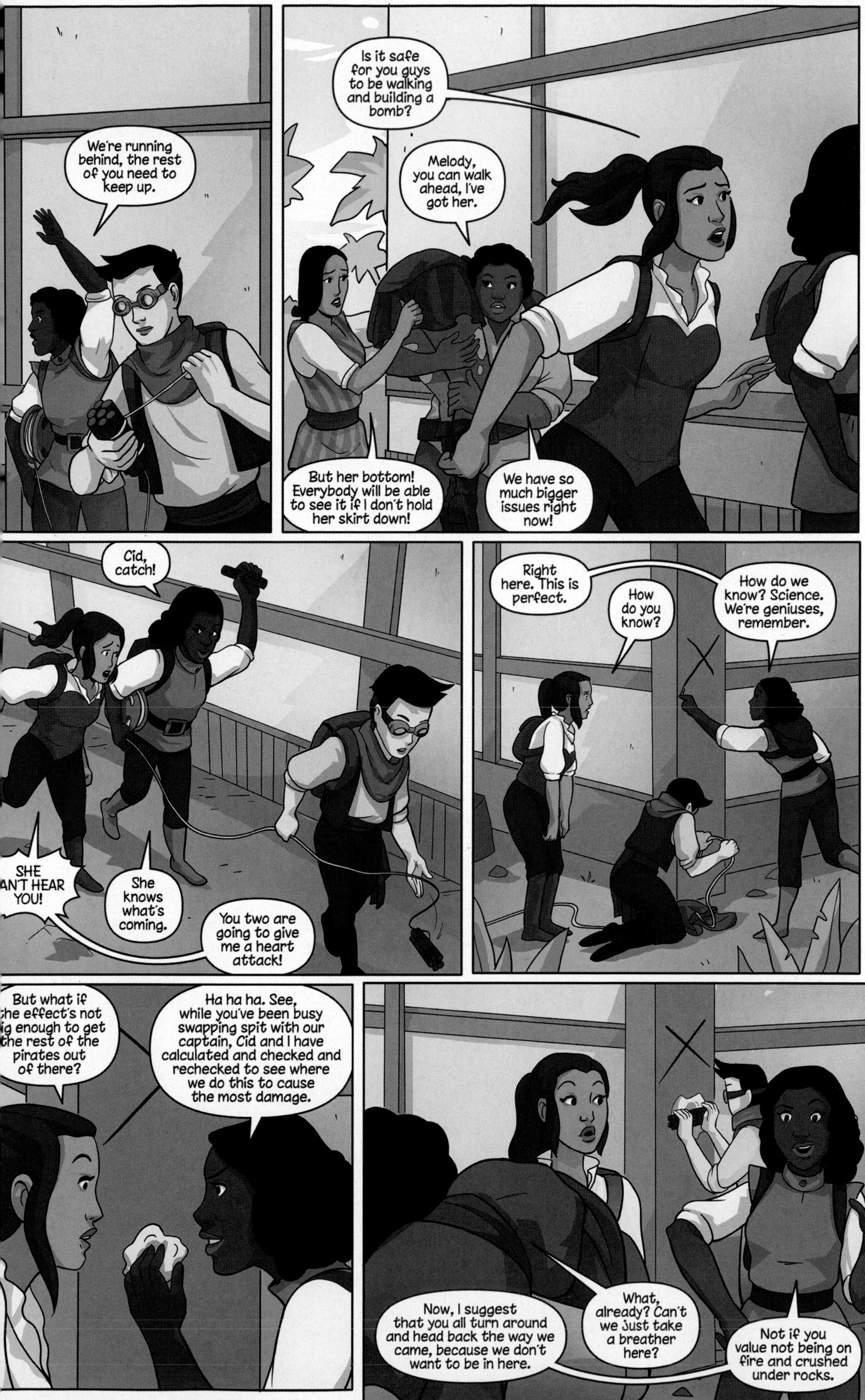
We're running behind, the rest of you need to keep up.
Is it safe for you guys to be walking and building a bomb?
Melody, you can walk ahead, I've got her.
But her bottom! Everybody will be able to see it if I don't hold her skirt down!
We have so much bigger issues right now!
Cid, catch!
SHE CAN'T HEAR YOU!
She knows what's coming.
You two are going to give me a heart attack!
Right here. This is perfect.
How do you know?
How do we know? Science. We're geniuses, remember.
But what if the effect's not big enough to get the rest of the pirates out of there?
Ha ha ha. See, while you've been busy swapping spit with our captain, Cid and I have calculated and checked and rechecked to see where we do this to cause the most damage.
Now, I suggest that you all turn around and head back the way we came, because we don't want to be in here.
What, already? Can't we just take a breather here?
Not if you value not being on fire and crushed under rocks.

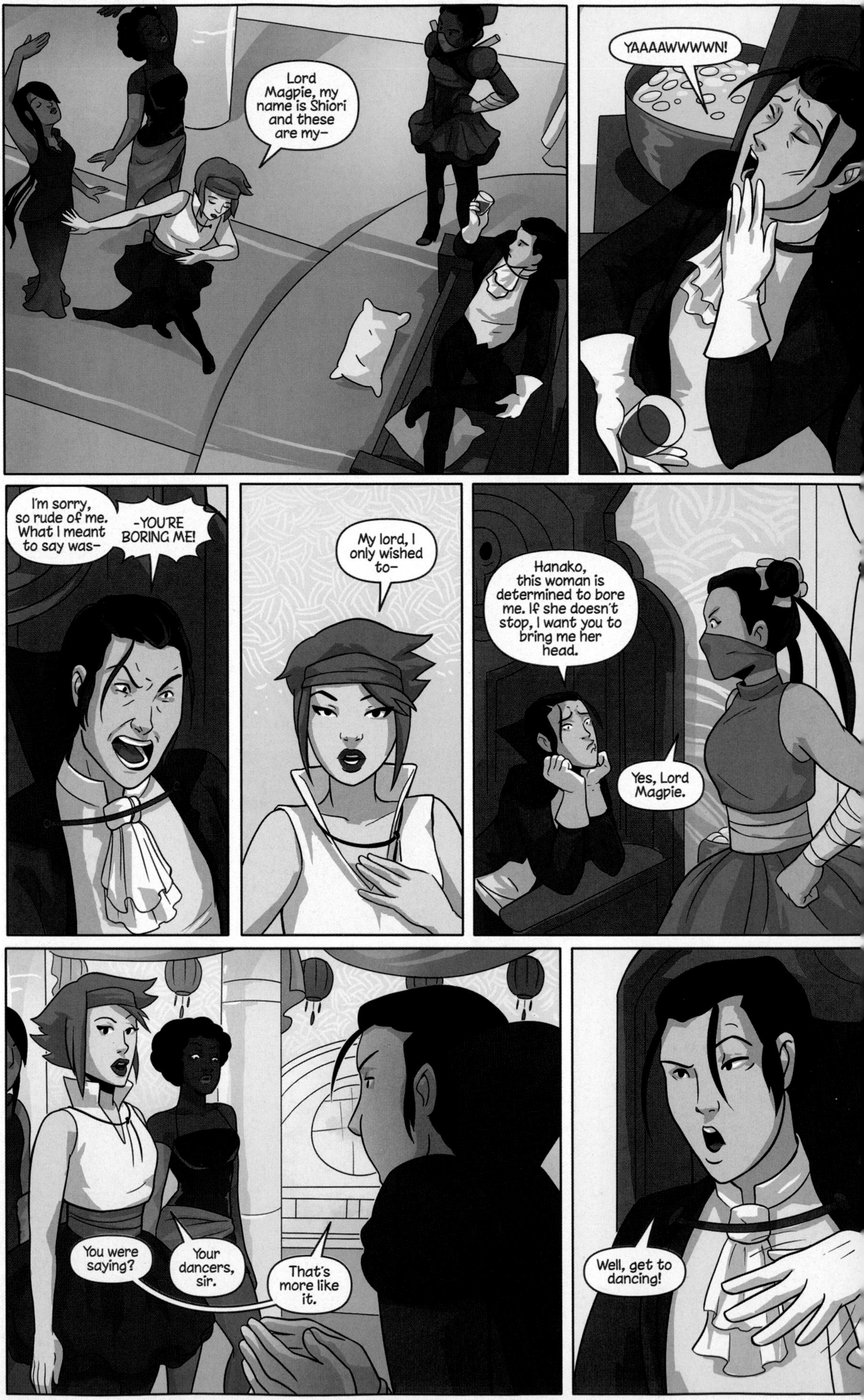
Lord Magpie, my name is Shiori and these are my–
YAAAAWWWWN!
I'm sorry, so rude of me. What I meant to say was–
-YOU'RE BORING ME!
My lord, I only wished to–
Hanako, this woman is determined to bore me. If she doesn't stop, I want you to bring me her head.
Yes, Lord Magpie.
You were saying?
Your dancers, sir.
That's more like it.
Well, get to dancing!

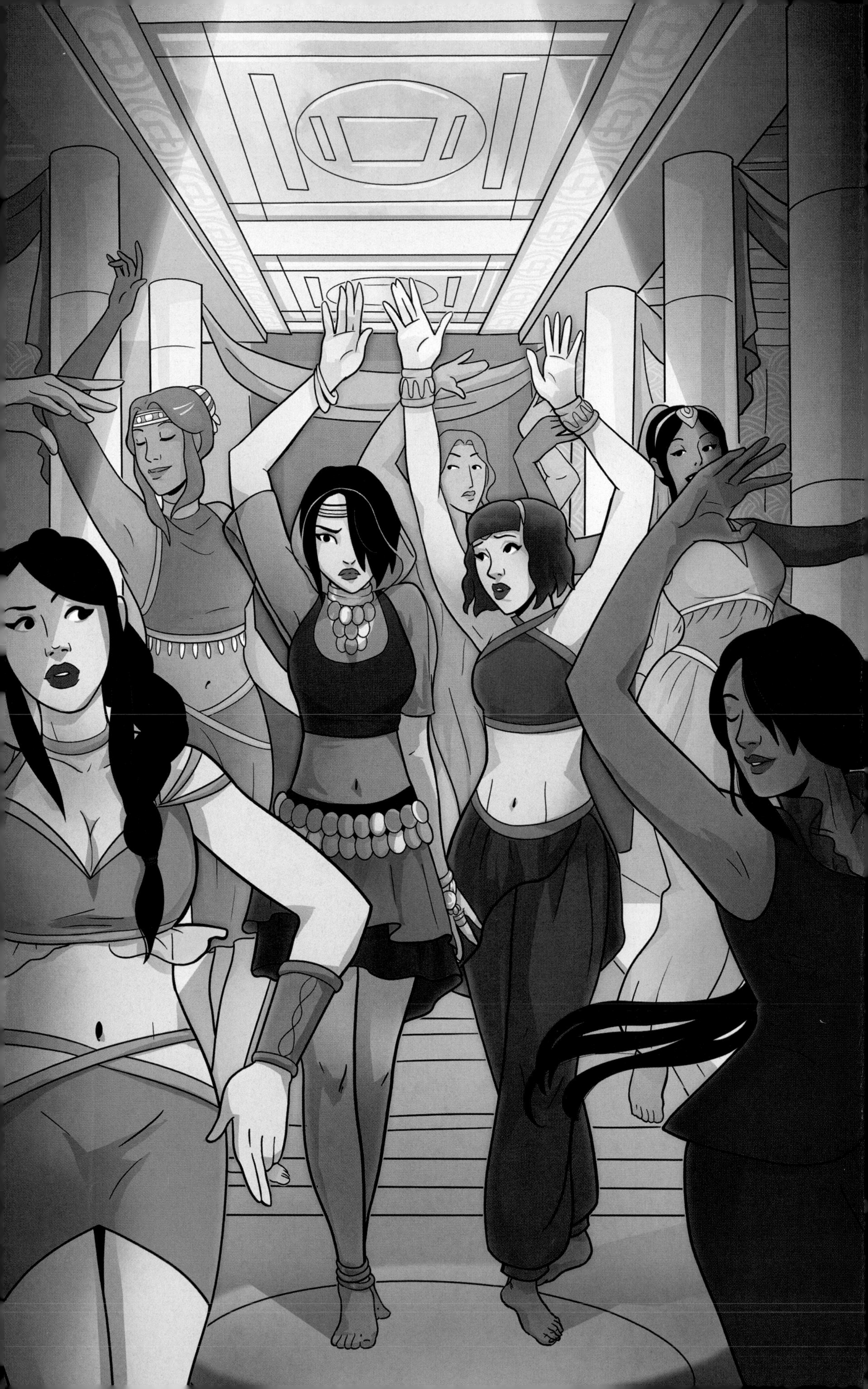

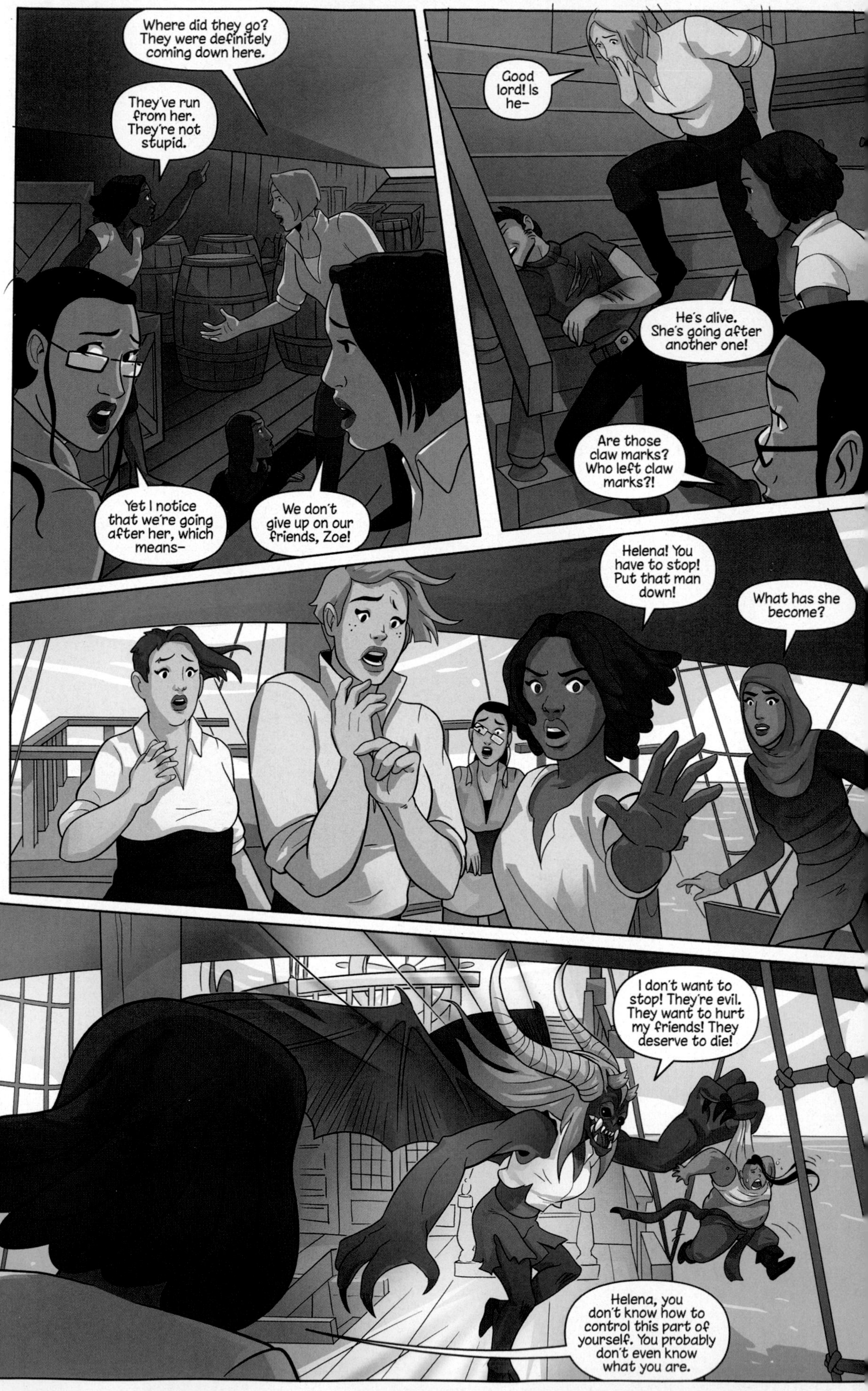
Where did they go? They were definitely coming down here.
They've run from her. They're not stupid.
Yet I notice that we're going after her, which means–
We don't give up on our friends, Zoe!
Good lord! Is he–
He's alive. She's going after another one!
Are those claw marks? Who left claw marks?!
Helena! You have to stop! Put that man down!
What has she become?
I don't want to stop! They're evil. They want to hurt my friends! They deserve to die!
Helena, you don't know how to control this part of yourself. You probably don't even know what you are.

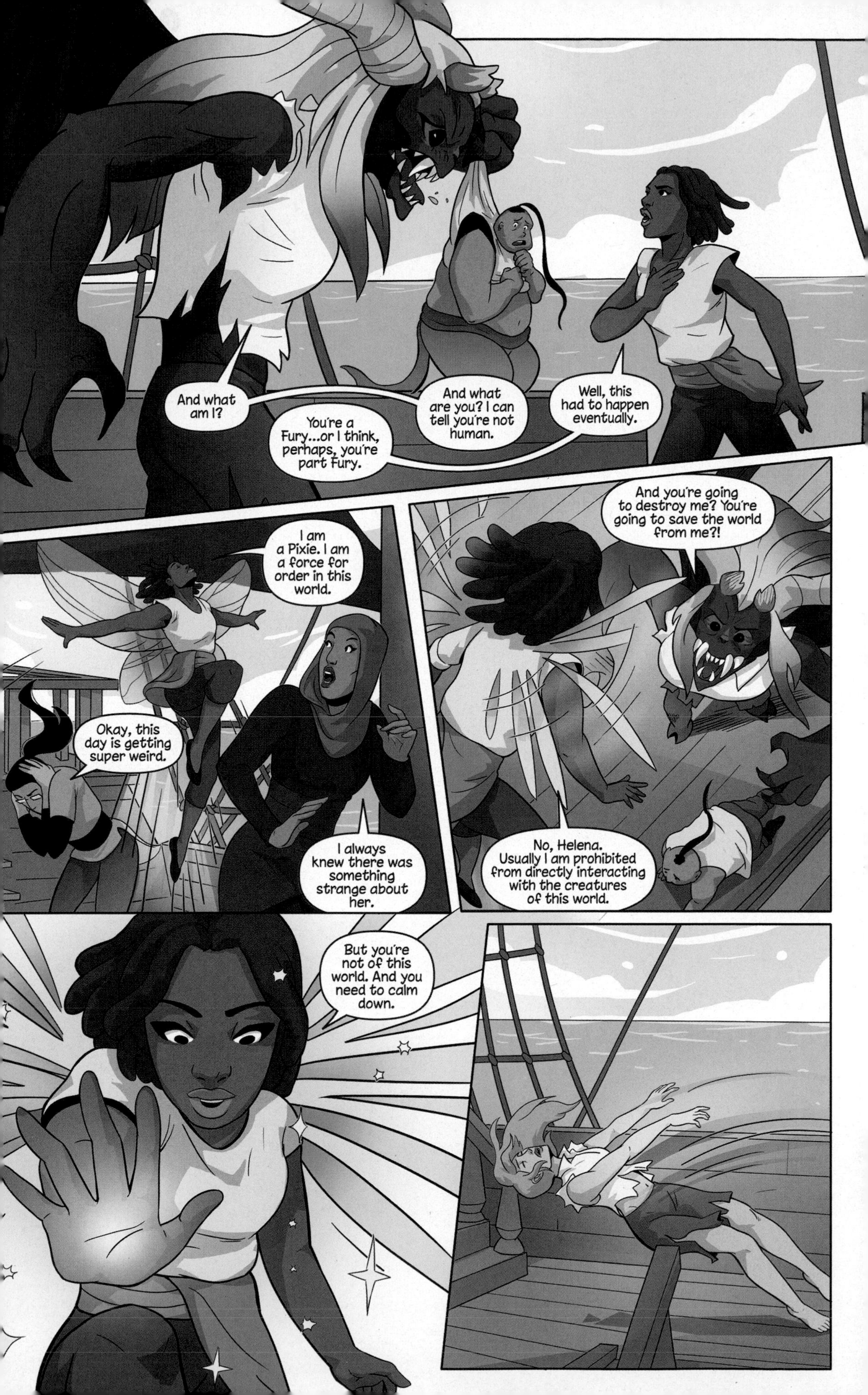
And what am I?
You're a Fury...or I think, perhaps, you're part Fury.
And what are you? I can tell you're not human.
Well, this had to happen eventually.
I am a Pixie. I am a force for order in this world.
Okay, this day is getting super weird.
I always knew there was something strange about her.
And you're going to destroy me? You're going to save the world from me?!
No, Helena. Usually I am prohibited from directly interacting with the creatures of this world.
But you're not of this world. And you need to calm down.

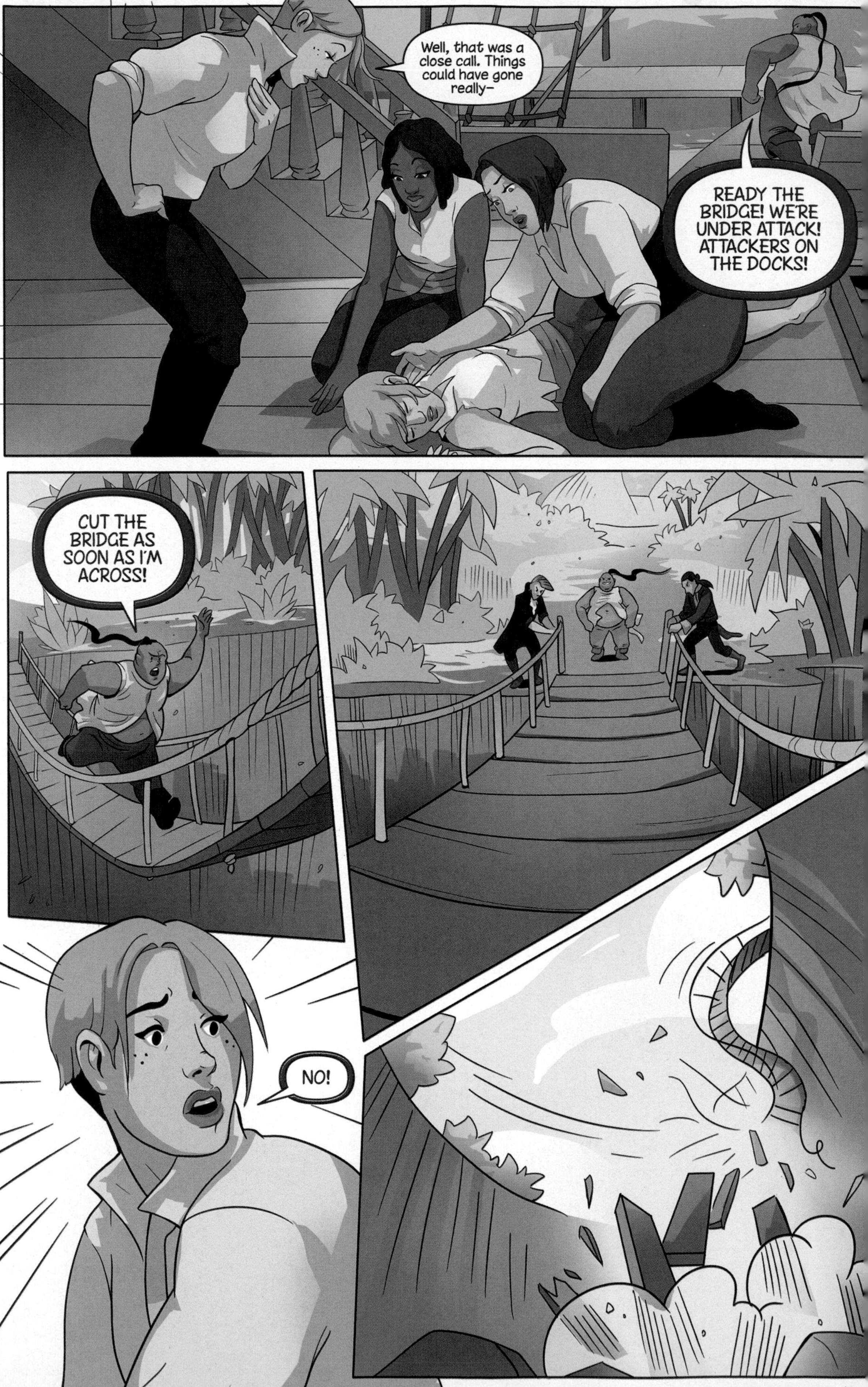
Well, that was a close call. Things could have gone really–
READY THE BRIDGE! WE'RE UNDER ATTACK! ATTACKERS ON THE DOCKS!
CUT THE BRIDGE AS SOON AS I'M ACROSS!
NO!

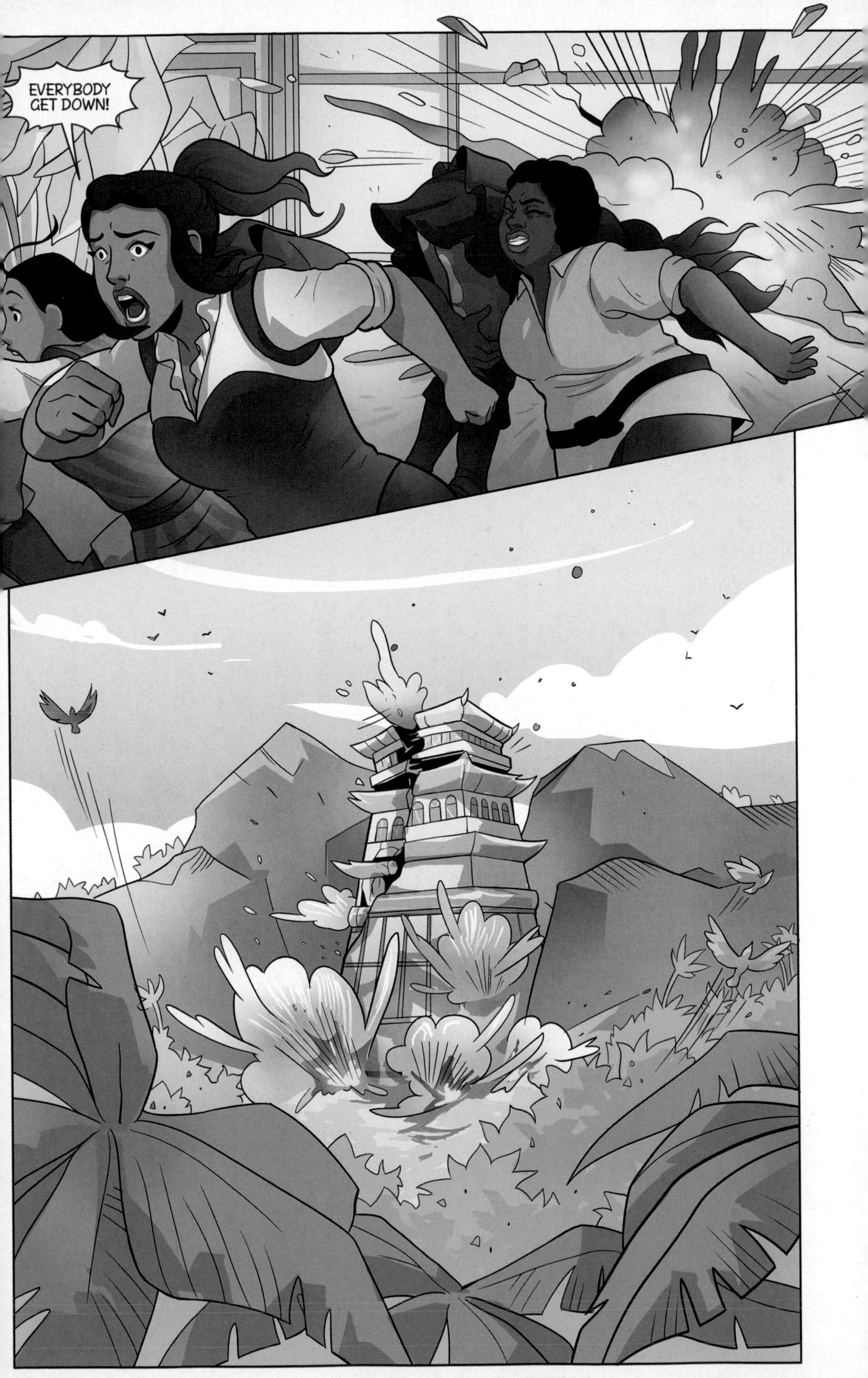
EVERYBODY GET DOWN!

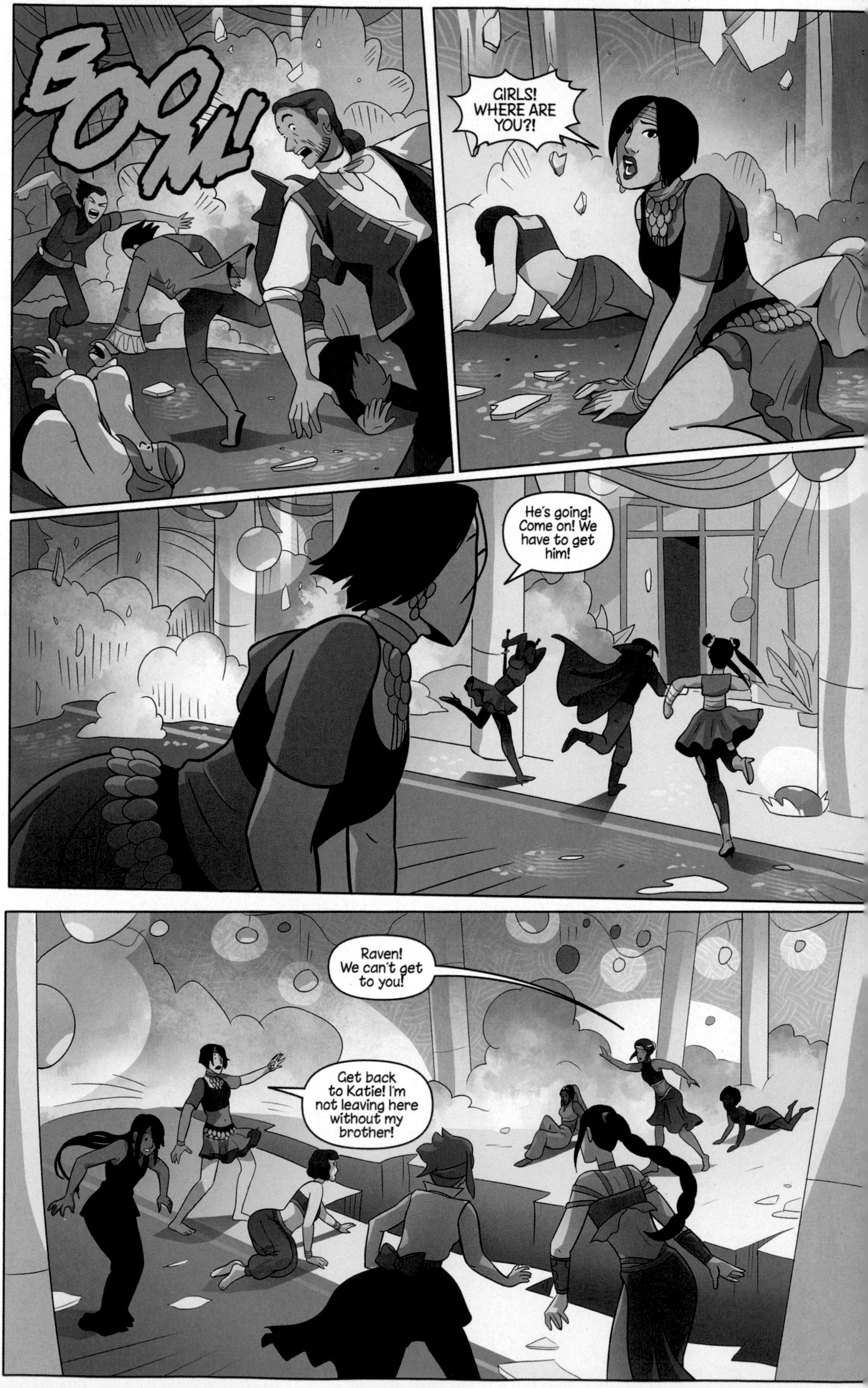
BOOM!
GIRLS! WHERE ARE YOU?!
He's going! Come on! We have to get him!
Raven! We can't get to you!
Get back to Katie! I'm not leaving here without my brother!

Princess

Raven

THE PIRATE PRINCESS

Year Two: Love and Revenge

Chapter Twelve: Let's be honest... the plan wasn't great

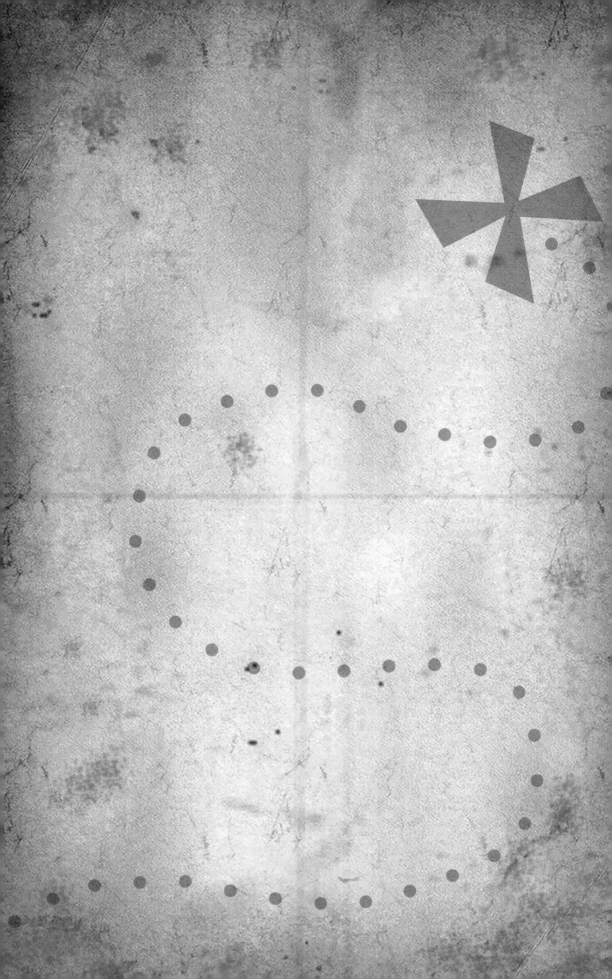

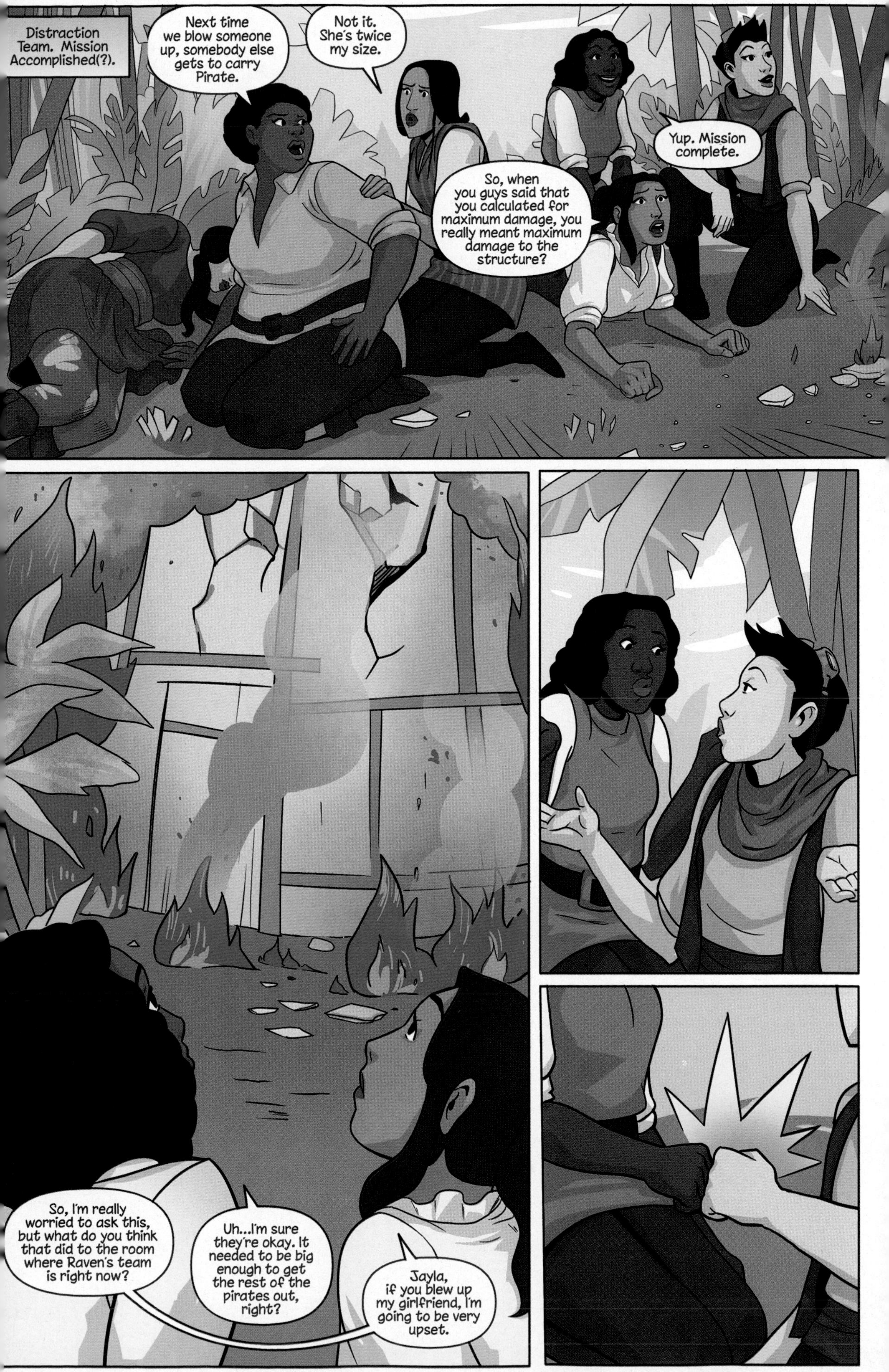
Distraction Team. Mission Accomplished(?).
Next time we blow someone up, somebody else gets to carry Pirate.
Not it. She's twice my size.
So, when you guys said that you calculated for maximum damage, you really meant maximum damage to the structure?
Yup. Mission complete.
So, I'm really worried to ask this, but what do you think that did to the room where Raven's team is right now?
Uh...I'm sure they're okay. It needed to be big enough to get the rest of the pirates out, right?
Jayla, if you blew up my girlfriend, I'm going to be very upset.

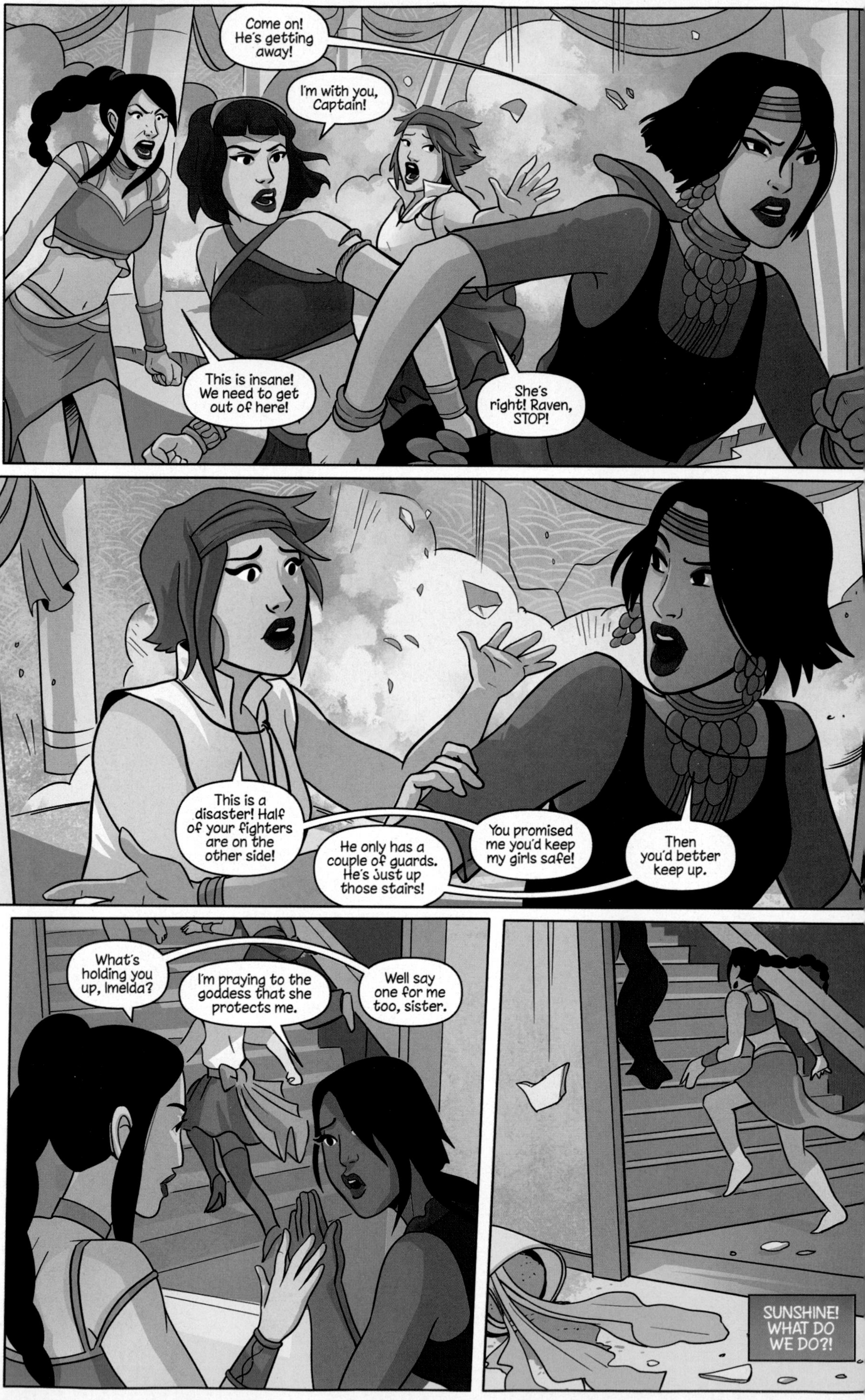
Come on! He's getting away!
I'm with you, Captain!
This is insane! We need to get out of here!
She's right! Raven, STOP!
This is a disaster! Half of your fighters are on the other side!
He only has a couple of guards. He's just up those stairs!
You promised me you'd keep my girls safe!
Then you'd better keep up.
What's holding you up, Imelda?
I'm praying to the goddess that she protects me.
Well say one for me too, sister.
SUNSHINE! WHAT DO WE DO?!

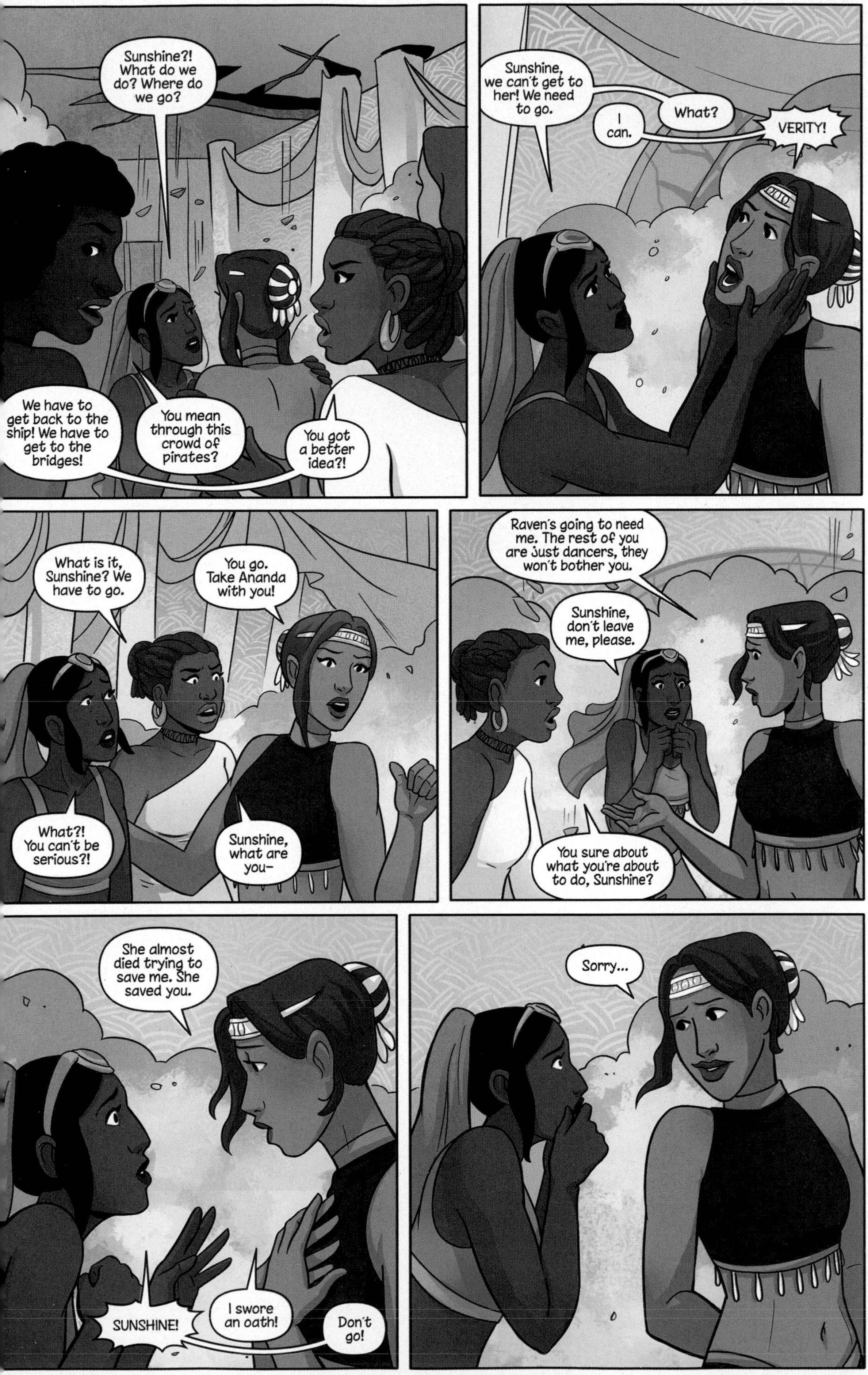
Sunshine?! What do we do? Where do we go?
We have to get back to the ship! We have to get to the bridges!
You mean through this crowd of pirates?
You got a better idea?!
Sunshine, we can't get to her! We need to go.
I can.
What?
VERITY!
What is it, Sunshine? We have to go.
You go. Take Ananda with you!
What?! You can't be serious?!
Sunshine, what are you–
Raven's going to need me. The rest of you are just dancers, they won't bother you.
Sunshine, don't leave me, please.
You sure about what you're about to do, Sunshine?
She almost died trying to save me. She saved you.
SUNSHINE!
I swore an oath!
Don't go!
Sorry...

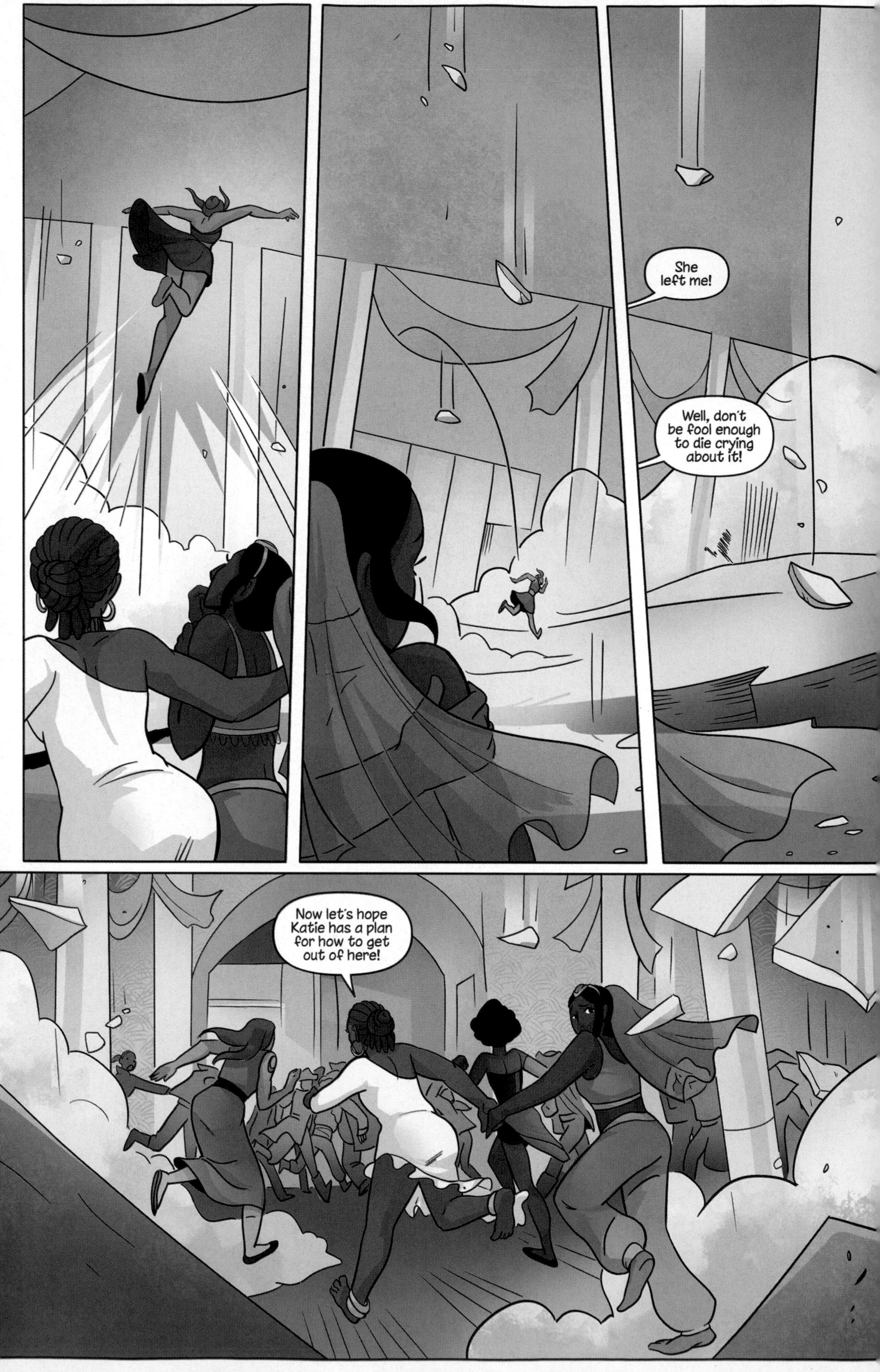
She left me!
Well, don't be fool enough to die crying about it!
Now let's hope Katie has a plan for how to get out of here!

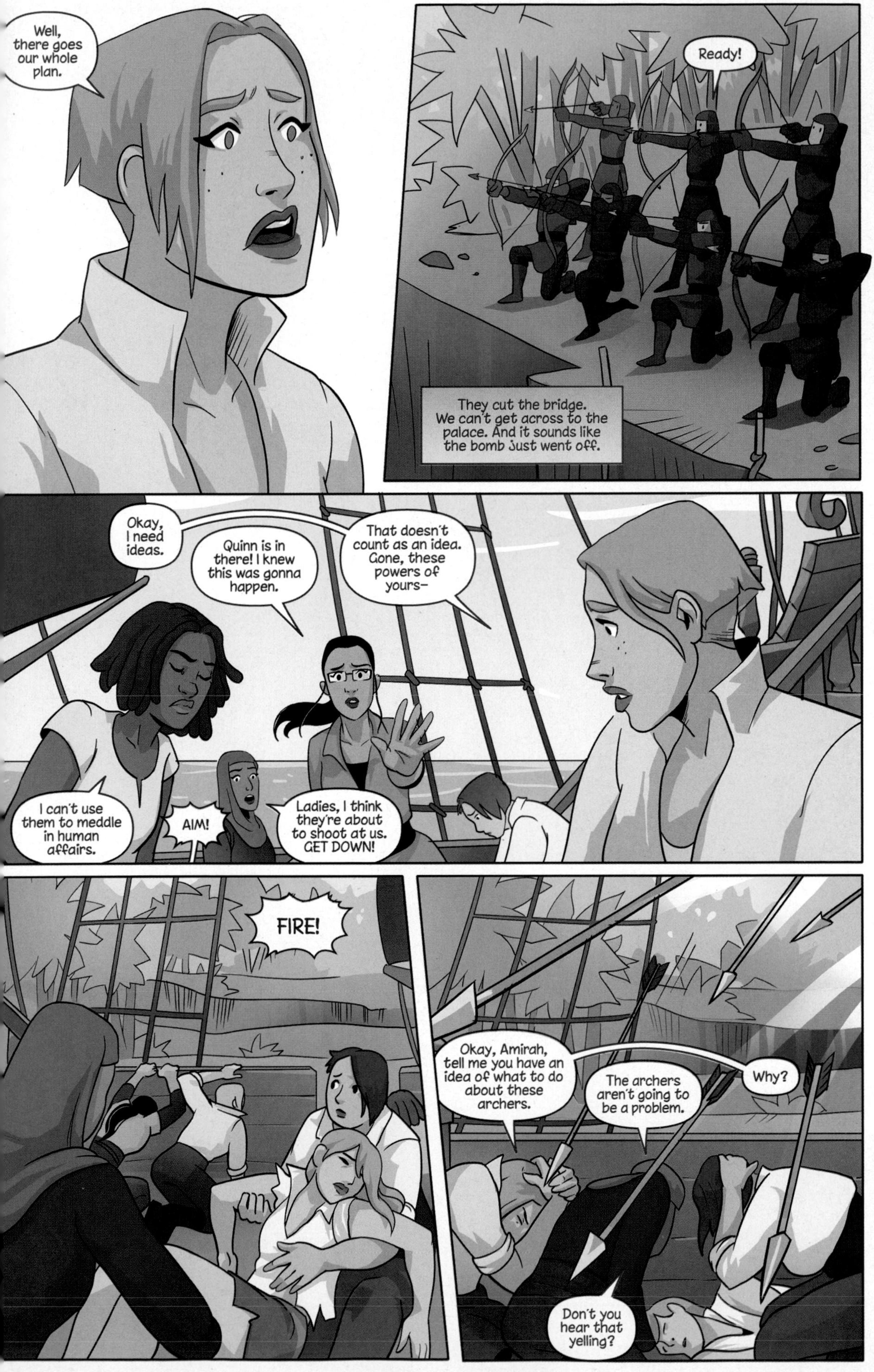

Well, there goes our whole plan.
Ready!
They cut the bridge. We can't get across to the palace. And it sounds like the bomb just went off.
Okay, I need ideas.
Quinn is in there! I knew this was gonna happen.
That doesn't count as an idea. Gone, these powers of yours–
I can't use them to meddle in human affairs.
AIM!
Ladies, I think they're about to shoot at us. GET DOWN!
FIRE!
Okay, Amirah, tell me you have an idea of what to do about these archers.
Why?
The archers aren't going to be a problem.
Don't you hear that yelling?

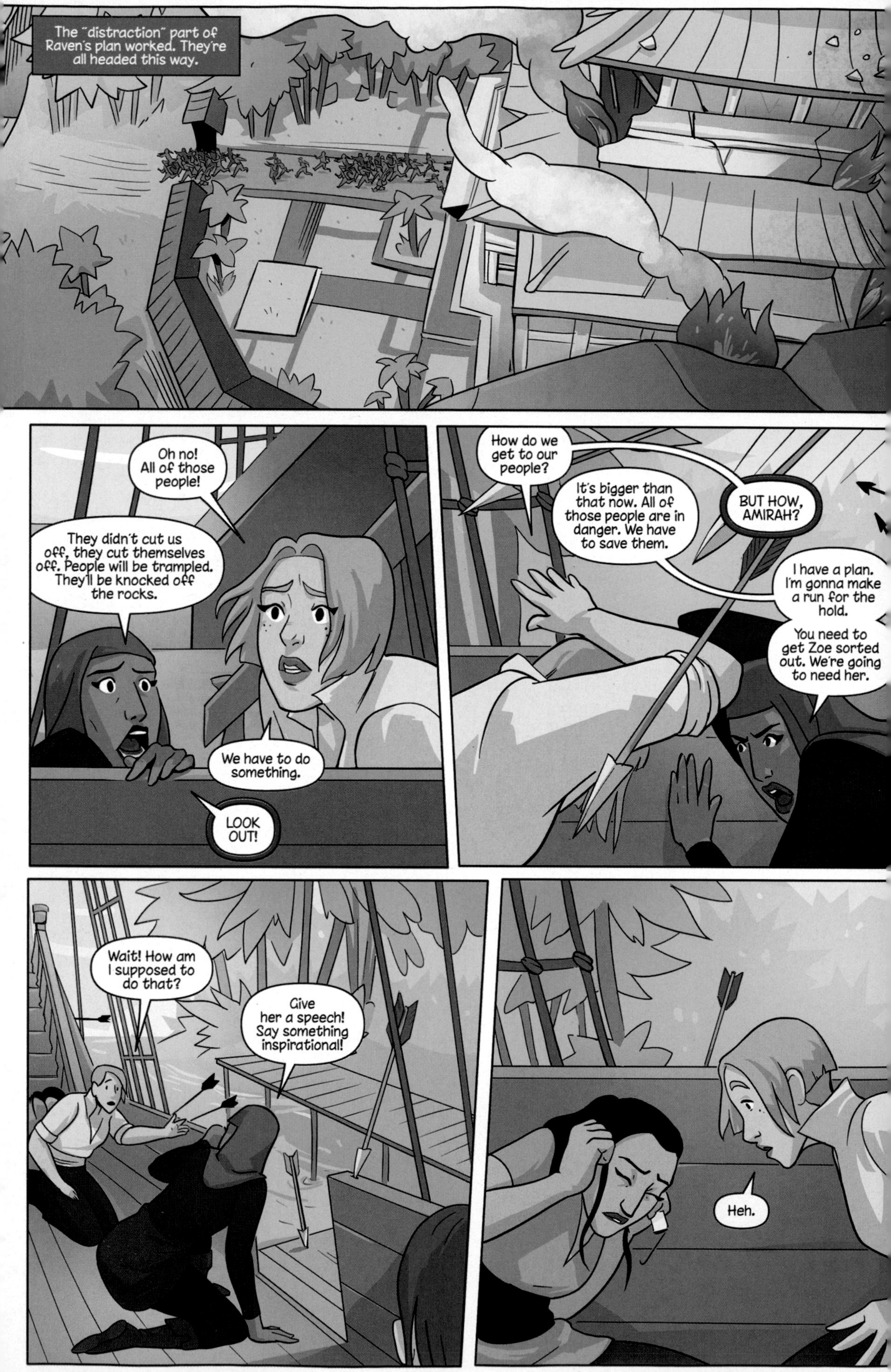
The "distraction" part of Raven's plan worked. They're all headed this way.
Oh no! All of those people!
They didn't cut us off, they cut themselves off. People will be trampled. They'll be knocked off the rocks.
We have to do something.
LOOK OUT!
How do we get to our people?
It's bigger than that now. All of those people are in danger. We have to save them.
BUT HOW, AMIRAH?
I have a plan. I'm gonna make a run for the hold.
You need to get Zoe sorted out. We're going to need her.
Wait! How am I supposed to do that?
Give her a speech! Say something inspirational!
Heh.

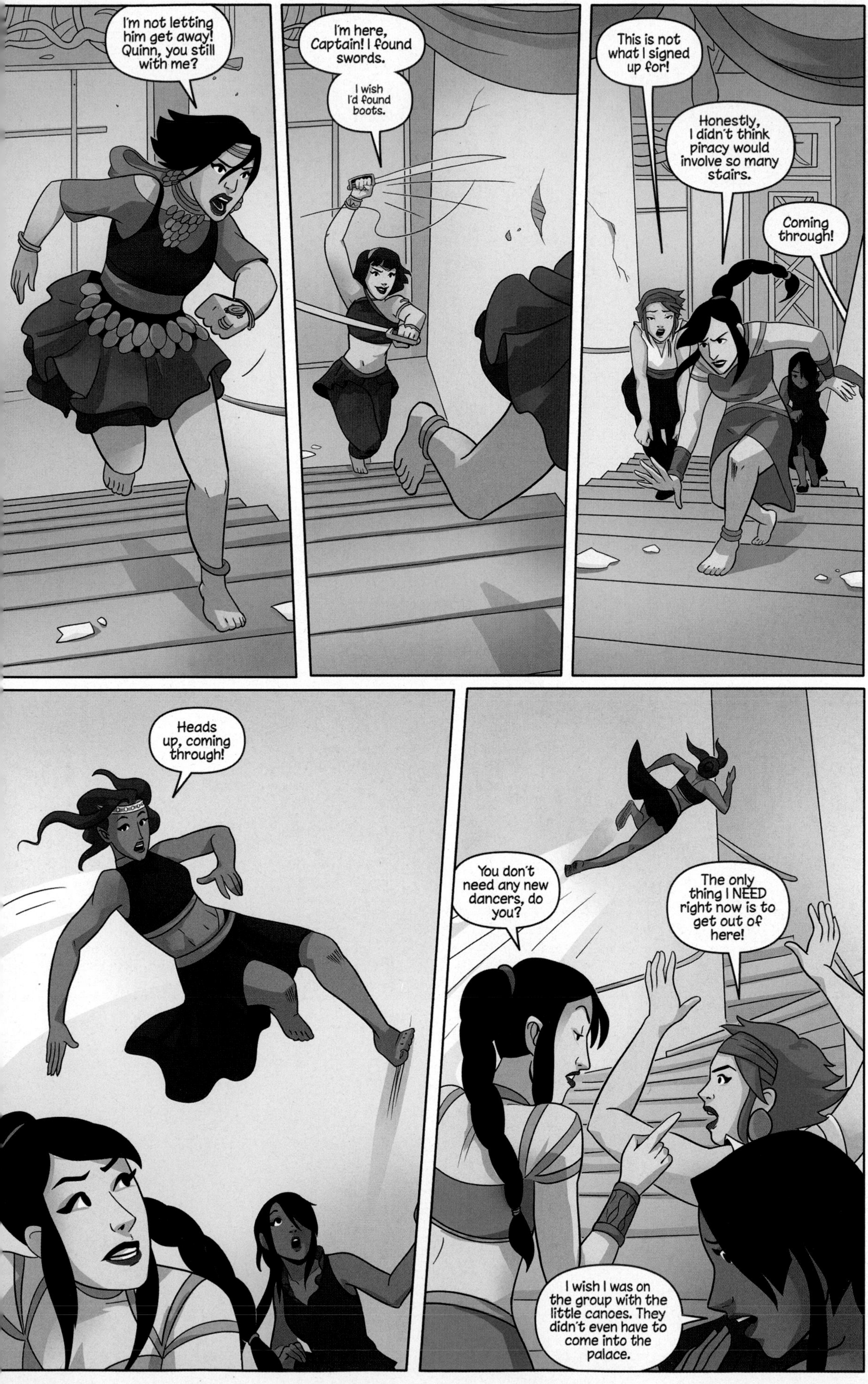
I'm not letting him get away! Quinn, you still with me?
I'm here, Captain! I found swords.
I wish I'd found boots.
This is not what I signed up for!
Honestly, I didn't think piracy would involve so many stairs.
Coming through!
Heads up, coming through!
You don't need any new dancers, do you?
The only thing I NEED right now is to get out of here!
I wish I was on the group with the little canoes. They didn't even have to come into the palace.

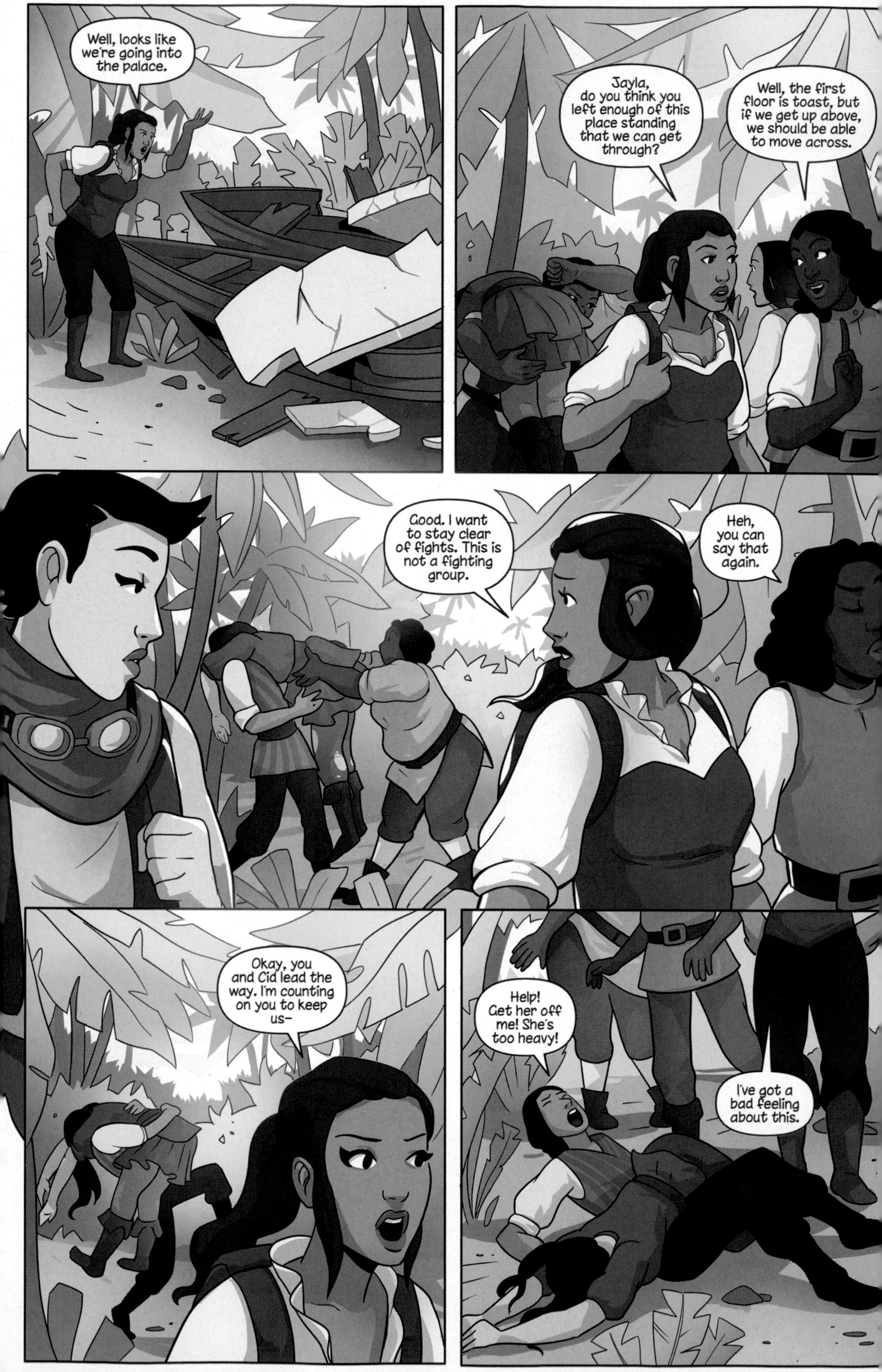
Well, looks like we're going into the palace.
Jayla, do you think you left enough of this place standing that we can get through?
Well, the first floor is toast, but if we get up above, we should be able to move across.
Good. I want to stay clear of fights. This is not a fighting group.
Heh, you can say that again.
Okay, you and Cid lead the way. I'm counting on you to keep us-
Help! Get her off me! She's too heavy!
I've got a bad feeling about this.

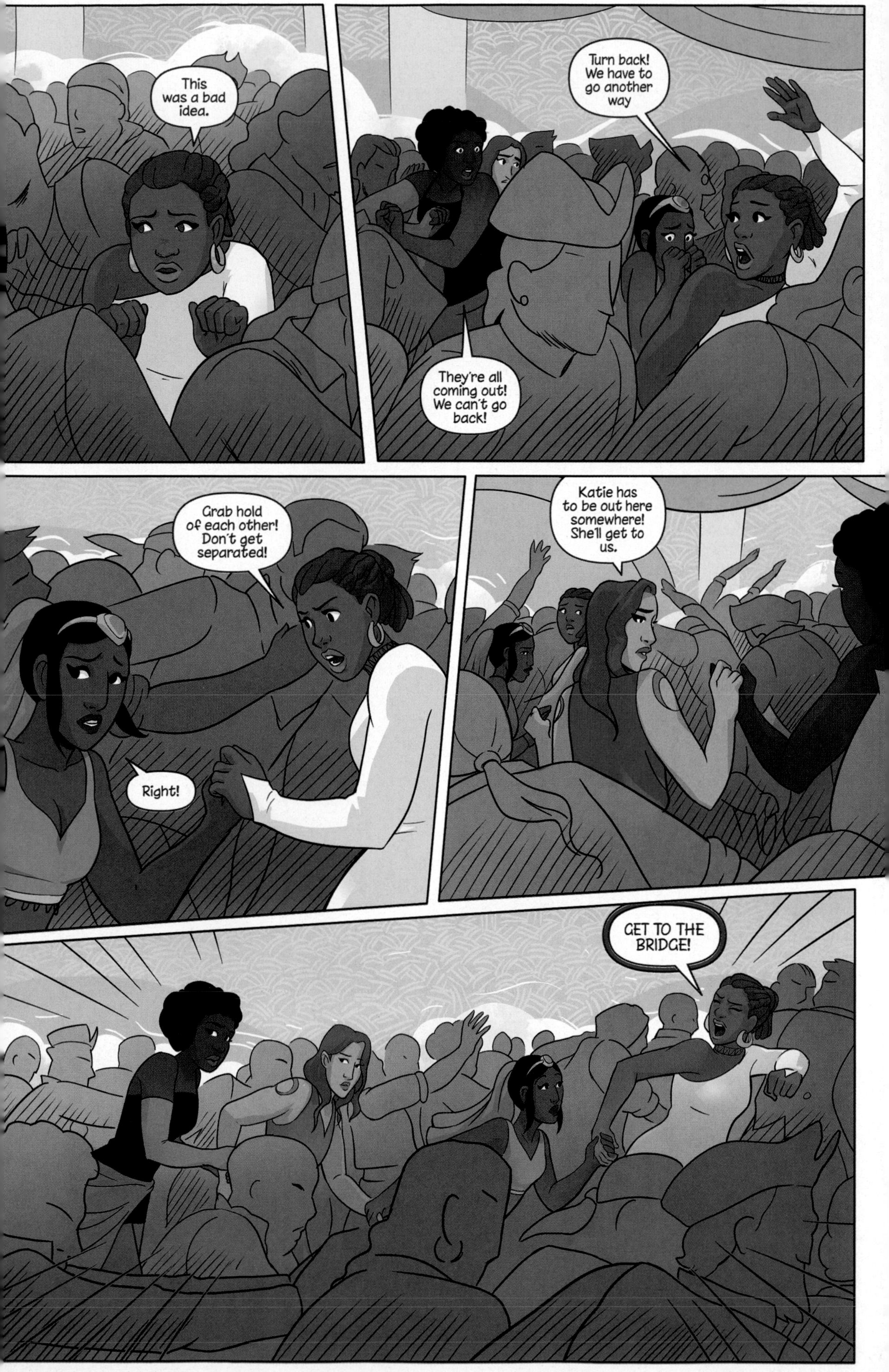
This was a bad idea.
Turn back! We have to go another way
They're all coming out! We can't go back!
Grab hold of each other! Don't get separated!
Right!
Katie has to be out here somewhere! She'll get to us.
GET TO THE BRIDGE!

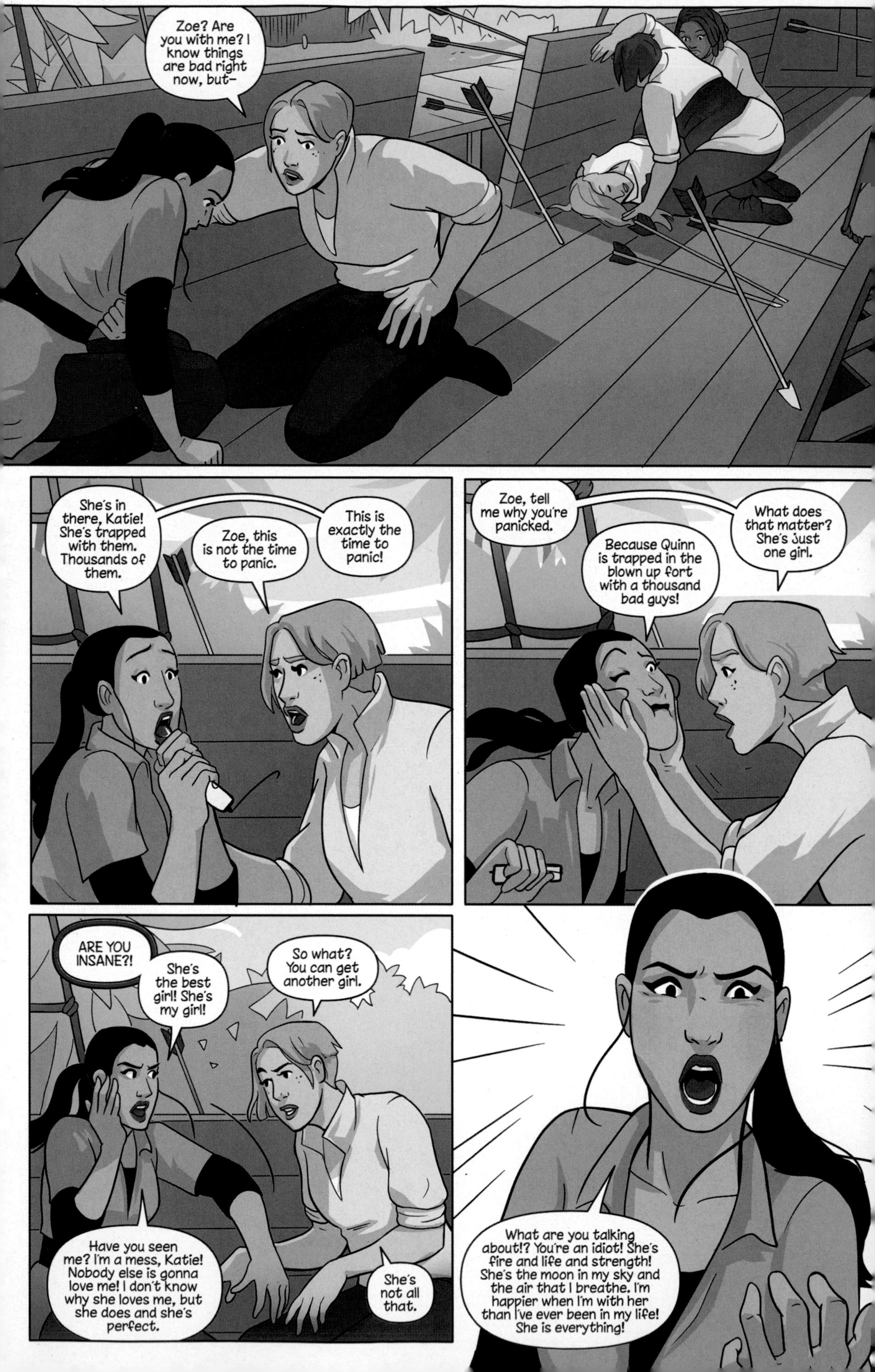

Zoe? Are you with me? I know things are bad right now, but–
She's in there, Katie! She's trapped with them. Thousands of them.
Zoe, this is not the time to panic.
This is exactly the time to panic!
Zoe, tell me why you're panicked.
What does that matter? She's just one girl.
Because Quinn is trapped in the blown up fort with a thousand bad guys!
ARE YOU INSANE?!
She's the best girl! She's my girl!
So what? You can get another girl.
Have you seen me? I'm a mess, Katie! Nobody else is gonna love me! I don't know why she loves me, but she does and she's perfect.
She's not all that.
What are you talking about!? You're an idiot! She's fire and life and strength! She's the moon in my sky and the air that I breathe. I'm happier when I'm with her than I've ever been in my life! She is everything!

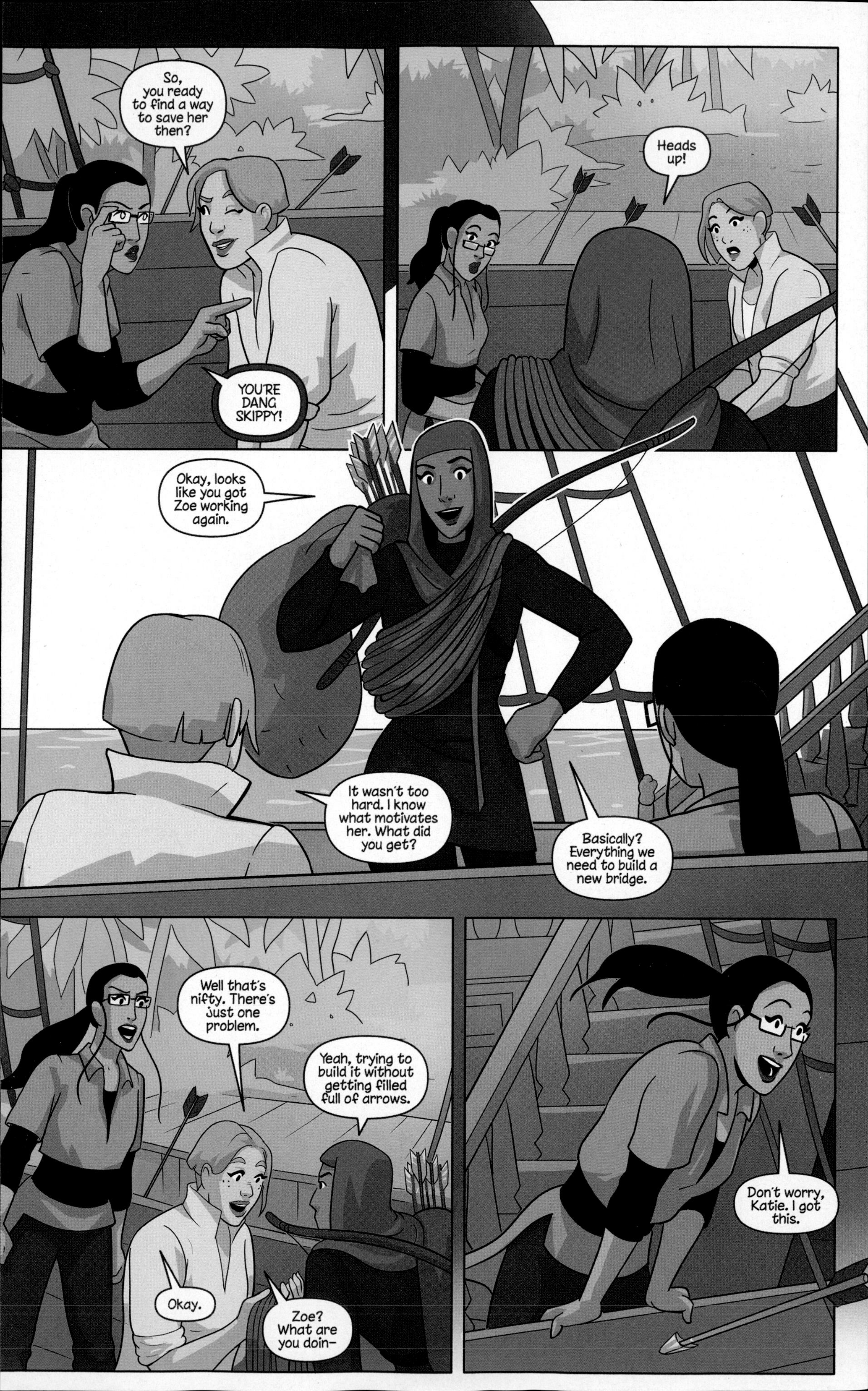
So, you ready to find a way to save her then?
YOU'RE DANG SKIPPY!
Heads up!
Okay, looks like you got Zoe working again.
It wasn't too hard. I know what motivates her. What did you get?
Basically? Everything we need to build a new bridge.
Well that's nifty. There's just one problem.
Yeah, trying to build it without getting filled full of arrows.
Okay.
Zoe? What are you doin-
Don't worry, Katie. I got this.

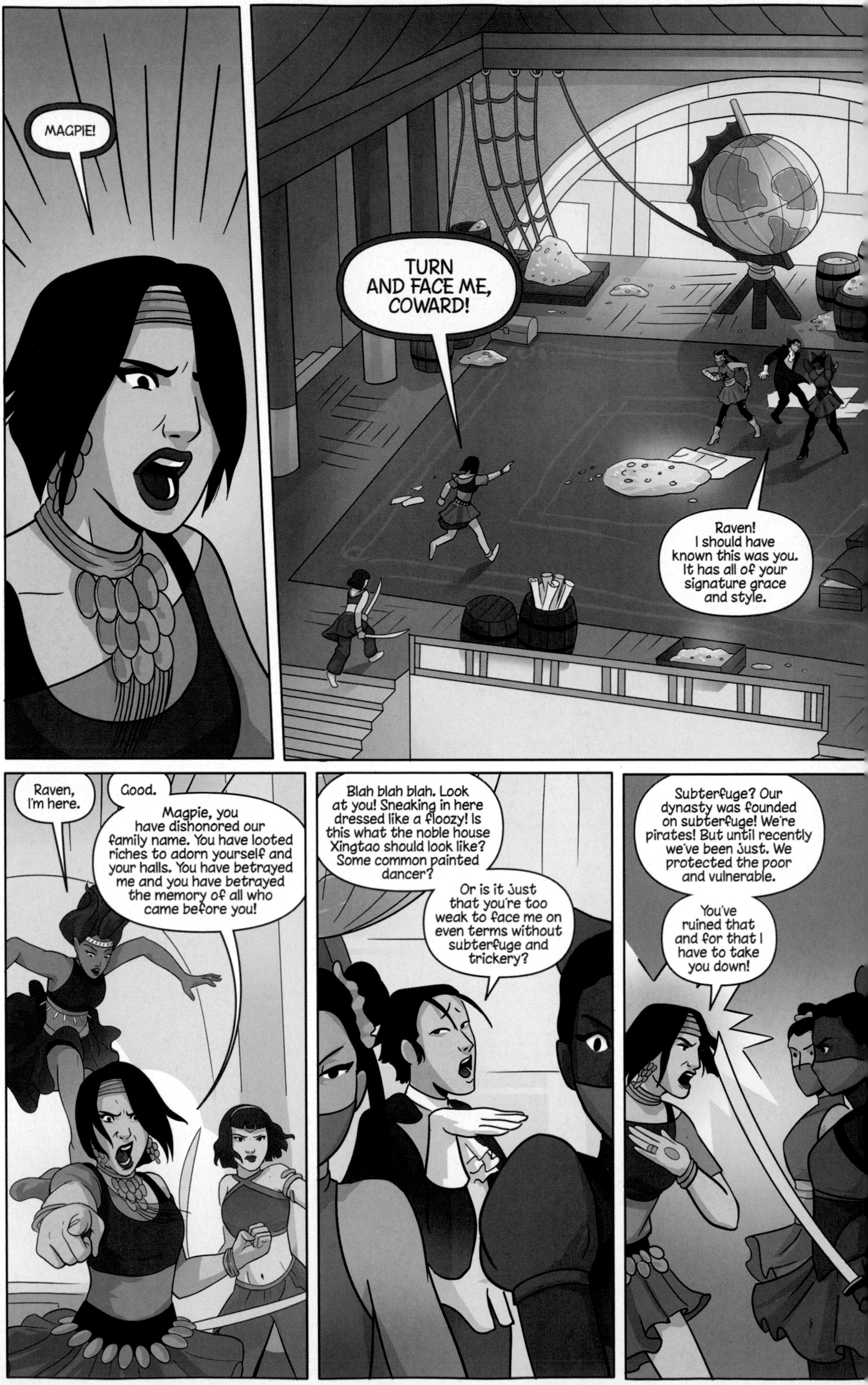
MAGPIE!
TURN AND FACE ME, COWARD!
Raven! I should have known this was you. It has all of your signature grace and style.
Raven, I'm here.
Good.
Magpie, you have dishonored our family name. You have looted riches to adorn yourself and your halls. You have betrayed me and you have betrayed the memory of all who came before you!
Blah blah blah. Look at you! Sneaking in here dressed like a floozy! Is this what the noble house Xingtao should look like? Some common painted dancer?
Or is it just that you're too weak to face me on even terms without subterfuge and trickery?
Subterfuge? Our dynasty was founded on subterfuge! We're pirates! But until recently we've been just. We protected the poor and vulnerable.
You've ruined that and for that I have to take you down!

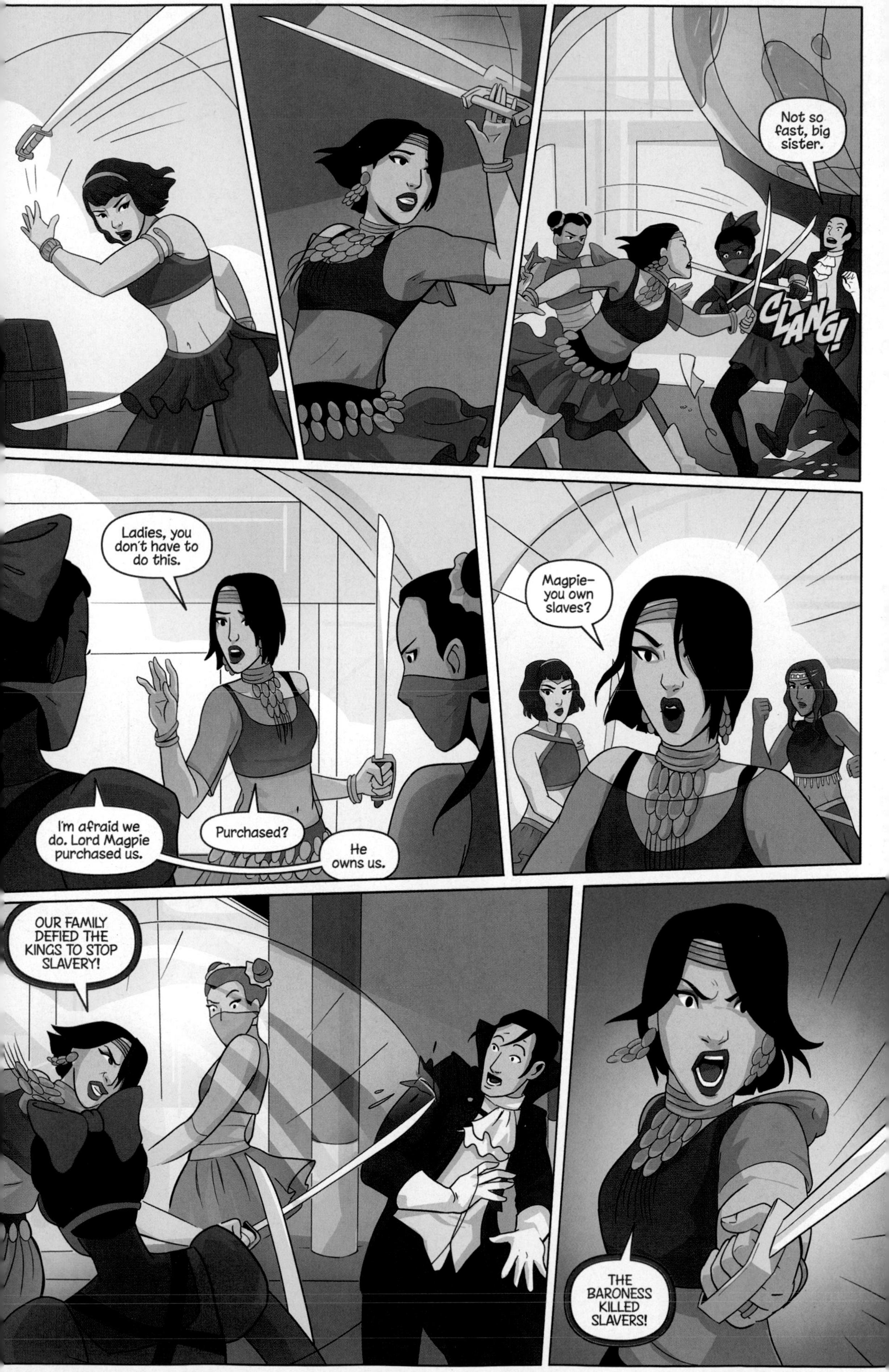
Not so fast, big sister.
CLANG!
Ladies, you don't have to do this.
I'm afraid we do. Lord Magpie purchased us.
Purchased?
He owns us.
Magpie– you own slaves?
OUR FAMILY DEFIED THE KINGS TO STOP SLAVERY!
THE BARONESS KILLED SLAVERS!

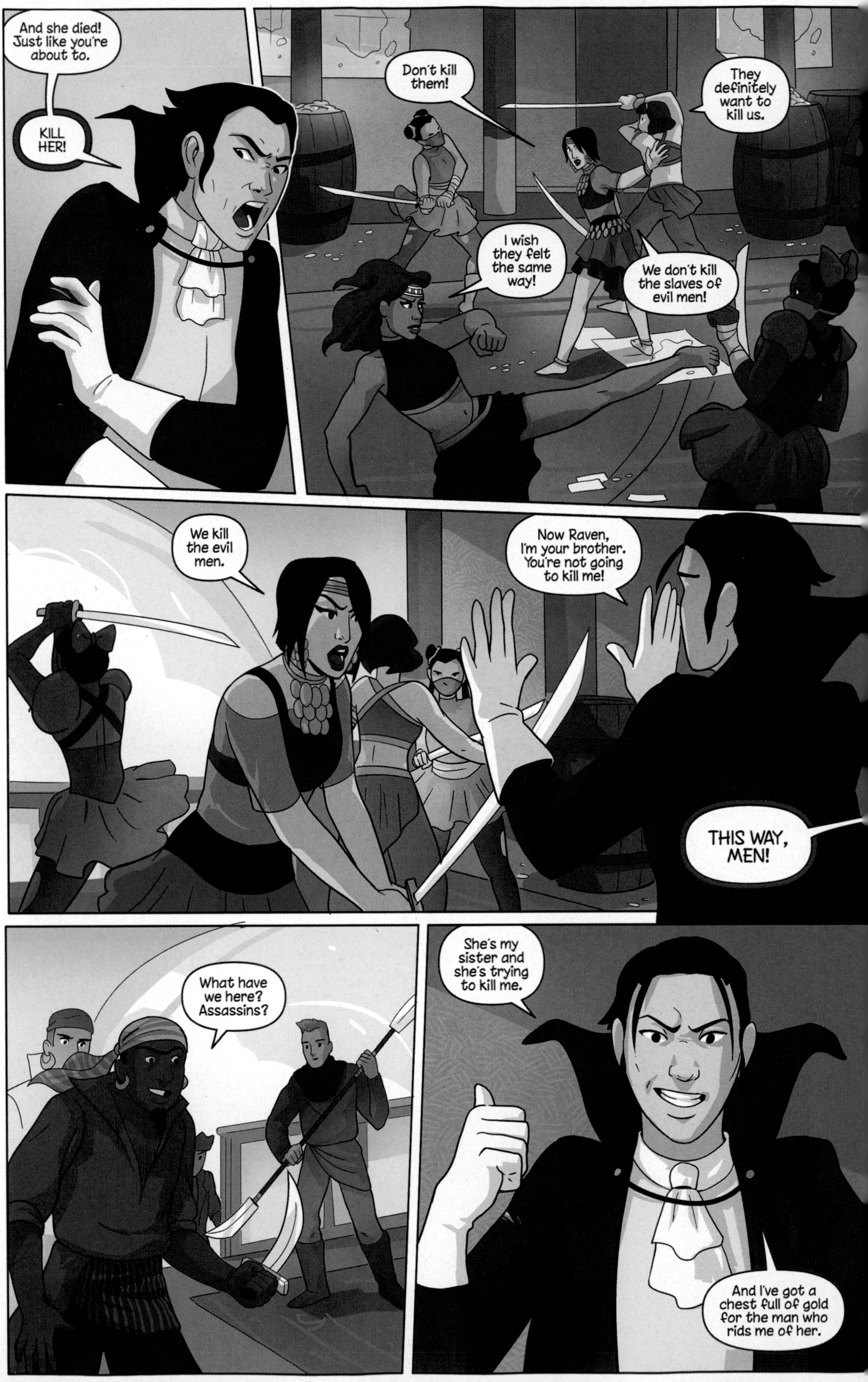
And she died! Just like you're about to.
KILL HER!
Don't kill them!
They definitely want to kill us.
I wish they felt the same way!
We don't kill the slaves of evil men!
We kill the evil men.
Now Raven, I'm your brother. You're not going to kill me!
THIS WAY, MEN!
What have we here? Assassins?
She's my sister and she's trying to kill me.
And I've got a chest full of gold for the man who rids me of her.

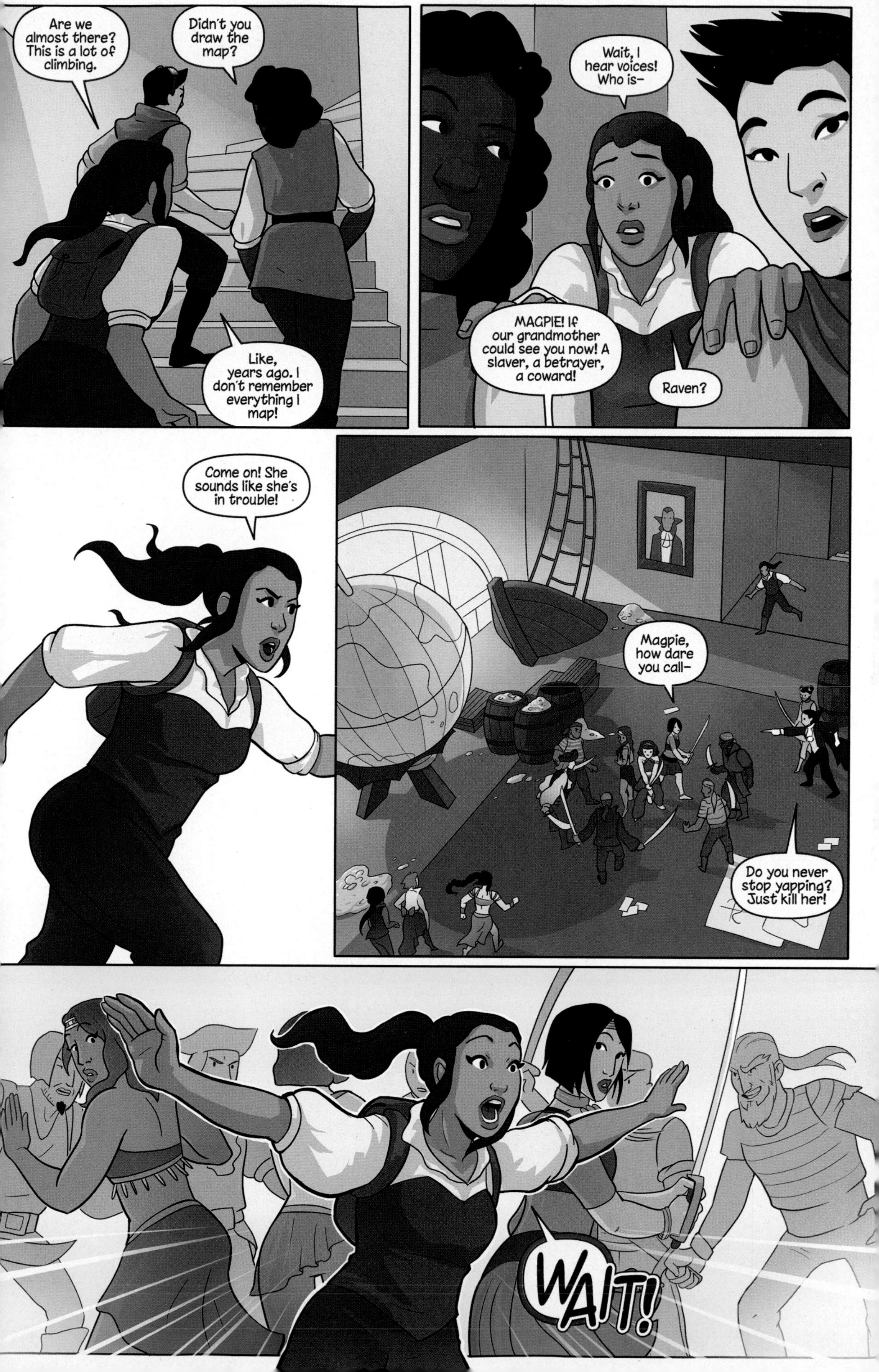

Are we almost there? This is a lot of climbing.
Didn't you draw the map?
Like, years ago. I don't remember everything I map!
Wait, I hear voices! Who is-
MAGPIE! If our grandmother could see you now! A slaver, a betrayer, a coward!
Raven?
Come on! She sounds like she's in trouble!
Magpie, how dare you call-
Do you never stop yapping? Just kill her!
WAIT!

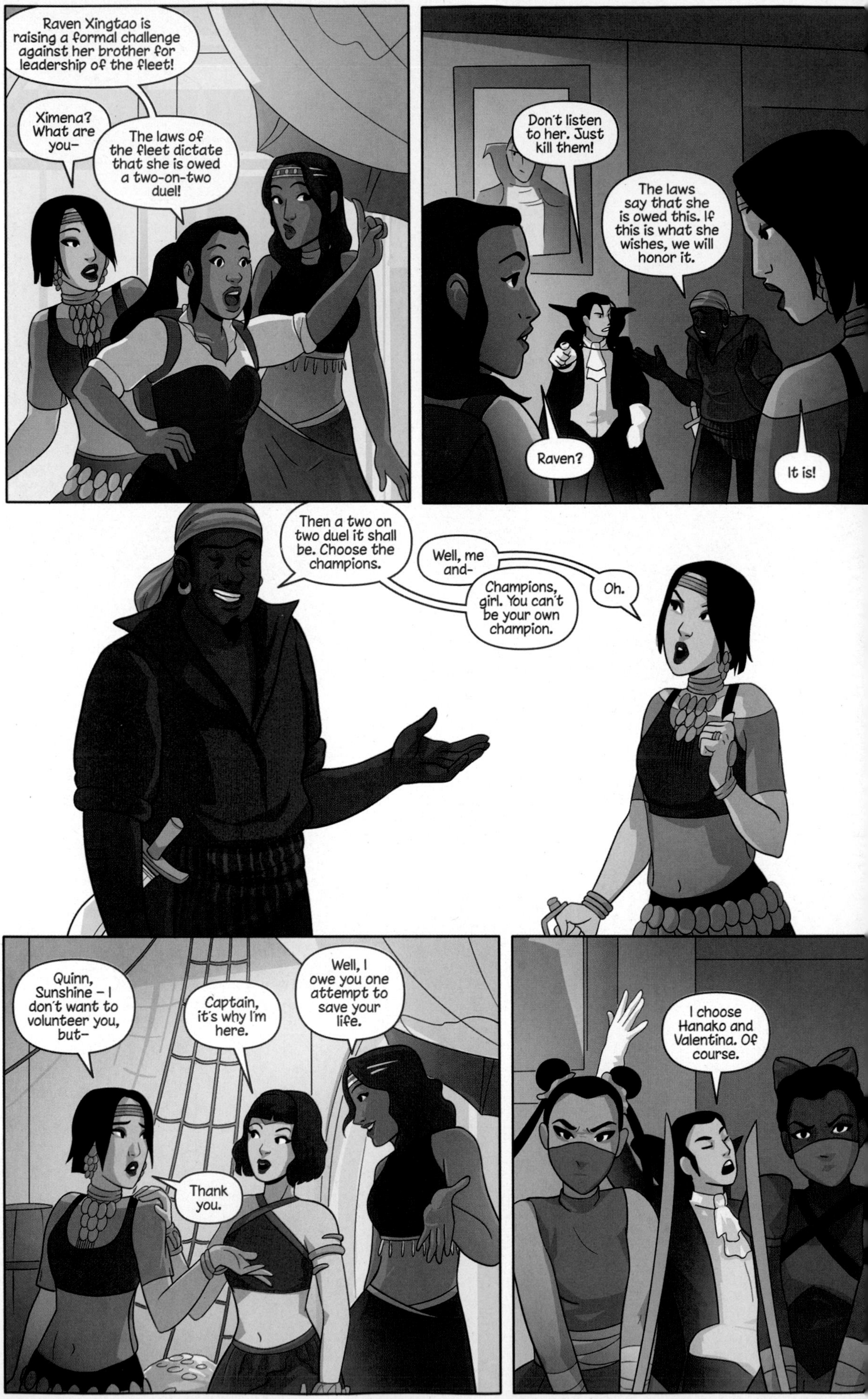
Raven Xingtao is raising a formal challenge against her brother for leadership of the fleet!
Ximena? What are you–
The laws of the fleet dictate that she is owed a two-on-two duel!
Don't listen to her. Just kill them!
The laws say that she is owed this. If this is what she wishes, we will honor it.
Raven?
It is!
Then a two on two duel it shall be. Choose the champions.
Well, me and–
Champions, girl. You can't be your own champion.
Oh.
Quinn, Sunshine – I don't want to volunteer you, but–
Captain, it's why I'm here.
Well, I owe you one attempt to save your life.
Thank you.
I choose Hanako and Valentina. Of course.

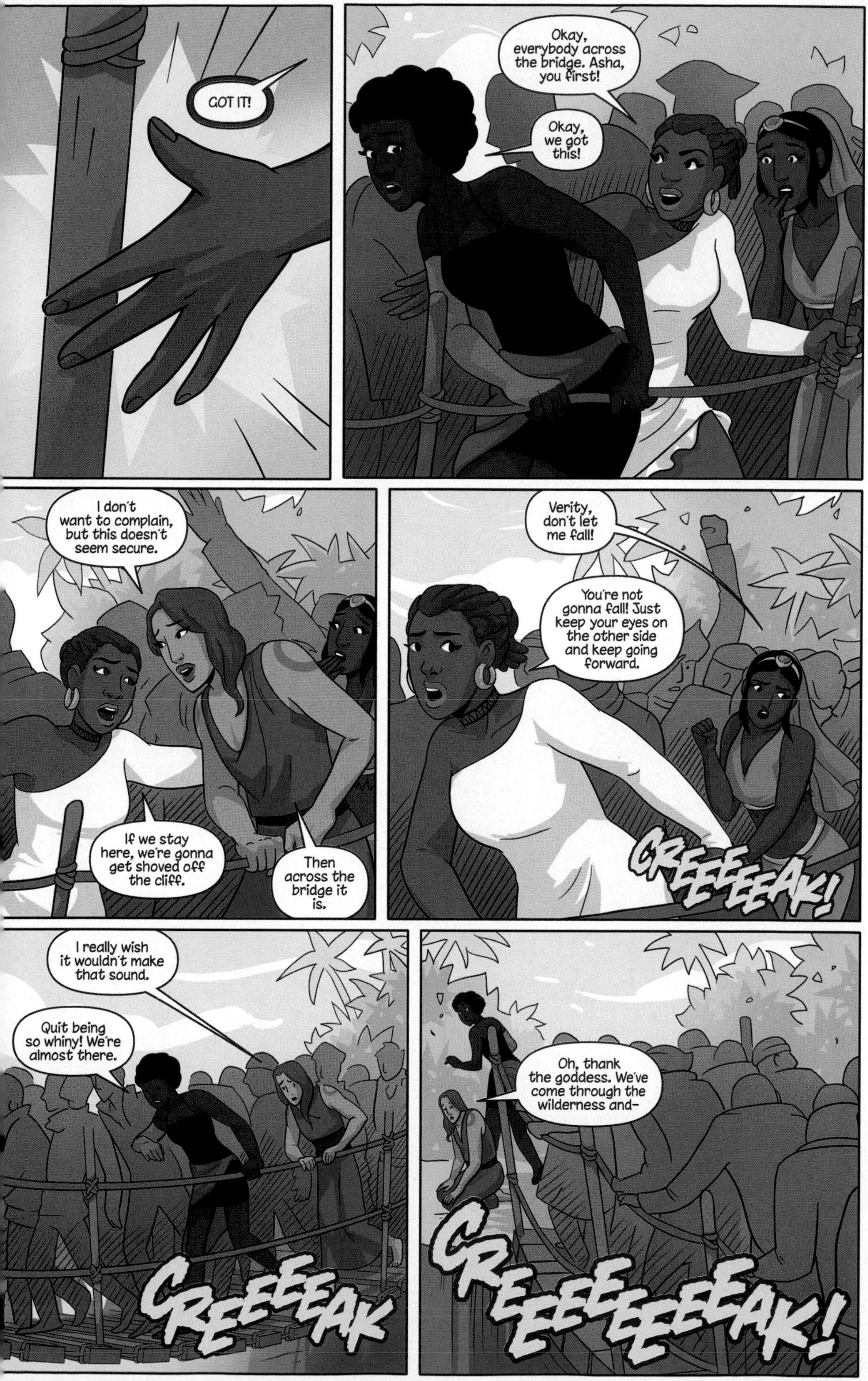
GOT IT!
Okay, everybody across the bridge. Asha, you first!
Okay, we got this!
I don't want to complain, but this doesn't seem secure.
If we stay here, we're gonna get shoved off the cliff.
Then across the bridge it is.
Verity, don't let me fall!
You're not gonna fall! Just keep your eyes on the other side and keep going forward.
CREEEEEEAK!
I really wish it wouldn't make that sound.
Quit being so whiny! We're almost there.
CREEEEEAK
Oh, thank the goddess. We've come through the wilderness and–
CREEEEEEEEEEAK!

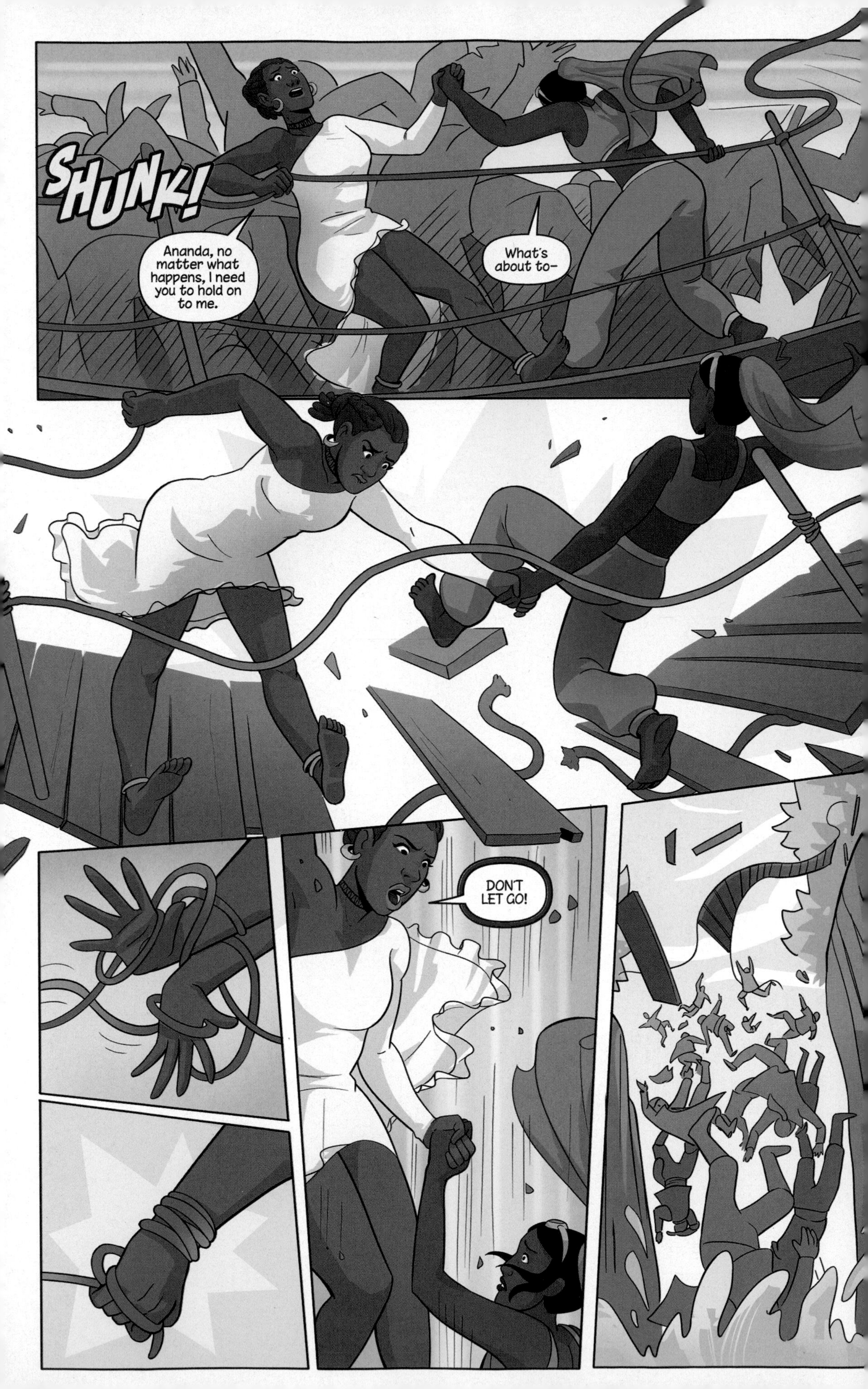
SHUNK!
Ananda, no matter what happens, I need you to hold on to me.
What's about to-
DON'T LET GO!

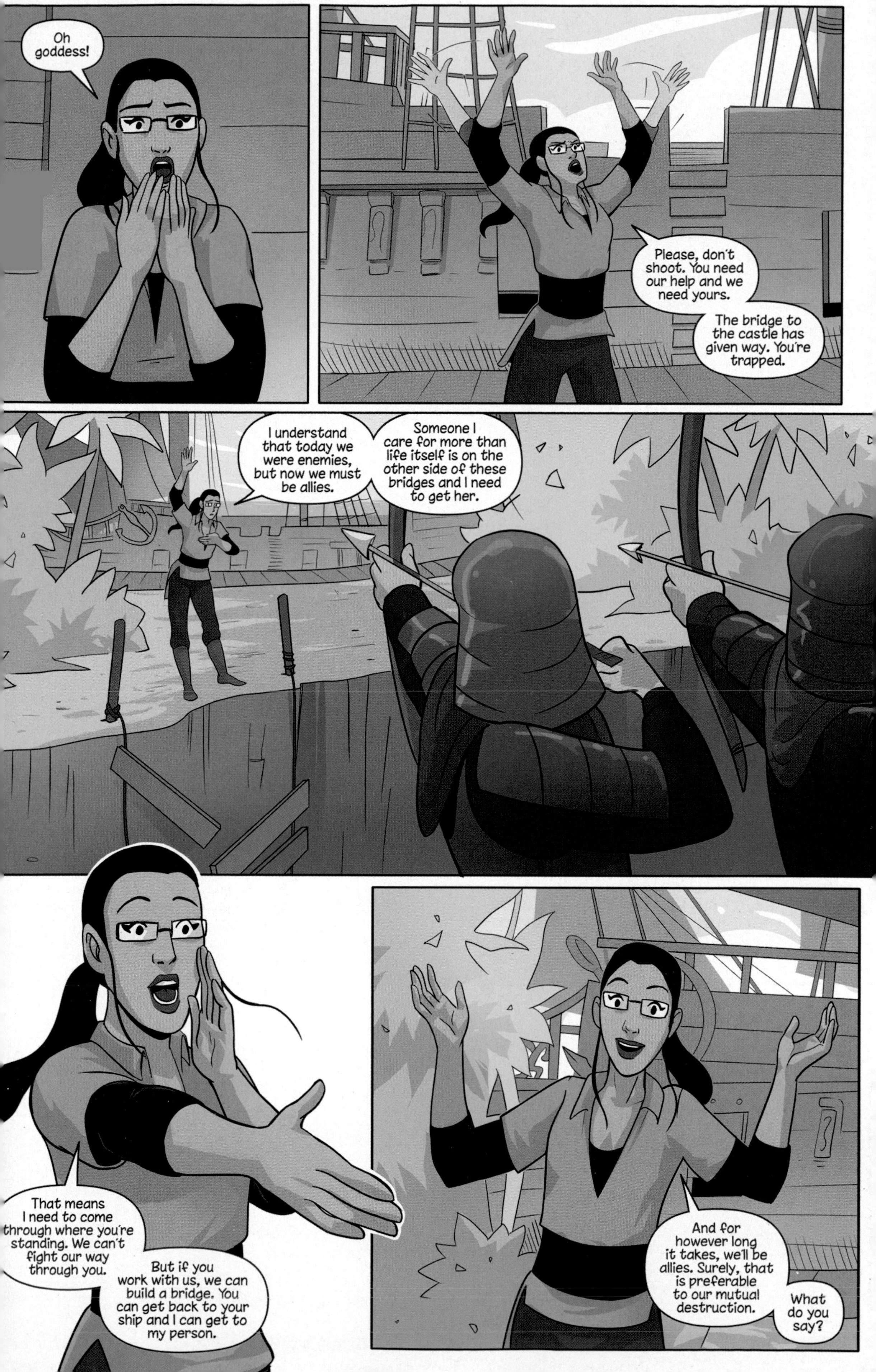
Oh goddess!
Please, don't shoot. You need our help and we need yours.
The bridge to the castle has given way. You're trapped.
I understand that today we were enemies, but now we must be allies.
Someone I care for more than life itself is on the other side of these bridges and I need to get her.
That means I need to come through where you're standing. We can't fight our way through you.
But if you work with us, we can build a bridge. You can get back to your ship and I can get to my person.
And for however long it takes, we'll be allies. Surely, that is preferable to our mutual destruction.
What do you say?

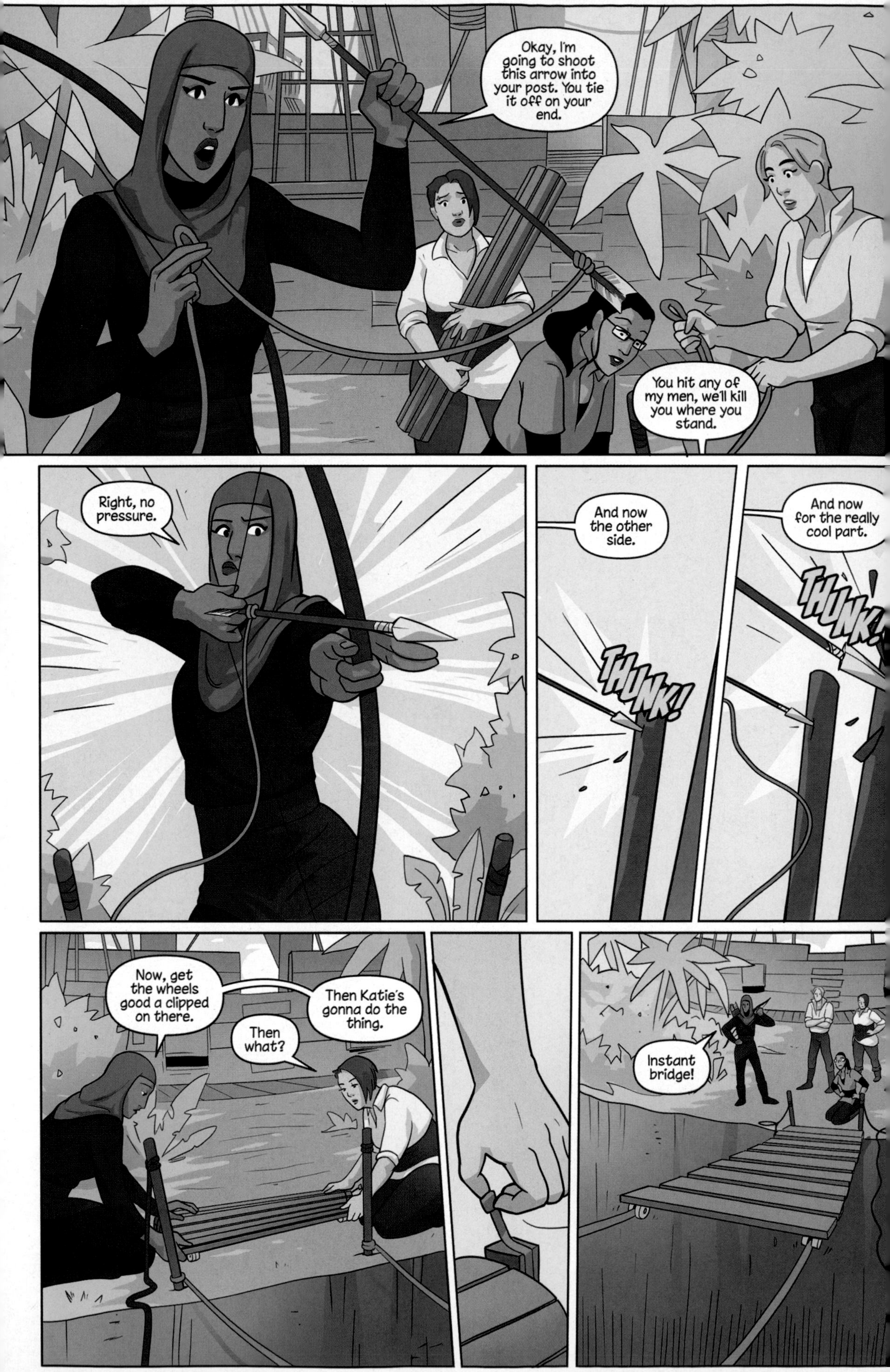

Okay, I'm going to shoot this arrow into your post. You tie it off on your end.
You hit any of my men, we'll kill you where you stand.
Right, no pressure.
And now the other side.
THUNK!
And now for the really cool part.
THUNK!
Now, get the wheels good a clipped on there.
Then Katie's gonna do the thing.
Then what?
Instant bridge!

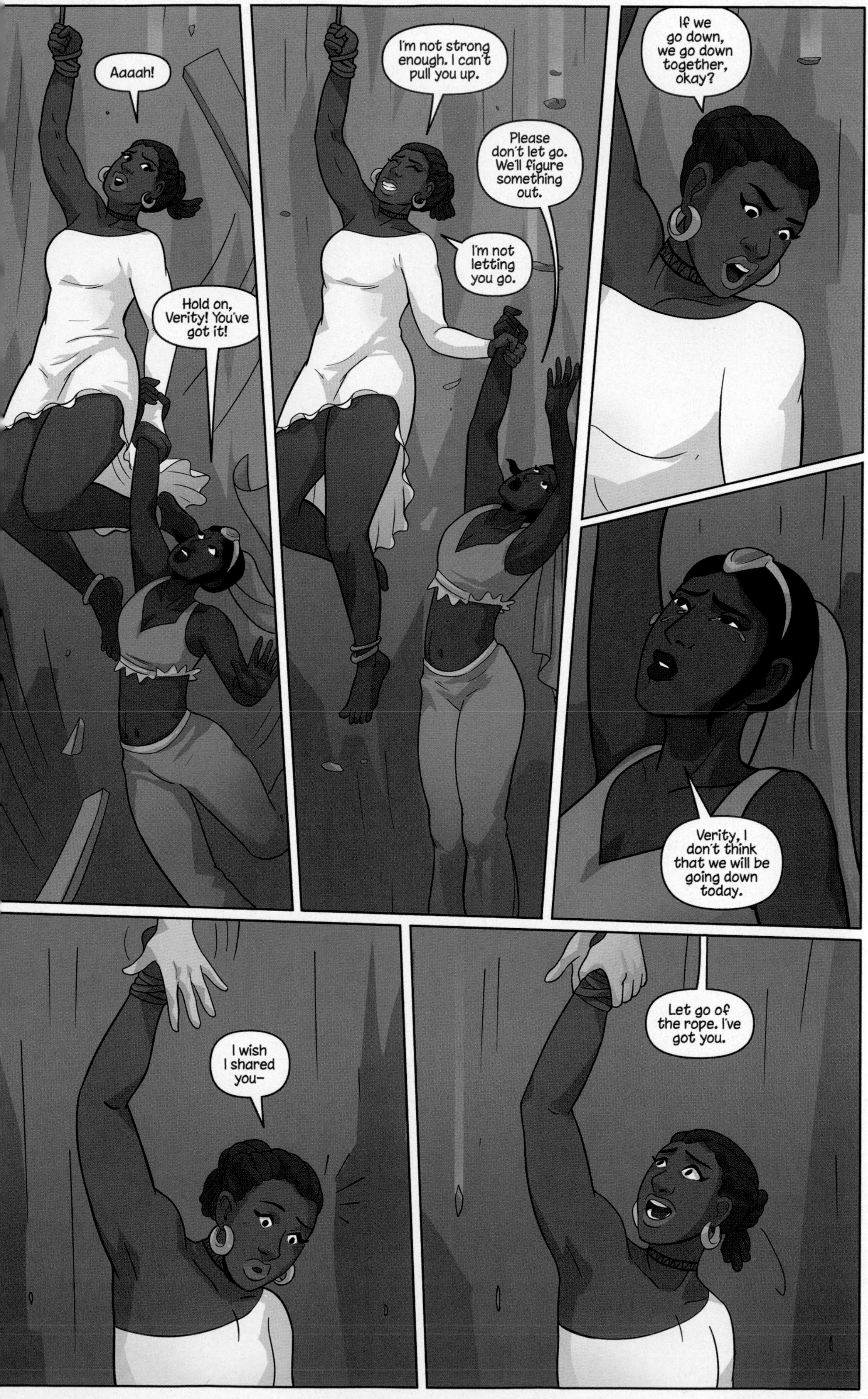

Aaaah!
Hold on, Verity! You've got it!
I'm not strong enough. I can't pull you up.
Please don't let go. We'll figure something out.
I'm not letting you go.
If we go down, we go down together, okay?
Verity, I don't think that we will be going down today.
I wish I shared you-
Let go of the rope. I've got you.

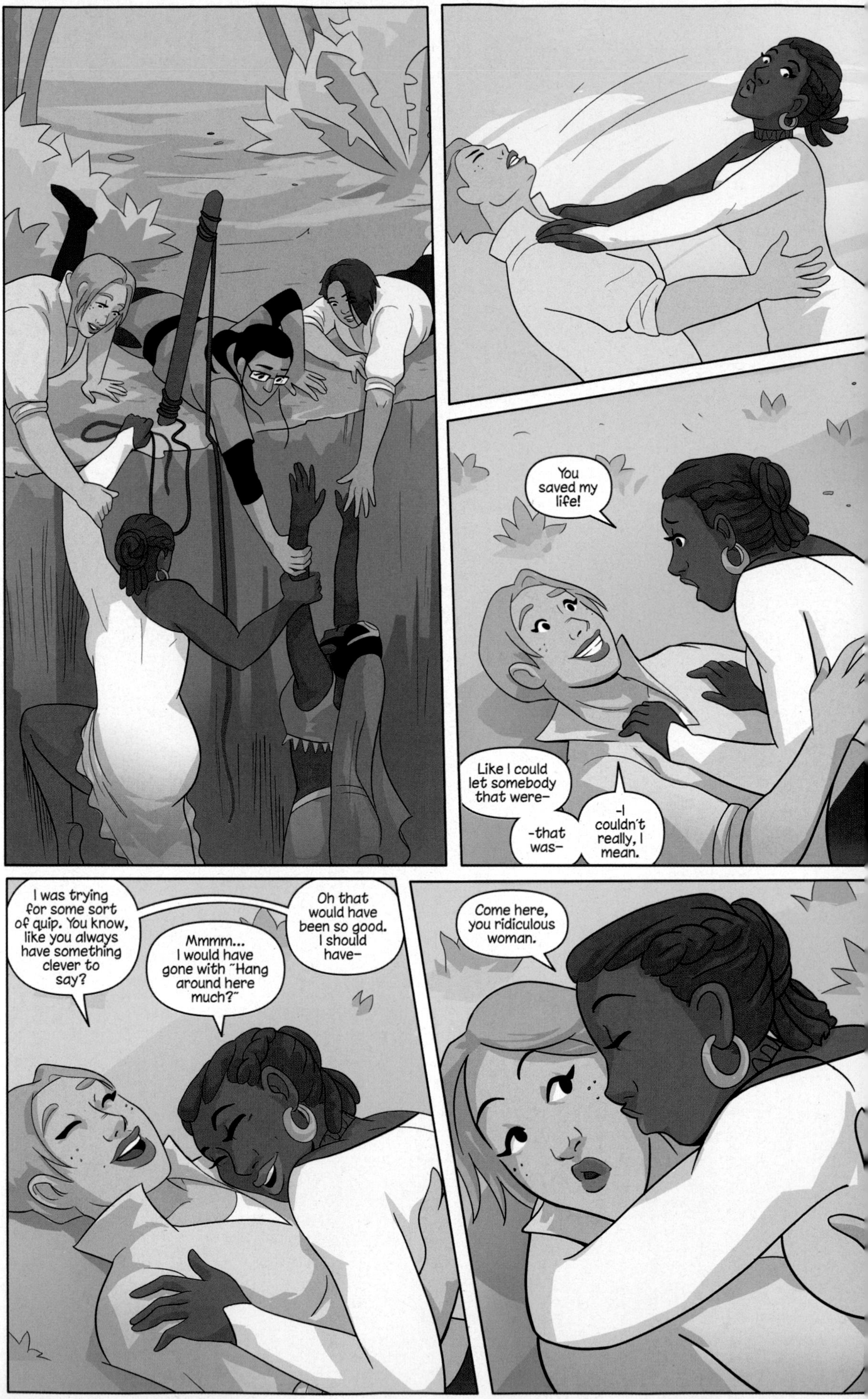
You saved my life!
Like I could let somebody that were-
-I couldn't really, I mean.
-that was-
I was trying for some sort of quip. You know, like you always have something clever to say?
Mmmm... I would have gone with "Hang around here much?"
Oh that would have been so good. I should have-
Come here, you ridiculous woman.

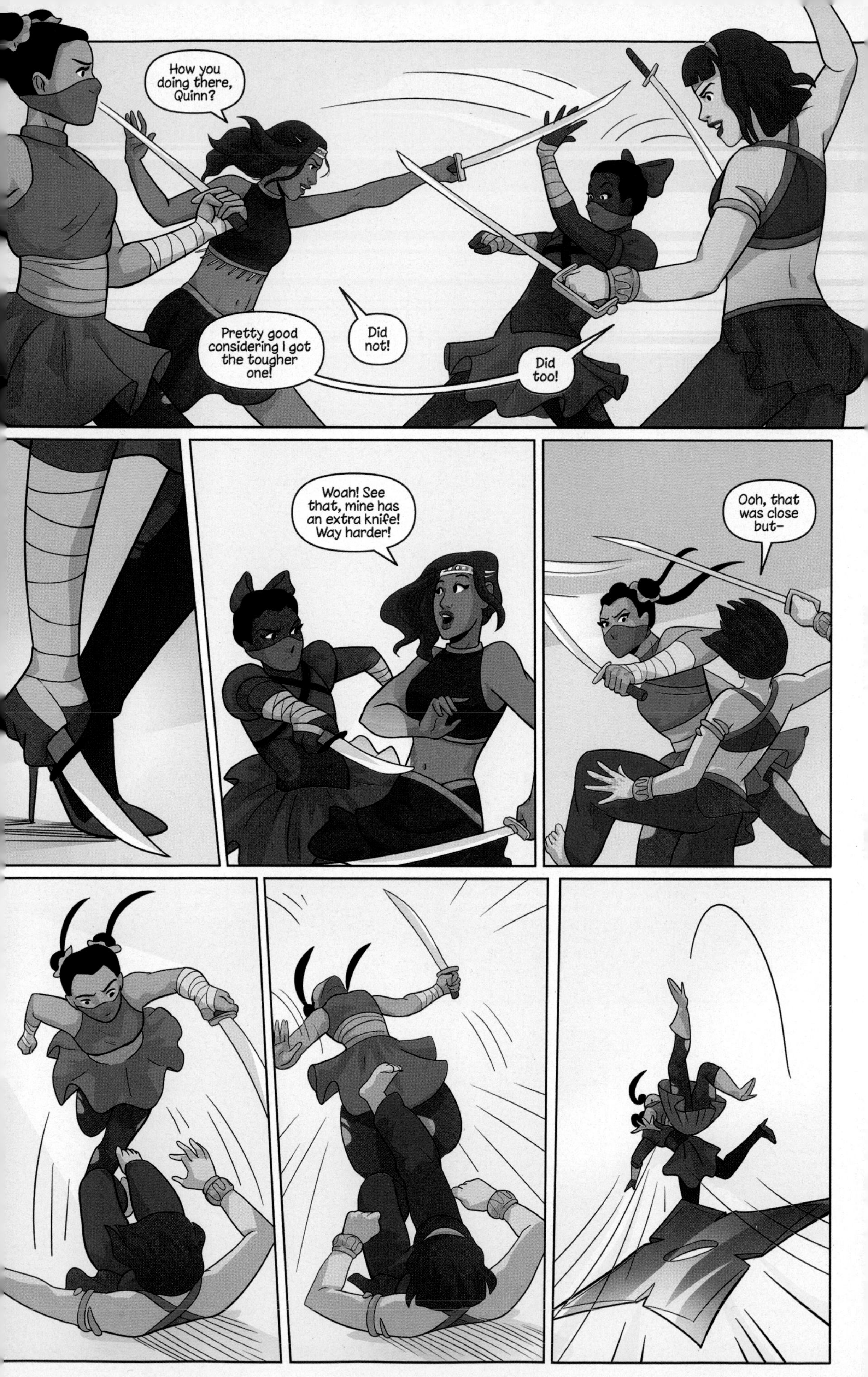
How you doing there, Quinn?
Pretty good considering I got the tougher one!
Did not!
Did too!
Woah! See that, mine has an extra knife! Way harder!
Ooh, that was close but-

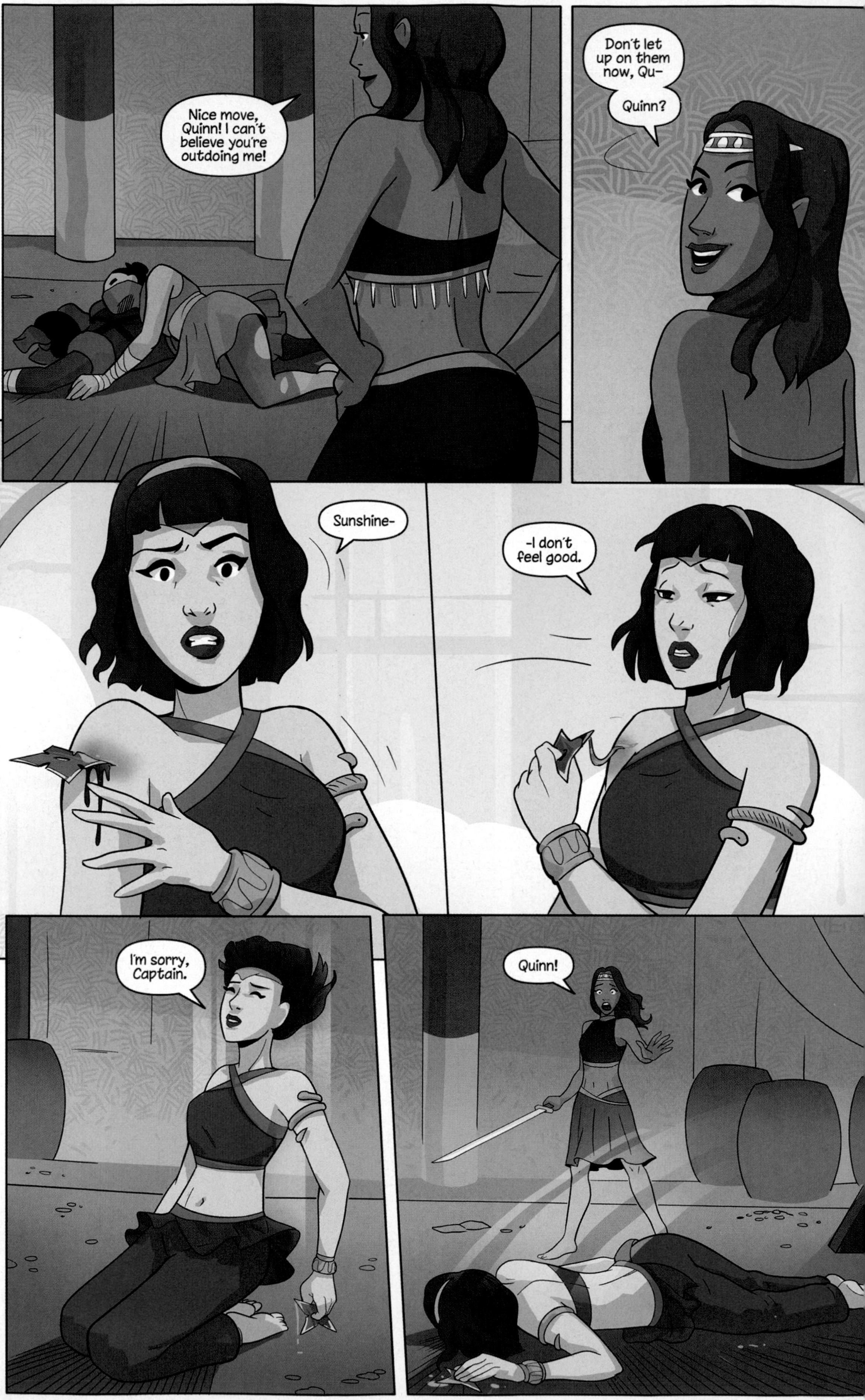
Nice move, Quinn! I can't believe you're outdoing me!
Don't let up on them now, Qu-
Quinn?
Sunshine-
-I don't feel good.
I'm sorry, Captain.
Quinn!

Raven: The Pirate Princess

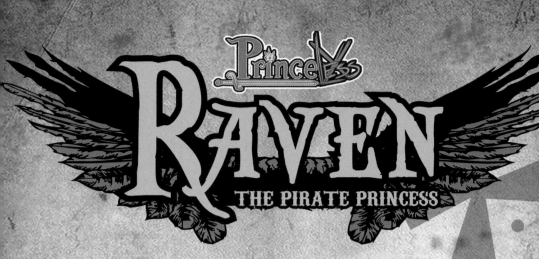

Year Two: Love and Revenge

Chapter Thirteen: Leader of the Fleet

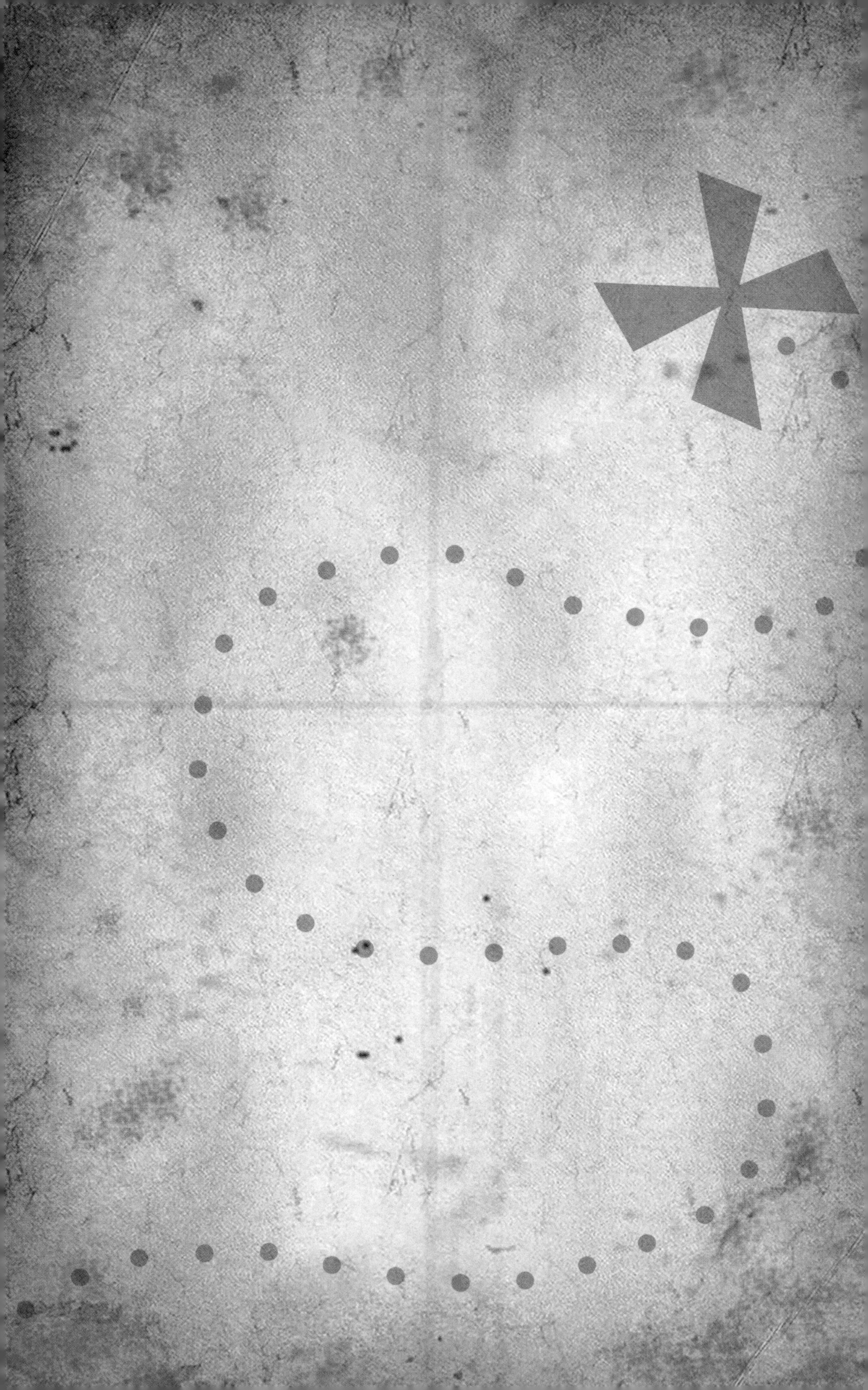

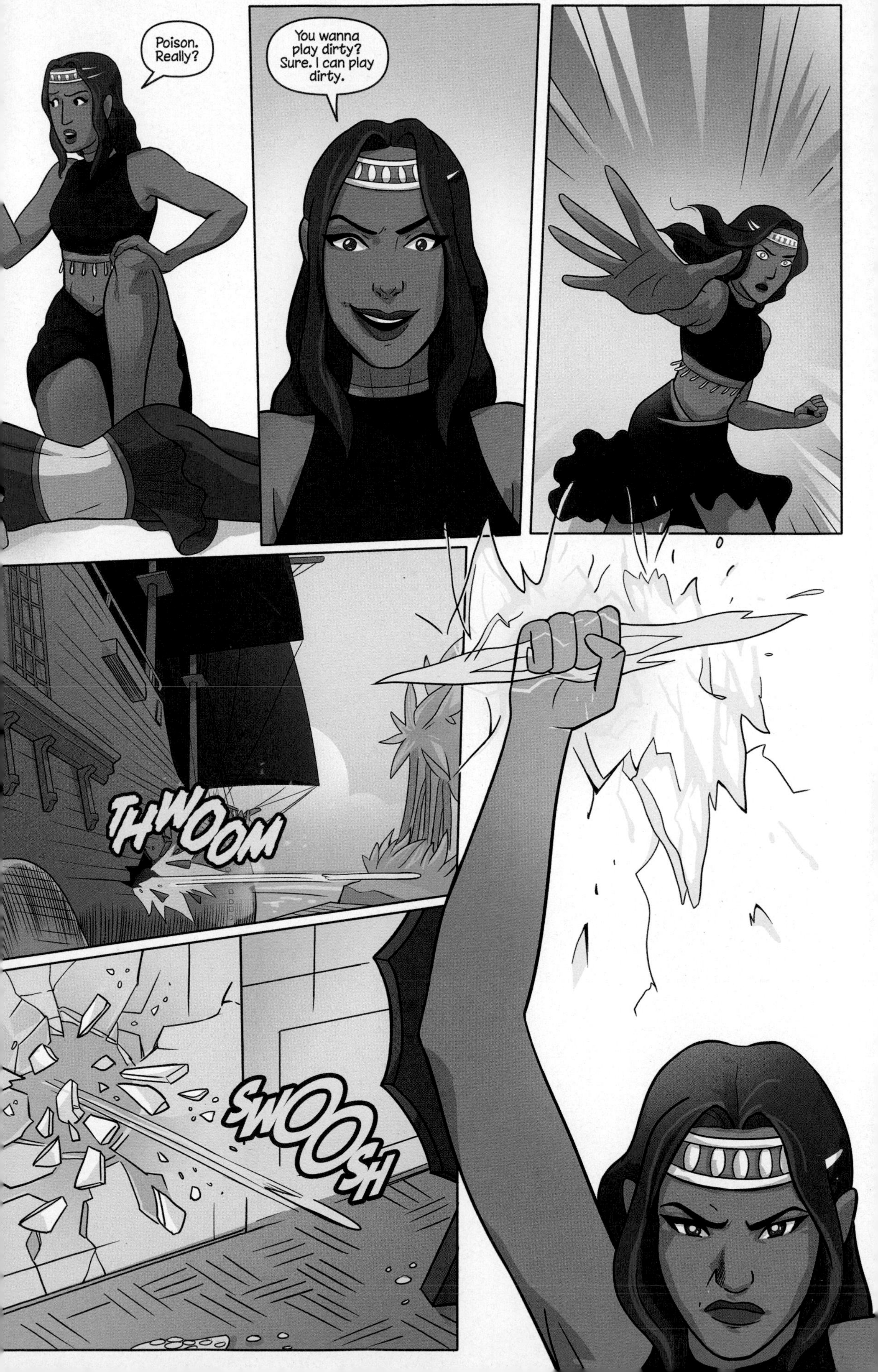
Poison. Really?
You wanna play dirty? Sure. I can play dirty.
THWOOM
SWOOSH

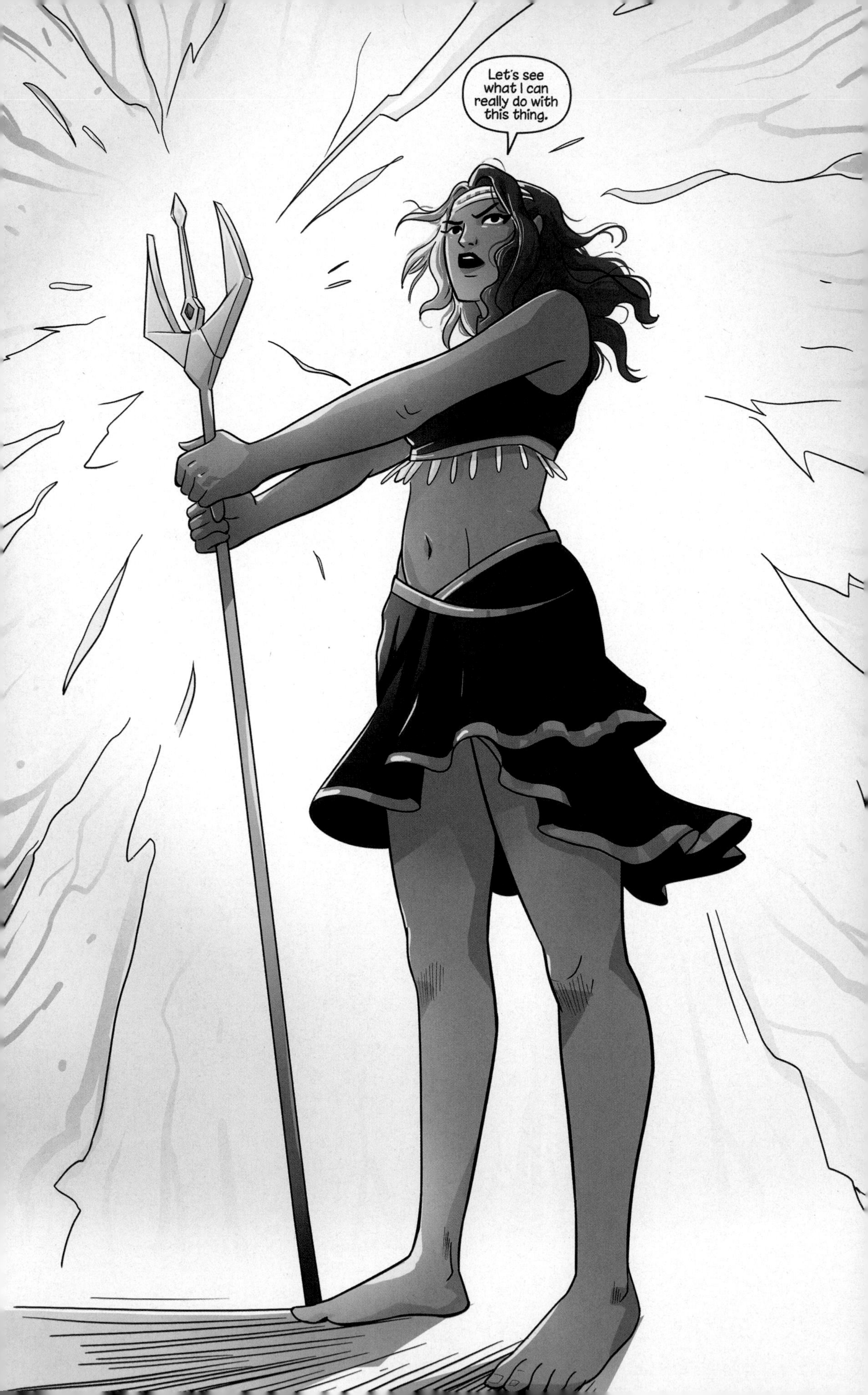
Let's see what I can really do with this thing.

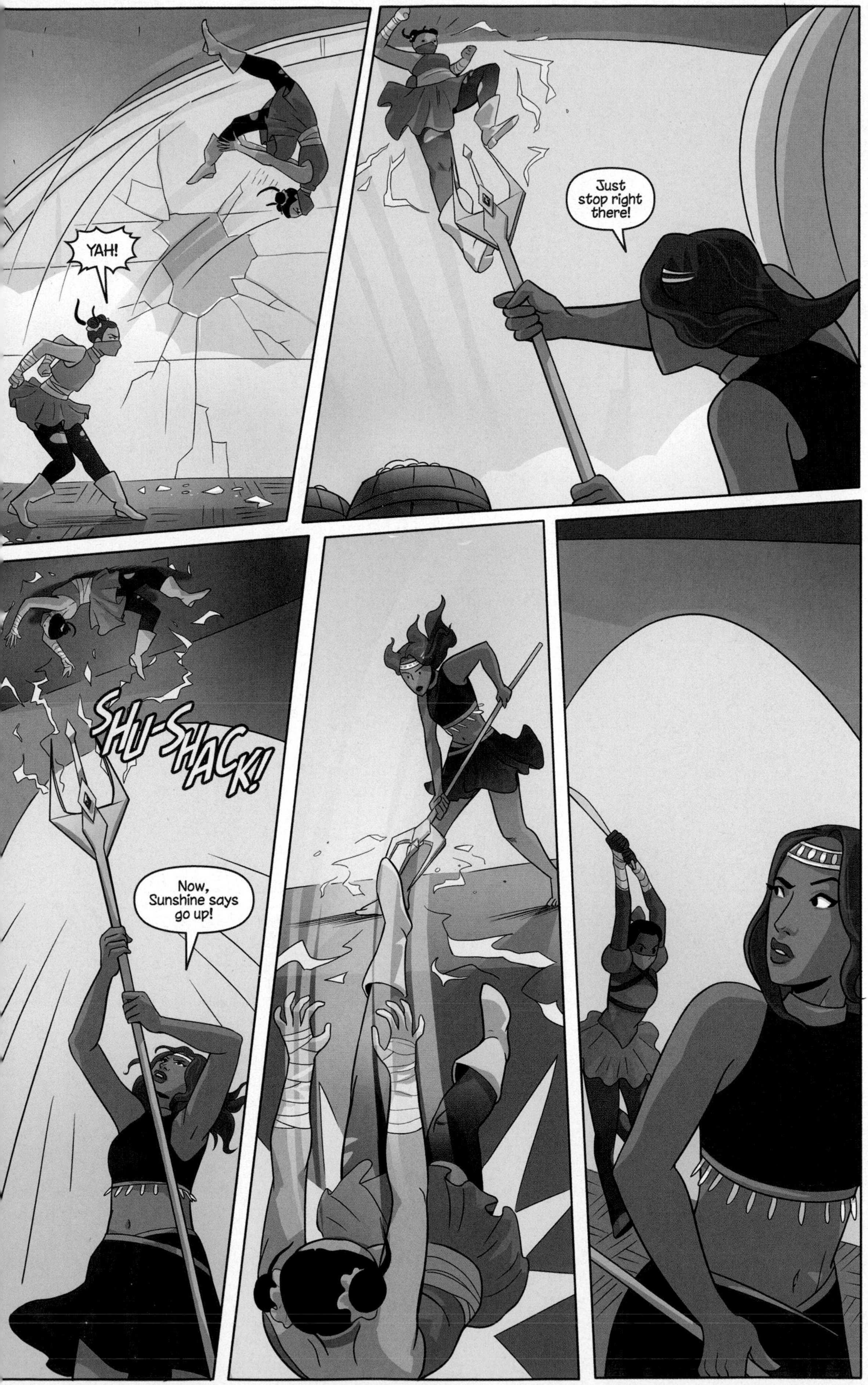
YAH!
Just stop right there!
SHU-SHACK!
Now, Sunshine says go up!

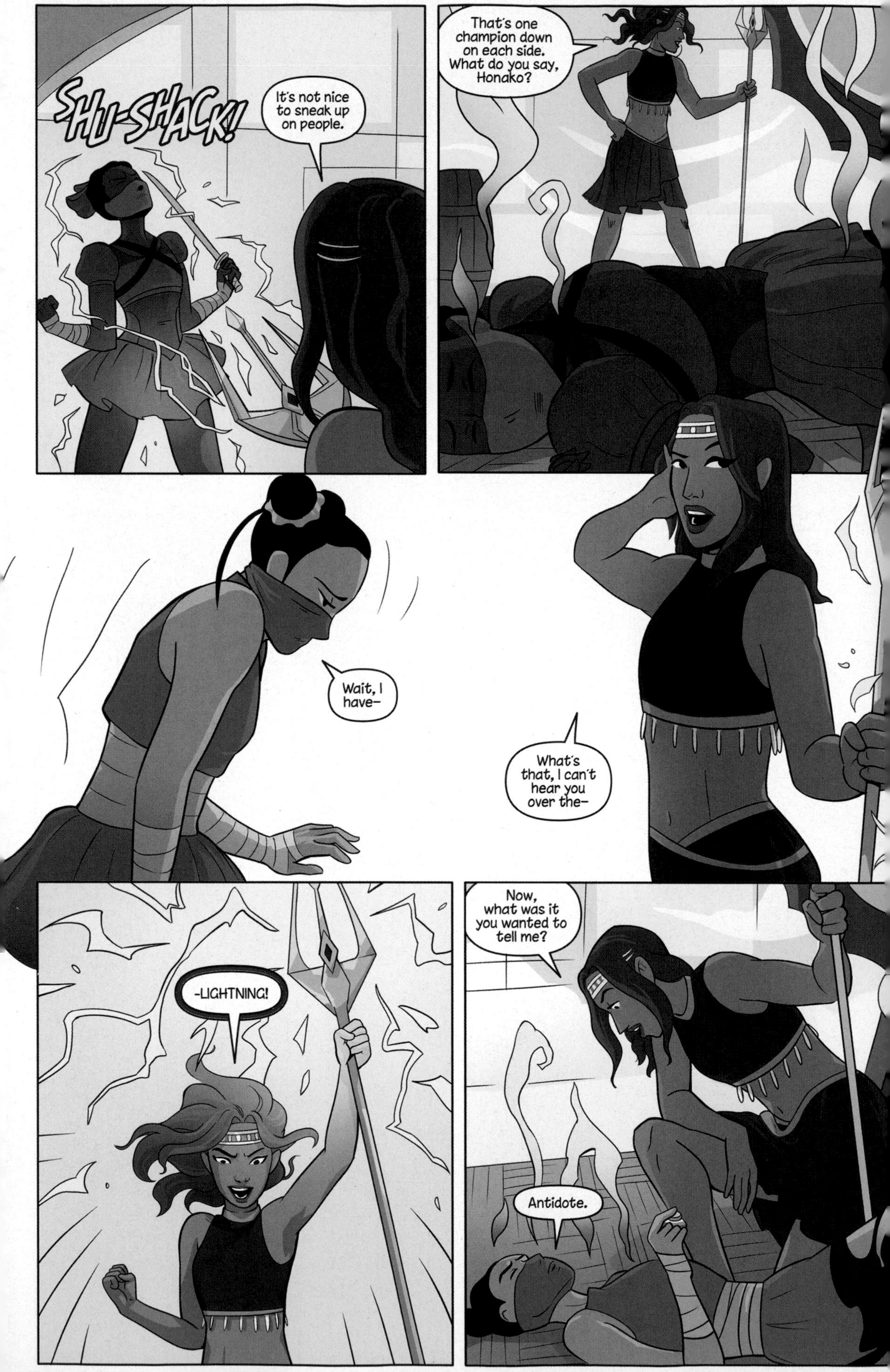
SHU-SHACK!
It's not nice to sneak up on people.
That's one champion down on each side. What do you say, Honako?
Wait, I have-
What's that, I can't hear you over the-
-LIGHTNING!
Now, what was it you wanted to tell me?
Antidote.

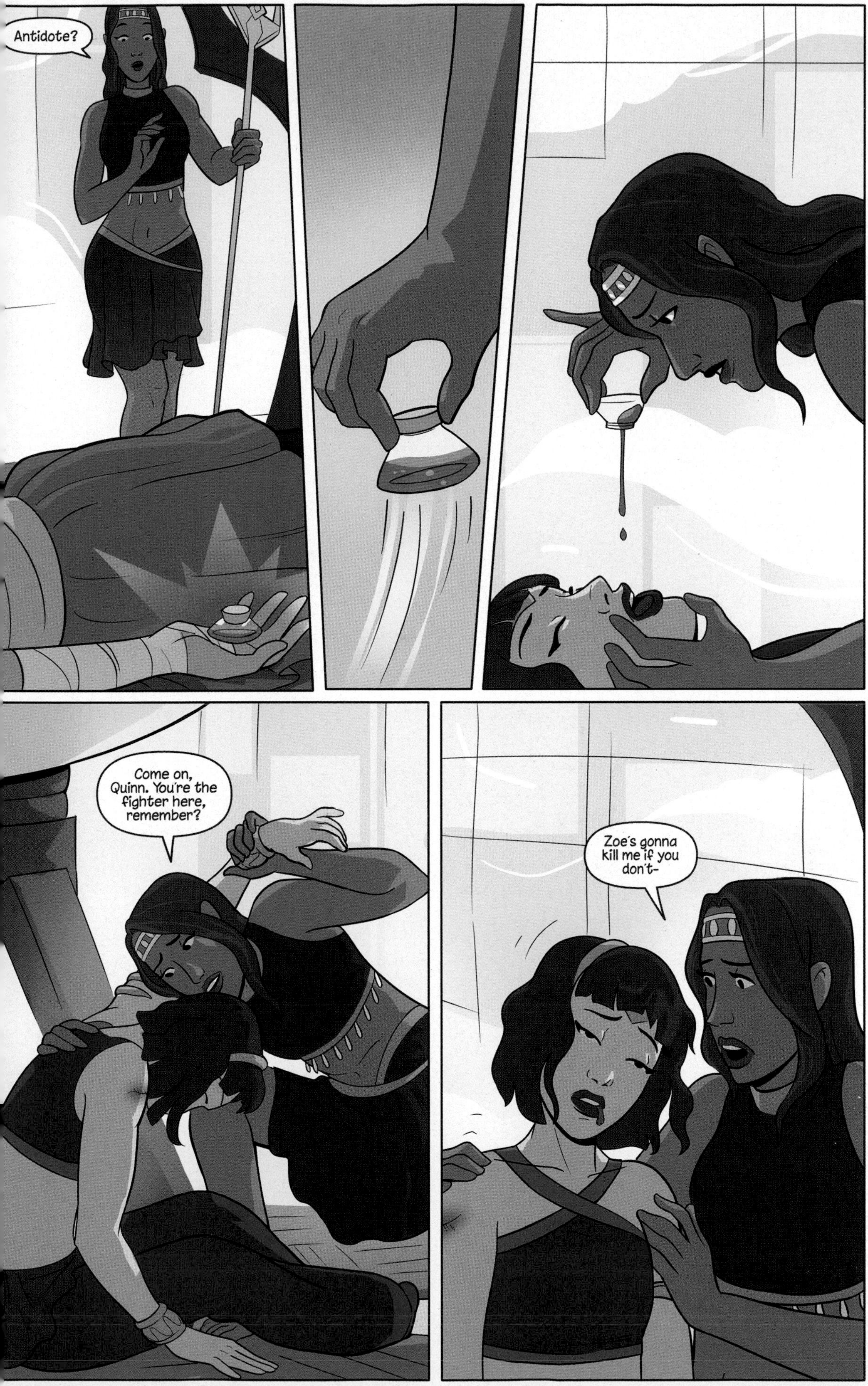
Antidote?
Come on, Quinn. You're the fighter here, remember?
Zoe's gonna kill me if you don't-

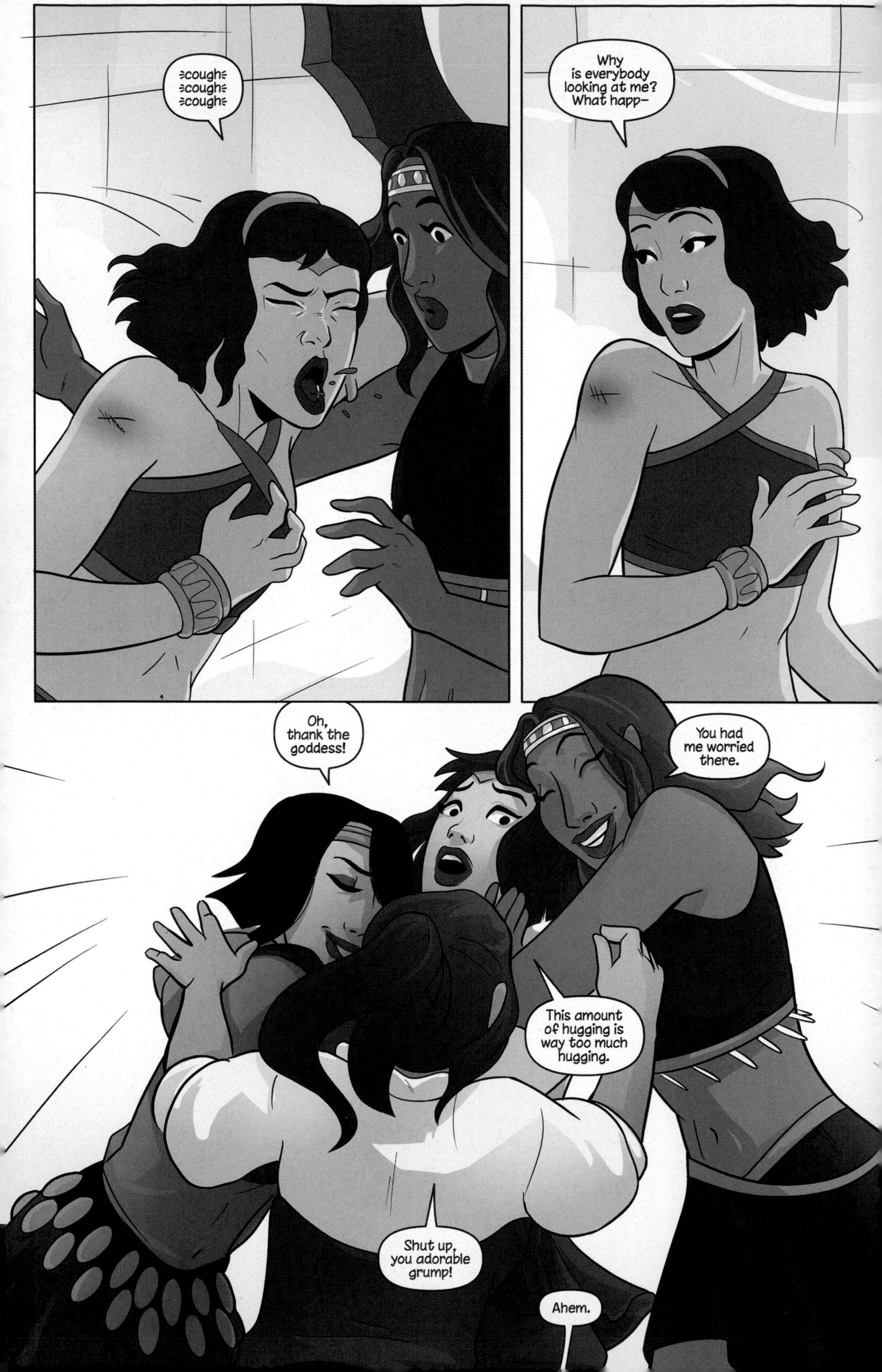
≈cough≈ ≈cough≈ ≈cough≈
Why is everybody looking at me? What happ–
Oh, thank the goddess!
You had me worried there.
This amount of hugging is way too much hugging.
Shut up, you adorable grump!
Ahem.

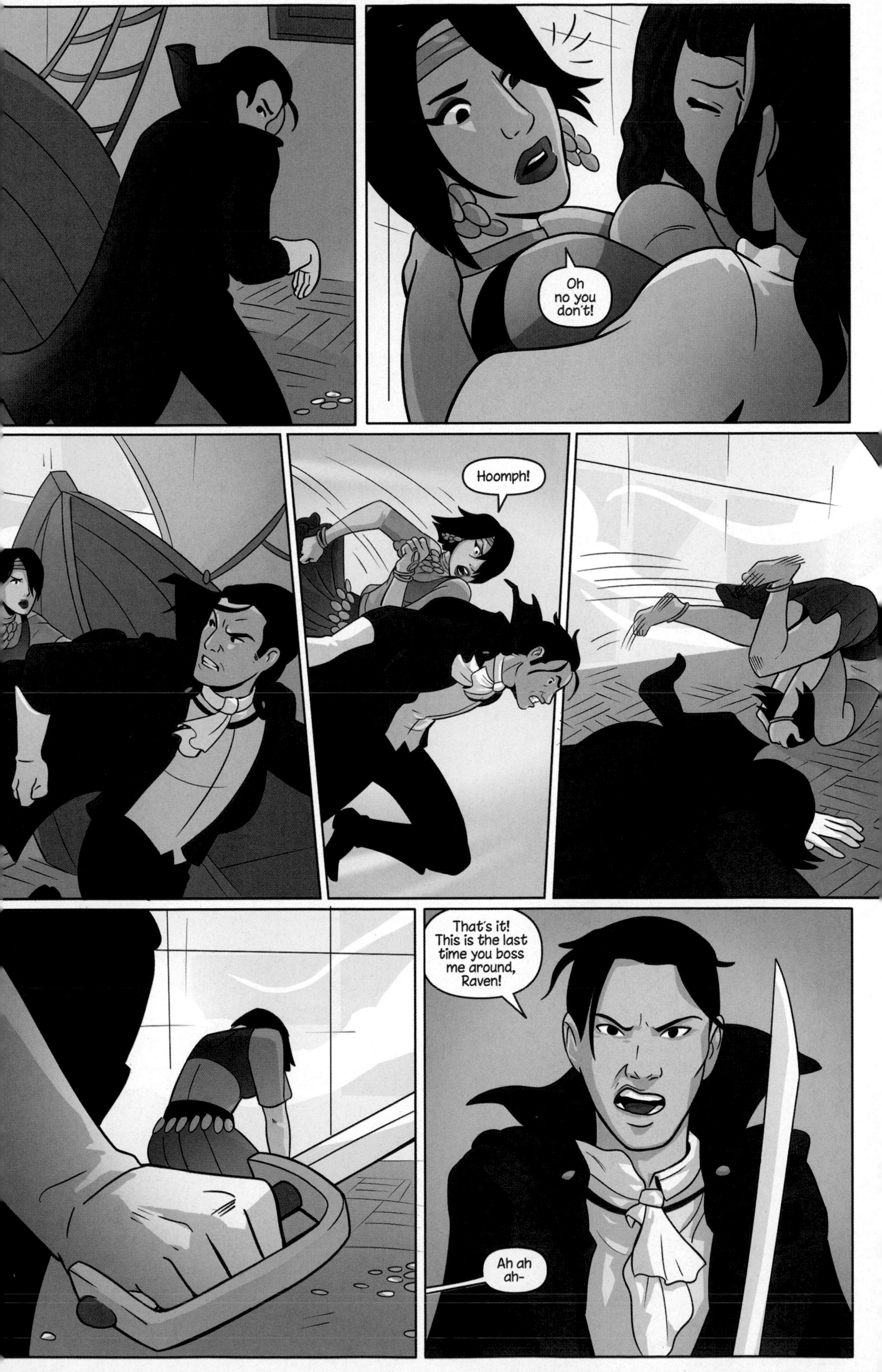
Oh no you don't!
Hoomph!
That's it! This is the last time you boss me around, Raven!
Ah ah ah-

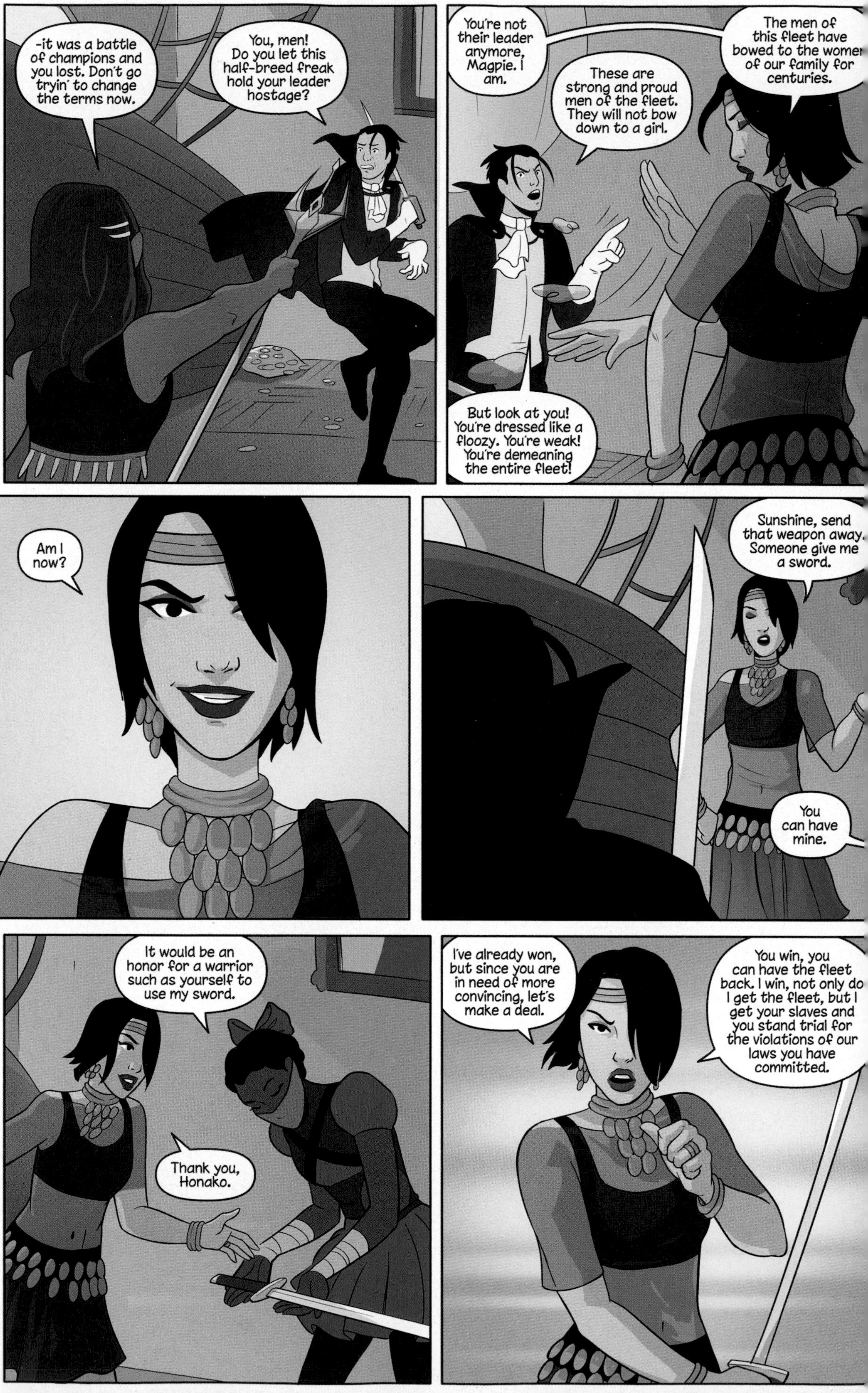
-it was a battle of champions and you lost. Don't go tryin' to change the terms now.
You, men! Do you let this half-breed freak hold your leader hostage?
You're not their leader anymore, Magpie. I am.
These are strong and proud men of the fleet. They will not bow down to a girl.
The men of this fleet have bowed to the women of our family for centuries.
But look at you! You're dressed like a floozy. You're weak! You're demeaning the entire fleet!
Am I now?
Sunshine, send that weapon away. Someone give me a sword.
You can have mine.
It would be an honor for a warrior such as yourself to use my sword.
Thank you, Honako.
I've already won, but since you are in need of more convincing, let's make a deal.
You win, you can have the fleet back. I win, not only do I get the fleet, but I get your slaves and you stand trial for the violations of our laws you have committed.

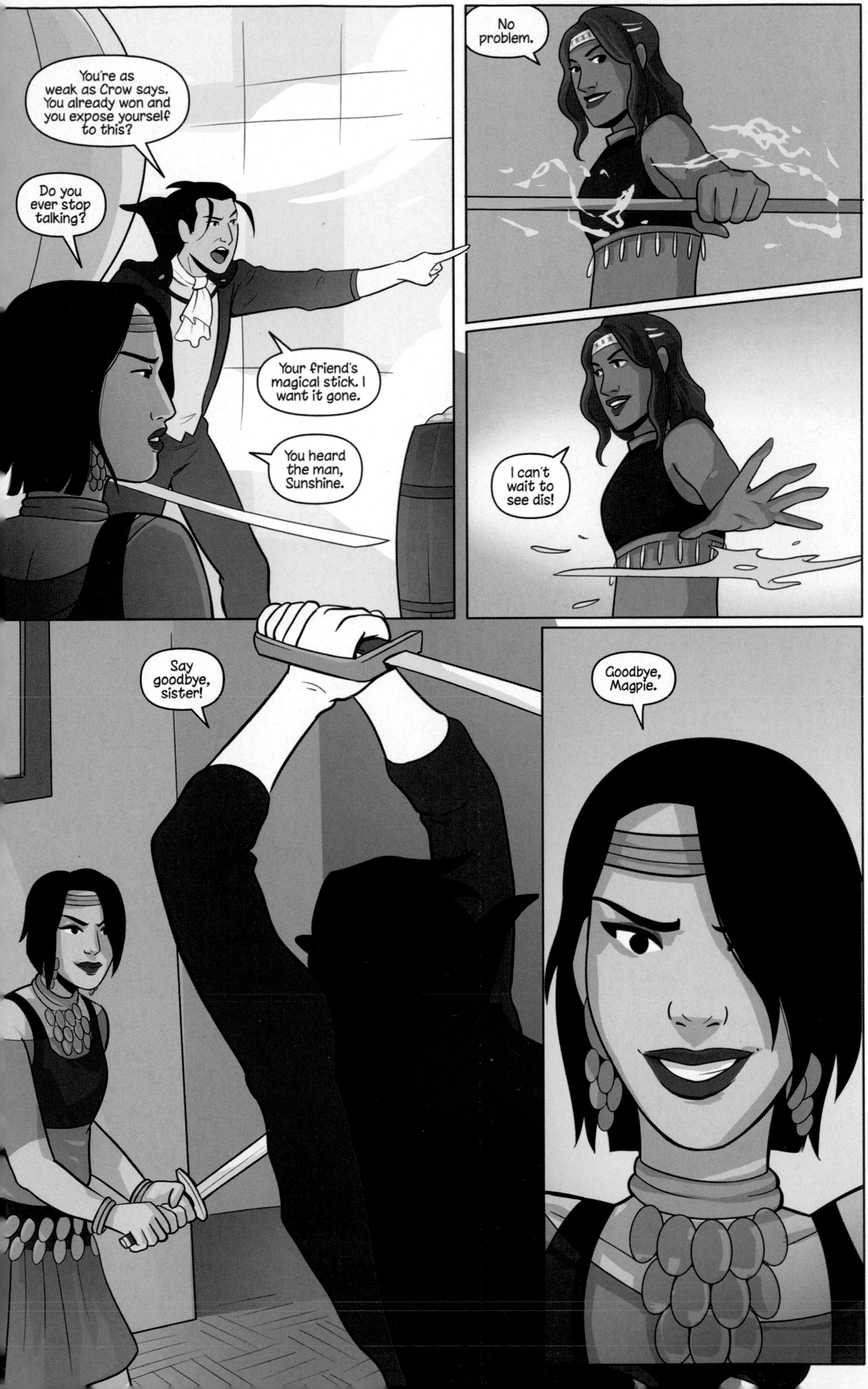

You're as weak as Crow says. You already won and you expose yourself to this?
Do you ever stop talking?
No problem.
Your friend's magical stick. I want it gone.
You heard the man, Sunshine.
I can't wait to see dis!
Say goodbye, sister!
Goodbye, Magpie.

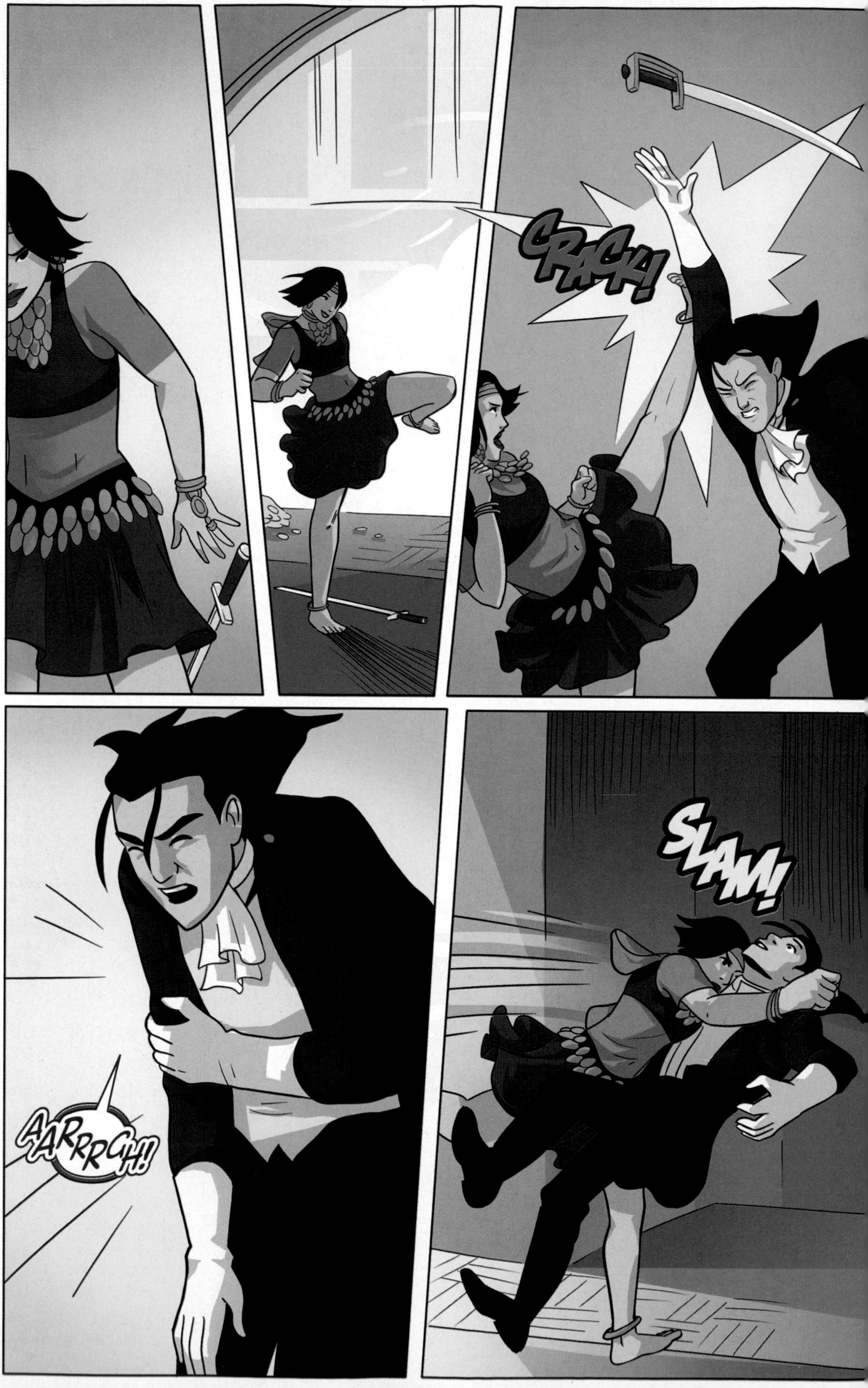
CRACK!
AARRRGH!
SLAM!

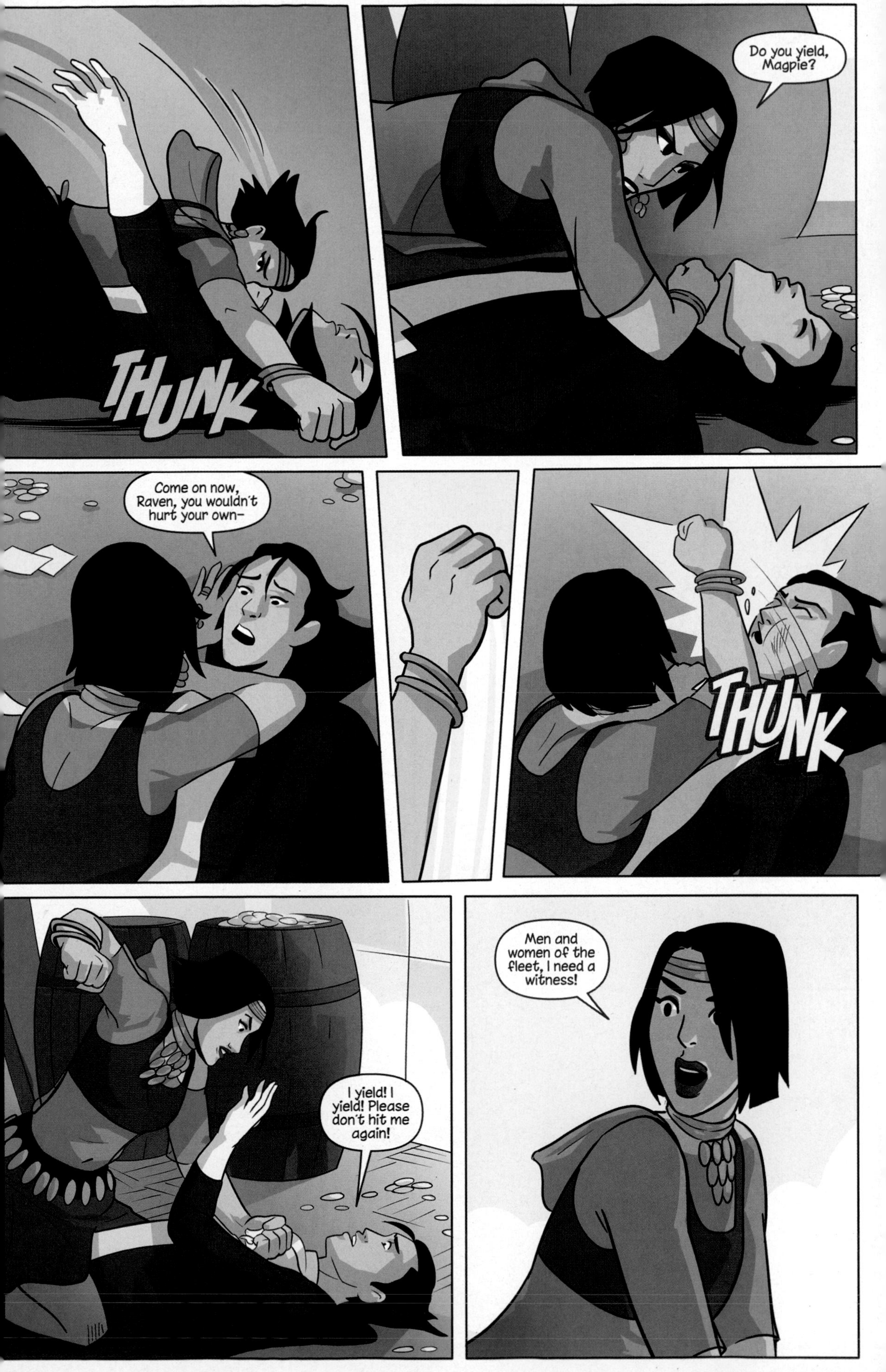
THUNK
Do you yield, Magpie?
Come on now, Raven, you wouldn't hurt your own–
THUNK
I yield! I yield! Please don't hit me again!
Men and women of the fleet, I need a witness!

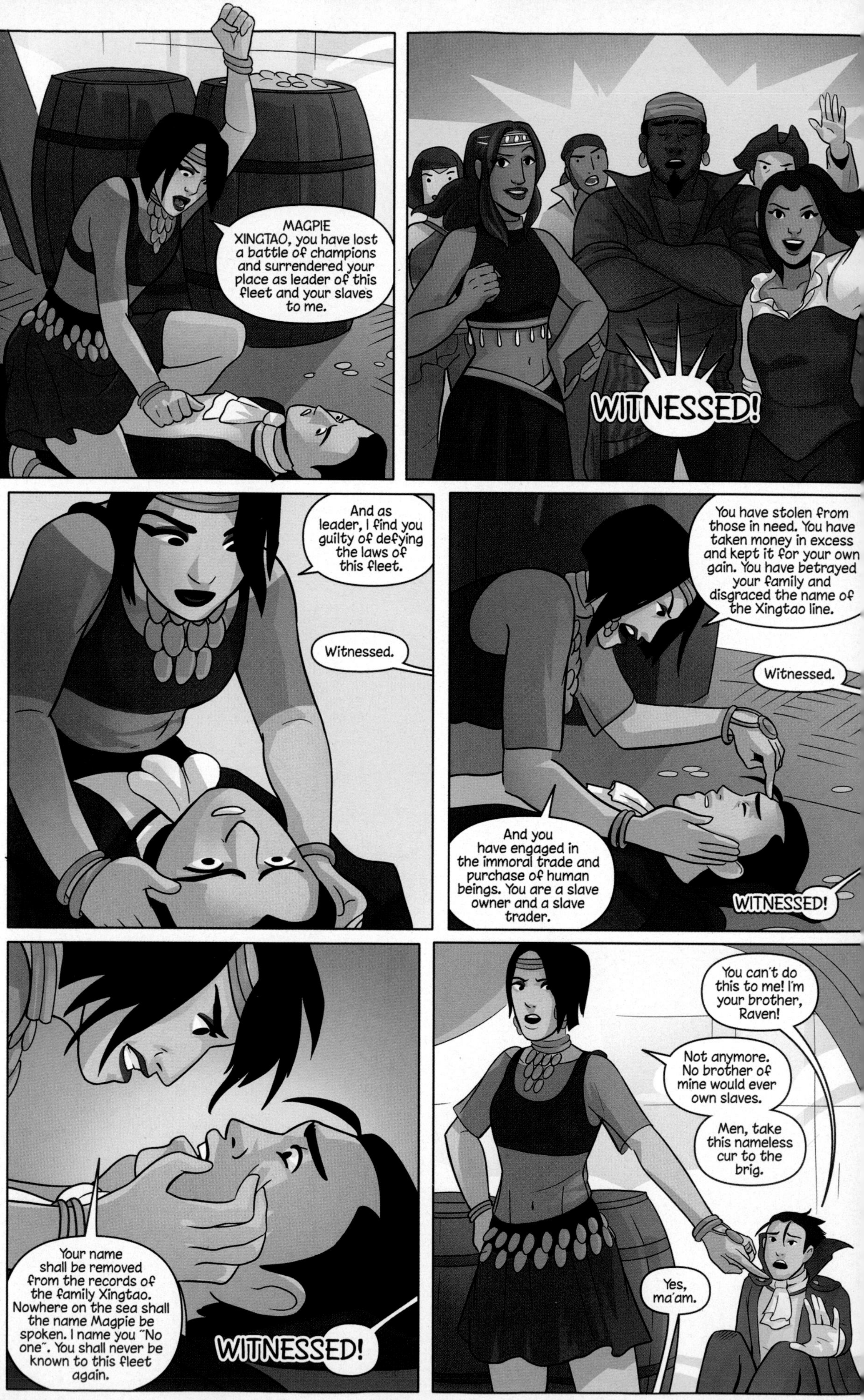
MAGPIE XINGTAO, you have lost a battle of champions and surrendered your place as leader of this fleet and your slaves to me.
WITNESSED!
And as leader, I find you guilty of defying the laws of this fleet.
Witnessed.
You have stolen from those in need. You have taken money in excess and kept it for your own gain. You have betrayed your family and disgraced the name of the Xingtao line.
Witnessed.
And you have engaged in the immoral trade and purchase of human beings. You are a slave owner and a slave trader.
WITNESSED!
Your name shall be removed from the records of the family Xingtao. Nowhere on the sea shall the name Magpie be spoken. I name you "No one". You shall never be known to this fleet again.
WITNESSED!
You can't do this to me! I'm your brother, Raven!
Not anymore. No brother of mine would ever own slaves.
Men, take this nameless cur to the brig.
Yes, ma'am.

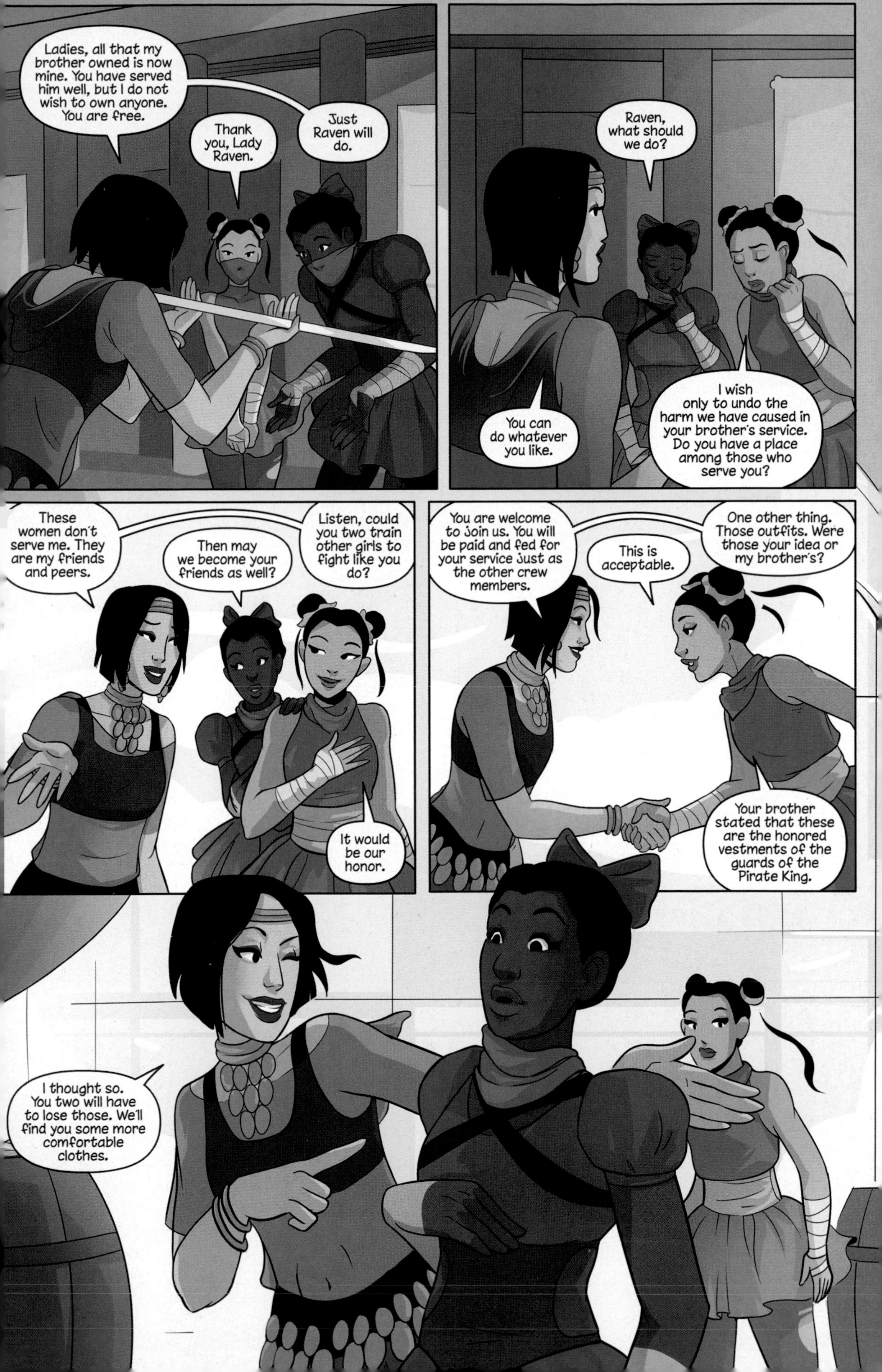

Ladies, all that my brother owned is now mine. You have served him well, but I do not wish to own anyone. You are free.
Thank you, Lady Raven.
Just Raven will do.
Raven, what should we do?
You can do whatever you like.
I wish only to undo the harm we have caused in your brother's service. Do you have a place among those who serve you?
These women don't serve me. They are my friends and peers.
Then may we become your friends as well?
Listen, could you two train other girls to fight like you do?
It would be our honor.
You are welcome to join us. You will be paid and fed for your service just as the other crew members.
This is acceptable.
One other thing. Those outfits. Were those your idea or my brother's?
Your brother stated that these are the honored vestments of the guards of the Pirate King.
I thought so. You two will have to lose those. We'll find you some more comfortable clothes.

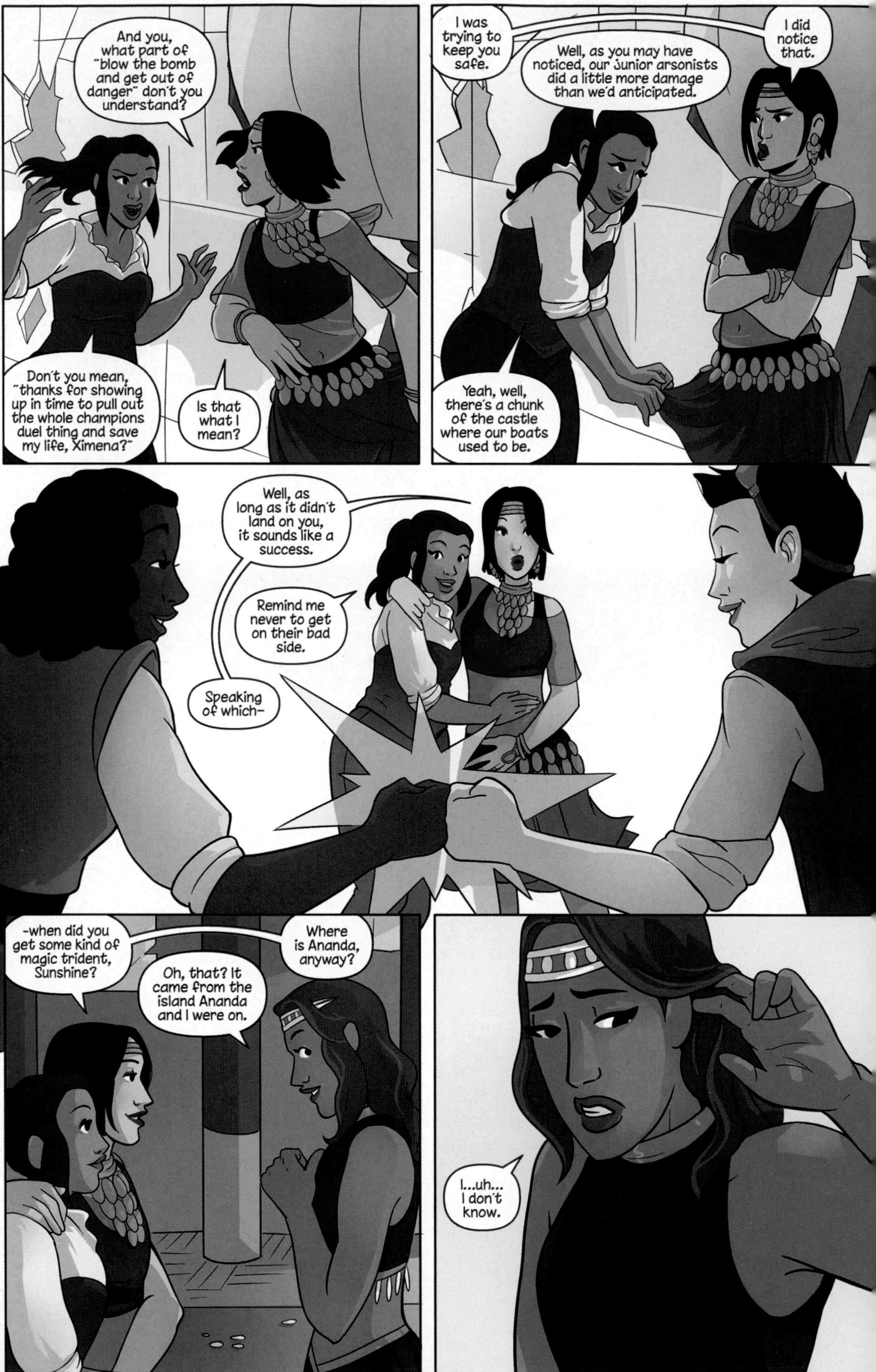
And you, what part of "blow the bomb and get out of danger" don't you understand?
Don't you mean, "thanks for showing up in time to pull out the whole champions duel thing and save my life, Ximena?"
Is that what I mean?
I was trying to keep you safe.
I did notice that.
Well, as you may have noticed, our junior arsonists did a little more damage than we'd anticipated.
Yeah, well, there's a chunk of the castle where our boats used to be.
Well, as long as it didn't land on you, it sounds like a success.
Remind me never to get on their bad side.
Speaking of which-
-when did you get some kind of magic trident, Sunshine?
Where is Ananda, anyway?
Oh, that? It came from the island Ananda and I were on.
I...uh... I don't know.

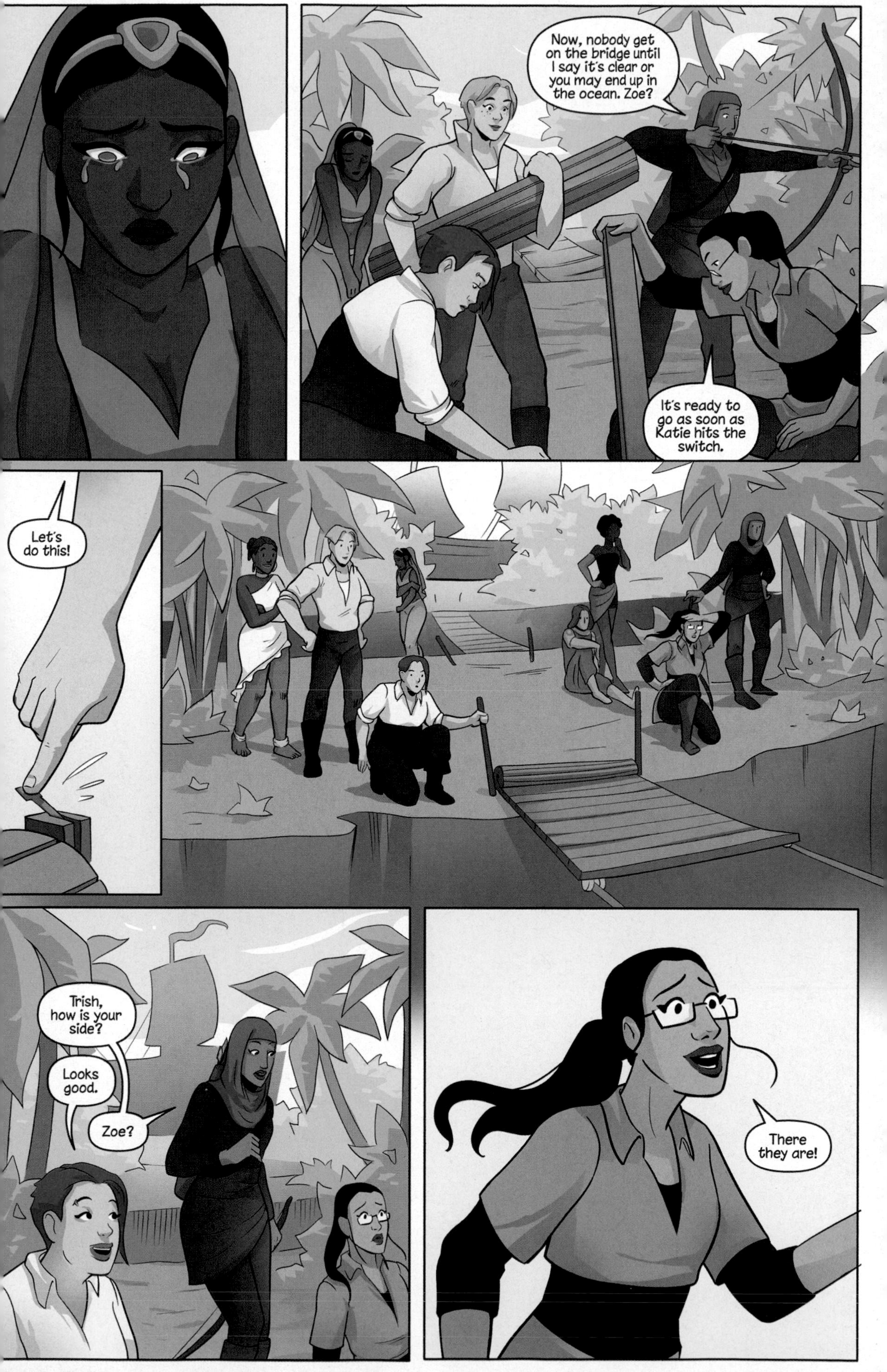
Now, nobody get on the bridge until I say it's clear or you may end up in the ocean. Zoe?
It's ready to go as soon as Katie hits the switch.
Let's do this!
Trish, how is your side?
Looks good.
Zoe?
There they are!

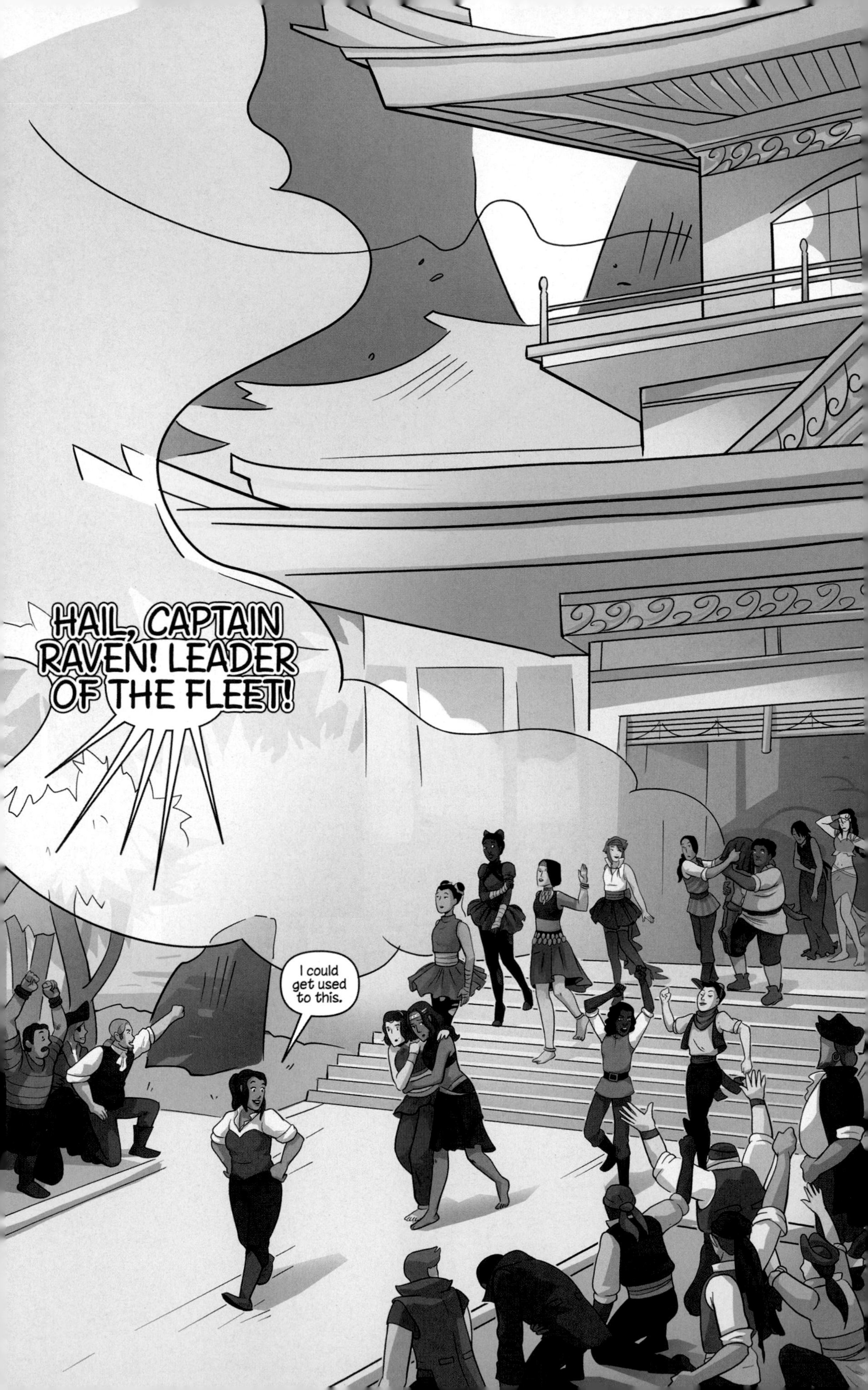
HAIL, CAPTAIN RAVEN! LEADER OF THE FLEET!
I could get used to this.

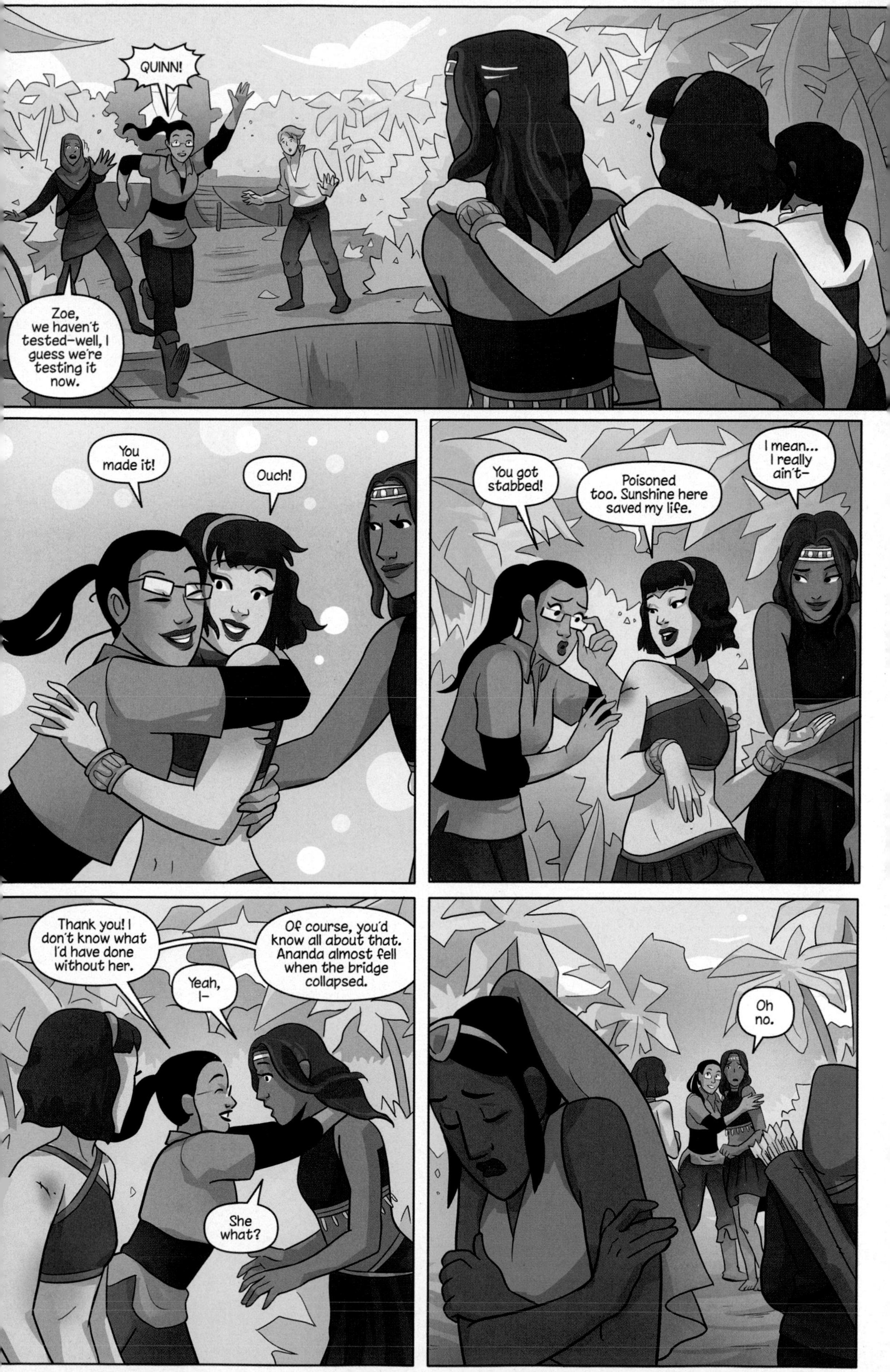
QUINN!
Zoe, we haven't tested—well, I guess we're testing it now.
You made it!
Ouch!
You got stabbed!
Poisoned too. Sunshine here saved my life.
I mean... I really ain't—
Thank you! I don't know what I'd have done without her.
Yeah, I—
Of course, you'd know all about that. Ananda almost fell when the bridge collapsed.
She what?
Oh no.

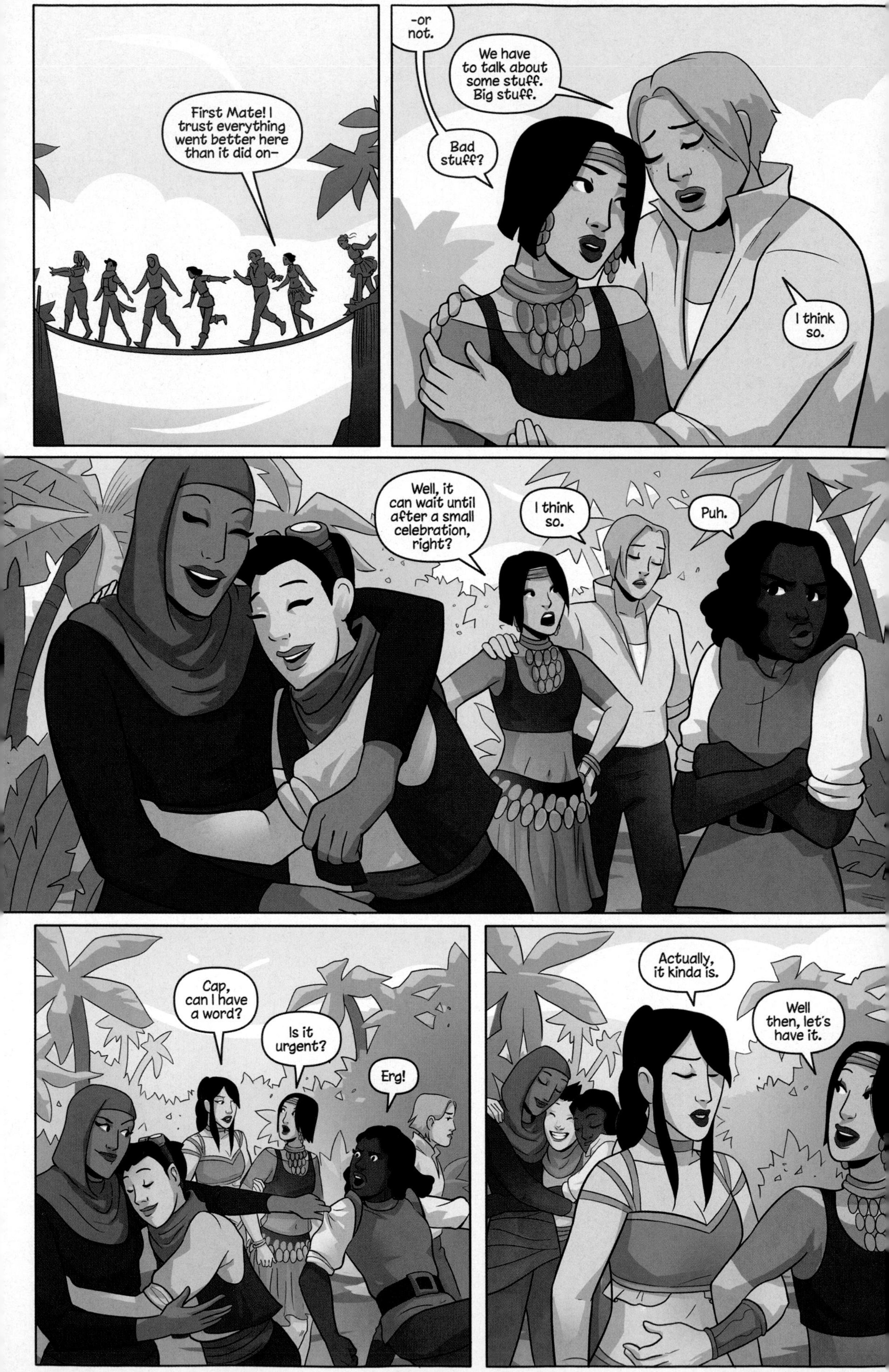
First Mate! I trust everything went better here than it did on–
-or not.
We have to talk about some stuff. Big stuff.
Bad stuff?
I think so.
Well, it can wait until after a small celebration, right?
I think so.
Puh.
Cap, can I have a word?
Is it urgent?
Erg!
Actually, it kinda is.
Well then, let's have it.

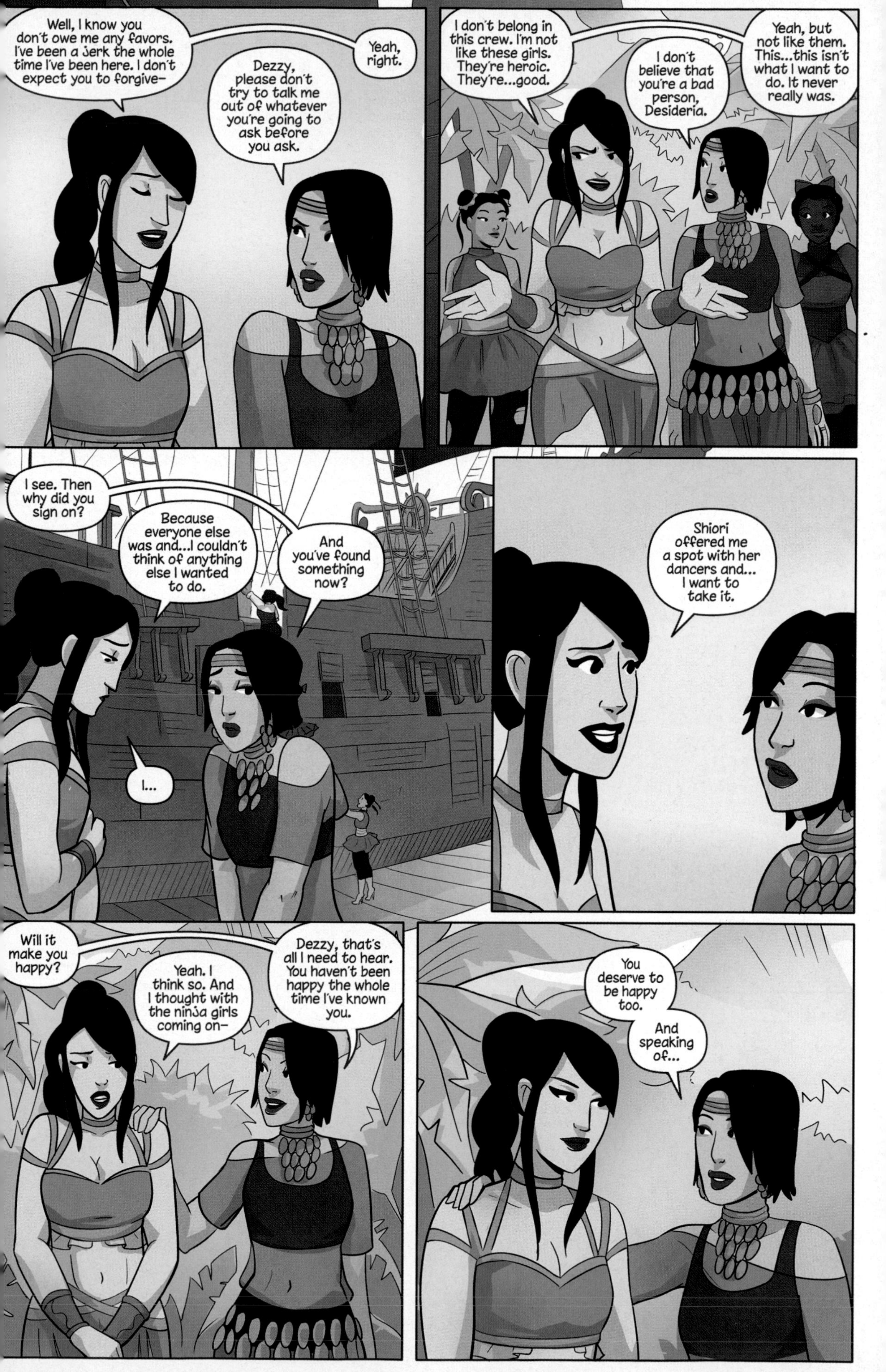
Well, I know you don't owe me any favors. I've been a jerk the whole time I've been here. I don't expect you to forgive–
Yeah, right.
Dezzy, please don't try to talk me out of whatever you're going to ask before you ask.
I don't belong in this crew. I'm not like these girls. They're heroic. They're...good.
I don't believe that you're a bad person, Desideria.
Yeah, but not like them. This...this isn't what I want to do. It never really was.
I see. Then why did you sign on?
Because everyone else was and...I couldn't think of anything else I wanted to do.
And you've found something now?
I...
Shiori offered me a spot with her dancers and... I want to take it.
Will it make you happy?
Yeah. I think so. And I thought with the ninja girls coming on–
Dezzy, that's all I need to hear. You haven't been happy the whole time I've known you.
You deserve to be happy too.
And speaking of...

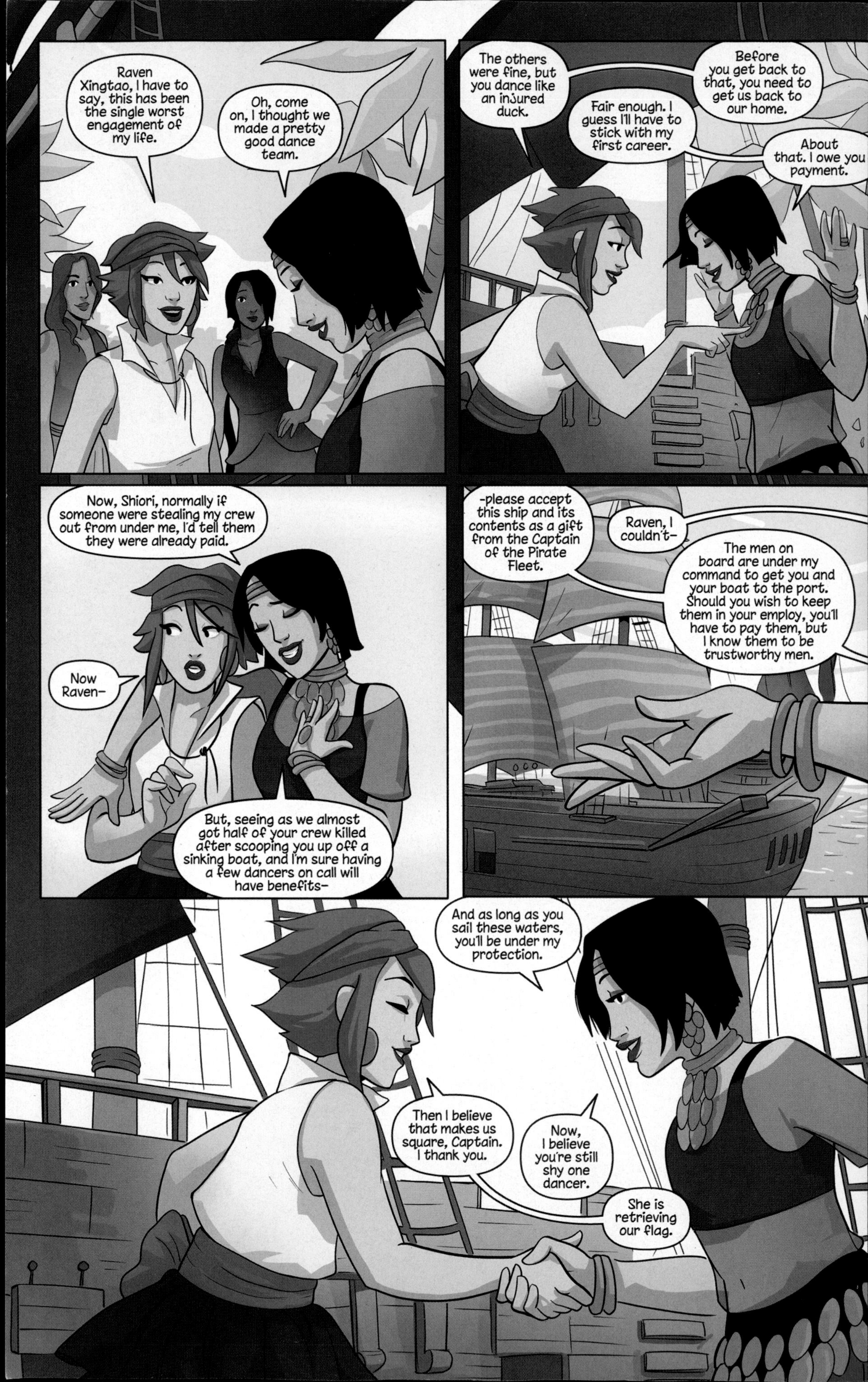
Raven Xingtao, I have to say, this has been the single worst engagement of my life.
Oh, come on, I thought we made a pretty good dance team.
The others were fine, but you dance like an injured duck.
Fair enough. I guess I'll have to stick with my first career.
Before you get back to that, you need to get us back to our home.
About that. I owe you payment.
Now, Shiori, normally if someone were stealing my crew out from under me, I'd tell them they were already paid.
Now Raven-
But, seeing as we almost got half of your crew killed after scooping you up off a sinking boat, and I'm sure having a few dancers on call will have benefits-
-please accept this ship and its contents as a gift from the Captain of the Pirate Fleet.
Raven, I couldn't-
The men on board are under my command to get you and your boat to the port. Should you wish to keep them in your employ, you'll have to pay them, but I know them to be trustworthy men.
And as long as you sail these waters, you'll be under my protection.
Then I believe that makes us square, Captain. I thank you.
Now, I believe you're still shy one dancer.
She is retrieving our flag.

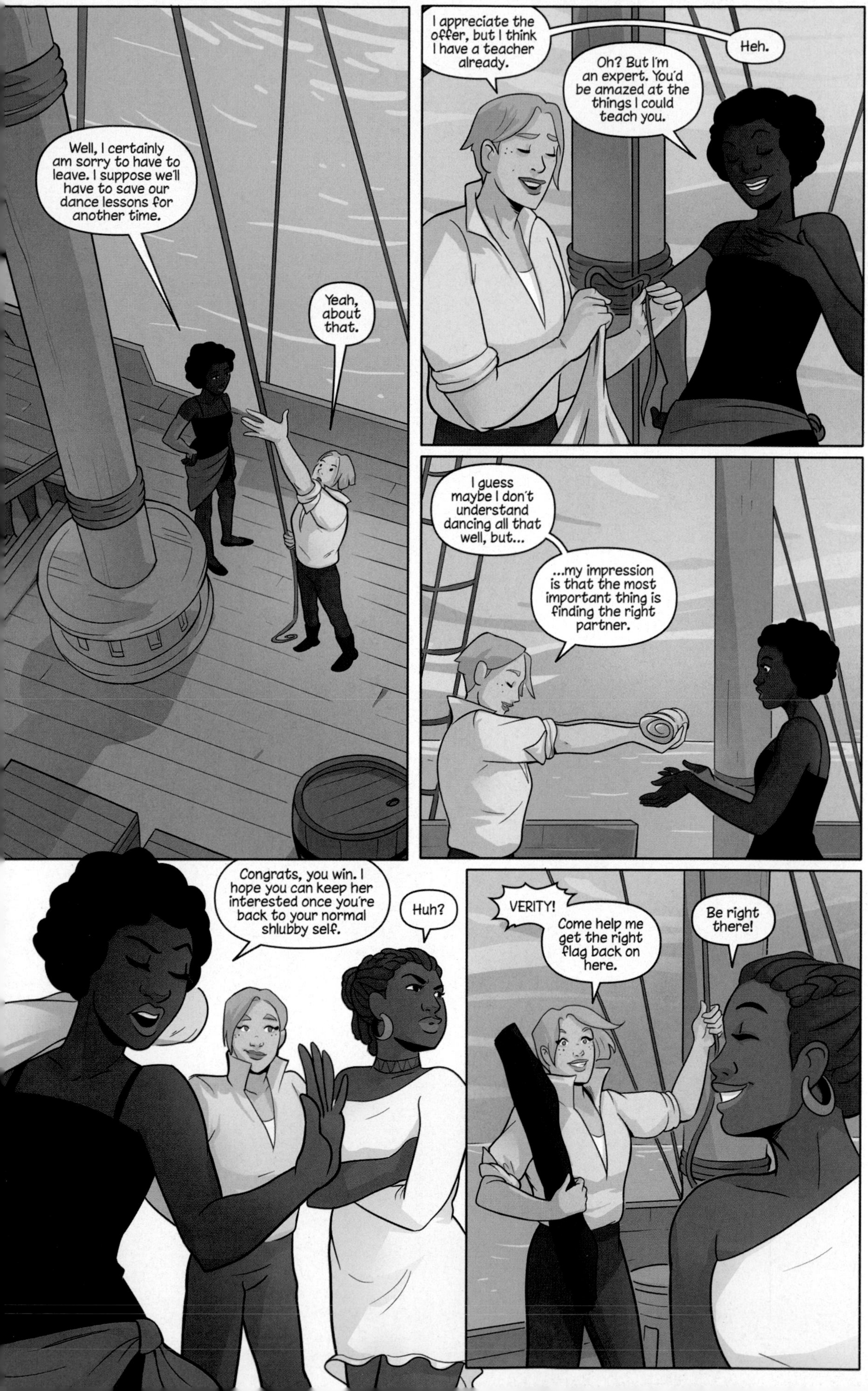

Well, I certainly am sorry to have to leave. I suppose we'll have to save our dance lessons for another time.
Yeah, about that.
I appreciate the offer, but I think I have a teacher already.
Heh.
Oh? But I'm an expert. You'd be amazed at the things I could teach you.
I guess maybe I don't understand dancing all that well, but...
...my impression is that the most important thing is finding the right partner.
Congrats, you win. I hope you can keep her interested once you're back to your normal shlubby self.
Huh?
VERITY!
Come help me get the right flag back on here.
Be right there!

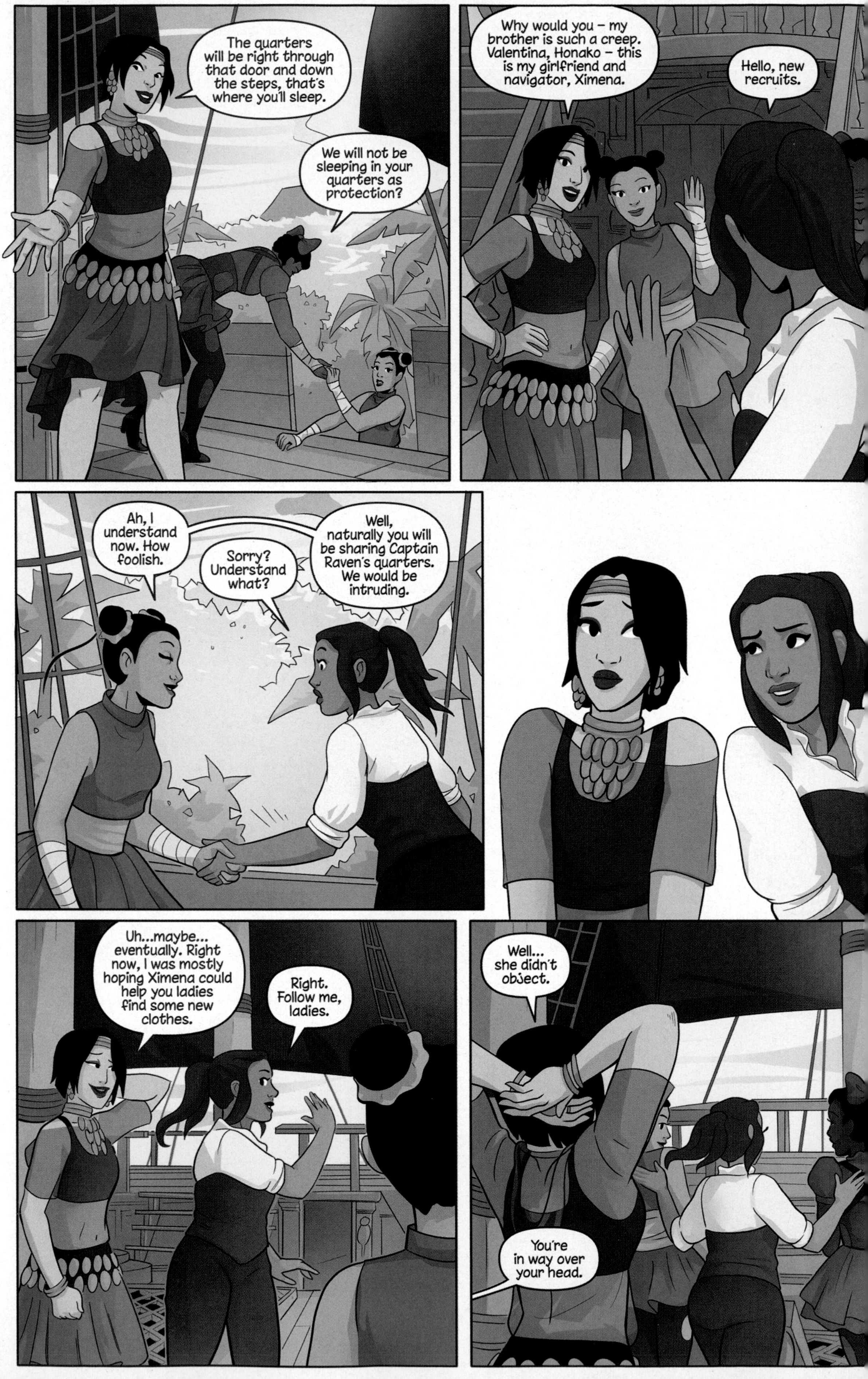

The quarters will be right through that door and down the steps, that's where you'll sleep.
We will not be sleeping in your quarters as protection?
Why would you – my brother is such a creep. Valentina, Honako – this is my girlfriend and navigator, Ximena.
Hello, new recruits.
Ah, I understand now. How foolish.
Sorry? Understand what?
Well, naturally you will be sharing Captain Raven's quarters. We would be intruding.
Uh...maybe... eventually. Right now, I was mostly hoping Ximena could help you ladies find some new clothes.
Right. Follow me, ladies.
Well... she didn't object.
You're in way over your head.

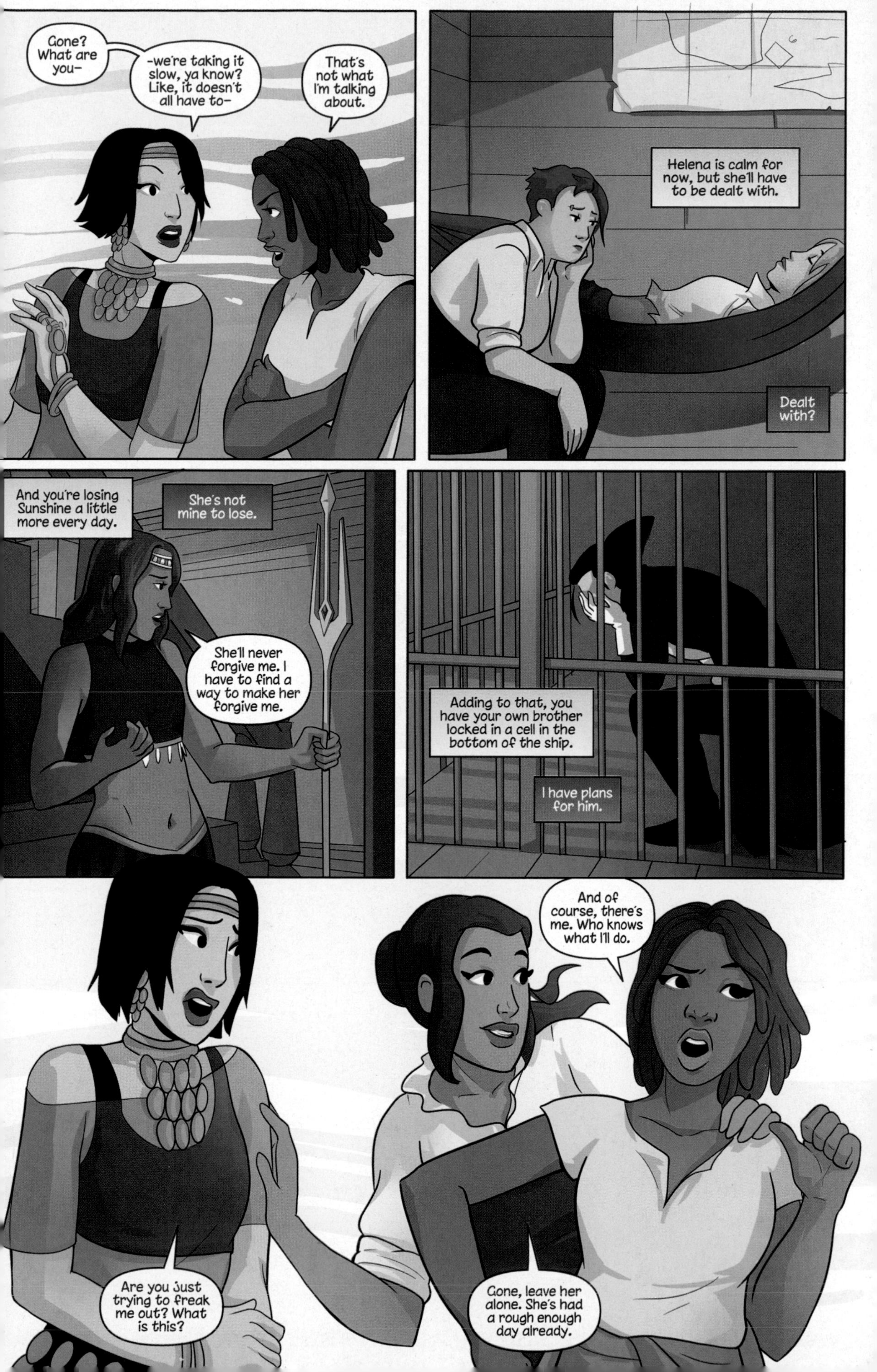

Gone? What are you-
-we're taking it slow, ya know? Like, it doesn't all have to-
That's not what I'm talking about.
Helena is calm for now, but she'll have to be dealt with.
Dealt with?
And you're losing Sunshine a little more every day.
She's not mine to lose.
She'll never forgive me. I have to find a way to make her forgive me.
Adding to that, you have your own brother locked in a cell in the bottom of the ship.
I have plans for him.
And of course, there's me. Who knows what I'll do.
Are you just trying to freak me out? What is this?
Gone, leave her alone. She's had a rough enough day already.

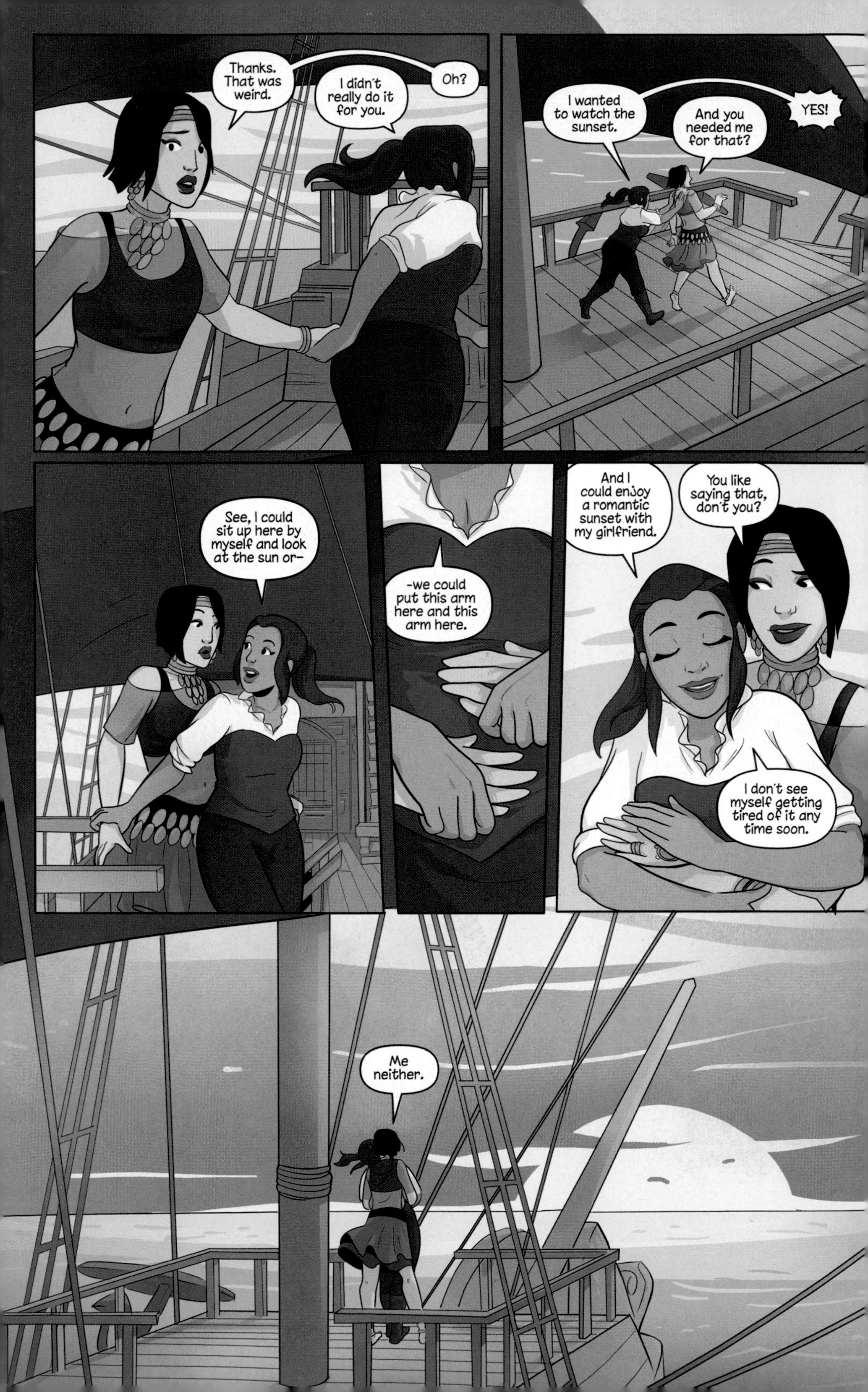
Thanks. That was weird.
I didn't really do it for you.
Oh?
I wanted to watch the sunset.
And you needed me for that?
YES!
See, I could sit up here by myself and look at the sun or-
-we could put this arm here and this arm here.
And I could enjoy a romantic sunset with my girlfriend.
You like saying that, don't you?
I don't see myself getting tired of it any time soon.
Me neither.